The Kaiyos Lex: Imperium

By

Bernard Lang

The Kaiyos Lex Imperium by Bernard Lang
Edition 01.01
Published by: Kaiyos Lex Publishing LLC
3644 Werk road #58086
Cincinnati, OH 45258

www.KaiyosLex.com

© 2020 Kaiyos Lex Publishing LLC
All rights reserved. No portion of this book may be reproduced in any form without permission from the publisher, except as permitted by U.S. copyright law.

For permissions contact:
Inquiry@kaiyoslex.com

ISBN: 978-1-953673-01-5

Chapter 1

Umbrian Republic Command Center;
Near Ischia, Aetnaeus

Dust and debris fell from the ceiling as the ground shook, adding to the thick haze which permeated throughout the command center. Analysts rushed between stations as a chorus of desperate voices echoed off the walls, the soft blue glow of their workstations casting strange shadows in the cramped confines of the underground bunker.

Praetor Gaius Aurelius Marcellus, the Umbrian Republic's newest field commander, was oblivious to it all. His attention was focused on the image floating in the center of the room.

Slowly spinning in front of him was Aetnaeus, the planet he had been tasked with defending from his merciless enemies, the Ascomanni.

His forces, represented by blue diamonds, wrapped around Aetnaeus's last functioning starport. Smaller groups of blue diamonds dotted other portions of the planet's sole continent, the only significant landmass on the planet. The rest of the map glowed an ominous red, indicating areas where the enemy had gained control.

A faceless voice cut through the din: "Praetor, the *Cerberus* just called in. Switching them to your channel, sir."

He nodded in the general direction of the update. In moments, his commlink flickered with a series of melodic tones, indicating a secure connection had been established.

"*Cerberus*, this is Ischia Actual," he said. "Confirm that you are ready to proceed to the designated coordinates."

"Confirmed, Ischia Actual, awaiting your command."

Marcellus's gaze shifted back to the map floating in the middle of the room. The largest set of blue diamonds outside of the perimeter were flashing, indicating friendly forces on the verge of being overrun. It was a situation that had occurred far too frequently over the last several weeks...

The battle for Aetnaeus had started six months ago, when a massive Ascomanni fleet had appeared in orbit. Facing long odds in space, Marcellus had dispersed his own fleet to preserve the scant naval resources available to him. With virtually no opposition in space, the enemy secured a beachhead planet-side.

His ground forces had done their best to prepare, but there was little they could do to counter the overwhelming fire support the opposing fleet brought to bear. Despite inflicting heavy casualties on the Ascomanni, his forces were unable to stop the invaders from establishing a base of operations on the planet.

With few remaining options, Marcellus took a chance and ordered his fleet to cut the enemy's supply lines and conduct hit-and-run raids on known Asco staging areas. As these tactics started to pinch the enemy's supplies, most of the enemy's ships withdrew to protect the convoys supporting their invasion.

This stroke of good fortune was not enough to turn the tide, however, as counterattacks aimed at eliminating the Ascomanni beachhead failed to make decisive gains.

After fifteen weeks of brutal, grinding combat, his forces had reached the point of exhaustion, and the Ascomanni's advances picked up speed. Only the dedication and discipline of his soldiers prevented the battle from becoming a complete rout.

A series of desperate holding actions bought time for a mostly orderly tactical withdrawal. Marcellus used that hard-won time to hastily reorganize his forces and establish a defensive perimeter around Ischia, a city nestled at the base of a dormant volcano, which had facilities suitable for planetary extraction.

This was done at great cost to the holding force, and many of those defenders became separated and surrounded during the retreat.

A few larger pockets had been able to hold out, and several frantic attempts had been successful in breaking out some of the larger groups of survivors. Marcellus did not have the resources to save them all, however, and one by one the smaller groups caught beyond the perimeter were being overwhelmed.

His adjutant, Valerian Barbatius, appeared at his side, breaking him free from his reverie.

"Praetor, Task Force Hyperion indicates that they cannot hold out much longer. Combat effectiveness is down to thirty-five percent. Aemilia is doing a great job holding them together, but there's only so much she can do."

Valerian had been with him from the beginning, since their time at the academy. He was tall, thin, and handsome, a fact which had gotten him into hot water more than once. With a dark, tan complexion and tawny golden-brown hair, he looked more like a celebrity than a soldier, and Marcellus couldn't help but be slightly jealous of his natural charm.

Val was also a stickler for the rules. While his compulsive nature would occasionally strain their relationship, he had a penchant for making order from chaos, and his mastery of organization and logistics had saved the day on more than a few occasions.

Marcellus nodded at his friend's report.

Task Force Hyperion was a group of several thousand soldiers, represented by the collection of flashing diamonds on his display. Located on a plateau near the abandoned industrial center of Syracuse, they had been cut off in favorable defensive terrain, with plenty of stores and equipment to sustain the defense.

Despite their strong position, the Asco had been relentless in their assault. As the weeks had gone by, the Task Force's leadership had been whittled away, until the most senior officer left was Aemilia Calvinus, a woman a few years his junior who he had met only once.

The memory of a young woman in her navy-blue dress uniform, fit and with shoulder length brunette hair, flashed to life, her blue-green eyes revealing an eagerness and confidence on the eve of battle.

Now she was facing long odds in a challenging situation. The Ascomanni had finally brought their full weight to bear against her soldiers, and time was running out to try and evacuate them.

"Communications, put me through to Tribune Calvinus."

"Understood, Praetor, patching you through now."

Task Force Hyperion; Near Syracuse, Aetnaeus

Sitting in the middle of a collection of trenches, earthworks, and strongpoints known as the Redoubt, Tribune Aemilia Calvinus tried to focus on the datapad in front of her. She did her best to block out the near-deafening sound of small arms and explosions as she scanned the latest report detailing the status of her forces.

Task Force Hyperion had started the campaign with three legions, each made up of ten thousand soldiers and five thousand Scutia battlemechs. Quintillius Varus, the most senior of the three legates commanding Hyperion's legions, was responsible for directing the Task Force.

It felt like a lifetime ago, Aemilia thought to herself.

With the added burden of managing the larger force, responsibility for the day-to-day operations of Varus's legion had fallen to his young Tribune.

She remembered being nervous over taking on such a large responsibility. When she shared her insecurities with her commander, Varus had expressed his confidence in her abilities, and Aemilia quickly grew comfortable in the role.

Destiny would have other plans, however.

Within the first few months of combat operations, Varus had been killed. Now, Aemilia was the most senior officer left. She found herself responsible not only for keeping her soldiers fighting, but also for keeping alive their fading hopes of rescue.

It was a difficult task, as Task Force Hyperion's position was growing more precarious by the hour. Aemilia was down to fewer than twelve thousand soldiers fit for combat, and she had less than three thousand of the Scutia, known more colloquially to her soldiers as 'scoots,' remaining.

Outside, the roar of battle increased as the enemy renewed their attack. Aemilia set the datapad down on the supply crate she was using as a desk, grabbed her range finder, and walked out of the camouflage-netted shelter from which she directed her forces.

She joined a few soldiers on the rampart surrounding her command post and looked down on the dusty red foothills below, where her forces were engaged with the enemy.

Tracers flashed between opposing positions as dusk set in, while larger munitions sprayed fountains of earth into the air. Two Asco frigates hovered over the enemy's rear area, providing direct fire support, while fresh formations of enemy troops prepared for another advance.

The Ascomanni were unrelenting.

With each attack, her defenders clung stubbornly to their positions. But despite their best efforts, they were steadily being pushed back, meter by meter, toward the summit of the plateau.

Making the situation worse, their stores of ammunition, medicine, and spare parts were becoming desperately low. Tanks and artillery batteries were only deployed in very limited circumstances, and the enemy was increasingly bold in exploiting their superior firepower.

Aemilia turned her attention to the latest flashpoint. Forty Asco tanks bore down on one of the outer defensive positions, while hundreds of foot soldiers advanced behind in support.

Aemilia's heart began to race, but she forced herself to calm down and trust her subordinate commanders to manage the defense.

Her chest tightened as a desperate call for fire support echoed over the command net. Gaps appeared in the Redoubt's energy shield, and the gentle *thrum* of its generator faded.

It was immediately replaced by the thunderous sound of artillery. The concussive force of the shots raced through the hilltop command center, and Aemilia's ears rang as she watched the battle unfold.

On the plains below, several rounds found their mark, knocking out a half-dozen tanks and scattering the accompanying Ascomanni infantry. The remaining enemy armor picked up speed, bearing down on the Umbrian frontline. Soon they entered the minefield surrounding the outer defensive works. EMP mines disabled more vehicles, and her soldiers engaged with portable missile launchers and accelerator cannons. More tanks burst into flame, but still the enemy came, heedless of their own losses.

As the Ascomanni pressure became overwhelming, her soldiers fell back as ordered.

Supporting fire from other positions attempted to suppress the enemy, but the retreat uphill was perilously exposed. Aemilia's stomach dropped as murderous fire poured into her retreating forces, with only a handful of Umbrians making it back to their secondary positions.

Turning away from the battle below, she activated her commlink: "All batteries, commence destructive fire on grid point Theta 2."

Again, the earth shook beneath her feet as a dozen artillery batteries focused their destructive might on the positions her forces had just vacated. Returning to the parapet, she watched as the attacking Ascomanni force disappeared in a sea of fire and death.

She did her best to try not to think about the wounded and dying Umbrians who had been left behind.

Just then, a flash of light on the edge of her peripheral vision caught her attention.

"Tribune, watch out!"

Before she had time to turn around, she was knocked from her feet by one of her soldiers. Dark shapes roared by overhead, and a series of teeth-rattling explosions tore through the Redoubt.

Aemilia shot to her feet and began assessing the situation. A pair of double-hulled Ascomanni dropships had snuck through the openings in the Redoubt's shields. They hovered nearby, pouring heavy fire into the Umbrian fortifications as they disgorged scores of troops.

"Verutum 1-4, we need immediate defensive fire support on my position," Aemilia barked into her commlink. Activating her combat suit, she turned to the handful of soldiers nearby and said, "Let's move, legionnaires, you're with me!"

Without waiting for confirmation, she set out toward the invading force.

"Shot out" came crackling over the command net, and a screeching whistle pierced through the air. She watched with satisfaction as her gun emplacements found the mark.

One dropship was torn in half by the impact, dropping straight down on the troops it had just deployed, while the other's aft end burst into flame as it spun out of control. The crippled dropship slammed into the Redoubt's shields and exploded, throwing flaming pieces of debris across the top of the plateau.

The Tribune and her soldiers raced through the narrow confines of the fortress's trenches. They came across an opening in the earthworks leading to a battered pillbox that jutted out from the walls of the Redoubt, and Aemilia ducked inside.

The fading rays of the sun poured through numerous holes in the walls and ceiling, and broken, motionless forms lay where they had fallen.

Aemilia paused for a moment, anxiously searching for any signs of life. It was too late; the bunker's defenders had all succumbed to their wounds.

There was nothing more she could do for these soldiers, Aemilia thought grimly to herself, but she could still save others from meeting the same fate. She gently pulled the body of one of her men from the bunker's firing slit and glanced out at the battlefield.

The pillbox looked down over a series of gullies and depressions that ran parallel to the outer walls of the Redoubt, providing a clear view of the newest Ascomanni incursion. A dozen hulking forms were providing suppressing fire near the burning wreckage of one of the dropships, while an equal number attempted to penetrate the fortifications.

The focus of their assault was a section of the Redoubt further down the trench, and return fire indicated more of her soldiers were still resisting at the point of attack.

She had an advantage, however, as the advancing force was exposed to the bunker's field of fire.

As the rest of her troops filed in, she issued her orders: "In sixty seconds, open up on the assault party. Once they are eliminated, shift fire to the rearward enemy force. As soon as they turn to engage you, I'll sally out with the forces on the rampart."

With that, Aemilia ran back out of the strongpoint and moved toward the enemy advance, passing more bodies as she went.

She came across a handful of Umbrian soldiers who were huddled behind the parapet, taking turns firing over the wall at their oncoming foes. Further down the line, a Scutia battlemech attempted to draw the Ascomanni's attention and slow their advance, its repeater cannon unleashing a torrent of fire as it attempted to suppress their enemies.

"Who's your commanding officer?" she shouted over the sounds of battle.

One young, anxious-looking soldier looked up, and, recognizing the Tribune, stuttered, "Centurion Accius was, ma'am, but he bought it as soon as those dropships started pounding on us!"

An explosion rocked the defensive positions as the scoot succumbed to concentrated Ascomanni fire. Screams of wounded soldiers echoed up the rampart, and the color drained from the young man's face.

"OK, listen up legionnaires, here is the plan," Aemilia roared. "In twenty seconds, a detachment to our left is going to pour flanking fire into the advancing Asco. Once the enemy base of fire shifts, we're going over the walls to annihilate whoever is left. How-oo?"

"*How-oo!*" came a chorus of voices.

"Good, check your gear. Ten seconds!"

Aemilia checked the pulse carbine built into the right forearm of her suit and activated the blade attachment on her left. In an instant, the blade burned red hot, ready to penetrate even the thickest enemy armor.

She spent the last few seconds steadying her nerves before her chrono finished its countdown and started beeping.

It was time.

The detachment in the bunker opened up on the Asco squad advancing on the Redoubt. Caught with their flanks exposed, the enemy soldiers attempted to find cover between themselves and this new threat, and the volume of fire directed toward the Tribune and her soldiers decreased markedly.

"That's our cue! Cut loose!" Aemilia yelled. With a roar, the Umbrians stood and fired into the Ascomanni. Caught in a crossfire, the advancing force was quickly torn apart.

The soldiers she had left in the pillbox switched their fire to the enemies who had been covering the assault squad's advance. Taken off guard by their sudden reversal in fortunes, the Ascomanni attempted to respond to this new threat by targeting the ruined bunker.

The Tribune saw her opening and called out, "Over the wall, let's go, legionnaires!"

Aemilia and her soldiers vaulted over the ramparts and charged toward the enemy.

It took the surprised Asco soldiers precious moments to react. Bright flashes of light reached out and struck some of the advancing Umbrians, but the legionnaires' return fire had an equally devastating effect on their entrenched foe.

The charging Umbrians let loose one final roar, and then they were amongst their enemies.

A lumbering, armored shape rose from a fold in the ground, suddenly standing in front of the Tribune. Without hesitating, Aemilia used her own kinetic energy to drive her blade into her enemy's chest. Blood and steam spurted from the wound, and together they toppled over into a small ditch.

Aemilia quickly scrambled to her feet and triggered a blast from her pulse carbine, punching a hole through her opponent's helmet and dropping the Ascomanni soldier for good.

Another soldier charged from behind, and she barely dodged a vicious blow from the butt of its weapon. She summersaulted underneath the alien's outstretched arms and whipped her bayonet up through the leviathan's left leg. It roared in pain as it clutched at its ruined appendage, only to be struck repeatedly in the chest by plasma fire.

The Ascomanni soldier collapsed to the ground and lay still.

As Aemilia stood, she found that the rest of her soldiers had cleared the remainder of the enemy from the plateau. Cheers rang out from the direction of the bunker.

The Fates had spared her again, Aemilia thought ruefully to herself.

She took a moment to catch her breath, her gaze drifting to the soldiers she had killed.

The Ascomanni were tall, almost two meters on average, and thickly built, with pale gray skin. When fully equipped, individual combatants could top out at over two hundred kilograms, and the soldier at her feet looked particularly muscular.

This incursion may have been over, but the Ascomanni had made several attempts to assault her command post over the last few days, each attempt coming closer to breaching the Redoubt than the last.

She marveled at the Asco's willingness to throw away soldiers on missions with such low chances of success or even survival.

The Tribune shook her head, glad that understanding the enemy wasn't her responsibility. Her only concern was holding the enemy at bay until the Praetor could come up with a plan to extract them.

Aemilia climbed back out of the gulch and surveyed the battlefield.

She spotted the young soldier she had spoken to on the rampart. He was kneeling not far from the bodies of two enemy soldiers. Leaning on one arm, the legionnaire was shaking as his body attempted to dissipate the adrenaline that had come with close quarters combat.

Aemilia caught his eye, and he offered a tight-lipped smile. She nodded in return. Despite their inexperience, her headquarters troopers had done well.

She called out for her soldiers to form up, and as the Umbrians gathered around, she issued a series of orders to tend to the dead and wounded and to begin shoring up the battered fortifications.

Satisfied that the situation was under control, she headed back toward her command section.

After vaulting back over the rampart, her commlink crackled to life: "Tribune, Ischia Actual would like a status update."

"All right, tell them I'll be right there."

Umbrian Republic Command Center;
Near Ischia, Aetnaeus

"Good work, Tribune," Marcellus said as Aemilia completed her update on the Ascomanni incursion. He could see her fatigue, and for a moment he felt a particular sense of kinship with the young officer, remembering a half dozen times where he too had stepped into a no-win scenario and still come out on top.

"The operation to relieve Hyperion will begin shortly," he continued. "Be ready to evacuate your forces. You've done a spectacular job, Aemilia, you're almost through."

"Understood, sir." The young officer gave him a wan smile and quick salute before disappearing from view.

With that, Marcellus switched to another frequency. "*Cerberus*, this is Ischia Actual, begin the operation."

The Praetor turned back to his tactical display, and in the blink of an eye, the URN *Cerberus* winked into existence in orbit directly above the flashing blue diamonds on Marcellus's map.

A smaller window appeared, showing the area immediately around the battlecruiser, while yet another tracked the missiles the *Cerberus* began launching at the surface. A timer was displayed, counting down from a minute and a half—the time remaining until impact.

Suddenly, the ground rocked violently and the lights in the command center flickered as another Asco artillery barrage hit nearby. The sea of voices in the command center faded with the echoes of the explosions, leaving only anxious whispers in their place.

"Sir, they've taken out Epsilon Three!" an analyst cried out.

"Carry on, soldier, let me know if they find any of the other locations," Marcellus responded coolly. The men and women of his headquarters unit quickly went back to their tasks, but the tension in the air remained.

Time was quickly running out, Marcellus mused. The Ascomanni were on to him.

The Praetor forced himself to focus on the task at hand and turned back to his display. As the *Cerberus*'s missiles cleared Aetnaeus's atmosphere, their casings split and fell away, each releasing thousands of small flechettes.

The kinetic energy of these tiny projectiles would blow through even the most well-armored vehicles and would leave scant trace of their targets. As the darts began to find their marks, Marcellus watched the map as the angry waves of red surrounding Task Force Hyperion faded away.

Now it was time for the next step.

Switching comm channels, Marcellus issued new orders. "Sagitta Wing, begin your approach. Make sure those transports reach their destination."

"Copy, command," came the anxious response. The map updated again to show three dozen fighters and three large transports leave the perimeter surrounding Ischia, on a direct heading for Hyperion's location. Another timer appeared, with a countdown that started at forty minutes.

"Hyperion, you have just over half an hour to get your people aboard those transports. After that, our window will close."

"Copy that, Ischia Actual."

Task Force Hyperion; Near Syracuse, Aetnaeus

Aemilia looked down at the pockmarked landscape that now surrounded the plateau. The rain of kinetic darts had completely obliterated the attacking Ascomanni force, leaving nothing but craters and wreckage. The two Ascomanni frigates that had been harassing her forces lay twisted and broken on the plains of Syracuse, with giant pillars of smoke and fire marking their final resting places.

She turned from the parapet and walked back into her dimly lit command post.

"All right, ladies and gentlemen, it's time to go. Marshall our remaining heavy weaponry north of the Redoubt, prep the wounded for transfer, and pull the scoots back to a tighter perimeter to cover the evacuation. Anyone or anything that is not at the landing zone in thirty minutes is getting left behind."

There was a chorus of acknowledgments, and a strong wind blew through the command center as Sagitta's squadrons passed by overhead.

Aemilia walked back out of the tent and moved down toward the landing zone, where three large transports had just set down. Already, engineers were loading equipment into the ships, while troops waited to board.

There was a great deal to do in a very short timeframe.

Umbrian Republic Command Center; Near Ischia, Aetnaeus

The Praetor anxiously skimmed through the latest status update. Sagitta had reached Task Force Hyperion and the evacuation was well underway. The Ascomanni had yet to counter, but Marcellus expected a response at any moment.

"Hyperion, this is Ischia Actual, what's your status?"

"Ischia Actual, Hyperion here. We are running ahead of schedule. Estimated time of departure, five minutes."

Marcellus checked the clock, which showed eleven minutes remaining. Things were going well, he thought to himself. So far anyway...

Suddenly a warning claxon wailed and the captain of the *Cerberus* came back on the line. "Praetor, the enemy is on to us! Three ships have dropped in and are on a heading to engage!"

"*Cerberus*, maintain comms discipline damnit!" Marcellus bellowed. "Get ahold of yourself, we've prepared for this."

On the tactical display, the squat forms of three new shapes appeared above Aetnaeus, while the vidfeed detailing the battlecruiser's position expanded to include the new enemy contacts.

Switching channels, Marcellus said, "*Echion*, that's your cue."

Bridge of the URN *Echion*, Orbiting Aetnaeus's Third Moon, Ostia

Archus Fabian Catus, commander of the Umbrian Navy's Third Fleet, gazed out into the inky blackness of the void while he paced impatiently behind his station. His hands were balled into fists behind his back, as he waited for the signal that would bring his ship into contact with the enemy.

As he brooded, he caught sight of his reflection in one of the *Echion*'s viewports. His features were plain, with a thin narrow nose and flat complexion. Deep creases crisscrossed his forehead, and worry lines were developing around his brows.

His eyes, however, were sharp and piercing, revealing an intelligence and determination that refused to be cowed by his own insecurities. He had *earned* the command of the Third Fleet, after leading numerous successful engagements against the Ascomanni. There was no time for self-doubt now.

All around him, his bridge crew were busily preparing for the coming engagement. His CAG stood nearby, overseeing his carrier's fighter wings, checking in with squadron leaders, and finalizing assignments. Other officers and sailors rushed about, but none showed any signs of panic or anxiety.

The Archus was proud of how far his crew had come over the last six months, but there were many tests still awaiting them before the Ascomanni threat could be contained.

The campaign for Aetnaeus had been a draining, drawn-out battle on the ground, but the situation in space was more complicated.

Massively outgunned, the Praetor had refused to give battle when the Ascomanni fleet first arrived. Instead, he had given Fabian the freedom to split his force, sending smaller groups to pinch the enemy's supply lines and engaging the enemy only where small numbers of Ascomanni ships found themselves isolated from their main fleet.

Technologically equal and tactically superior to the Ascomanni, the Umbrians were more than capable of bloodying their enemies' noses. However, the sheer weight of numbers the Ascomanni had available prevented Fabian from having a decisive impact in space. For every enemy ship he destroyed, another took its place, while each of his lost or damaged ships diminished his ability to influence the battle.

"Archus, the Praetor indicates that the enemy has taken the bait. Three enemy destroyers have engaged the *Cerberus*."

"Understood," Fabian said.

The *Cerberus* was more than capable of handling a single Ascomanni destroyer, Fabian mused, but facing three alone would leave it hard pressed. It would not be long before the battlecruiser was forced to withdraw, and without its support, the transports evacuating Task Force Hyperion would be destroyed as they attempted to escape.

Fortunately, he had planned for just this type of reaction.

Fabian tapped a series of commands into his command console and addressed his crew. "All hands, action stations. Combat with the enemy is imminent."

Flashing lights and a low, dull claxon rang throughout the ship, reinforcing the urgency of his command. Within thirty seconds, his section heads reported that the crew was ready. The Archus allowed himself a small smile. That was the fastest time his sailors had managed yet. The moment passed, and his brow furrowed as he turned back to the task at hand.

"Navigation, take us in."

In the blink of an eye, the colossal supercarrier, the pride of his fleet, flashed into orbit.

The red-brown terrain of Aetnaeus's only continent contrasted sharply with its navy-blue oceans. Below and to the right were the three enemy destroyers, moving together to engage the larger Umbrian battlecruiser. From this distance, the *Cerberus* was only a speck on the backdrop of the planet below.

Fabian watched as his fighters and bombers deployed, milling about only long enough to form up and advance toward the Ascomanni destroyers in unison. Six hundred starfighters descended on an unsuspecting enemy.

The Ascomanni were slow to react. The lead destroyer had just entered the outer edge of the *Cerberus*'s weapons range, and the space between the two lit up with explosions, tracers, and the contrails of missiles and torpedoes. One of the trailing destroyers turned to face the new threat from his fighters, while the third slowed indecisively without changing course.

Within minutes, his squadrons reached the rear-most enemy destroyer, and it attempted in vain to protect itself from the swarm of small craft. He watched as his pilots looked to exploit the destroyer's weak points while avoiding its counter-fire.

Tiny flashes of light appeared wherever the Ascomanni's defenses found one of his fighters.

Each represented a man or woman under his command who would not be returning to the flight deck after the battle.

Fabian's mouth went dry. There was no such thing as a bloodless war, the Archus thought to himself, and his pilots accepted that. Each had trusted him to lead them with purpose and integrity. The sacrifices of his flight crews would not, *could not*, be in vain.

After a ceaseless pounding, the Ascomanni warship's armor finally gave way, and Fabian watched as a series of explosions ripped through its hull. The destroyer's engines flickered and died, and all defensive fire from the ship ceased as it lost power and began drifting toward Aetnaeus.

Fabian turned to his second in command. "Procurator, calculate the destroyer's re-entry, and inform Ischia Actual of its trajectory and expected impact zone."

"Aye, sir!" Grinning at their initial success, the younger officer acknowledged Fabian's order and began his calculations.

The Ascomanni attempted to regroup after the loss of their first ship. The destroyer that had engaged the *Cerberus* appeared worse for wear, venting atmosphere from several locations along its hull. The undamaged ship attempted to position itself to the other's port, away from the planet, where it could screen its wounded counterpart from the *Echion*'s fighters.

The *Cerberus*'s captain had taken the initiative, however, and the Umbrian battlecruiser bore down on the fleeing Ascomanni ships.

Fabian moved quickly to shut the door on his escaping foes. "Flight Group Echion, concentrate your fire on the leading ship. *Cerberus*, you've got the other one. Do not let them get away!"

Having issued his orders, the Archus stepped back and gave his subordinates room to carry them out.

Echion's fighters disabled the first ship within a few minutes, while a lucky shot from one of *Cerberus*'s batteries struck the second destroyer's magazine, creating a massive fireball that faded as quickly as it appeared in the merciless vacuum of space.

With a few more well-placed shots from the *Cerberus*, the disabled Ascomanni ship broke apart. Fires ravaged the derelict for the briefest of moments before the ship's atmosphere was totally consumed.

The Archus sat back heavily into his chair, satisfied with his ships' performance. The Ascomanni destroyers were no longer a threat to the *Cerberus* or to the transports below.

Umbrian Republic Command Center;
Near Ischia, Aetnaeus

Cheers and whistles sounded throughout the command center as the last enemy warship was destroyed, and Marcellus was satisfied with the result. The Ascomanni would think twice before engaging another ship sent to provide support to his ground forces.

"All right, let's begin Phase Two. Inform *Neptune* and *Vulcan* to proceed."

Valerian nodded and turned to the communications officer.

Two more Umbrian warships entered orbit over isolated pockets of friendly ground forces, and, repeating their earlier success, quickly decimated the surrounding Ascomanni from space. As the dust settled, two smaller groups of transports left Ischia to evacuate these forces.

Marcellus was counting on the Asco to hesitate before attempting to engage either of the new combatants, lest they stumble into another trap.

Fabian had enough resources to cover the retreat of both ships if it came to it. They wouldn't have the strength to drive off significant opposition though, and the transports would not survive without the URN's protection.

The ground rumbled beneath his feet yet again, pulling his attention back to his immediate surroundings. The Ascomanni were getting closer.

His commlink crackled to life. "Sagitta Lead to Ischia Actual. We have Hyperion on board and are heading for orbit."

"Understood, Sagitta, good work out there. *Echion*, *Cerberus*, keep the lane open as the transports withdraw and follow them out."

A series of acknowledgments met his orders, and the Praetor watched as the transports cleared Aetnaeus's atmosphere and jumped to lightspeed. *Echion* recovered her fighters as well as Sagitta's, and then both Umbrian warships disappeared from the orbital display.

Cheers rang out again as his staff celebrated Task Force Hyperion's successful escape.

Their celebration would be cut short as the ground bucked even more violently beneath them, throwing those standing from their feet and choking the bunker's air with even more dust and smoke.

"Praetor, Epsilon Two and Five just went dark! They're gone, sir!" Valerian called out.

Marcellus nodded and gave himself a few seconds to think.

"All right, everyone," he said, raising his voice above the din, "all secondary and tertiary functions and associated personnel are to fall back to the backup command site and prepare for our arrival. As soon as *Neptune* and *Vulcan* complete their objectives, all remaining staff will follow."

A frenzy of activities began to unfold. Only a handful of officers providing direct support to the front continued at their stations.

Turning to his adjutant, Marcellus continued: "I need you to go with them Valerian. Make sure the Viceroy's residence is up and running by the time we get there."

For a moment, his trusted aide looked ready to argue with him, but Valerian merely nodded and moved off to oversee the transfer. Confident that Val would ensure everything was in order, the Praetor drifted off into his own thoughts as his staff hurried about their tasks.

The Ascomanni had clearly caught on to his trick, he mused. The six Epsilon locations were dummy command posts staffed with skeleton crews. Their goal was to keep Marcellus's command center safe and the enemy guessing by spewing an endless stream of false orders on dummy frequencies.

Each had received sporadic artillery fire for the last few days, but over the last couple of hours, the rate of bombardment had picked up dramatically. It looked like the Ascomanni had finally decided to cut the head off the snake.

As minutes passed and the number of staffers left in the command center dwindled to the single digits, Marcellus overheard a series of reports from the other transport groups. Each had successfully evacuated their intended targets, though *Neptune*'s transport group had to sacrifice their Scutia battlemechs to cover the retreat, and *Vulcan*'s transports had been unable to salvage any of their evacuees' heavy equipment.

Both ships jumped to lightspeed as soon as their transports were away. The evacuations had concluded successfully.

"All right, ladies and gentlemen, we've done what we needed to do here, time to pack it in. Inform the secondary command center that we are falling back. ETA, fifteen minutes."

As his remaining staff executed their assigned tasks, he took one last look at the map of Aetnaeus and the forces the Ascomanni had arrayed against him. His vengeful enemy would soon marshal all its remaining might against the perimeter around Ischia, and there was little time to exploit this victory if he wanted to get the remainder of his forces off the planet.

Marcellus bowed his head and whispered, "I will find a way to get us home."

Suddenly warning strobes filled the room with a bright red light, and a deafening wail filled the bunker. One of his officers pointed to the map and screamed, "Sir! We have bogeys heading straight for us! They've found us!"

"We've got missiles incoming!" shouted another.

Above, the ripping, tearing noise of the bunker's point defenses competed with the alarm as they attempted to shoot down the incoming munitions. A series of explosions shook in the distance as the emplacements found their mark, but they could not intercept all of the missiles racing toward the bunker.

Time slowed for Marcellus as two deafening explosions threw him through the air and brought the bunker's roof down on top of him.

Chapter 2

Umbrian Republic Command Center;
Near Ischia, Aetnaeus

Blinking away blood and dust, Marcellus came to in the ruined remains of his command center. Dark shapes moved slowly about in the red glow of the bunker's emergency lighting. His combat harness had activated at the last moment, encasing him in his protective armor. His helmet's heads-up display flashed with words and images that he couldn't understand as a muffled voice tried to speak over the ringing in his ears.

Still dazed, he attempted to get to his feet, but as soon as he moved, a searing pain shot up his left leg.

Muffling a scream, Marcellus realized that his leg was trapped beneath a section of the bunker's ceiling.

The pain helped the Praetor focus, and Marcellus finally began to make sense of his surroundings. The symbols displayed on his HUD finally swam into focus, and he recognized his vital signs as reported by his suit's diagnostics. A timer counted down from ten seconds and the muffled voice of his armor's AI assistant resolved into words he could understand.

"…execute automatically in 10… 9… 8… Warning, Warning: Significant trauma to left leg. Heart rate and blood pressure elevated. Applying sedative and immobilizing extremity. Command will execute automatically in 4… 3… 2… 1…"

There was another sharp pinch as his armor locked in place around his damaged limb, but it was immediately followed by a wave of pleasant heat which faded away with the pain. Marcellus shifted, attempting to free himself once more, but was unable to budge the fallen rubble which was pinning him in place.

"Praetor! Over here, quickly!"

The shapes he had observed before converged on him. Another brief flash of pain overcame the sedative as the debris holding him down was lifted away. Marcellus rose as best he could with his leg forcibly extended and found himself standing in the midst of three of his praetorians, the most elite of his soldiers, hand-picked to serve as shock troops and bodyguards.

In the dim light of the ruined bunker, Marcellus recognized the individuals standing around him as Gaius, Thana, and Cornelius, soldiers who had been with him for years before the campaign on Aetnaeus had begun.

"It's good to see familiar faces," Marcellus said. "What about the others? Have you found any other survivors?"

"I'm sorry, sir, none of the others made it. Are you OK?" Gaius asked.

"My leg appears to be broken, but otherwise just some bumps and bruises," Marcellus responded.

"Not exactly, sir," Thana said as she knelt next to Marcellus. "You've got a piece of rebar going through your upper thigh. We'll need to remove it to allow your suit to seal the wound."

Marcellus looked at his damaged leg and spotted the metal bar. No larger in length or diameter than his thumb, it stuck out of the top of his armored thigh. Turning his torso slightly, he gingerly felt out the length protruding from the back of his leg and found it to be of a more substantial length. Marcellus took a deep breath, gritted his teeth, and, with a quick jerk, pulled the rod out of his leg.

Immediately his helmet erupted with new alarms: "Warning, Warning: Heart rate elevated. Puncture wound detected. Applying bio-sealant."

"Yeah, yeah..." Marcellus muttered as blood and a blue foamy substance began to bubble out from the hole in his leg. In moments, it had hardened into a durable purple gum covering his wound.

Shifting his weight to his damaged leg, Marcellus tried to get a feel for how badly he would be impaired. He was surprised to find that he still had a decent range of motion and that the pain was manageable.

The ground shook violently, and additional debris clattered down from the ruined ceiling.

"All right, praetorians, what's the situation?" Marcellus asked.

"The enemy has broken through the perimeter and they're driving straight for this location. Prefect Invictus and the rest are above, holding a defensive perimeter around the entrance to the bunker, but we're in danger of being overrun," Gaius said.

"Let's get moving then. Cornelius, give me a hand."

With that, they began working their way back up to the entrance. As they neared the surface, Marcellus's connection to the command net was re-established. A hundred discordant voices poured over his commlink:

"Sigma Two-Seven to command, we're being…"

"Phoenix flight has dropped payload on target, good effect. Returning to…"

"Arafa Three-Six requesting immediate fire support in sector…"

Marcellus did his best to block out the noise and switched to the praetorians' encrypted frequency: "Leo Six, this is the Leo Zero, give me a sitrep."

"It's good to hear your voice, Zero, you had me worried there! The Asco point of attack was north of the command center. They massed enough force to penetrate the first and second lines of defense. We are currently counterattacking with the mobile reserve, but we're still losing ground. How long until you reach the surface?"

"We are closing in on it now. ETA, three minutes. Zero Alpha should have the secondary command post up and running, but I need to get back there ASAP."

"Understood, I'll have a dropship standing by. Leo 6 out."

The four Umbrians reached the final stairwell leading out of the derelict bunker. Night had fallen, and the harsh white light of an illumination round spilled down the stairs, while the muted sounds of battle became an earsplitting roar.

They hurried up to the surface and emerged into a maelstrom of explosions and small arms fire.

Immediately surrounding the bunker's entrance were a pair of battlemechs, while the silhouettes of two dozen praetorians could be seen scattered amongst makeshift fighting positions nearby.

A deep, throaty roar drowned out the sounds of battle and twin shadows, a pair of Umbrian fighter-bombers swooped low overhead, their cannons flashing as they strafed the advancing enemy.

Just as quickly as the fighters had come and gone, a larger shadow was cast over the exit. They were buffeted from above as wind whipped at their armor. A dropship came to rest a few feet above the ground, and Marcellus waved for his three rescuers to follow him as its bay doors slid open. Once they were onboard, the dropship's door slid shut and they accelerated away from the fight.

Wrapping his fist on the cockpit's bulkhead, Marcellus called up to the pilots. "Notify the secondary command center that we'll be arriving imminently. Make sure they have everything prepared for Operation Omega."

Umbrian Republic Supply Depot;
Near Ischia, Aetnaeus

Standing at the entrance of a nearby motor pool, Prefect Invictus Flaminus drove his blade through the barrel of his adversary's weapon before spinning to deliver a crushing blow to the Ascomanni soldier's knee. With a grunt, the bulky armored form toppled to the ground before Invictus finished it off with a burst from his pulse carbine.

Turning quickly, he triggered another salvo at two more enemies who attempted to flank one of his soldiers. Their smoking forms collapsed to the pavement and lay still.

The intensity of battle receded momentarily, and his praetorians took advantage of the lull to form a defensive perimeter around the garage. Another illumination round soared through the night sky, allowing the Prefect to get a better grasp of his immediate surroundings.

Satisfied that the situation was under control for the time being, Invictus activated his commlink: "Leo One-Six, what's your status?"

"Leo Zero is away, we've fallen back to our secondary positions. We've got some heavy armor on location and are holding for now."

"Good work, One-Six. We're heading to you now. Gather Two-Six and Four-Six for a briefing in ten minutes. Leo Six out."

With that, he walked out of the motor pool and started searching for Primus Aria Fulvia Nobilior, the last of his subordinates. He found her a short distance away, huddled with a medic around a pair of wounded soldiers.

She patted one of the wounded men on the shoulder and stood as the Prefect approached.

"Prefect Invictus," she said, offering one of her standard tightlipped greetings.

Aria was athletically built and strikingly beautiful, with silver-blond hair highlighting her bronzy skin. A stony expression belied her beauty, which vacillated between dour and severe. In all the time he'd spent with her, he'd never once seen her crack a smile or make a joke.

"The Praetor is on his way back to the Viceroy's residence. While he gets organized, we need to do something about the breach in the perimeter. Round up your cohort and move to the RV. Vetus, Antonia, and Sextus should be waiting for us by the time we arrive."

"Understood, sir," she replied curtly.

Aria turned and issued a couple of commands to the soldiers nearby, who quickly formed up and began working their way toward the rendezvous point. As her praetorians began to move out, she swung back to face Invictus, waiting silently for his next order.

Invictus shook his head at his peculiar subordinate. "All right, let's get moving Aria. I told Vetus we'd be there in ten minutes, and you know how pissy he gets when we're late."

Aetnaeus Viceroy's Mansion; Ischia, Aetnaeus

With Cornelius's continued support, Marcellus limped into the grand entryway of the Viceroy's mansion, former home to Aetnaeus's civilian administrator. As his eyes adjusted to the light, he was taken aback by the grandeur of the residence. The white marble foyer was flanked by two sweeping staircases featuring gilded balustrades, while serene landscapes and other works of fine art decorated the walls.

This beauty was the backdrop for barely organized chaos.

Nearly every square meter of space had been utilized: workstations and displays had been set up on portable tables running along the walls, while crates of supplies were stacked wherever spare room could be located.

Before Marcellus could flag down one of his officers, Valerian appeared and rushed over to the Praetor's side.

He threw Marcellus's other arm over his shoulder and said, "Damnit, sir, this is why you shouldn't have sent me back with the others. You always get yourself into trouble when I'm not around."

Smiling ruefully, Marcellus responded: "It's good to see you too, Val. I needed to be sure everything would be up and running here, and it looks like you've done a fine job."

Cornelius passed the Praetor off to Valerian, and Marcellus shuffled around to address the three praetorians who had pulled him out of the ruined bunker.

"Gaius, Thana, Cornelius; thank you. Vetus made the right choice sending you three down after me. Without your help, I wouldn't have made it out of there."

Cornelius laughed and said, "Well, sir, next time you feel like having a ceiling dropped on you, make sure to let us know in advance."

Valerian cast the Praetor a sideways glance, one Marcellus had seen before, and the other two praetorians winced at their comrade's unsuccessful attempt at humor.

Thana punched Cornelius in the shoulder. "Shut up, you idiot!" she said before turning back to Marcellus. "Thank you, Praetor. Is there any way we could get a ride back to our unit?"

"Of course, Valerian here will make sure you get back to your cohort."

Together, the three praetorians saluted and walked back out of the mansion, while Valerian and Marcellus turned and headed deeper into the structure.

"All right, Val, out with it," the Praetor demanded.

A grin spilled onto Valerian's face. "So, you pick all your praetorians by hand then, sir?"

Marcellus laughed as they worked their way toward their way deeper into the viceroy's mansion.

Umbrian Republic Defensive Perimeter; Near Ischia, Aetnaeus

Prefect Invictus huddled behind the smoking remains of an Ascomanni tank while Primus Sextus kneeled next to him, his arm broken and immobilized by a bloody med-wrap. A portable holotable provided a tactical readout of the battlefield, showing the position and composition of friendly forces and known enemy units.

The situation still wasn't good. An angry red dagger, representing thousands of Asco soldiers, had been driven through the defensive perimeter. The enemy had advanced all the way to the outskirts of Ischia itself. The Ascomanni hadn't begun to roll up the perimeter's flanks, but if Invictus couldn't seal the breakthrough, the Umbrian defenses would eventually start to collapse.

Invictus had come up with a simple plan to blunt the Ascomanni assault. He had redeployed his four cohorts, two on either side of the breach in the perimeter. One cohort would penetrate the enemy's lines from each side, while the second unit would screen their flanks and help hold the regained territory until reinforcements could arrive.

Things had been going well. Sextus's command neared their final objectives, while Aria's forces had already reached the rally point. All that stood in their way was Elevation One Thirty-Four, a low rise in the terrain that the Umbrian Republic had heavily fortified.

Sextus's initial attack on the fortification had attempted to take advantage of the advance's speed, hoping to keep the enemy off balance. The Ascomanni had been ready, however, and they had defended the hill tenaciously.

Somehow, they had managed to reprogram a series of automated Umbrian gun emplacements that dotted the elevation's defenses. Worse still, the Ascomanni had waited until the Umbrians were very close before activating them.

The result was bloody. Fifty-two praetorians had been killed, while another seventy-five had been wounded. Sextus's cohort had already started the battle understrength with four hundred and sixty soldiers. For a tightly knit, elite unit, such losses in a single engagement were difficult to deal with.

Triage had been set up behind the same tank Invictus was using as an impromptu command post, and many of the wounded needed to be evacuated quickly if they were going to survive. Two dropships had attempted to pull the wounded out, but they'd taken heavy damage from the Asco defenses and were forced to withdraw.

As the Prefect poured over the tactical readout before him, it was clear that storming the hill again would result in heavy casualties. Even if they successfully pried it from the Ascomanni's grasp, they would be too weak to hold it if the enemy counterattacked.

Attempts to raze the fortification entirely would also be difficult, as the structure was protected by a kinetic barrier which would stop anything short of an orbital bombardment. Furthermore, the same automatic turrets which had proven so deadly for his men would prove equally dangerous to attacking aircraft.

The only remaining option Invictus saw available to him was a low-level infiltration of the strongpoint. A handful of praetorians might be able to sneak into the fortifications and take the guns offline. It was risky, and he'd need a solid team...

He turned to look at his wounded subordinate.

Rugged, strong jawed, and serious in expression, Salvius Sextus was approximately his age, and had seen his fair share of combat prior to joining his command. Despite his best efforts to stay on top of the situation, Invictus could tell that Sextus was struggling under the weight of the sedative that had been administered for his broken arm. His eyes occasionally drifted from the display, half lidded, before he wiped at his face with his free hand.

Sextus was clearly in no condition to make the assault, but maybe that would be for the best. While his insertion team made their approach, Sextus and what remained of his cohort could distract the enemy by laying down a heavy base of fire on the Ascomanni position.

Once the guns had been silenced, the praetorians would overrun the enemy and make contact with Aria's unit, sealing the hole in the perimeter around Ischia and encircling the Ascomanni spearhead.

Invictus shook his head. That strategy would rely on skill, speed, and no small amount of luck, but it was the best he could come up with. He turned to Sextus and laid out his plan.

Aetnaeus Viceroy's Mansion; Ischia, Aetnaeus

Marcellus's senior commanders had been gathered in a beautiful, partially covered amphitheater overlooking the Viceroy's vineyard. It was a brilliant, clear night. Light from Aetnaeus's moons illuminated tall purple foliage, which clung to trellises lining the rolling, reddish-brown hills. Cercyon, Ischia's dormant volcano, towered off in the distance, its imposing bulk blocking out a section of the night sky.

It would have been easy to lose focus amid this idyllic vista, if not for the constant thunder of combat in the distance.

As Marcellus hobbled in, Valerian called the room to attention. Marcellus waved his commanders down and took his place at the central podium.

"Ladies and gentlemen, first off, I want to thank you all for doing a fantastic job over the last nine months. Our losses have been steep, but each of you has kept your units fighting, and together we have kept the Ascomanni at bay.

"Despite all of your efforts, our hard-earned respite will soon come to an end. It's only a matter of time before our enemy brings irresistible force crashing down on the perimeter around Ischia. We simply do not have the strength to hold out indefinitely."

Marcellus watched the faces of his leaders. Most showed signs of fatigue, but only a few showed any indication of despair. They all knew that this would be the inevitable outcome.

"As you all know, the war has already seen too many setbacks. We have been pushed steadily back from the Frontier, making the Ascomanni pay a steep price in blood for each world they take from us." "However," he continued, "the outcome is always the same. Another colony lost. Another world's resources left to fuel our enemy's conquest of our people.

"The Triumvirate believes we must hold Aetnaeus to the bitter end, that only by showing the Asco the fullness of our resolve can we pause their advance."

His audience began to shift in their seats and whisper to one another. Valerian took a half step forward, but Marcellus held up a hand to forestall his adjutant's rebuke.

Raising his voice, Marcellus called out over the hubbub: "I happen to disagree!"

The amphitheater quieted down again, and the Praetor was satisfied that he had his subordinates' full attention once more.

"For too long, we have fought our enemy as if we were their equal. We are not. They are many, while every day there are fewer of us to man the ramparts. Unless we change course, the Ascomanni will wash over us with sheer numbers alone!

"If we have any hope to repel this threat, we must shepherd our resources. Each of our soldiers must equal a hundred of the enemy! Every ship must be worth ten of theirs! For too long we have sat and waited for the Ascomanni to come to us, only to engage in pitched battles that we are unable to win. We *must* find a way to take back the initiative, to hit the enemy where they are vulnerable while avoiding their heaviest blows.

"Before we can do that, however, we have to get as many of our soldiers and as much of our equipment off Aetnaeus as possible. To enable such a massive undertaking, we have spent the last month prepositioning transports around the perimeter. It'll be cramped, but these ships have the capacity to evacuate our remaining forces.

"There are several problems to overcome before that can happen though. The space above the planet is contested. A large-scale evacuation would be identified immediately, and the Third Fleet does not have the strength to go toe to toe with the enemy. We cannot hold the perimeter and evacuate at the same time, and we cannot allow the Ascomanni to know our intentions, lest they cut off our escape route.

"To solve for these problems, we have formulated a plan that we believe offers the best chance for success in this difficult situation." Marcellus paused, inhaling deeply before continuing: "To save the forces defending Aetnaeus, we must destroy her. I'll turn it over to Valerian to explain Operation Omega."

With that, Marcellus limped over to the nearest seat, while Valerian typed a few commands into a remote. The whispers in the audience picked up again, but the tension and anxiety Marcellus had felt upon entering the room had been replaced with curiosity and determination.

The amphitheater's projector sparked to life, and before them appeared an image of the perimeter around Ischia. Valerian cleared his throat and began the presentation.

"To facilitate our withdrawal from Aetnaeus, we have been drilling shafts through the base of Cercyon for the last three weeks. Robotic boring machines have drilled to within four hundred meters of the volcano's magma chamber. Already, pressure is building on these weak points between Cercyon's molten heart and the surface, and soon they will fail.

"Once that happens, an incredible amount of force will push back up this channel, and the volcano will shoot a thick cloud of ash and dust into the atmosphere. It is under this umbrella that we will evacuate."

Valerian turned and looked at Marcellus, but Marcellus gave him a quick shake of the head.

"For operational security, that is all we have for you at this point," Valerian continued. "Based on the seismic readings we are getting from the boring machines, we believe this eruption will trigger in anywhere from two to six hours. Detailed plans for each of your units have been sent to your datapads."

Marcellus stood and hobbled back to the dais. He gestured out at Cercyon in the distance and said, "The volcano will mask our retreat, but we still must hold off the enemy long enough to disengage. Once the eruption has begun, elements of Archus Catus's fleet will repeat the tactics we used earlier today. However, instead of remaining in orbit, they will skirt through the atmosphere before slingshotting back out of the system."

Marcellus's throat began to grow raspy, and he quickly wrapped up the briefing: "This tactic should leave the enemy disorganized long enough for our escape. All Umbrian Republic forces will be evacuated from the system by this time tomorrow. Are there any questions?"

One of his legates stood. "Praetor, what about the rear area units? The ones in closest proximity to the volcano?"

"Those units have already been loaded into transports and will be the first ones out," Marcellus responded.

A wing commander, Tulla Cornelia, stood next and asked, "What about the ground-based fighters and bombers?"

"Good question. Two assault carriers will jump in and recover all craft incapable of reaching the rendezvous point on their own. The rearguard will also be evacuated directly to the carriers before we depart."

She nodded and sat down.

Marcellus answered a few more questions. When no one had anything left to ask, the meeting broke up, and the Praetor and his adjutant walked back toward the command center.

Elevation One Thirty-Four, Umbrian Republic Defensive Perimeter; Near Ischia, Aetnaeus

Invictus stabbed his bayonet into the base of the sentry's skull. The red-hot blade hissed as he whipped it through the Ascomanni's neck, and the sentry gurgled and collapsed.

All around them, Ascomanni soldiers engaged the remnants of Sextus's cohort. They had deployed a smokescreen, which, together with the thunderous noise of battle, had masked the infiltration team's advance and gummed up the enemy's sensors.

Invictus and his small team had already penetrated the outer perimeter and were slowly working their way up the trenchworks in the direction of the pillboxes and bunkers that sat at the top of the hill.

Invictus waved the rest of the infiltration team forward.

After ten minutes of slowly and deliberately working their way toward the summit, they finally came to the entrance of the hill's primary fortification. The eight praetorians stacked up at the entrance, and Invictus tapped his tech specialist on the shoulder.

Nodding, he kneeled and pulled a small spherical drone from his bag and rolled it around the corner. A new image appeared in each of their HUDs, showing the camera feed from the drone.

The bunker was an open, two-storied structure, with its lower level built into the hill. The bottom level was cluttered with workstations and monitors. Two sets of staircases on either side of the lower floor led up to a gunnery deck, which expanded outward in three directions.

The gunnery deck was thick with Ascomanni soldiers, but only four Ascomanni were present on the lower level. One of them in particular drew Invictus's attention.

This Ascomanni was not wearing the heavy power armor associated with the shock troops they normally faced. Instead, it wore a slimmed-down set which appeared similar to the Umbrian's own combat suits.

Invictus began to draw up a plan. "All right, praetorians," he whispered in his helmet, "we'll lead with a wave dampener to cover our entrance. The first four in will take out the Asco on the lower level, while the remaining four split into teams of two and clear the gunnery deck from both sides. Am I clear?"

A chorus of whispered *how-oo*'s echoed across the channel. Nodding, Invictus pulled a rectangular device from his belt and flicked it on. Leaning around the corner, he slid the wave dampener across the bunker's floor.

"Execute, execute, execute."

The praetorians streamed silently into the bunker; the heavy sounds of their movement were reduced by the dampener, leaving nothing more than a dull thud to reverberate through the attackers' feet with every step.

Invictus was first in, and his plasma cannon blew a hole through the nearest Ascomanni soldier.

The smaller Ascomanni Invictus had noticed before reacted quickly, dropping and throwing itself to the left.

Invictus moved faster.

Before it could sound the alarm, he knocked it out with a blow to the back of the head.

The other members of the infiltration team poured into the room and burned down the other two Ascomanni soldiers. Four praetorians split off and headed in pairs for the stairs on either side of the lower level. They waited for a moment, pausing only long enough to sync up.

The stairwell teams then breached the upper level of the bunker. Few of the Ascomanni soldiers heard the praetorians over the sounds of their own weapons, and the tightly packed mass of Ascommani were torn apart in a grisly kaleidoscope of plasma fire and blood.

Invictus jogged over and picked up the dampener and switched it off. In an instant, the sounds of battle came rushing back, providing a momentary and unwelcome sense of disorientation.

"Clear!" a voice echoed through the team's headsets.

"Clear down here," another voice called out.

Invictus quickly set two of his soldiers on the gunnery deck, while two more covered the entrance they had entered through. The remaining soldiers were detailed to watch their prisoner. He then moved to the center command console where he found his specialist kneeling and furiously tapping away on a diagnostic panel.

"Can you disable the guns from here?" he asked.

With a vengeful grin, the specialist turned and said, "I can do you one better, sir. I can restore the guns back to their default programming. They'll tear the Asco apart!"

"Those guns are still chewing up our people. How long?" Invictus demanded.

"Sixty seconds, no more," the specialist responded.

"Get to it then."

Leaving the specialist to work, he turned and walked over to the prisoner. Still unconscious, it looked even less like the Ascomanni up close. In fact, if it weren't for the difference in armor, it would look a great deal like an Umbrian.

Ascomanni biology had been a hot topic from the outset of the war. They were warm blooded bipedal beings, with gray skin, pale violet eyes, and flared nostril slits. With redundant vital organs, thick skeletal structure, and substantial muscularity, the Ascomanni were dangerous adversaries.

The form at his feet definitely did not fit the description.

"Keep it sedated," Invictus said to the guards. "Command is going to want to see this."

A voice rang out across the bunker: "Prefect, I've got it! The turrets just finished their boot sequence. We can fire them up on your command."

Turning back to the center of the room, Invictus quickly moved to the command console. He nodded once to the technician: "Do it."

Invictus watched the console as the gun emplacements turned on the Ascomanni. Short controlled bursts tore through the enemy defenders. Within thirty seconds, any Ascomanni exposed to the guns had been neutralized.

Invictus keyed the bunker's communications array and selected the appropriate frequency. "All right, Leo Four-Six, that's your cue!"

Outside, the *how-oo*'s of three hundred voices echoed off the slopes of Elevation One Thirty-Four. Sextus's praetorians rose from their fighting positions and charged up the hill. The Ascomanni broke and ran, but between the auto turrets and Sextus's vengeful warriors, they were quickly cut down.

The Ascomanni breach in the perimeter had been sealed. Sextus arrived and began requesting dropships to evacuate his wounded, while Invictus prepared a short report for the Praetor and arranged for the prisoner to be transferred to the Viceroy's mansion.

Other Umbrian troops would mop up the pocket of Ascomanni forces trapped behind the Umbrian defensive line, and once that was complete, the praetorians would be relieved.

Invictus's praetorians would have to hold for a while more, but the night's fighting was almost done.

Aetnaeus Viceroy's Mansion; Ischia, Aetnaeus

Marcellus sat in the Viceroy's elaborate quarters while Invictus finished up his report on the night's activities. His subordinate looked surprisingly spry despite enduring hours of combat, his pale brown eyes radiating energy while his trademark happy-go-lucky disposition was still firmly planted on his long, narrow face. Somehow, even his red-gold hair, kept slightly longer than regulation allowed, seemed to bounce and flow in Aetnaeus's gentle breeze.

Marcellus smiled at the vid feed of his friend and said, "Good work, Vic. Once you're relieved, redeploy your cohorts to the spaceport. The *Aegis Fire* will be waiting to take our praetorians to Safe Haven."

"Understood, Praetor, we'll see you there." With that, Invictus saluted and ended the transmission.

Marcellus checked his chrono and found that he still had an hour or so to rest before the earliest projections for the eruption. He walked to the bathroom, located the sink, and splashed some cold water over his face.

As he opened his eyes, he was startled by the sight of his reflection. He looked almost haggard, his thick black hair a tangled mess, while dirty smudges and numerous small nicks and abrasions marred his face. He ran his hands up and over his face, massaging the hollows of his cheeks and taking a moment to relish the tactile pleasure of his stubble grating against his fingertips.

He barely remembered the fresh-faced twenty-something he'd been upon leaving the academy all those years before. Square jawed and with strong cheekbones, he'd prided himself on the dashing figure he'd cut in his dress uniform.

While his features had withstood the test of combat, he saw a gauntness to his appearance that had escaped his notice previously.

Marcellus chuckled to himself. If that's all he'd suffered after numerous brushes with death, he could hardly complain. He walked gingerly to the room's massive bed and sat down. But, before he could remove his combat harness, there were two quick raps on the door.

"Come in," Marcellus called out.

The door slid open and Valerian walked in.

"Valerian, what can I help you with?" Marcellus asked.

"Please forgive the intrusion, sir," his adjutant replied tentatively. "But something has been bothering me. During the briefing, why didn't you tell the others about the bomb?"

Marcellus's cheerful disposition faded.

"What we are attempting to do has never been done before. There will be consequences, and they will be mine alone to face. Those men and women need to concentrate on defeating our enemies, not the idea of being hauled before a court martial or some stupid Senate subcommittee."

Valerian reluctantly nodded. "So, it's just you and I who are in the loop?"

"No. Fabian and Invictus are aware of the plan as well. If things go poorly, Invictus will take command of the ground troops, and Fabian will have overall command of the theater. No matter what happens, they will need you, Val. You have kept us going, kept the machine from grinding to a halt, for much longer than I thought possible."

"I've done what I could for Umbria, sir, no more or less than you should expect from any of your soldiers."

Valerian's stiff response caught him off guard, but he chalked it up to his friend's anxiety.

Marcellus simply nodded and said, "There's one more thing I need you to do, Val. Invictus captured a prisoner when he sealed the perimeter. I need you to make sure it gets transferred to the Combined Intelligence Directorate."

"Since when do the Asco surrender?" Valerian asked, a bewildered look on his face. "Moreover, what do you expect to learn from some mindless shock trooper?"

"He said this one is different. Apparently, it looks more like us than them. It's all very hazy, but this could be a member of a separate Ascomanni leadership class or maybe even a distinctive sub-species. It'll be up to CID to figure out the specifics."

"Understood, sir. I'll make the arrangements. In the meantime, I'd recommend you get some rest. How's the leg?"

"Good, the doctor wrapped up the fracture point. It'll bear weight with only minor discomfort, and the nano-mesh will help it heal faster than it would on its own."

"Glad to hear it. I'll wake you once the…" Valerian trailed off as the ground began to shake. Smiling repentantly, he looked at Marcellus and said, "Well, sir, I guess there is no rest for you today."

Marcellus grinned back. "Call down to the command center and get them to raise Fabian on the comms. It looks like Cercyon is ready to do its part."

Bridge of the URN *Echion*, Outer Edges of the Aetnaeus System

A nervous anxiety was building up within Fabian's chest as he gave his report: "We are set, Praetor. There's not much left to do at this point. The captains of the *Vulcan* and *Neptune* know the plan and are ready. The Third Fleet has been assembled and we're prepared to cover the withdrawal."

"Good work, Fabian. I need you to detach two corvettes and a patrol ship from the fleet. The corvettes will evacuate my command staff, and I'll be evacuating on the patrol ship."

"Praetor, why not have a larger capital ship pick you up?" Fabian responded. "The patrol boat is fast, but it doesn't have the armor or shielding to protect you from the Ascomanni."

"Speed is paramount. I'm not sure if this plan will work, and I will not doom more of our sailors than necessary if it doesn't."

With an exasperated sigh, Fabian relented. "As you wish. You know, you are a real pain in the ass sometimes, sir."

Thirty billion kilometers away, Marcellus laughed. "You better not talk to your next CO like that, Fabian."

"Well then, you better survive so you can reprimand me yourself!" Fabian replied, grinning. His expression grew sober. "It's been an honor to serve with you, sir."

Marcellus's voice softened: "The honor has been mine, Fabian. For the Republic, Archus."

With that, the Praetor and his subordinate exchanged salutes for what could be the last time, and the vid feed winked out.

"For the Republic..." Fabian whispered to himself in reply.

He swiveled in his chair and addressed his communications officer: "Give me an open channel to the fleet."

The officer nodded and a moment later a green light appeared on Fabian's console.

"Men and women of the Third Fleet, this is Archus Fabian Catus. In a few short minutes, we will begin the effort of extracting our brothers and sisters from Aetnaeus. I expect a significant encounter between the URN and the Ascomanni fleet. We have the element of surprise, but the enemy will inevitably respond."

"Over the last six months, each and every ship in this fleet has been tested, and your mettle has been proven beyond doubt. Although we retreat, we withdraw with our strength intact, having inflicted grievous wounds on our foes."

"Today, we shall pull our comrades from the fiery pits of hell and shatter any who dare to stop us! Tomorrow, we drive the Ascomanni back into whatever cesspit they crawled out of! Fight well, brave sons and daughters of Umbria. For the Republic!"

The bridge around him erupted in response, with four dozen voices calling out together: "For the Republic!"

The anxiety bubbling in his stomach was still present, but Fabian allowed himself a tight smile. For better or worse, the Third Fleet was ready.

Aetnaeus Viceroy's Mansion; Ischia, Aetnaeus

Standing on a balcony overlooking Cercyon, Marcellus watched as a giant plume of ash spewed out of the once dormant volcano, marring the first rays of the morning sun. Valerian, his ever-present friend and aide, stood next to him taking in the view while ash and soot fell from the sky like snow.

As they watched, streams of soldiers and equipment were heading to the starport, while more still gathered in fields that were thick with camouflaged freighters and troop transports.

The evacuation had begun.

"Any word from the front, Val? Are the Ascomanni on to us yet?"

"Not yet, Praetor. There have been a few probing attacks, but nothing serious. The CAP has also been guarding the perimeter tight. They've already downed at least a dozen enemy surveillance drones."

Marcellus nodded and remembered the wing commander from the briefing earlier in the day. Her squadrons were orbiting over the perimeter as they spoke, eagerly watching for any sign of approaching Ascomanni. Her pilots had acquitted themselves well during the campaign on Aetnaeus. If he survived the battle, he'd make sure to recommend her for promotion.

Together they stood and watched events unfold in a small bubble of peace. A gentle breeze rustled through the surrounding vineyards; the sounds of rustling leaves just audible over the noise of his forces' retreat.

This brief reprieve was broken, however, as a massive shockwave rocked the Viceroy's mansion. Glass shattered and wind whipped through the mansion as two massive shapes punched through the ash cloud.

As quick as a bullet, two Umbrian battleships, the *Neptune* and the *Vulcan*, tore through the space overhead on perpendicular vectors.

The kilometer and a half-long weapons of war unleashed a withering barrage on their unsuspecting enemy. The ground kicked and buckled under the force of their bombardment, as if the planet itself were being torn apart.

The ships were gone just as quickly as they had appeared. Their disappearance created a vacuum in the battlespace, and an eerie calm fell over the city.

Three new shapes descended from the clouds, these much smaller in size. Two short, squat corvettes approached the Viceroy's mansion, while a thin, winged patrol ship followed from the rear.

As the ships neared their destination, an alarm began to wail. *Air raid*, Marcellus instinctively thought to himself.

Marcellus and Valerian fell prone as the corvettes disgorged a swarm of missiles. They screamed over the mansion and raced toward the front. A series of explosions rippled over the outskirts of the perimeter as approaching Ascomanni fighters and bombers were destroyed.

"Well, if they didn't know before, they're most certainly on to us now!" Marcellus exclaimed. "Let Fabian know that the first phase is complete, and then get the headquarters troops on those corvettes!"

Valerian got back up to his feet, saluted, and rushed off.

Marcellus lingered a moment longer, watching as the three ships passed by overhead. They kicked up clouds of debris as they set down in the grand gardens lining the approaches to the mansion. Before the dust had even settled, men and woman began transferring equipment to the newly arrived vessels.

The Praetor took one last look out over the terrain his soldiers had fought so hard to defend, then headed toward the exit.

Bridge of the URN *Echion*, Outer Edges of the Aetnaeus System

Fabian watched as Vulcan and Neptune pulled back into formation following their strikes on Aetnaeus. Two boxy, octagonal forms also hung off the starboard bow. They were assault carriers, ships designed to deploy troops and provide close air support during a planetary invasion. They would enter Aetnaeus's atmosphere to recover the ground-based air force squadrons and provide additional fire support where needed.

The first wave of the Praetor's troops was almost ready to launch, and Task Force Icarus, made up of the *Echion*, *Cerberus*, the battleship *Orcus*, and a handful of destroyers, frigates, and light cruisers, would jump into orbit over Ischia to protect them. The remaining ships of the Third Fleet hung further back. They would provide a flexible tactical reserve which could be employed to counter the Ascomanni response as necessary.

Fabian's second in command approached and said, "Archus, we've received word from Ischia Actual. Transports are launching now."

"All right, time to get started."

Fabian switched to his fleetwide frequency: "Task Force Icarus, we jump in thirty seconds." He turned to back to his XO and said, "Procurator, take the ship to general quarters. Navigation has the coordinates."

A claxon wailed throughout the *Echion* as her crew prepared for combat, and, half a minute later, the ship flashed into orbit over Aetnaeus, joined by the other sixteen vessels of Task Force Icarus.

Below, an angry cloud of volcanic ash had covered the southern end of the planet's only continent. As Fabian watched, four dozen ships punched through the clouds, pulling tall spires of dust and soot into the upper atmosphere behind them.

The Ascomanni did not wait long to react.

Fabian's executive officer called out, "Archus, ten ships are coming around from the far side of Aetnaeus. Enemy strength is estimated at five frigates, three destroyers, a pair of cruisers, and a battleship."

"All right, have the destroyers and frigates screen the transports. Order *Cerberus* and *Orcus* to form up with the light cruisers and keep us close. Flight group Echion should stick with the screen and engage any enemy fighters that approach. Once they have achieved space superiority, they can attack the Ascomanni heavies at will."

His subordinate nodded and passed on the Archus's orders.

There was nothing to do now but wait. Fighters and bombers swooped across the forward spars of his vessel's hull, while his screening ships moved to protect the fleeing transports.

As the Ascomanni grew closer, a new shape punched through the clouds below, almost too small to track with the naked eye. As it cleared Aetnaeus's atmosphere, it slowed, reoriented, and headed straight for the enemy fleet. With a new burst of energy, it ripped across space before striking a distant target.

"Sir, the enemy battleship has been struck by some sort of projectile!"

A display appeared showing a magnified view of the oncoming Ascomanni ships. In the rear of the enemy fleet, the massive battleship had been eviscerated by whatever object had hit it.

The mighty ship's engines continued to push forward, but the damaged hull could not absorb the force. Fabian looked on with a mixture of elation and horror as the once proud warship folded in on itself like two hands on an old analog clock.

As the sections of the hull came into contact with one another, the ship's reactor exploded, creating a massive shockwave which ripped through one of the nearby Ascomanni ships. That cruiser's hull plating crumpled under the force of the blow, and its running lights flickered and died.

The remaining Ascomanni ships loosened up, drifting further away from each other in order to reduce the chance of additional collateral damage.

"Archus, Ischia Actual just sent us a short transmission. It appears we just witnessed the operational debut of the 'Longbow,' some kind of surface-launched capital ship killer. They sent a questionnaire asking us to rate the weapon's efficacy and said, 'Good hunting.'"

Fabian grinned at his XO. The message was probably Valerian's work, he thought to himself. Val had that type of rye humor which could grate on you just as easily as it would make you smile.

In this case though, the new and the unexpected were more than welcome. Undoubtedly his Ascomanni counterpart would have something new to think about before committing additional forces.

"Contact *Orcus* and the other capital ships. Tell them to move in and finish the job. Flight Group Echion is clear to engage as well, but keep the screen with the transports. CID believes there could be upwards of one hundred Asco capital ships within operational distance of Aetnaeus. We can expect additional enemy forces at any time, so as soon as we mop up what's left out there, pull everyone back into a tighter perimeter above Ischia."

His XO saluted and walked back over to the communications station to relay the orders.

Fabian pulled up a large-scale map of space Icarus inhabited, while a second display featured telemetry from *Orcus*. The evacuation ships had formed up with the screening force and were only a minute or two away from their jump point.

Meanwhile, his heavier combatants had just entered the maximum range of their weapons and let loose a withering barrage on their disorganized adversaries. The *Orcus* supported enough heavy mass drivers to quickly reduce an Asco destroyer to space junk, and his light cruisers were packed with cells of ship-to-ship missiles. *Cerberus* was no slouch either, and together they quickly destroyed two Asco frigates and disabled a destroyer.

They had now entered the enemy's optimal range, and return fire from the Ascomanni lanced out to meet his forces. Point defense turrets worked overtime to intercept as many of the incoming missiles and projectiles as possible, but some inevitably found their way through.

One light cruiser took a pair of hits to its starboard engine nacelle, and the boxy structure twisted and bent inwards under the force of the impact. The cruiser began to list to port, and the ship's captain reduced engine output to correct the drift.

The *Orcus*'s captain responded by positioning his ship in front of the Umbrian attackers. Rotated ninety degrees on its long axis and turning perpendicular to the line of advance, the battleship looked like a great shield from Umbria's distance past.

Its reinforced armor plating was much better able to handle the punishment dealt out by the Asco destroyers and frigates. Hits from enemy weapons tore chunks out of the ship's armor, but few fully penetrated.

Cerberus surged under the *Orcus*'s protective umbrella and drove through the heart of the enemy formation, straight at the remaining enemy cruiser. Surrounded on all sides, all of her gun emplacements could engage the enemy. The battlecruiser lit up like a miniature star as its full complement of weapons reached out and struck the enemy.

Explosions rippled through the enemy fleet as *Cerberus* bore down on the remaining functional Ascomanni cruiser. A collision looked inevitable, and Fabian leaned forward, his stomach churning as he watched. At the last possible moment, the Ascomanni captain lost its nerve and veered to the left. The Umbrian battlecruiser took advantage and slid to the right, pulling alongside the enemy vessel.

Once more, *Cerberus* lit up the darkness of space. The bridge crew around him gasped as the battlecruiser's weapons penetrated one side of the Asco ship and ripped out the other, spewing fountains of fire and debris out into space.

Cerberus accelerated away as secondary explosions continued to wrack the cruiser before it finally succumbed in another massive explosion.

The remaining Ascomanni ships scattered in an attempt to get away, but by this time, *Echion*'s fighters and bombers had finally reached the fray. Within a few minutes, all of the surviving Ascomanni ships had been destroyed.

Soon Fabian's captains reported in, and he was satisfied with the result. They had destroyed ten enemy ships at the cost of one heavily damaged light cruiser. The hull integrity readings for his remaining ships put them well within range for continued combat operations.

"Procurator, have one of the frigates escort our damaged ship to Safe Haven, then reform the Task Force over Ischia," Fabian said. "Also, send word to the assault carriers that the path has been cleared."

"Aye, sir."

On the large-scale map of the area around his ships, Fabian watched as both the screening force and his capital ships began to circle back toward the *Echion*.

"Were there any complications with the first wave of transports?"

"No, sir," his XO responded. "Everyone got away cleanly this time."

"Good. Rotate the flight group through so they can refuel and rearm, but make sure to keep a solid CAP out there. We could have additional Ascomanni on our hands at any moment."

With that, Fabian leaned back into in his chair and watched as a pair of assault carriers flickered into orbit and began their descent.

URN Patrol Ship *Aquila*, Aetnaeus's Viceroy's Mansion; Ischia, Aetnaeus

Captain Claudia Critonius, master of the URN *Aquila*, looked up from a console and nodded in the Praetor's direction.

"The line is secured, sir."

Marcellus nodded at the young woman, a twinge of remorse echoing through his conscious. He had been shocked by how young she looked upon first meeting the ship's commander. He assumed that she'd only just earned her commission, and with it, her first command. Then again, perhaps he was just getting old, he thought ruefully to himself.

Either way, Captain Critonius and her crew were in for a steep challenge.

"Thank you, Captain." Marcellus said to the young officer, feeling a temporary pang of guilt as he sat at her appropriated workstation.

She nodded and worked her way aft, to the back of the patrol ship's cramped interior. The captain and her crew vacated the bridge for other parts of the ship to give the Praetor some privacy.

With a standard complement of eight officers and sailors, the *Aquila* was designed to monitor the Frontier. Its job was to observe and report back, and its limited internal space prioritized sensors over weapons.

However, what it lacked in firepower it made up for with superior range, speed, and communications equipment. The *Aquila* was a runner, not a fighter, designed to be the URN's eyes and ears in the vast expanses of the Frontier.

Those traits were exactly what he was looking for, and why he had ignored Fabian's advice. If he was going to pull this off, Marcellus needed speed above all else.

Doubt began to creep into the edges of his consciousness. For all intents and purposes, Marcellus had removed himself from the operational picture, turning the logistical nightmare of evacuating his soldiers over to Valerian.

Was this convoluted, crazy plan really the best way he could serve the men and women under his command?

Marcellus shook his head. He could ill afford to doubt himself now, so he buried his concerns away. Valerian was a logistical genius, by far the best in the entire Umbrian Republic military. If there was anyone in the galaxy who could pull this off, it would be Val.

With that being said, Marcellus still wanted to maintain awareness of the overall situation, lest some new complication put a kink in his plan. Data feeds were streaming from the corvettes which were parked nearby, keeping him informed of the evacuation's progress.

So far, things were going smoothly. That might have worried him before, but he had learned to take good news where he could find it. The first wave had departed over two hours ago. It had contained about eighty thousand support troops as well as nearly sixty thousand critically wounded soldiers on a pair of hospital ships that had been docked in Ischia's main starport.

Marcellus was also satisfied that the Longbow weapon system had been field tested successfully. They'd only received one unit, but it showed promise for the future. Such a weapon, especially in larger numbers, might enable the Umbrians to better resist future planetary assaults, and help take some of the pressure off their overstretched Navy.

But the best news by far was that the second wave of transports was ready to go. This would be the largest group of transports, carrying over a quarter of a million men and women and thirty legions' worth of heavy equipment and Scutia battle mechs.

Enemy pressure on the perimeter was almost nonexistent, and it had grown worse for the Ascomanni after the assault carriers *Celeres* and *Spatha* had taken up position over Ischia.

These ships were purposefully built to support ground operations, with a significant number of weapons emplacements located on the lower hull. Moreover, their fighter complement had allowed his ground-based flight groups to relocate to the carriers' increasingly crowded hangar decks without ceding air superiority to the Ascomanni.

In four to six hours, all of his remaining forces would be evacuated.

Two things continued to weigh on the Praetor's mind, however.

Scans indicated that the pressures within Cercyon were growing. So far, steam from the water table had propelled mostly ash and dust into the atmosphere. However, their artificial eruption was beginning to accelerate beyond their ability to manage, ceding control of the situation back to nature.

The original shafts which had been bored to the magma below were expanding as heat and pressure liquefied more and more rock. A violent eruption could endanger those still on the ground, and it increasingly looked like it was a question of *when* and not *if* that would occur.

As dangerous as the situation could become, Marcellus was even more concerned by the fact that the Ascomanni had not sent additional ships to contest the invasion.

Intelligence had indicated that a substantial number of Asco warships were within a few hours' distance of Aetnaeus. Either the Ascomanni commander had too few ships to overcome Task Force Icarus, or they were waiting for the next batch of transports to leave.

As Marcellus thought about it, he grew increasingly uncomfortable. The enemy was traditionally very aggressive, and they had not hesitated in the past to commit assets to a no-win engagement, just to keep the Umbrians off balance.

He sent a quick message to Valerian asking him to call as soon as he could. It had no sooner been sent than an encrypted channel appeared on the console in front of him.

"Valerian, thanks for getting back to me so quickly…. You look like hell!"

His subordinate looked haggard, the strain of his task weighing heavily on him. "Things have been a little hectic as of late, sir…" Valerian said, smiling wanly across the vid stream.

Marcellus's demeanor grew serious: "I understand, Val, you have done a fantastic job, and I've tried my best to stay out of your hair. Thousands of our soldiers owe you their lives. But that's not why I bothered you. Have you seen Fabian's reports?"

"Yes, sir. Let me guess, you think it's strange that we haven't seen any more Ascomanni fleet activity since Icarus first arrived?"

"Yeah. They are always aggressive, but they were almost fanatical at Battipaglia and Tivoli. This situation is totally counter to our experiences to this point in the war."

"Perhaps you made the right call by giving Fabian free rein to throw sand in their gears. I'm sure Longbow helped as well, they can't possibly know that was our only operational unit." Valerian paused for a moment, deep in thought. "But you're right, subtle is not a tactic our enemy has used against us to date."

Marcellus took a beat to gather his thoughts. "I'm about to ask the impossible, Val."

"More impossible than slipping half a million soldiers off Aetnaeus?" he responded drily.

"Yeah, Val. We need to accelerate our timeframe. I need you to delay the second wave, and we need to consolidate the third and fourth waves. Pull the perimeter back to the city itself, and use three legions' worth of scoots to hold the line. Anything and everyone not in a container or on a transport by that time is getting left behind."

"Sir, I… But what about…?" Valerian stammered. He was silent for a moment. "I can do it, but it's going to be messy. We'll need to start pulling frontline units out now via dropship. The *Celeres and Spatha*'s decks are going to get crowded very quickly."

"I understand. Ditch some of the fighters if you have to. Our people come first."

"Even with only scattered pockets of resistance, the Ascomanni are going to take advantage of the situation. We will suffer heavier losses."

"I know, Val, I know…"

Valerian paused again, as if making some quick calculation, before continuing.

"Praetor, we can get everyone on a ship within two hours. If you believe that is the best course, we will make it happen. But I must advise against your own reckless plan. Your soldiers need you. Umbria needs you. Please, have the *Aquila* leave with the rest of the transports."

"You have your orders, Valerian. I trust you to see them out."

His friend's face dropped, but Valerian nodded dutifully as the Praetor closed the channel.

Bridge of the URN *Echion*, Orbiting over Ischia, Aetnaeus

Fabian was not surprised when he learned the Praetor had delayed the launch of the second wave. He shared the Praetor's concerns. With each passing minute, he was more convinced that certain annihilation was but moments away.

The Third Fleet had spent the last nine months playing tag with a dramatically superior adversary. Convoy raiding and minor engagements were the norm. Where Ascomanni capital ships were found, they were found in large numbers, and his captains were instructed to stay well clear.

Their naval victories had been relatively isolated affairs, resulting in a moderate number of losses for the enemy. But that would not have made much of an impact on the vast fleet the Ascomanni had started the battle with. Why hadn't they attacked his task force yet?

The welfare of his sailors and pilots weighed heavily on him, and the long wait was growing intolerable. Worse still, Fabian realized he was losing his composure, like some fresh-faced ensign right out of the naval academy.

He willed himself to calm down. The hours-long delay was almost up. If the enemy was going to contest the evacuation, it was now or never. The men and women of his command were counting on him. The soldiers evacuating Aetnaeus were counting on him. When the enemy came, he had to be ready and in control. Lives depended on it.

His communications officer turned and called out: "Archus, Ischia Actual indicates that the evacuation transports are lifting off now. *Celeres* and *Spatha* have formed up at the head of the formation and are leading them out."

Fabian nodded, not trusting himself to speak.

There were gasps of astonishment and awe amongst the bridge crew as hundreds of ships began to emerge from the ever-increasing shroud of volcanic ash below. Once they reached Task Force Icarus, the warships began to form up in a protective sphere around the vulnerable transports. *Echion* pulled into the center of the formation.

Navigation threw a plot on the primary monitor, showing their path and a timer showing their estimated arrival time. They began their journey to the jump point. Five minutes. That was all that separated his forces from safety.

Fabian was sure that it would be the longest five minutes of his life.

He stared at the clock, willing it to go faster. Four minutes remaining. Three minutes. Slowly Fabian began to allow himself some small sliver of hope. Perhaps the Ascomanni had been caught napping. Perhaps they really would get away scot free.

It was not to be.

Fabian saw it unfold in front of him, and, before his brain could even begin to process the sounds of the alarms blaring around him, he knew they were doomed.

There, blocking their exit, was the largest Ascomanni fleet any Umbrian had ever seen. It seemed to stretch in all directions as far as the eye could see. Hundreds and hundreds of ships sat before them.

There would be no escape.

Frantic calls poured in across the fleetwide channel, and his bridge crew sat in stunned silence.

Fabian snapped back to the present.

He had to do something; he had to act!

The Archus pulled himself out of his chair, opened a channel to the fleet, and started issuing orders in a calm, icy voice.

"Sailors, remember your duty. We are two minutes away from the jump. Task Force Icarus, move to the front of the formation. Pull the CAP in close and deploy fighters. We must keep the enemy away from our transports. We can do this. For the Republic!"

A handful of crew members murmured it back, but the spell had been broken. His officers and sailors were back in the moment and concentrating on the task at hand.

"Procurator, contact the rest of the Third Fleet, tell the *Vulcan* and the *Neptune* to jump in on opposite sides of the enemy formation. We need a distraction."

His XO nodded and moved off to transmit the orders.

The opposing fleets began to reach out for one another. Salvos of high explosives filled the darkness of space. There was no time to do anything, to try anything. They had been found out, but Fabian would be damned if he would not see the transports to safety.

Suddenly, a new message began to play fleetwide. Marcellus appeared, and in a loud, commanding voice said, "All ships, under no circumstances are you to deviate from your orders. I expect each of you to follow Archus Fabian's directives without hesitation."

With that, his cryptic message ended, but a new channel, this one open and unencrypted, began to play. "To all URN forces, this is Praetor Gaius Aurelius Marcellus. My ship has suffered catastrophic engine failure and is unable to leave the surface. I need immediate assistance!"

Thirty seconds had elapsed. *Vulcan* and *Neptune* had arrived with the rest of the Third Fleet. One of Task Force Icarus's destroyers, the *Dolabra*, exploded as it was struck by overwhelming fire from the enemy. Ascomanni fighters whipped through the Umbrian formation, and a transport fell victim to a coordinated attack run. But on the master display, something interesting was happening. Dozens of enemy ships were breaking off and heading for the surface of Aetnaeus.

The *Orcus* charged forward, once again positioning itself between friend and foe. As Fabian watched, explosions riddled the battleship's hull, but still she fought on. Each burst against the hull was a blow that could have struck one of the fleeing transports or a smaller warship.

Finally, she could take no more. Her captain accelerated into the enemy's midst as the battleship's core went critical. For a moment, *Orcus* shone brighter than Aetnaeus's sun, and then, was no more. Ten thousand souls, gone in an instant.

One minute left. Twelve transports had been destroyed. Only seven ships of Task Force Icarus remained. A wireframe display showed the mounting damage *Echion* was taking. But the remaining transports were going to make it.

Then, Fabian's heart sank. A colossal enemy ship winked into existence immediately in front of them: a three-kilometer-long Ascomanni dreadnought.

Before he could react, the *Cerberus* flashed before them, fires raging from dozens of holes in her hull. She struck the titanic vessel amidship. The *Cerberus*'s superstructure peeled off at the point of impact as her engines drove the ship's frame deep into the enemy's bowels. Explosions rocked the dreadnought as it split down its centerline and began listing.

Thirty seconds. The first transports reached the jump point and made it away. Dozens remained. Fabian found his voice. "Recall all fighters, order *Vulcan* and *Neptune* to break contact."

One of his light cruisers rammed an approaching enemy destroyer, pushing it into a nearby Asco cruiser. The force of the impact crushed the Umbrian ship's neck. Focused fire from surrounding Ascomanni vessels tore all three ships apart, both friend and foe alike.

Ten seconds. The rest of the transports were away, but eighteen of the evacuation ships had been lost. Fabian's XO appeared, ashen faced, and said, "All wings recovered, Archus. Casualties north of sixty percent."

Fabian put a hand on his subordinate's shoulder, lost for words.

The chrono hit zero, and the stars elongated into an impenetrable wall of white light as the remaining Umbrian ships slipped away.

URN Patrol Ship *Aquila*, Somewhere over Aetnaeus

Electromagnetic counter measures bloomed from the *Aquila*'s hull as pursing Ascomanni fighters launched missile after missile at the fleeing patrol ship. The vessel rocked as near misses exploded around them.

A single, rear-facing torpedo tube belched a response. Fifty meters out, the torpedo dissolved into a fine mist of tetrahedral objects. The chasing Ascomanni fighters had no time to avoid them and flew straight through this lethal fog. They began to disintegrate as air rushed through the tiny holes caused by hundreds of impacts.

One fighter's left wing snapped off, and it summersaulted into one of its wingmen. Both ships exploded. Another started rolling gently toward the ground below, its pilot clearly incapacitated or killed, while the fourth simply came apart midair.

Behind them, the horizon burned in a terrifying swirl of fire and ash as a concentrated orbital bombardment turned the city of Ischia into a cauldron of molten metal and liquefied concrete. Anyone who'd been left behind would have perished instantly in the midst of such destruction.

Marcellus was still numbed by what he saw. Five hundred and sixty-three enemy ships had appeared in orbit, the largest Ascomanni armada ever observed. Somewhere in the logical part of his brain, he knew he was lucky that any of his soldiers and sailors had made it out, but that was cold comfort now.

"Praetor, we have enemy fighters vectoring in on us, but they are still a way's out. We're ready to begin our climb," Captain Critonius called out.

"Good work, Captain."

Claudia was silent for a moment, and then asked the question which had been nagging at every member of the *Aquila*'s crew: "I beg your pardon, sir, I mean no disrespect. But why are you here? Or more precisely, why are we? Surely you would have been safer on an assault carrier, or even one of the corvettes."

"That is a good question, Captain. You may have heard that we artificially caused the volcano to erupt. But that isn't all we did. Another drilling rig bore a separate tunnel even further toward the planet's crust, until it could not go any further without risking the premature detonation of its payload."

"It's payload, sir?" she asked quizzically.

"Yes, we've been field testing a number of prototype weapons during the battle here on Aetnaeus. One of the last items I received was a prototype antimatter warhead. The designers had originally intended it to be used in space, but I had a different idea."

The *Aquila*'s helmsman turned and said, "Captain, we've begun our ascent. A minute fifteen before we leave the atmosphere."

Claudia nodded, but was still distracted what Marcellus had shared. Seeing the confusion and apprehension he had caused his young captain, he decided it was time to share the details of his plan.

"Sailors," Marcellus said, addressing the *Aquila's* crew, "as you may be aware, the tide of war is currently turned against us. We have been driven from planet after planet in the Frontier, with no hope of victory in sight. Today, we were forced to abandon Aetnaeus, but for the first time we bloodied the enemy's nose and managed to get away."

Marcellus's gaze hardened as he continued: "But that is not enough. We need time to rally our strength and come up with a plan for victory. Left unopposed, the Ascomanni will use this planet and its resources to advance on the next world, and the next one after that.

"After all the blood we've shed defending this world, I will not see it turned into yet another staging area for our enemy's advance." He paused for a moment, aware of the magnitude of his actions. "I am going to destroy Aetnaeus."

A handful of the ship's crew gasped, but Marcellus continued anyway, a deep-seated anger and resentment finally bubbling to the surface.

"The Triumvirate would throw away my soldiers' lives, *your* lives, to show the Ascomanni we'll fight to the end. I have no interest in presiding over such a wasteful and tragic event. To triumph, we cannot be content to idly throw our lives away for the Republic; we must make the Ascomanni pay dearly for them!

"From this day forward, when those wretched monsters hear the word Aetnaeus, they will shudder in dread! If Umbria is to fall, if the Republic is to burn, then the Ascomanni will burn with us! Today, the nine of us will send a message to our enemies…"

"Make that the ten of us," a familiar voice interrupted from the entrance to the bridge.

Marcellus snapped around to find Valerian standing in the doorway.

"What are you doing here, Valerian?!" Marcellus exclaimed.

"Well, sir, since you're too stubborn to listen to reason, I decided I couldn't let you make this decision alone. I'll be right here with you, no matter the outcome."

Marcellus smiled broadly and embraced his friend. "You are a lunatic, you know that, right?"

"I'm just following your example, Praetor," Valerian responded.

Before Marcellus had a chance to reply, a signal started beeping from the console Marcellus had appropriated. He quickly sat back down and typed a command into his keyboard.

"Helmsman, I need you to put us outside the orbit of Aetnaeus's moon. How long will it take to plot the jump?"

"I've got a preset series of coordinates, sir. It'll just take a few moments to line us up on the right vector."

"Good, we might make it. Sailors, I just activated the antimatter bomb buried in the planet's crust. The force of the explosion will crack the planet's surface and release an immeasurable amount of energy. It's set to go off in ten seconds," Marcellus continued. "Please bring up any remaining feeds from surveillance assets around and above Ischia."

"I've got an observation satellite, sir," the *Aquila*'s sensors officer called out.

"Good, put it up."

As the Ascomanni's gigantic fleet hovered above the planet, an impossibly bright flash lit up the display. A shockwave expanded out from the epicenter of the explosion, thousands of kilometers in diameter.

The planet's surface fractured, and a jet of superheated rock blasted through Aetnaeus's atmosphere and into space. Like the fist of an angry god, it destroyed everything in its path. In seconds, it reached the satellite, and the vid feed dissolved into static.

The *Aquilla* began to shake violently. Marcellus anxiously called out, "Helmsman…"

"Got it, sir!"

The *Aquila* flashed into brilliant light, reappearing a millisecond later outside the orbit of Aetnaeus's sole natural satellite. They had survived, but as the patrol ship turned to face Aetnaeus, it was clear that the planet, and anyone on or around it, had not.

A full quarter of the planet had been pulverized, with gigantic pieces of Aetnaeus floating above its now-exposed core. Gravity pulled the smaller chucks back down to its surface, showering the ruined world with a thousand shooting stars.

Any trace of the Ascomanni was lost in the hail of debris.

Together they sat in stunned silence.

Minutes passed before Marcellus finally broke the spell.

"Captain, take us to Safe Haven."

Bernard Lang

Chapter 3

URN *Aquila*, Somewhere in the Frontier

Three days later, the *Aquila* finally arrived at its destination. Marcellus watched as the patrol ship drew ever closer to the peculiar system's only planet: an expansive blue-green gas giant, orbiting its dim, magenta-colored star. A multitude of moons circled the gassy planet, while an expansive asteroid belt was caught in the middle of the two titans' gravitational pulls.

This was Safe Haven, and it was vital to the Republic's war effort. As much as a fifth of all Umbrian war material was created from the system's facilities.

Its asteroid belt housed the largest shipyards and exoplanetary factories the Umbrians had ever developed, feeding off the metal-rich rocks around it. Even from this distance, Marcellus could make out the shape of a nearly completed capital ship floating amongst the belt's facilities.

The gas giant, Aurae, provided the fuel for these massive works. The planet itself was rich in Helium-3, the primary fuel used in Umbrian fusion reactors. Refineries and storage tanks dotted its upper atmosphere, converting Aurae's gases into usable fuel before transporting it to the belt.

Aurae's moons were also vital to the system's sustainability. The elliptical nature of the largest moons' orbits created enough tidal heating to support the development of settlements.

Eurus, the biggest, had a thick nitrogen atmosphere with an atmospheric pressure similar to that of Umbria itself. This allowed the Umbrians to construct massive domed communities which were sealed against the environment and closely regulated to ensure they were comfortable for Umbrian habitation. Geothermal energy was used to cultivate produce in large, kilometer square greenhouses across the moon's surface, feeding both the planet's populace and the system's workforce at large.

Its second moon, Notus, contained a massive subterranean ocean beneath its frozen exterior. A passage had been bored through the moon's exterior, which led to a domed city, Caurus. Suspended within the planet's crust, the city's desalination plants processed Notus's salty internal sea, transforming it into potable water.

The system's crown jewel, however, rested inside the atmosphere of the gas giant itself. The *Aquilla* punched through Aurae's turbulent atmosphere and began its final approach. It was here, still obscured by the swirling blue haze, that a massive artificial harbor had been constructed.

At its center, a city-sized spheroid floated serenely against the backdrop of Aurea's clouds. This was the anchor point. It was made up of a solid inner core of iron and nickel, surrounded by an outer core of liquid metal. This artificial mantel swirled around the anchor's interior, creating an intense magnetic field which protected the harbor from Aurae's fierce radiation and tempered the worst of the gas giant's storms.

As the *Aquila* entered the harbor, Marcellus found his tired and bloodied command.

Two dozen platforms were scattered in a ring around the anchor point. The transports carrying his army had docked alongside. Each contained miniature cities, where all the amenities Umbria's soldiers and sailors might need could be located.

Here his battered warriors would find the time to heal their wounds and catch their collective breath before returning to the front. Lost equipment would be replaced by the factories in the asteroid belt beyond, and new recruits would be brought in to fill the gaps in their ranks.

Instead of heading to one of the platforms, however, Marcellus directed Claudia to head for an oblong structure hovering over the anchor point. This was the Citadel, which managed every aspect of the Umbrian Republic's operations in the system.

The *Aquila*'s master gently eased her ship into the tight confines of the Citadel's docking bay, and Marcellus and Valerian prepared to disembark.

The Citadel, Safe Haven; System: Classified, Frontier Space

As Marcellus and Valerian walked down the ship's ramp into the Citadel's hangar, they were greeted by an honor guard of praetorians in full dress uniforms, with Invictus at the head waiting to receive them. As they approached, the praetorians snapped to attention, and Invictus saluted. Marcellus returned the salute before smiling broadly and taking his friend by the shoulder.

"It's good to see you made it out in one piece, Invictus."

"You as well, Praetor, I cannot express how relieved I was when we spotted the *Aquila*. I thought you had gotten yourself killed for sure."

Marcellus was taken aback by Invictus's earnestness, but decided not to press the issue. "It was close, Vic, but the two of you aren't rid of me yet."

"Looks like the Asco missed their chance," Invictus replied more jovially. "I bet we make them regret it later. Now, if you'll follow me, everyone's waiting for you in the command center."

Marcellus nodded, and together, the three began walking toward the Citadel's control center.

"We shouldn't fool ourselves, we got really lucky. How the hell did intel miss a fleet of nearly six hundred Ascomanni ships?" Valerian spat, anger clearly evident in his voice. "If we would've known what we were up against, we could've—"

"You did a fantastic job, Val," Marcellus said, gently chiding his aide. "There's nothing else you could've done. Given the size of the enemy force, it's a miracle any of us made it out at all."

"You got that right," Invictus said somberly. "Task Force Icarus was badly mauled. Fabian is a good commander, perhaps the most skilled Archus we have, but I think his losses are eating at him, Marcellus. You may want to speak with him."

They reached the central elevator shaft that would take them to the facility's central nervous center, and they boarded the lift to the command deck.

"I will, Invictus. How many transports did we lose?"

"Eighteen transports were destroyed, but about a quarter were carrying equipment and supplies. Still, we lost over forty thousand in the evacuation."

A pit grew in Marcellus's stomach as he thought about how helpless his soldiers must have felt as they met their end. They had died in the cramped compartments of troop transports, where they could not fight back, could not resist.

The Fates had cut their lives short, but once again allowed him to walk away in one piece.

In a soft voice, Invictus continued, as if reading his superior's mind. "You were never going to save them all, Marcellus. This is total war, on a scale our people have never known. We have lost whole worlds to these bastards. You must remember that."

"And because of your leadership, these men and women lived to see another day," Valerian added. "For the first time in the war, a fleet, *a whole army group*, fought the Ascomanni for extended periods and survived."

Invictus nodded in agreement. "We train our people as well as we can, but there is no substitute for the real thing. The three of us learned that at Varese."

Marcellus reluctantly nodded as his mind drifted to memories past.

Varese.

At that time, he was just a legate, commanding the Ninety-Third Legion—Legio Gigas, the giants. Valerian had served as his second in command, and it would be on Varese that he would first meet Invictus.

Together with four other legions, they were responsible for holding the planet, a resource-rich world that had only recently been discovered in the outer edges of the Frontier.

The battle started disastrously for the Umbrians. Thirty ships of the Second Fleet had been tasked with supporting the ground forces on Varese. After a pitched battle against a numerically superior Ascomanni fleet, the surviving Umbrian warships were forced to withdraw after taking heavy losses.

Eight weeks of intense ground combat ensued. Marcellus quickly became the highest-ranking officer left on the planet. They were cut off, with no access to reinforcements or resupply. Communication with the War Council, the official term for Umbrian High Command, was tenuous at best. Worse still, they rapidly expended their supply of heavy munitions and fuel just to keep the enemy at bay.

The situation appeared hopeless, so Marcellus took a gamble and threw out the rulebook. Varese had a very quick day/night cycle of only a few hours. The Ascomanni, for all their strengths, were not particularly adapt night fighters, and he took advantage of this weakness to launch a series of raids behind enemy lines.

Ammo dumps and fuel depots were destroyed in the dark of night by quick hit-and-fade attacks. Soon, the pressure against the front began to slacken. The Tribune of the Forty-Sixth Legion, Invictus Flaminus, distinguished himself during these actions. Marcellus would come to rely on him to complete the toughest assignments.

Valerian's outstanding organizational abilities kept his dwindling forces mobile by salvaging what they could from enemy stores. For another three months, they frustrated the Ascomanni's attempts to consolidate their control of Varese.

Despite their success, the situation had become critical as time dragged on. Constant and relentless battle had worn his legions' strength down to a small fraction of their original numbers.

Believing that they had been left for dead, Marcellus and his remaining officers decided that they would launch one final strike on the enemy's primary headquarters on the planet. The goal was to neutralize the Ascomanni leadership element and beam a signal back to command.

A report was drawn up which contained the experiences they had gathered over the last few months, details on how best the enemy might be countered, a record of the legions' actions and accomplishments, and personal messages his surviving soldiers wished to have passed on to loved ones back home.

With less than six thousand Umbrians remaining, Marcellus assaulted the Ascomanni's primary stronghold on the planet, an abandoned mining facility they had converted for their own purposes.

Speed and stealth were priorities, and by the time the Ascomanni garrison was alerted, his soldiers had already penetrated the outer perimeter.

The assault quickly devolved into a savage free-for-all in close quarters. Marcellus's soldiers spread through the facility, staging ambushes and delaying enemy reinforcements. In this fashion, the Ascomanni were kept from marshalling a significant number of troops in any one place.

Meanwhile, Marcellus, Invictus, and a hundred hand-picked legionnaires breached the control room. The enemy commander was gigantic, even by Ascomanni standards, and he was personally responsible for the death of many Umbrians as they swarmed through the access points made in the walls of the control center.

In the end, Marcellus and Invictus cornered the behemoth. Knowing that he could not escape, the Asco general lured them into a tight corridor lined with unused mining equipment. The cramped confines prevented them from effectively using their plasma carbines, and the Ascomanni brute took advantage to charge the pair.

The Ascomanni general threw Invictus against a wall and interposed himself between the two Umbrians. The enemy commander moved to finish Invictus off, but Marcellus rushed forward and drove his blade through the enemy's power armor, severing the appendage just above the knee.

Their opponent roared in pain, groping wildly at its missing limb. Invictus took advantage to jump on the creature's back and drive his bayonet through its chest. With a final, muted gasp, their enemy toppled to the floor and was still.

Marcellus's soldiers mopped up the remaining Ascomanni and prepared for the inevitable counterattack. In the control room, Valerian was able to successfully reach High Command for the first time in over a month and a half.

The War Council was shocked to find that anyone had survived on Varese. Within hours, a URN Task Force under the command of Archus Fabian Catus had appeared in orbit. They scattered the few Ascomanni ships that were present and pulled Marcellus and his soldiers from Varese.

They had started the battle with a little over forty-two thousand soldiers. Only a tenth of that number would be evacuated.

"Praetor, are you still with us?" Valerian asked.

Marcellus blinked. While he had been daydreaming, the lift had reached its destination. Invictus looked at him with amusement, while Valerian seemed concerned.

"Yes, I'm fine, Val. I just drifted off for a moment."

"Well, I'm sure you are tired, sir, but we're here, and the others are waiting for you."

The doors to the lift opened, and the three of them walked down a short corridor to the command center.

"*Echion* is in dry dock out in the ring, so Fabian is on the line. We've also gathered Safe Haven's magistrate, senior medical officer, and head of the CID's local intelligence department," Invictus said.

"Good, there are some things we need to take care of immediately."

With that, they entered a large rectangular room. The long side of the space was packed full of workstations, with analysts and supervisors pouring over all types of data. On the opposite side, transparent panels ran the entire length of the wall, allowing those inside to gaze out over Safe Haven's platforms and the swirling azure clouds of the gas giant beyond.

"Attention on deck," Valerian called out. Everyone stood at attention, but Marcellus waved them off.

Invictus jabbed Valerian with his elbow and whispered, "See, he just *hates* all the formality of High Command. If you ever really want to piss him off, schedule a formal inspection for the whole army group."

Valerian just rolled his eyes as they approached a raised platform set in the middle of the room.

Three people waited for them, while a vid feed of Archus Fabian was displayed nearby. Valerian introduced each of them in turn: Gnaeus Publicola, the most senior medical officer in the system, Julia Flavia, one of the most skilled engineers in the Republic Armed Forces and the magistrate of Safe Haven's industrial facilities, and Mallius Theodorus, the local section head of the Combined Intelligence Directorate.

After brief introductions, Marcellus took charge of the meeting and said, "All right, thank you all for meeting on such short notice. First, I want to see to the disposition of our forces. Fabian, you're up first."

"Over the–" Fabian's voice cracked as he started to speak. His face pinched up a bit before he exhaled and began his report again. "Over the course of the campaign on Aetnaeus, Third Fleet destroyed twenty-one enemy capital ships of cruiser size or bigger, and another thirty-four destroyers, frigates, and corvettes.

"Prior to the evacuation, we had roughly a dozen ships put out of action, but only four, one light cruiser, a destroyer, and two frigates, were completely lost." Fabian's voice became strained once more as he continued. "Task Force Icarus started the battle with one supercarrier, battleship, and battlecruiser apiece, as well as four light cruisers, six frigates, and four destroyers.

"One of the light cruisers was heavily damaged during the initial encounter and withdrew to this location for repairs. Only the *Echion*, another light cruiser, and three frigates survived the second stage of the evacuation. The battlegroups attached to the *Vulcan* and *Neptune* took some damage, but no ships were lost before they disengaged.

"The Third Fleet has been reduced to a strength of seventy-two ships, with twelve requiring substantial repairs, including the *Echion*. I expect these vessels to be back in fighting condition in about six weeks."

"Regarding the Third Fleet's fighter complement, the air wings assigned to *Falacer*, *Decima*, *Celeres*, and *Spatha* are at or above ninety percent strength." Fabian's voice cracked again as he finished his report. "Flight Group Echion is down to thirty-eight percent. Getting it back up to its full complement will take several months."

Marcellus looked intensely at his subordinate and said, "Fabian, you did a fantastic job during the campaign. On more than one occasion, you saved us from certain destruction. You should be proud of how your command performed."

Fabian nodded meekly, without saying anything else. It was clear he was doing his best to maintain his composure.

Marcellus hid a frown. Fabian had been well recommended for command of the Third Fleet, having successfully defeated the Ascomanni in a number of smaller engagements, but his experience managing large units had been limited prior to his promotion. Not everyone was capable of handling that responsibility. He'd have to watch Fabian closely. If he didn't see signs of improvement, and soon, he'd need to have a tough conversation with his fleet commander.

"All right, Valerian, your turn, please summarize the results on the ground."

Valerian took a half a step forward and began to speak. "The battle for Aetnaeus was by far the largest in terms of forces fielded since the Umbrian Republic first encountered the Ascomanni at Battipaglia. Sixty legions were deployed, as well as sizable support detachments of artillery and armor. When air force personnel were factored in, our total strength exceeded eight hundred thousand men and women planet-side.

"We lost approximately one hundred and twenty thousand during the initial invasion and about the same during the withdrawal to and defense of Ischia. Two legions were completely destroyed, with another eight at less than forty percent of their original strength. The remaining formations are anywhere between fifty-five to eighty percent of their table numbers.

"The attached air wings started the battle with twelve hundred craft of all types, and finished with just under seven hundred. However, attrition was higher in material losses than pilots and flight crew, as many of our pilots who had to bail out were recovered and returned to action.

"A quick headcount was tallied upon our arrival, and it looks like we've managed to extract just over six hundred thousand of our personnel from the planet.

"As for the losses we inflicted on the enemy, we estimate that over three million Ascomanni soldiers were deployed to Aetnaeus. We expect the vast majority of these soldiers died over the course of the battle, or with Aetnaeus's destruction. A detailed breakdown will be compiled after a thorough review of available after-action reports and reconnaissance imagery."

Valerian offered a tight-lipped smile as he finished. "As grave as our casualties have been, we inflicted significant losses on the enemy."

"All right, thanks for the overview, Val." Marcellus turned to address the image of his fleet commander: "Fabian, reinforce your flight crews with the squadrons *Spatha* and *Celeres* pulled from Aetnaeus. It'll be easier to train experienced pilots in carrier operations than replace them entirely. That'll get *Echion* back in the fight faster. I'll smooth it over with their parent organizations."

"Understood, sir."

Marcellus watched Fabian closely. His demeanor seemed to lighten just slightly, but his posture was still stiff and uncomfortable.

"OK, Doctor Publicola, what is the situation with the wounded?"

The short, elderly man spoke in a soft gravelly voice. "The most critically wounded on the *Salubritas* and *Clementia* received priority and have been transferred to the more extensive medical facilities here at Safe Haven. The remaining wounded have been prioritized for transfer to our facilities based on the gravity of their injuries.

"Additional casualties were sustained during the evacuation, and these soldiers have been backfilling the beds emptied on the hospital ships. The total number of patients is estimated at eighty-five thousand. I'll make sure to provide your adjutant with updates regularly."

"Thank you, Doctor. I appreciate you and your staff's quick work, and I'm sure my soldiers will be well cared for in your charge," Marcellus said.

The Praetor turned his attention to the middle-aged woman responsible for maintaining the system's factories and shipyards.

"Magistrate Flavia, Valerian will provide you with a detailed total of the equipment we need to get back to full fighting strength. I know we've asked a lot of you and your workers, so I trust your judgment in prioritizing your existing production needs with this new request."

"We'll do our best to get you back up and running as quickly as possible, sir."

"I appreciate it, Magistrate." Marcellus turned and gazed out the window as he continued: "We have weathered a tremendous storm together, but there will be more battles to come. Fabian, I need you to send a force back to Aetnaeus. Keep it tight while you ascertain whether any Ascomanni forces remain in system, but we need to evaluate the effectiveness of Operation Omega."

"Understood, Praetor."

"Theodorus, I would appreciate any support CID can provide in determining where that massive fleet came from. Please work with Fabian to chase down leads and identify targets of opportunity for future strikes."

"We'll make it happen, Praetor. It'll be good to hit these bastards back."

Marcellus gave Valerian a sideways glance. The Combined Intelligence Directive had a checkered reputation amongst Umbria's armed forces. They would need to watch this man carefully.

"All right," Marcellus continued, "there is clearly much to do here to re-equip and reorganize our forces. However, I'm entrusting that task to Fabian and Valerian. Invictus and I will be returning to Umbria. I've sent word to the War Council requesting a meeting with my peers."

Surprise rippled across some of the faces in his audience, and for good reason.

The War Council was made up of the twelve most senior officers in the Umbrian Military. These men and women were primarily responsible for strategic planning, intelligence gathering, logistics, and procurement.

The Council advised the Triumvirate and the Senate, the Republic's executive and legislative bodies, respectively, on military matters, but left command of the Republic's armies and fleets to the six Praetors who had been selected to lead Umbria's forces into battle. Pulling all of these individuals away from the war was no small undertaking, and, as such, meetings of this type seldom happened.

Marcellus shrugged off his audience's reaction and continued. "Additional reports on the state of the war and the battle for Aetnaeus will need to be provided to the Senate and Triumvirate, and if there is to be any fallout over the destruction of Aetnaeus, I alone will bear it.

"In my absence, Fabian will take overall command of my forces, with Valerian as his second. While we are gone, please keep me informed of developments here. If you encounter any issues do not hesitate to escalate them directly to me. Invictus, select eight praetorians to join us for the trip. Fabian, I'll need you to detach a corvette for transport."

"I'll take care of it, sir," the Archus responded.

"Good, that's it ladies and gentlemen. Thank you all for your time."

With that, the meeting broke up.

Valerian escorted him to his temporary quarters, a luxurious stateroom whose excesses made Marcellus uncomfortable. After Valerian left, he removed his combat harness and lay down in the absurdly comfortable bed.

His uneasiness with the room's gaudy appointments was soon forgotten as he drifted off to sleep.

***

Tracers flashed through a reddish black sky as Marcellus found himself standing alone on top of a tall hill. The haunting, skeletal ruins of a city could be seen in the distance. All around him lay the broken bodies of his soldiers, while Ascomanni, too numerous to count, swarmed up the sides of the hill.

Before they could reach the Praetor, a bright flash appeared on the horizon, annihilating the city as Marcellus was flung into space. Marcellus grasped at his throat as he began choking and gasping for air.

As he drifted further into the starless abyss, the planet below him split, as if it had developed a devilish grin. As he watched, it transformed into the hideous visage of the Ascomanni general he had defeated on Varese. With cold, callous laughter, the maw of his vanquished foe expanded, and Marcellus was consumed by the darkness.

Marcellus bolted upright, panting and dripping with sweat. Someone knocked at the door of his stateroom again. Grabbing the dagger he always kept close at hand, he approached the door and activated the camera to the exterior.

Marcellus exhaled sharply with relief and opened the door.

The orderly standing in front of him appeared to be taken off guard by the Praetor's sudden appearance. "Sir…uh, um, sorry for the interruption," he stammered, "but your adjutant asked that I deliver your dress uniform, sir."

"Perfect, thank you."

The young man saluted and beat a hasty retreat. Marcellus threw his freshly pressed uniform on the bed and took half an hour to get himself cleaned up. For the first time in nine months, he truly felt refreshed and ready to face the day.

Marcellus sat down at the desk in his temporary quarters and activated the integrated console. There were a handful of messages waiting for his review, but one jumped out for immediate action. He hit a series of buttons and Fabian appeared on his display.

"Praetor, what can I help you with?"

Marcellus examined the man's face, concerned by his subordinate's dull expression. He'd hoped some time would help Fabian gain some perspective on the recent battle. Perhaps he'd hoped for too much.

"You've confirmed the initial assessment, Fabian?"

"Yes, sir, Operation Omega completely obliterated the enemy fleet contesting the evacuation. A passive sensor array in orbit around the moon of Ostia confirmed there were no space-time distortions leading away from the planet after the detonation, save for the *Aquila*'s."

"That is almost too good to believe, Archus. Has there been any sign of the Ascomanni since?"

"No, it's possible that they had scouts in the outer system that we didn't detect, but no Ascomanni ships have approached the planet since Aetnaeus was destroyed."

"And the planet itself?"

"See for yourself, sir."

A new image appeared. It was Aetnaeus, or what was left of her. The planet's atmosphere had been blown away, and Aetnaeus's oceans were already starting to freeze. The surface seemed to ripple as an endless shower of meteorites rained down from orbit. But most impressively, a full quarter of the planet had been jettisoned into space, leaving an angry, jagged wound which still glowed where its core was exposed.

"Damn… OK, how many ships do you have on station, Fabian?"

"As much of *Vulcan*'s and *Neptune*'s battlegroups as could be mustered. About sixty ships, mostly screens."

"I need you to do something unorthodox. I want you to use your available ships to pull the debris from the battle back down into Aetnaeus. Either the planet's core or its freezing oceans will swallow all evidence of what happened there."

"Sir…?" Fabian asked quizzically.

"Fabian, we have fought this war as if we were fighting ourselves, an enemy who thinks like we do, is bound by the same logic and rules as we are, and who values the same things we do. In the end, we've been playing right into the enemy's hands."

"By removing the evidence of what happened," Marcellus continued, "we deny our enemy information about what transpired and introduce uncertainty. We keep them from knowing how badly we hurt them and how little we suffered. And maybe, just maybe, those bastards will start to fear *us*."

"Understood, sir, I'll make it happen."

"Good, thank you, Fabian. Before you go though, I want to reinforce something I said earlier at the debrief. I am alive today because of you and your sailors, and so are all of the soldiers under my command."

Marcellus gave his subordinate as penetrating a look as he could muster over the vidfeed and continued: "I know you've probably run things through your head a hundred times to figure out what you could have done differently, but this is war. Everyone who puts on the uniform made the decision that defending our people and our way of life is more important than their own survival."

The Praetor watched Fabian's face as he spoke. Hidden behind the stony surface of a man facing his superior was someone who was grieving. Marcellus softened his voice as he tried to bring his point home.

"You are an extremely skilled tactician and leader, Fabian. I have no doubt that you are the best choice to lead my fleet..."

Marcellus paused and considered his final words with great care.

"...but if you doubt your own skill and judgment, you owe it to your sailors to turn the reins over to someone who can make the hard decisions. I'll be back from Umbria in three weeks. There is no shame in choosing reassignment, but if that is your choice, I want the name of the individual you believe is better qualified to lead your men and women into battle."

Fabian looked sucker-punched, but quickly regained his composure. "I understand, Praetor."

"Good, you're in charge until I return, Fabian. I trust you."

With that, he ended the call with his troubled Archus and slumped back into the chair with a heavy sigh. Fabian was the best naval mind the Umbrians had, but if he couldn't pull himself out of the pool of self-doubt he was drowning in, he'd need to be replaced.

Fabian's raw skill and success on the battlefield would count for nothing if he didn't believe in himself. Unless overcome quickly, his uncertainty and indecision would lead to disaster sooner, rather than later.

There was another knock on the door of his stateroom.

"Come in!" Marcellus called.

The door slid open and Invictus entered with two praetorians.

"Fancy digs, sir," Invictus said as he scanned the room. "I hate to pull you away, but..."

"Really, Vic?" Marcellus replied with a grin.

"No, not really. Wouldn't want you to get too cozy. You're already starting to look a little thick around the midsection..."

"Well then there's no time to waste, Prefect. Lead on," Marcellus said, smirking, as he gestured out the door.

Invictus smiled wryly and, with the Praetor in tow, led the group to the ship that would take them home.

URN *Hasta*, Approaching Umbria, Capital of the Umbrian Republic

Marcellus stood on the bridge of the corvette *Hasta* and looked down on the placid, green-blue world before them. It was Umbria, the epicenter of their great civilization, the planet of his birth, and his home.

It was the first time he had returned to his homeworld in over a year, since shortly after the fall of Varese. He recalled how the Umbrian Republic, so desperate for good news in the fight against the Ascomanni, had welcomed him back as if he were a returning conqueror.

The report that his officers and soldiers had assembled on Varese was broadcast publicly, and overnight Marcellus became a household name. The Senate promoted him to Praetor, granting him a fleet and an army despite his youth.

Marcellus did what he thought best at the time. In a speech broadcast across the Republic, Marcellus had shared the story of his soldiers' resistance on Varese and declared that, although it would not be easy, the Ascomanni horde could be defeated.

Recruitment soared after his speech, and he spent another three months speaking to rallies and crowds in support of the war. With great fanfare, he was then sent out to the Frontier to engage the enemy.

Marcellus had looked forward to seeing the capital again, but it appeared that destiny had some cruel trick to play on him.

"Something's wrong, Marcellus. Very wrong," Invictus said softly.

Marcellus nodded in agreement. Hundreds of ion engines twinkled like tiny blue stars in the space around Umbria. The ships were overwhelmingly freighters and transports, with only a handful of warships interspersed throughout. Many bore the scars of battle.

As they approached Umbria, one of the freighters exploded. Shuttles and patrol ships raced to the scene, but there was nothing to do and no one to save.

"Gods... What the hell is going on?" Marcellus asked quietly. He turned to the corvette's captain and asked, "Have you gotten ahold of anyone at orbital command?"

"Sir, it's a mess," the *Hasta*'s commander called out. "Communications is still holding for someone at the Castellum."

"Set course for Perugia, we won't do anyone any good in space."

"Understood, sir."

The *Hasta* began the descent, and the view beyond the bridge began to glow as they entered Umbria's atmosphere. In a few minutes their destination came into view. There, with the sun rising to the west, was Perugia, the capital of Umbria and her Republic.

Kilometer-high spires rose by the dozens through a light morning fog, their plated exteriors glowing a soft amber-gold with the first warm rays of the morning's light.

Transparent tubes weaved elegantly between these giants, carrying freight and passengers to destinations throughout the city. Personal craft zipped through Perugia's air lanes while the giant, luxurious airships of the extravagantly wealthy hovered amongst the clouds.

Another day was just beginning in the beating heart of the Republic.

Without warning, four Umbrian interceptors roared past the corvette's bridge, and Marcellus heard the *Hasta*'s communication's officer speaking quickly into his headset. Two of the fighters looped around and fired warning shots over the bow.

Marcellus leapt down into the comm officer's station and ripped the headset off the young man's head.

"Attention, Umbrian flight group, who am I speaking to?"

"This is Pugio Leader to unidentified Umbrian corvette. Return immediately to orbit or we will be forced to consider you hostile."

Marcellus lost his cool.

"You listen to me, you mindless drone, this is Praetor Gaius Aurelius Marcellus. I did not defeat marauding armies of Ascomanni just to be threatened by the likes of you! Unless you want to clean latrines for the rest of your military career, you will break off and escort my ship to the Castellum. I expect you to comply immediately."

There was a pause on the other end as the flight leader undoubtedly rushed to confirm his voice pattern. In the space of thirty seconds, Pugio Lead was back.

"Praetor, my deepest apologies, but we've been ordered to prevent any ships from entering the capital's airspace. We are vectoring you to the nearest available landing pad."

Marcellus glanced at his helmsman, who gave him a nod in return. "We've received the coordinates, Pugio Leader. Care to tell me what the hell is going on?"

"You'll have to wait on the higher-ups for that, sir. We have no idea. I can tell you that ships have been arriving all night."

"Understood. *Hasta* out." With that, he handed the headset back to its original owner.

The corvette and her new escorts veered to the north and approached a dense cluster of buildings with a distinctly more utilitarian feel. This was the Castellum, the seat of the Umbrian armed forces' War Council and the nerve center of the war against the Ascomanni.

Without another word, Marcellus stalked out of the bridge and worked his way toward the rear of the ship. It was time to find out what was going on.

The Castellum; Perugia, Umbria

Five minutes later, the *Hasta* set down on a large rectangular landing pad, and Marcellus and his praetorians disembarked. Marcellus was surprised to find that no one was waiting to meet them.

Invictus saw his Praetor's agitation and laughed. "That's what you get for being such a hard ass to those poor pilots. Apparently, they couldn't round up a welcome party brave enough to face you."

Marcellus gave his subordinate a look, and Invictus realized how concerned his commander was. "This way, Praetor," Invictus said. "We can take the tubes to get to the Ops Center."

"Lead the way, Vic. Double time, praetorians."

Together the ten Umbrians jogged to the nearest station, and after checking in with the guards, they boarded a tube shuttle heading deeper into the headquarters complex.

Additional guards were waiting when they reached their destination, but these wore full combat suits.

Marcellus could feel their anxiety as they patrolled the landing platform. He spoke briefly with the officer on duty, who promptly allowed them passage.

As Marcellus and his troopers walked in, they entered a maelstrom of activity. Soldiers were rushing about everywhere, and the din of activity was amplified as it echoed off the walls of the building's grand entryway.

The entrance to the Castellum's main building contained an open-air atrium. Each level of the structure was connected to an elliptical ring accessing the space, and the rings grew in size the higher one went within the building. This created a funnel-like structure of curving terraces that stretched from the bottom floor all the way to the skylights set in the rooftop.

The walls were lined with murals of Umbria's military history, and half a dozen historic aircraft hung suspended in the open space within the atrium. Planters containing fauna from dozens of the Republic's worlds dotted the terraces, and each ring contained gently sloping ramps leading to the ones above and below.

To move quickly between levels, a series of lift shafts were located on the walls immediately to the left and right of the main entrance. The primary operations center, Marcellus's ultimate goal, was located on the topmost floor.

The Praetor pulled Invictus aside and issued orders as softly as he could.

"This place is a powder keg, Vic. I've never seen the Castellum like this! You can feel the fear and apprehension rippling through the room. I need you and the rest of the praetorians to find the armory and suit up."

"But... Praetor..." Invictus stammered.

Marcellus cut him off and kept going.

"Once that's done, send two praetorians up to join me in the Ops Center, but you and the rest should patrol the atrium. I need you to engage with these people, to project an image of strength and certainty. The only thing more dangerous than a panicky mob is a panicky mob of soldiers."

"What the hell is going on, Marcellus?" Invictus asked, concerned. "Do you know something?"

"No, brother, but it's clear that things are spinning out of control. Once I know more, I'll pass it along, but for now, I need you to follow orders."

Invictus drew himself up, saluted, and he and the eight praetorians headed off to the armory located on Level Three. Marcellus turned and boarded a lift, which quickly began the ascent to the Operations Center.

As he looked out over the atrium, he did his best at coming up with a rough number for all of the people milling around. The size of the crowds indicated that many of these men and women had left their duty stations, and that pointed to a breakdown in discipline across the board.

What the hell was going on? Marcellus asked himself. Something had clearly gone horribly wrong, but no one seemed to know what it was.

The doors of the elevator slid open as he reached Level Fourteen, and Marcellus was immediately greeted by four legionnaires in full combat gear. Each had their weapons trained on him.

"This is a restricted level. No one is allowed access. Return immediately to the appropriate level," the nearest legionnaire said.

"I am Praetor Gaius Aurelius. Who is in command, soldier?"

"Praetor Aulus Festus. Now, please, take the lift back to a lower level."

"Take me to him. Now."

The legionnaire looked like he was going to press the issue, but before he could respond, Marcellus could hear a faint buzzing echo in the soldier's helmet.

"Understood," the legionnaire seemed to say to no one in particular. "Praetor, please come with us."

Marcellus nodded, and the four soldiers formed up around him as they walked to the Operations Center. Marcellus couldn't help but feel more like a prisoner being escorted to his cell than an honored guest being shown the way.

They approached two more legionnaires guarding a pair of large, ornate doors. They nodded as his group approached, and the doors slowly opened.

They walked into a large room filled with all of the equipment necessary to oversee the Republic's war effort. Like the atrium, it was elliptical in shape, and the room's walls gave way to floor-to-ceiling windows as it came to a point opposite of the entrance. They provided a beautiful view of the capital's glittering skyline, but Marcellus was too distracted to notice.

All around, officers and technicians sat at their posts, working diligently. None dared look up as the group of five passed. As worrisome as the melee in the lobby had been, Marcellus found himself even more concerned by the self-imposed silence he observed here.

They finally reached the center of the room, where concentric circular displays projected a graphical representation of Umbrian space. The details of various military units floated over their designated locations, and blue and red haze showed who controlled specific portions of their little corner of the galaxy.

As they drew closer, a figure could be seen standing amongst the projectors, and Marcellus's heart caught in his throat.

There, in the middle of display, stood Praetor Aulus Festus.

Festus was short by Umbrian standards, only about one and a half meters in height. One eye sparkled green, while the other, an artificial replacement, glowed red, contrasting strikingly against the otherwise bland features of his ocher-colored face. Prostheses covered his chest and had replaced his left arm, mechanical repairs to wounds he had survived early in the war.

Marcellus had only met Praetor Festus once, but every member of the Umbrian Republic's armed forces knew of him. Aulus had a reputation for strict discipline, bordering on the sadistic, and his tactics, while effective, often cost his forces a steep price in blood.

The older man turned and grinned as the group approached, and Marcellus's skin crawled involuntarily beneath his uniform. Festus nodded once to his men, and two of the legionnaires left to return to their post near the lift. The remaining two stood behind and on either side of Marcellus.

"Praetor Aurelius, it's good to see you!"

Marcellus saluted and said, "It's good to see you as well sir. Forgive my impetuousness, but what exactly is going on?"

A dark shadow stole over the older man's face. "You don't *know*? I have terrible news to share then. Tratirne has fallen."

"Tratirne?!" Marcellus exclaimed. "But...when? How?!"

"An Ascomanni fleet, numbering over three hundred ships, jumped in-system thirty-six hours ago. They smashed the First Fleet and over twenty legions on the planet. Worse still, there was no warning. Tratirne's civilian population hadn't been evacuated. Praetor Asinia did the best she could to buy the civilians time, but we only got a couple hundred thousand off world before the battle ended."

Marcellus was devastated. Tratirne had a prewar population of over half a billion souls. Moreover, the planet sat just inside the edges of the Frontier, and was the closest world attacked by the Ascomanni yet.

"It gets worse," Festus continued. "Several key members of the War Council were visiting Tratirne when the Ascomanni attacked. They didn't make it out..."

"Does the Senate or the Triumvirate know about this yet?" Marcellus asked.

Aulus turned and folded his hands behind his back. "No, and with luck, they won't know until it's too late."

"Too late for what, sir?"

The diminutive cyborg began to pace in front of Marcellus and said, "Aurelius, for too long the politicians have sent us to die fighting a war we cannot win. It's time we seek compromise and accord with the Ascomanni. To do that, I'm taking control of the Republic."

Marcellus's blood ran cold. He shifted his stance slightly and adjusted the cuffs of his shirt behind his back, using the motion to subtly press a button on his wrist communicator.

"But, sir... Every attempt we've made at communicating with the Ascomanni has been met with bloodshed. Why do you believe you can get them to listen?"

"You actually deserve some of the credit for that, Aurelius. You see, the prisoner you apprehended on Aetnaeus was very cooperative. Unfortunately, I don't have time to share the whole story, as my men are about to storm the Senate Chambers."

Aulus turned back to face the young praetor as he continued. "I need to know, Praetor, are you with me, or should you be locked up with what's left of the Council?"

"Aulus..." Marcellus started. A flicker of anger flashed over Praetor Festus's face. Marcellus caught himself and began again. "Praetor, what are you going to do if the senators or the Triumvirs resist?"

"We are talking about the survival of our people, Aurelius!" the older officer thundered. "There will be blood, but better to sacrifice a few lives for the sake of the whole."

"I understand, sir, but if we finally have an opportunity to end the war, why can't the government be trusted with such a task?" Aulus stirred, but Marcellus pressed on anyway. "I beg your pardon, I know you must surely be growing impatient with me, but I am loath to think that we should have to spill the blood of our own people."

A smile spread across Festus's face, but it was devoid of any warmth. "I commend you for your fortitude, Gaius Aurelius. Truly you have the composure and bravery of a man twice your age. But you've played your hand. You will be detained until this is all over. Once I have saved Umbria, you will be released."

"Saved?" Marcellus responded, no longer hiding his disgust. "Perhaps, but at what cost?"

Aulus snorted. "Don't make me reconsider my initial assessment of your worth, Aurelius." He waved his hand dismissively. "Take him to the detention level. Put him in with the others."

Before Festus's men had a chance to react, the doors to the Ops Center blew open.

The men and women manning the Operations Center's posts screamed and dove for cover.

Marcellus took advantage of the opportunity. He lunged at the guard to his left, twisting him in front of the other legionnaire just as he fired his weapon at Marcellus.

The plasma round struck the hapless guard in the chest, and the young praetor threw the smoking corpse at the remaining soldier.

As Aulus's henchman struggled to get out from under the body of his deceased comrade, Marcellus quickly drew his dagger and charged, driving his blade through the man's forearm. The legionnaire's weapon malfunctioned, and a vicious electrical discharge left him convulsing on the floor.

Suddenly, a heavy blow struck Marcellus from behind and sent him flying. He rolled over to find Aulus standing over him with a pistol.

"You will not ruin my—"

Without hesitating, Marcellus kicked out at the older man's leg, bending it in a direction it was never designed to go.

Aulus bellowed in pain, and Marcellus took advantage to drive his dagger into the shoulder joint of Festus's prosthetic arm. He yanked upwards, and with a pop, the robotic appendage was severed completely, pistol and all.

Aulus collapsed to the floor with a groan and clutched at his broken leg with his remaining good arm.

Marcellus spun around to find Thana and Cornelius, two of the praetorians who had pulled him from the bunker on Aetnaeus, jogging toward him.

"Good work, sir!" Thana called out. "Prefect Invictus secured the lifts and the terrace outside. The Ops Center is secure."

Gasping for air, Marcellus flashed his soldiers a quick grin. "Thanks, Thana, looks like I owe you two again."

"Not at all, sir, you did all the hard work," Cornelius replied with a grin. "What do you need us to do?"

"Watch the good Praetor," Marcellus said grimly.

He walked back toward the entrance to the room and raised his voice to address the men and women who still huddled behind their workstations.

"Soldiers of Umbria, Praetor Aulus Festus was planning a coup to overthrow the duly elected government of the Republic. There is still much to do to prevent his plan from succeeding," Marcellus continued, "but I would ask that at this time you file out of the Operations Center and wait on the terrace outside. If you are a member of the communications section, please stay at your stations."

The men and women who had furiously sought shelter at the sounds of explosions and gunfire slowly began to stand and walk toward the exit. Four soldiers stayed and approached Marcellus.

"Thank you for stepping forward," Marcellus said sincerely. "I know things are confusing right now, but I need you to get me a secure link to the head of the capital's garrison force."

One of the four, the most senior from her insignia, nodded and said, "We'll make it happen, sir. Is there anything else?"

"Not at this time."

She gave Marcellus a tight-lipped smile and the foursome went back to their stations.

Marcellus activated his wrist comm again and called out to Invictus: "Vic, just giving you a heads-up, you're about to have thirty new guests out on the terrace. Please keep them in place while we figure everything out."

"Understood, Praetor. Oh, and Marcellus? Cornelius is sharing the helmet feed from their breach. That was a solid job taking Aulus and his men down. Your soldiers are mighty impressed by their commander right now."

"I'll claim it was faked," Marcellus said into his comm with a grunt. "How'd you fair coming up the lift?"

"We told them we were their relief. They were confused long enough for us to take them down." Invictus's voice quivered for a moment. "Unfortunately, two of them didn't make it."

"You did what you had to do, Vic. Once I've contacted the Capital Guard, we're going to need to storm the detention level. They are holding the Council there."

"That'll stretch us pretty thin, sir. We'd be hard pressed to keep the Ops Center under control while taking D-Level."

"I know, but we can't rely on anyone else for the time being. We're it."

"Understood, Marcellus. I'll wait for your word."

Marcellus turned and walked back to the communications section. The same woman who had spoken earlier popped her head up over her console and said, "Praetor, I have a link to the Prefect of the Capital Guard."

"Good, thank you, soldier." Marcellus leaned over the station and said, "Prefect, I need you to listen very carefully, we have no time to waste. Praetor Aulus Festus was plotting a coup. I have him in custody at the Castellum, but your soldiers need to lock down the capitol building immediately!"

The image of the garrison's commander alternated between shock and disbelief as he processed Marcellus's words.

"Uhh...umm, of course. We'll...we'll deploy immediately. I'll contact you again once we've secured the building."

With that, Marcellus cut the channel and turned back to the anxious technicians sitting around him. "Thank you for your help, troopers, we may have just averted a catastrophe. Please remain at your posts. If you get any news from the garrison commander, provide one of my praetorians with the update and they will pass it along."

He walked back toward his soldiers and said, "Thana, Cornelius, I need you to hold the Ops Center. Bind the prisoners and keep an eye on them. You'll have support just outside the door, but if you are in danger of losing this position, I need you to destroy the comms section and prevent the enemy from freeing Praetor Festus."

Cornelius's eyes widened as he realized what his Praetor was asking them to do, but Thana put a hand on her friend's shoulder.

"It won't come to that, Cornelius, but if it does, we need to make sure these traitors cannot communicate with any remaining conspirators." Thana said. She turned back to her commander and gave him a quick salute. "We've got the situation here under control, sir. Good luck."

Marcellus nodded before heading back out the exit, where he found his soldiers managing the crowd that had gathered on the terrace outside. He waved to Invictus, and the leader of his praetorians jogged over.

"What's the plan, Marcellus?"

"Keeping the Operations Center secure is key, but we can't foil this plot alone. We need to release whatever's left of the Council. They'll be able to help us identify those troops that Aulus brought with him to the capital," Marcellus responded.

"OK, so I guess just you, me, and a pair of the remaining praetorians. That'll leave four to secure the terrace with two more in the control center."

"That's the best we're going to do, Vic. Let's get going."

"Yes, sir."

Invictus turned to the remaining praetorians and passed the orders along. Two peeled off and followed Marcellus and Invictus to the lift, while the rest patrolled amongst the personnel detained on the terrace.

As the group of four began their descent, Invictus realized his commander was still unarmed.

"Sir, should we stop at the armory so we can get you suited up?" Invictus asked.

"There's no time. Speed is of the essence, Prefect."

"Like he needs it anyway…" one of the praetorians mumbled under her breath.

Marcellus ignored it, but Invictus struggled to suppress a laugh. "Your soldiers take pride in fighting for the toughest son of a bitch in the URA, Praetor."

Marcellus finally allowed himself a slight smile. "All right, enough," he said softly, taking any sting out of the rebuke. "Let's focus on the task at hand. There are normally two dozen MPs guarding the detention blocks, but we don't know what their status is or how many of Praetor Festus's soldiers might still be guarding the level."

The lift passed the atrium's ground floor and proceeded into the sublevels. The bright vibrancy of the morning's light was replaced with a sterile white glare as they passed underground and continued further and further into the depths of the Castellum. Finally, eight levels down, the lift came to a stop.

The party walked out into a wide hallway. Black scoring marred the walls, while the lights flickered sporadically. They slowly and carefully proceeded down the hallway with Invictus in the lead.

Soon enough, they came upon a security checkpoint, where the detention level split off at equal intervals into eight separate cell blocks. Corpses were strewn everywhere, and the sickly smell of blood and charred flesh fouled the air. Two of the bodies were clad in combat armor and bore the insignia of Festus's personal guard, the rest wore the uniforms of the Castellum's security force.

"Check for vitals," Marcellus whispered.

The party fanned out across the room. Marcellus approached one guard who had propped himself up against the wall. He had been shot in the gut, and as he approached, the wounded soldier issued a gruff, gurgling cough.

Kneeling next to the guard, Marcellus called out, "I've got a live one here."

One of his praetorians rushed over and gave the wounded guard a sedative. She continued to evaluate him for a few more seconds before turning to Marcellus and shaking her head. There wasn't anything they could do.

As the Praetor went to stand, the guard reached a bloodied hand out and grabbed his forearm. The guard looked at Marcellus with half-lidded eyes as he struggled to speak.

With a halting voice that was barely audible, he said, "There were six. They opened fire after we refused…access." The guard was overcome by a fit of coughing, and blood began to drip from the corner of his mouth, but he continued: "They have them in Cell Block Three."

Marcellus lowered himself to the floor next to the dying guard. With the utmost care, he lifted an arm up and over the soldier's shoulders and gently pulled him closer.

"You've done well. Rest now, soldier," Marcellus said, his voice quivering.

There was nothing more to say and nothing more to do. Together they sat there for a few more moments until, with a final, shuddering gasp, the soldier's grip on Marcellus's arm loosened.

Marcellus gently pulled his arm away so as not to disturb the deceased. He closed the man's eyes and said, "Find your way to the Fields of Elysium, son of Umbria. We will bring your murderers to justice."

The sea of emotions that had been boiling within him since confronting Praetor Festus was consumed by a white-hot, all-encompassing fury. What Umbrian could murder his fellow soldiers? How could they have left this man to die alone in this dank basement?

A rage more powerful than anything he had experienced before drove all thought and reason into the recesses of his mind.

There was only one thing that mattered now: justice.

Marcellus shot to his feet, a crazed look in his eyes, and ran to the entrance to Cell Block Three. Invictus saw his commander's disposition and chased after him, with the two remaining praetorians lagging behind.

Marcellus descended a short series of steps before coming across the first pair of Aulus's men who were standing guard at the entrance of the cell block. He slowed his approach and forced a smile as they noticed him.

One trained his weapon on the Praetor while the other approached Marcellus, held out a hand, and said, "This area is off limits. Identify yourself immediately."

"Praetor Festus sent me to interrogate the War Council. We need to determine the strength and disposition of the Capital Guard prior to launching our attack on the Senate Chambers."

The soldiers relaxed slightly, and the leader of the two said, "We were not informed of your visit, sir. I'll need to call this in. State your name please."

Marcellus's smile broadened. "Of course, I wouldn't expect anything less." With a low, guttural snarl he roared, "My name is Kairon, the ferry man, and I am here to drag you to hell!"

Marcellus pulled his blade and drove it twice into the soldier's chest before spinning him around and throwing him into his comrade. The two clattered to the floor, and the uninjured soldier quickly attempted to regain his feet. Marcellus delivered a swift kick to the man's helmet, and the soldier collapsed limply to the ground.

Marcellus continued down the cell block. There were more scorch marks on the walls, and he passed the bodies of two more guards before finally reaching his destination. The final two legionnaires stood flanking the door to a large holding cell at the end of the hallway.

Marcellus waved as he approached and said, "Gentlemen, good to see you. Praetor Festus has sent me to interrogate the prisoners. Please check with your comrades up the way for confirmation."

The two collaborators turned to look at each other, and Marcellus wasted no time to strike. He threw his dagger at one of the conspirators and watched with satisfaction as the blade sank into the man's shoulder.

Taking advantage of the confusion, the Praetor charged the other, tackled him, and slammed his head against the floor, cracking the visor on the soldier's helmet.

Marcellus turned to make sure the other legionnaire was out of the fight, only to find that he had gotten to his feet and was bringing his plasma carbine to bear.

There wasn't enough time. Marcellus would not be able to reach him before the soldier pulled the trigger.

He closed his eyes and prepared for the end.

The sound of a plasma carbine echoed off the walls of the cell block, followed by the noise of a body crumpling to the ground.

Opening his eyes, Marcellus found his assailant lying still on the floor, with Invictus standing further back down the corridor.

Marcellus sat on the cold metal floor plating, panting heavily from exertion. Sweat ran down his forehead and stung his eyes. He blinked away the irritation, and slowly the rage that consumed him bled away.

He stood and turned to his friend and subordinate. "Thanks, Vic, I thought I was done for sure."

"We're even now, Marcellus," Invictus said, his voice heavy with anger and concern. "What the hell were you thinking? What you did was reckless, and it put all of us at risk!"

"I know. But the sight of that guard…bleeding out, all alone. I snapped."

"You're in command. You are supposed to be in control. Your soldiers' lives depend on it!" Invictus shouted. "You're no good to anyone dead."

Marcellus looked at the floor as shame washed over him. Vic was right, and he knew it. "I'm sorry Invictus. You are absolutely right."

It was Invictus's turn to feel awkward, and, after a few seconds of uncomfortable silence, he muttered, "Yeah, well... At least it worked out. This time, anyway." He reached out an arm, and Marcellus grasped it. "Let's free us some VIPs."

Marcellus nodded. "We have a coup to foil after all."

He tapped a few keys on the panel next to the holding cell, and the door shot open.

Chapter 4

The Castellum: Perugia, Umbria

Standing in the Operations Center, Marcellus looked out over Perugia's skyline. The sun was now high in the sky, and faint tendrils of smoke wafted up between the capital's skyscrapers. The situation was still fluid, but things were finally beginning to settle down.

The Capital Guard, well trained and in superior defensive positions, had turned the tables on the conspirators. Many had surrendered. The few who did not were quickly defeated, but not before some minor damage had been done to the buildings adjacent to Capitol Hall and the Senate Chambers.

That still left the disaster unfolding in Umbria's orbit to tend to. The most senior member of the War Council present, Chief Armaments Magistrate Maniah Glabria, had taken charge of the situation.

Originally a civilian bureaucrat in the Magistracy of the Army, Maniah still carried herself with the dignity and poise of someone who had served in uniform. Marcellus guessed she was in her mid-fifties, and her amber colored hair was streaked with silver and white.

Magistrate Glabria had been rattled by Praetor Festus's attempt to seize power, but Marcellus was shocked by how quickly she seemed to shake it off and focus on the pressing needs of the present.

On Marcellus's advice, she had ordered the ships carrying refugees to land in the lush plains to the east of Perugia.

A tent city was already springing up amongst the long yellow grasses of the plain. Prefabricated barracks built to support Umbria's legions were now being used to provide shelter to the refugees from Tratirne. Food, water, and medicine was being rushed to the survivors from the capital and other nearby cities.

Despite the spate of good news, there was still no definitive word from Tratirne. Praetor Festus's version of events had not been borne out by reality, and more transports and freighters continued to jump into orbit. The captains of these vessels reported that resistance was still being offered by Praetor Asinia's soldiers prior to their departure.

Given the time it took to return to Umbria using an indirect route, her forces were still resisting as of the day before. However, the only warships that appeared tended to be light and heavily damaged, which did not bode well for the fate of the First Fleet.

The commanders of the Seventh and Fifth Fleets had been ordered to make for Tratirne with all speed, but were told not to jeopardize their vessels unless they found a favorable situation to exploit or that committing forces would aid in the assumed evacuation of the planet.

Back in the Ops Center, Marcellus had offered his praetorians' services to Magistrate Glabria. She had ordered them to help secure the Castellum. Working with the remaining guards, Invictus had quickly detained any other soldiers who had come to the facility with Praetor Festus.

Many of those men and women would have had no idea what their commander had planned, but until the coup had been fully investigated and all of the conspirators identified, they were to remain detained.

It had been a long day already, and it was bound to grow longer still, Marcellus thought to himself.

He had sent a brief message to Valerian, informing him of events and indicating that his return may be delayed. But with the chaos around him still needing to be tamed and only a handful of his own soldiers available, there was little for Marcellus to do but stay out of the way and wait.

As he gazed out over the city, his wrist began to buzz. Marcellus activated his communicator and was not surprised to hear Invictus's voice.

"Praetor, you've got incoming, it looks like the Triumvirate has arrived and they are on their way up to you. You might want to give the Council a heads-up."

The doors to the Ops Center swung open, and three figures, clad in ornate robes, swept into the room. A gaggle of aides and bodyguards followed closely, like children chasing after their parents.

"Too late, they are already here, Vic. I'll let you know how it goes."

The members of the War Council had lined up to meet the Triumvirs, and Marcellus walked over to join them. The three Triumvirs came to a stop before the members of the War Council, and Marcellus was suddenly very conscious of his grimy appearance. Dirt, sweat, and blood marred his dress uniform, but the situation had not allowed him time to clean himself up.

The Triumvirate served as the executive body of the Umbrian Republic. Each Triumvir was elected to a term of six years by a complex algorithm that gave a proportionally weighted score to each planet in the Republic. The winner of each planet's popular vote would win the entirety of that planet's score, and the candidate who received a simple majority of the score would be elected.

To ensure the executive branch's responsiveness to their people, these elections were staggered, with a new Triumvir being selected every two years. In practice though, the turnover amongst the Triumvirate since the start of the war had been non-existent.

Magistrate Glabria took a half step forward to greet them: "Welcome to the Castellum, Triumvirs, I'm sure you have many questions. We will provide you with what information we can, but details are still coming in on a number of important subjects."

Triumvir Aula Eppia, the oldest both in age and in time in office, responded, saying, "Thank you for receiving us so quickly, Maniah. I am sure many things demand your attention, but the Triumvirate must be informed of the events unfolding on our own doorstep."

She was an elegant woman who had passed middle age with grace. Still vibrant and full of energy, she was the keystone of their people, keeping a diverse Republic of eighty worlds and countless minor outposts together in this time of crises.

Her demeanor grew stormy as she continued, but Marcellus suspected it was more at the subject of the conversation than any anger at the magistrate herself.

"The Senate is demanding information, and the public is still waiting for an official statement explaining the damage to the city center and the near-constant stream of ships landing in the plains. The news analysts are already concocting all sorts of wild scenarios, and we desperately need to provide people with a clearer picture of what's going on."

"I understand, Triumvir. What I can share is that Tratirne has been attacked, and Praetor Aulus Festus attempted to seize control of the Republic," Magistrate Glabria said. "How the two are related, if at all, is still unknown at this time."

The Triumvirs looked aghast by the news.

"Aulus tried to overthrow the government?!" one of the two remaining Triumvirs, Vibius Sestius, gasped.

Triumvir Sestius was a tall, middle-aged man with a regal look about him. Having been elected in the last cycle before the Ascomanni were first encountered, he was well known for having a modest and sensible disposition.

However, the discovery of a hostile alien race and a consistent stream of bad news from the Frontier had slowly broken this once promising politician.

In the face of such uncertainty, he clung desperately to his position as Triumvir. He had barely been re-elected to a second term, and rumors of corruption and cronyism were widespread. He had grown more insular and paranoid as the years had gone by, and the news of the attempted coup had the career politician on the verge of hysteria.

"If a Praetor could plot against us, how can we trust that other members of our officer corps have not forsaken their oaths to the Republic?!" he shouted in panic.

The last of the three, Triumvir Decius, put his hand on his peer's shoulder. "Calm yourself, Vibius. We would most likely be dead by now if the conspiracy was more widespread."

Sestius looked at his colleague with a curious blend of dread and scorn. "That is not funny, Publius! We face a crisis!"

Publius Decius, a famed explorer and military man, had been elected after Sestius, and had just recently won a second term. His popularity within the Republic's military and the public at large gave him outsized influence for being the junior member of the Triumvirate.

He was a handsome man, who had maintained his fitness levels following his retirement from the military. He wore the marks of age with dignity; the worry lines and crows' feet marking his face did little to distract from his presence. His silver-black hair was still thick and full, and at the present, was brushed back to the nap of his neck, just meeting the collar of a well-appointed suit coat he wore under his official attire.

Fortunately, at least as far as Marcellus was concerned, he used this power to limit the frequency with which the Senate and his fellow Triumvirs meddled in the war against the Ascomanni. Marcellus had great respect for the man, and being so close to the Triumvir was equal parts thrilling and terrifying.

Decius's brow furrowed, but before he could say anything in response, Triumvir Eppia cleared her throat. "Gentlemen, please. This is not helpful." She turned back to Magistrate Glabria. "We are deeply concerned by these events, Maniah. Is there anyone you can spare to brief us more thoroughly?"

The magistrate nodded. "As he played a central role in foiling Festus's plot, I can think of no one better than Praetor Aurelius. He has just returned from the Frontier, where his unorthodox tactics have resulted in a tremendous victory for the Republic."

Marcellus was shocked, but quickly regained his composure. He stepped forward and addressed the Triumvirate, saying, "I would be happy to provide you with a detailed report of today's events. There is a briefing room across the veranda that would be suitable for our purposes. We can begin at your convenience."

"Ha! The Hero of Varese! A man famous for losing," Sestius spat sarcastically. "Our young praetor looks worse for wear, Magistrate. Is this the best you can provide us?"

Marcellus's cheeks burned with embarrassment, and he looked down at the floor.

"You show your own ignorance, Vibius. This man has demonstrated his worth before our enemies, which is more than can be said for the three of us. We'd be fortunate to receive his counsel," Decius retorted.

"How dare you…" Sestius began to sputter, but Triumvir Eppia once again cut them off.

"We appreciate your willingness to assist us, Praetor. However," she said with a motherly smile, "I think we can spare half an hour to let you clean yourself up. We will be waiting in the briefing room you specified."

A wave of gratitude and relief washed away his shame, and Marcellus thanked the Triumvir for her consideration. Without any further notice, the Triumvirs turned and left the Ops Center with their attendants in tow.

Marcellus slowly exhaled and tried to get his heart rate back under control. He had been close to the Triumvirs before, but he'd never actually interacted with them. And now he'd need to provide a briefing on the day's events...

Sensing Marcellus's unease, Magistrate Glabria approached, a knowing smirk on her face, and said, "I apologize for throwing you to the wolves, Praetor."

"It's no problem at all, Magistrate, I know you've still got a lot on your plate here. I would ask that you send me what information we have been able to put together on the situation at Tratirne."

"Done. One word of warning before you go, Praetor. I would advise you to use caution in dealing with the Triumvirs. Sestius's paranoia is getting worse by the week, and although Decius has been very supportive of the war, he delights in his popularity with the people. He could easily see you as a tool to further increase his growing cult of personality across the Republic."

"I understand, Magistrate. Thank you for the heads-up. If I might, could I bother you for one last thing?"

"Of course, what do you need?"

"Can you point me to the nearest officers' quarters? The Triumvirs made me acutely aware that I really need to grab a shower..."

Magistrate Glabria laughed.

***

In a fresh uniform and armed with a data pad full of information, Marcellus pushed open a pair of ornate doors and entered the briefing room.

It was a large, circular space, well-lit with a domed ceiling and plentiful seating to accommodate large groups. The spacious rows of benches that gently curved around the room could accommodate fifty people, but now, only a dozen or so occupied the space.

In the center of the room, the Triumvirate paced back and forth, while their aides huddled in small groups. Sestius and Decius were arguing, and the former, with his back toward the door, failed to notice the Praetor's arrival.

"...trust any of them at this point?! For all we know, this could have been a ploy deliberately intended to put us off guard and force us deeper into their arms for protection."

Marcellus cleared his throat. "Forgive me, Triumvir Sestius, but I assure you that this took us all by surprise."

Sestius spun around, mouth agape as he stuttered. "Praetor...I...I didn't hear you come in." His surprise faded and a nasty look stole over his face. "It is very rude to eavesdrop on your betters, boy."

"I beg your pardon, Triumvir," Marcellus responded. "But I wanted to provide you with the information you requested as soon as possible."

Triumvir Eppia stepped in before Sestius could escalate further and said, "Thank you for your timely return, Praetor. I'm sure there is much to cover, but I for one would like to start with the events surrounding Aulus's attempted coup."

Decius nodded in agreement. "We must ensure that Perugia is secure and that the government is no longer threatened."

Sestius just grunted and took a seat opposite his peers. His aides scurried to his side while everyone else found a seat.

Marcellus walked to the center of the room and activated a small pedestal located there. The lights dimmed and four metallic disks emerged from the stand and floated toward the ceiling. They formed a perfect tetrahedron before orienting back toward the middle of the room and projecting a soft blue light.

Marcellus tapped a few keys on his datapad, and a three-dimensional image appeared featuring the telemetry data from the *Hasta* as they approached the planet.

"Honored Triumvirs, I arrived in the Umbria system at approximately five o'clock this morning. Upon our approach, we noticed several hundred civilian ships in orbit over the planet. Despite repeated attempts to get in contact with planetary control, we were unable to get landing clearance. On my orders, the crew of my corvette brought us to the surface anyway."

Sestius scoffed imperiously, but said nothing. Marcellus waited a moment more before continuing.

"On our approach to the planet, we were intercepted by a flight of fighters. After I identified myself and explained my purpose, the flight escorted my ship to the Castellum. I disembarked with nine of my praetorians."

The image changed as they switched to surveillance imagery from the Castellum itself.

"Praetor Aulus Festus had returned to Umbria two days ago. He was already here at the Castellum as the first evacuation ships began to arrive from Tratirne, and he ordered orbital control to keep the new arrivals from landing on the planet. He only began executing his plans after receiving a report on my party's approach from the flight that intercepted us.

"Unsure of our intentions, he accelerated his timeline. He summoned the members of the Council present at the Castellum to the Operations Center, where his soldiers arrested them. They were then taken to the Detention Level of this facility.

"The guards on that level, loyal sons and daughters of Umbria, denied Aulus's troops access to the cellblocks and attempted to apprehend them. A firefight developed, and eventually all twenty guards on that level were killed. Two of Aulus's conspirators were killed and three members of the Council were also wounded in the exchange. With D-Level secured by the rebels, the Council was transferred to a large holding cell and the remaining conspirators took up position to guard the cell block.

"Praetor Festus had spent his time since returning to the capital pre-positioning additional loyalists in locations around Capitol Hall and the Senate Chambers. In order to coordinate his attempted coup, Aulus sealed the Operations Center and confined the on-duty members of its staff to their posts. All non-essential personnel on the remaining levels of the Castellum were ordered to return to their barracks.

"With the Castellum secure, he communicated the timeline to his loyalists, who began preparations to seize key facilities across the capital, including Capitol Hall and the Senate Chambers."

Marcellus paused briefly to provide the Triumvirs with the opportunity to ask questions if they had any, but a stunned silence was all that met his words.

"Upon landing, it became clear to me that something strange was going on, a feeling only reinforced by the absence of any technical or security personnel on our landing platform. We proceeded with all haste to the Castellum, where we were granted access by security after presenting credentials.

"On entering the building, I was further disturbed by the sense of fear and unease that hung over those individuals we passed. Soldiers milled about at will, and the sounds of frantic conversations echoed off the atrium's walls.

"Out of an abundance of caution, I dispatched my praetorians to the armory to gear up. Once they were equipped, they were to patrol the atrium and attempt to bring order to the situation. In the meantime, I headed to the Ops Center."

"On my arrival, I was confronted by a pair of conspirators in battle armor. They initially denied me passage, but brought me to the rouge Praetor after he was informed of my presence. Once in the Ops Center, Aulus informed me of the fall of Tratirne and his plans to seize control."

"During this time, I opened a channel to my subordinates, who retook this level by direct assault and subdued Aulus. I immediately contacted the Capital Garrison and informed them of the pending attack. Once that was done, I took a handful of soldiers with me to liberate the Council members located in the detention level. After a brief struggle, we secured their release.

"In hindsight, we were very fortunate that Praetor Festus had not had sufficient time to secure the Castellum. A hovertruck carrying forty of his best soldiers was en route, but was intercepted by the Capital Guard after we informed them of the plot. Those conspirators refused to surrender, and their vehicle was destroyed by the same flight group that had intercepted my ship on our approach."

Marcellus paused again, waiting for feedback from his audience. It was Triumvir Eppia who found her voice first.

"Gaius Aurelius Marcellus, the Republic owes you a profound debt. Your actions today prevented the collapse and destruction of our entire civilization."

Decius nodded in assent. "You show a clarity of thought that is exceptional for a man your age, Praetor." He cast a sideways glance at Triumvir Sestius and said, "Any remaining doubt about the Senate's decision to elevate you to your current rank must surely be put to rest now."

"Yes, yes. Your story is full of the type of clear-cut, black-and-white heroism that fools like Decius eat up," Sestius retorted. "However, I have one very important question to ask you, young Praetor. Why did you return to Umbria in the first place? Our last reports from the War Council place you on Aetnaeus, gallantly leading your army against the enemy."

"I had requested a meeting of my peers and the full War Council to discuss recent developments following the successful evacuation of Aetnaeus."

"Oh, so you ran from the enemy again?"

Marcellus's temper flared as the Triumvir's words gnawed at him, but he forced himself to remain calm.

"No, sir. Faced by an unrelenting and superior enemy, I chose not to sacrifice my soldiers' lives for a planet we had already lost. After inflicting grievous loses on the enemy, I successfully withdrew my forces from the planet."

"Giving the Ascomanni yet another planet from which to stage further attacks on the Republic?" Sestius snarled. "Perhaps you should reconsider your sycophantic mewing for this young pup, Decius."

Decius opened his mouth to speak, but Marcellus lost control of his anger and cut the Triumvir off.

"Again, you are incorrect, sir. After evacuating Aetnaeus, I destroyed the planet. Aetnaeus's destruction resulted in the total annihilation of a fleet of nearly six hundred Ascomanni ships and millions of Ascomanni soldiers. The enemy will have no new staging area, no added resources to fuel their conquest of our people."

The smug grin on Sestius's face was quickly replaced by one of astonishment and disbelief.

"Praetor, you did what?!" exclaimed Triumvir Eppia.

"I used a prototype antimatter bomb to fracture the planet's crust." He tapped a few keys on his data pad, and images of the evacuation of the planet and its ultimate destruction began to play.

Marcellus keyed another command before continuing. "A complete report of the campaign and its conclusion has just been sent to your aides. I suspect that it will take some time for you to process the news I have just shared."

"You have exceeded your authority, Praetor!" Sestius bellowed. "Guards! Arrest this man!"

"Belay that order!" Decius shouted back. "You forget your place, Sestius! The Senate gives the Praetors wide discretion in prosecuting the war against the Ascomanni, and rightly so! If it is the Senate's wish to remove the Praetor for his actions, then it is their prerogative to do so. You, however, are in no position to order his detention."

"Enough! Do you two not grow tired of your bickering?" Triumvir Eppia interjected. "I admit, I find the Praetor's actions disturbing, but we should not rush to judgment. Moreover, Decius is right about the Praetors' privileges. It is not constructive to continue this line of discourse, Sestius."

"Always you rush to Publius's aid, Aula! I have been mocked and belittled long enough! I am returning to Capitol Hall, and I promise you have not heard the end of this!" Sestius roared before storming out of the room.

His entourage quickly gathered their possessions and followed him, and Marcellus was immediately reminded of the sketch comedies he'd been fond of as a youth. As the last member of Sestius's following filed out, Triumvir Eppia stood.

"Do not judge him too harshly, Praetor. The war has taken a steep toll on him," she said.

"The responsibilities of leadership weigh heavily on him," Decius agreed. "That is no reason to take it out on you, however."

He turned and looked at Triumvir Eppia, and she nodded.

"Despite Sestius's absence, I would ask you to continue your briefing, Praetor. We still must know what fate has befallen Tratirne and the forces defending her."

"I understand, Triumvirs, and I appreciate your willingness to defer judgment." Marcellus typed a few more commands into his data pad, and a series of tables replaced the images from Aetnaeus.

"We've determined that part of the reason we haven't been able to contact Praetor Asinia or her fleet is that a series of deep space relays have been destroyed. This is very disturbing, as the arrays are controlled by an algorithm which manages their positions directly from the Castellum. As you know, they move at random in a parsec square area of space to prevent the enemy from tracing the origin and destination of our signals. How the Ascomanni were able to locate these relays so quickly is a mystery.

"While the Council sees to the repair of the long-range communications network, civilian survey vessels have been commandeered to take the place of the missing relays. We have also received an update from the vanguard of the Seventh Fleet, which just reached Tratirne. A detailed report has not yet been received, but preliminary analysis shows that our forces continue to resist the enemy, while the planet's evacuation is well underway.

"Regarding the battle, it is known that the enemy struck with little notice. However, that is not to say that the attack was a complete surprise. Asco scouts were spotted on the edges of the system prior to the assault. First Fleet had a few hours to prepare, and ambushed the Ascomanni upon their arrival. They managed to stall the assault for some time before being forced to retreat.

"The Ascomanni have shown some uncharacteristic restraint in deploying their forces. They have taken a more measured approach than they have in the past, making sure not to become overextended or leave their supply lines exposed. Instead they deliberately worked their way through our orbital defenses and secured a beachhead on the planet from which they can steadily reinforce their strength."

Marcellus walked back to the pedestal in the center of the room and tapped a few buttons. The lights came back on and the holographic projectors floated back to their resting place.

"That is all the information we have available at this time, Triumvirs. As the War Council receives additional details from the front, it will be passed to your offices for review."

"Thank you for the thorough briefing, Praetor Aurelius, but something bothers me," Decius said. "You indicated that Festus believed Tratirne had already fallen. However, due to the loss of the comms relays, he could not have had that information. I find the discrepancy most odd. Did he mention anything else that seemed peculiar?"

"Preator Festus believed he had an opportunity to end the war. When I asked him why he thought he would be successful where so many others have failed, he made a reference to an unusual Ascomanni soldier my forces had detained on Aetnaeus."

"Why did you capture this individual, Praetor?" Triumvir Eppia asked. "I was under the impression that, with a few exceptions, Ascomanni soldiers were not very intelligent."

"They are extraordinarily well-disciplined, Triumvir, and you are correct, they show little in the way of individual initiative. However, the subject we apprehended appeared to be very different than the Ascomanni it led. In fact, its biology seemed to be very similar to our own."

The Triumvirs exchanged a quick glance. In a flash, a tingling sensation ran up Marcellus's spine.

"Did Festus have contact with this prisoner, Praetor?" Decius asked, his facial features hardening into an unreadable mask.

"I believe so, sir."

Umbria's leaders exchanged another look.

Eppia thanked Marcellus again for his time and for sharing what information he could, and the two Triumvirs took their leave.

As the doors closed behind the last member of the Triumvirs' entourage, Marcellus was left alone in the expansive briefing room to consider the meaning of the day's events.

Chapter 5

Umbrian Orbital Grid Two Gamma Zeta

Three hours later, Marcellus was piloting a jumpship headed toward high orbit, while Invictus slept in the co-pilot's chair. Their destination was one of the Intelligence Directorate's automated data processing annexes. Records showed that Praetor Festus had visited this location prior to his attempted coup, and Marcellus wanted to know why.

After the briefing with the Triumvirs, he had asked Magistrate Glabria for quarters for his soldiers, and she provided five rooms for Marcellus and his praetorians. These guest rooms were normally reserved for distinguished visitors, but none of the praetorians took issue with their sumptuous new accommodations.

While the others took time to rest, grab food, and visit the Castellum's rec center, Marcellus had been pouring over information relating to Festus's time on Umbria. The traitorous Praetor had returned from the Frontier onboard his personal battlecruiser, the *Fortuna*, and brought two cohorts of legionnaires with him to the surface.

Interestingly, Festus's soldiers were originally quartered at a barracks complex on the outskirts of the capital instead of closer to the Castellum or the city center. After finding lodging for his troops, he had met with the Director of Naval Intelligence. As soon as that meeting had concluded, records showed the Preator had boarded a shuttle and departed without filing a flight plan.

Marcellus had requested the flight log from that particular ship, but it wasn't immediately available. It had been deployed to bring supplies to the refugee camp in the plains around Perugia, and it was several hours before the shuttle returned from its mission.

Once it returned to the Castellum, Marcellus had wasted no time requisitioning it for his own purposes.

Finally, their destination came into view. The space station had a large rectangular body, with two long cylindrical sections protruding at equidistant points from the lower hull. Hangar bays and living quarters were located in each of the spars, and the sections were joined by a catwalk that provided access between the two.

Something more pressing grabbed Marcellus's attention, however. Patrolling around the station were two Umbrian frigates. Marcellus gave Invictus a hard nudge with his elbow.

"Hmm... Wha... I'm awake," Invictus grumbled. He rubbed the sleep from his eyes for a moment and looked out of the cockpit. "Uhhh... Marcellus...? Why are there warships guarding a glorified library?"

"I was going to ask you the same thing," Marcellus replied uncertainly.

As they approached, the station requested their clearance codes. Marcellus transmitted his information, and to his relief, they were granted permission to dock in the station's starboard hangar.

They neared the rightmost spar and its docking bay doors slid open. Marcellus set the shuttle down gently, and the hangar doors closed quickly behind them, dropping the hangar into total darkness.

Intelligence Annex Delta-Five;
Orbiting above Umbria

Marcellus toggled the shuttle's floodlights, and together, he and Invictus disembarked into the unlit hangar. Beyond the shuttle's searchlights, the interior of the hangar remained shrouded from view. Marcellus turned to look at Invictus, and the latter shrugged uncomfortably.

Suddenly, there was movement to their right, and Invictus lunged forward.

The sounds of a scuffle quickly ended as a surprised voice called out: "Hey! What's going on?!"

A moment later, Invictus dragged a young-looking orderly into the light. He wore the uniform of the Combined Intelligence Directorate, and his face paled noticeably as he came face to face with the pair of soldiers.

"Mind telling us what the hell is going on?" Marcellus growled.

"Oh uh, sorry about the hangar, sir. We've been having some mechanical issues..."

No sooner had the orderly spoken than the hangar's lights flickered and came on, revealing a drab, utilitarian interior.

"I guess maintenance finally got it sorted," the orderly mumbled. "So, uhm...welcome to Intelligence Annex Delta-Five Praetor. I assume you are here to see the prisoner?"

Marcellus gave Invictus a quick glance, and the latter gave an almost imperceptible shrug.

"That's it exactly. Please take us to it immediately."

"Of course, Praetor. Unfortunately, I must ask that your subordinate stay with the ship, as he does not have the appropriate clearance to receive information on this topic."

Invictus began to object, but Marcellus put his hand on his friend's shoulder. "I'll be all right, Vic. Stay here. I'll be back as soon as I can."

Invictus extended his arm, and the two grasped each other's forearm. Invictus nodded and headed back up the ramp without another word.

The orderly seemed to have recovered from his earlier scare, and said, "Thank you for your understanding, Praetor, and again, I apologize for the fiasco with the hangar lights. Everyone's been on edge since they brought her aboard. Strange things have been happening.

"What kind of strange things?" Marcellus asked.

"Power fluctuations, unexplained mechanical breakdowns, mostly minor issues. The only major problem we had was when our link to HQ was severed for several hours yesterday. The problem's been resolved, but...well, I'm sure you know how superstitious people can get."

Marcellus nodded and did his best to keep his expression blank. A communications blackout? In the timeframe surrounding the attempted coup? Very suspicious.

The orderly led Marcellus through a series of corridors before they finally came to a lift located in the center of the spire. Together, they boarded the elevator and began their ascent into the heart of the station.

"So, what have you been able to uncover so far?" Marcellus probed.

"It's fascinating really!" the orderly said, his voice raising in pitch with excitement. "She speaks our language, and appears shockingly similar to us in appearance. A sample of her genetic material was retrieved and is in the process of being sequenced. This could be a watershed event for our understanding of exo-species biology!"

"Who all is aware of these developments?"

"Well, sir, with the exception of the Directors of the CID, and the team examining the prisoner, no one does. Not even the Triumvirs. However, two days ago, the Director of Naval Intelligence ordered us to clear you and your fellow Praetors for access to our program. Another Praetor arrived shortly thereafter."

"And that man had direct communication with the prisoner?"

"Yes, sir, they had quite a lengthy conversation."

"What did they discuss?"

"Unfortunately, the audio recordings were corrupted, so we are not exactly sure. He left immediately after meeting with her, though."

"I see. Who's responsible for the team here?"

"Doctor Mirabella Urbanus is in charge. I'm sure she will find some time to provide you with a short overview of her team's work."

"Excellent, I look forward to meeting her."

Marcellus's mind was racing, but each trail of thought led to darker and more disconcerting places.

What had Festus uncovered here? The disgraced Praetor's words haunted him. Had he found the key to finally bring the war to an end? If so, why seek to overthrow the government?

The lift finally came to a stop, and the doors slid open to reveal a large, two-story chamber. A catwalk ran around the whole room, connecting the first and second levels. The whole space was bathed in a cool blue light, and the soft whir of machinery echoed off the cavernous walls of the space.

The floor below was full of computers, medical equipment, and scientific instruments. The floor was elevated, and large portions had been removed, exposing thick cords running beneath the remaining pathways. In the middle of the space sat a box made of an opaque white material. Armed guards in full combat gear stood watch around the perimeter.

Together, the pair walked down a flight of stairs to the primary workspace below. The room was cold; Marcellus could see his breath as the orderly led him past rows of mainframe clusters and storage terminals.

After a short walk, they finally came upon a group of scientists who were pouring over biometric data displayed on a series of charts. One saw the pair approaching and called out to their leader.

As the head scientist came into view, Marcellus caught a glimpse of his new host and suddenly felt as though someone had knocked the wind out of him.

Mirabella Urbanus was young for someone who held such an important post, perhaps no more than two or three years younger than Marcellus himself. She was of average height but pale for an Umbrian, her skin a pastel orange, with rust-colored freckles dotting her face. A shock of curly, auburn hair framed her features and rested gently on her shoulders.

She smiled as he approached, and the Praetor lost himself in her midnight blue eyes.

"Greetings, Praetor Aurelius, I am Doctor Mirabella Urbanus. My team and I are responsible for studying the prisoner your forces retrieved."

Marcellus stared for a moment too long without response, and her smile faded somewhat.

Blushing at his own foolishness, Marcellus hurriedly introduced himself. "It is a pleasure to meet you, Doctor. I am Praetor Gaius Aurelius. I would like to ask you a few questions about the prisoner and Praetor Festus's visit the other day."

"Of course, this way please."

The doctor led him closer to the cell set in the middle of the room, and Marcellus saw an opportunity to learn more about his beautiful host.

"So, Doctor, you must be very bright to have received this assignment so young. What is your discipline of study?"

Mirabella's brow furrowed and she gave Marcellus a piercing glare. "I assure you, Praetor, I earned my position here. I have multiple doctorates in the fields of chemistry, exo-biology, and biomedical engineering, and my work studying the Ascomanni has dramatically increased our knowledge of our enemy."

Marcellus flushed again. "I apologize, Doctor, I meant no disrespect. I'm afraid my social skills have atrophied somewhat with my time spent at the front."

Seeing the Praetor's discomfort, it was Mirabella's turn to feel self-conscious.

Marcellus struggled to stay focused as her skin blushed pale red with embarrassment, highlighting her freckles. "I'm sorry, sir," she said apologetically. "I've overcome my fair share of superiors who felt like I was too young to have advanced so quickly on my own merit. I can be a bit oversensitive on the subject."

Thankfully for Marcellus, the awkward exchange came to an end as they reached a large console just beyond the prisoner's cell. Mirabella began typing furiously, and the opaque walls of the cell became translucent.

The room was meagre in its amenities, featuring a small table, two chairs, a simple bed, and a latrine. Each was made of the same shiny metallic alloy, devoid of any personal touch or warmth. And sitting on the bed was—

A jolt ran through Marcellus's body as he caught sight of the prisoner.

She was sitting upright with her hands in her lap, staring vacantly at the floor. She wore a simple white jumpsuit which accentuated the amethyst color of her skin. Boney ridges ran from the nape of her neck to just above each eye socket, with a braid of jet-black hair running in between, stopping just above the small of her back.

"Is...is she Ascomanni?" Marcellus asked.

"No," Mirabella responded. "She is something different. We have not encountered anything like her before."

She tapped another series of commands into the console and images of the muscles, organs, and skeletal structure of an Ascomanni soldier were displayed.

"We believe that the Ascomanni developed on a dense, high-gravity world, which resulted in their impressive skeletal strength and muscle mass. Their natural attributes have been further augmented by cybernetic enhancements which increase individuals' strength and durability. Finally, neural implants override the decision-making and behavioral portions of the Ascomanni's brain, resulting in obedient and reliable soldiers."

"Are you suggesting that the Ascomanni are some type of organic, mindless drones?" Marcellus interjected.

"No, not entirely, they maintain a general awareness of self and are capable of interpersonal communications and relationships. The implants serve more as a circuit breaker, prohibiting individuals from acting against the commands of their superiors by manipulating their pain receptors."

"Doctor, I've encountered Ascomanni with excellent tactical awareness and the ability to adapt under pressure. That may not be true of your average foot soldier, but to write them all off as less than sentient is a dangerous mistake."

"You're right of course, Praetor." Mirabella nodded in agreement. "It appears that the Ascomanni have some kind of caste or class system. It's not exactly that straightforward, but I won't bore you with the technical details. Like the Ascomanni general you defeated on Varese. He demonstrated the same physical enhancements as the run-of-the-mill shock trooper, but his cognitive abilities did not appear to be limited by the cranial implants we see in less important subjects."

"OK, so how does this relate to our prisoner?"

"Like the Ascomanni, she appears to share certain genetic traits with us. However—"

"Wait, say that again?" Marcellus interrupted.

"The Ascomanni and this new race of aliens share certain genetic characteristics with Umbrians."

"You mean...we are related to them?!"

"Yes, distantly. Our species originated from a common gene pool." Mirabella frowned. "Surely you knew this already, sir. Clearance for this working group is predicated on having been thoroughly briefed on the Oracle program."

Marcellus was stunned. He reached for a nearby stool and dropped heavily down upon it, jaw agape. In an instant, Doctor Urbanus's revelation shattered his understanding of the universe.

The vast, merciless hordes arrayed against his people *were somehow related?!*

How was this possible? The people of Umbria maintained an unbroken record of their history since they had developed written language. There was no evidence of other sentient species on Umbria. Even as they had reached out to the stars, they failed to encounter other advanced lifeforms on the habitable planets they had discovered.

A gentle hand laid itself on Marcellus's forearm, and he snapped out of his musings to find Mirabella staring intently at him, worry clearly showing on her face.

"I'm sorry, Praetor, it can be a lot to take in all at once. I was unaware that you were in the dark about Oracle."

Marcellus gulped and raspily replied, "I appreciate your concern, Doctor. It'll take some time for me to fully digest what you've just shared."

"That was my mistake, and I'm afraid I've said too much on the topic. Information surrounding the Ascomanni's origins is highly sensitive, and I would ask that you keep it to yourself."

"Understood." Marcellus cleared his throat and returned to his feet. "Is there anything you can tell me about this new species?"

"I am able to give you a general overview on what we've uncovered so far. She has shared that her people call themselves the Pasarga. Aside from that, her responses have been cryptic and self-serving. We have determined they have received significant cybernetic enhancement. This improves their reflexes, motor skills, and cognitive abilities.

"Based on the results of our scans, we believe that these changes must be made to individual specimens after they reach full maturity. The quality of their augments is far superior to that which we have observed in the Ascomanni. Where Ascomanni implants seem haphazardly installed and can malfunction, causing crippling damage or death to the subject, the prisoner's seem to work in perfect symbiosis with their host."

"So the Ascomanni are the brawn, and these...Pasarga are the brains?"

"That could be it, Praetor. But they are only weak in comparison to the Ascomanni. Their muscularity is equivalent to our own, and their added dexterity would make them capable adversaries on the battlefield. I would think they would make for excellent scouts or spies, in addition to having the capacity for strategic thinking and execution. I'm surprised you were able to capture this one alive."

"It was a close-run thing, Doctor. The Prefect of my praetorians stunned her prior to her apprehension. However, the Ascomanni accompanying her inflicted heavy losses on my soldiers."

Mirabella was taken aback. "Oh…umm. I'm sorry to hear that. I mean… Forgive me, that was a trite thing to say… I'm sorry for your loss, Praetor."

"It's OK, Doctor, the right words are often hard to find. I appreciate the sentiment." His gaze shifted back to the alien sitting in the middle of the room. "Praetor Festus spoke with the prisoner. Is there any way I could do the same?"

"Yes, sir, we can arrange that. However, I must ask that you turn over anything that she might be able to use against you."

Marcellus nodded. He unbuckled his belt and detached the ornamental plate before refastening it. He also began to unfasten his wrist communicator. Mirabella produced a simple plastic container, and Marcellus deposited a handful of useful gadgets and knickknacks into it. Finally, he produced his dagger and set it down gently in the bin.

Mirabella's eyes widened at the sight of the blade. "Do you always carry that with you?"

Marcellus smiled back roguishly and said, "Only when I'm not in power armor."

"Right… OK, well please come this way. We will be able to see into the cell, but the room will appear milky from within. If you need assistance for any reason, just call for help."

With that, she led him to the door of the cell.

A guard waved a scanning device over the Praetor's body. When the results came back clear, he gave the doctor a nod. She typed a code into the lock by the door and a retinal scanner appeared. Mirabella looked into the scanner and there was a soft click as the door unlocked.

"Good luck, Praetor," Mirabella whispered softly.

Marcellus opened the door and walked into the cell. The Pasargan did not turn to face him or show any other sign of interest in his arrival. Marcellus grabbed a chair and pulled it closer to the prisoner.

"Praetor Gaius Aurelius Marcellus. It is an honor to receive you," she said, finally turning to face him.

Pale yellow eyes with narrow, slitted pupils gave the Praetor a penetrating look. The prisoner's soft, almost melodic tone of voice took Marcellus by surprise, but he did his best to keep his features emotionless.

"That is kind of you to say. You clearly know my name, but I am afraid I don't know yours," Marcellus replied.

"My name is unimportant, Praetor. I am but a single grain of sand in the vast desert arrayed against you."

Marcellus smiled. "I expect you are being modest. Still, I insist, it would be impolite to proceed without first knowing your name."

The prisoner flashed him a smile full of razor-sharp teeth. "Your persistence is admirable, Praetor. I will indulge your curiosity. My name is Atossa."

"Atossa. That is a beautiful name. I'm sure there is much we will learn from you, Atossa, but I am primarily concerned with a guest who visited you recently."

"Praetor Aulus Festus."

"Yes."

"He was an interesting man. Praetor Festus's augmentation may have kept the body from dying, but it did not stop the mind from decaying. He was quite receptive to what I had to say."

"And what might that have been?"

"Your species faces a simple choice. You can choose to continue to resist, and face your ultimate destruction, or you can submit, and be consumed. Either way, in the end, you will succumb."

"Neither of those options sounds very appealing, Atossa. You say we will be destroyed or consumed. By what exactly?"

A remorseless grin spread across the strange woman's face.

"There are ancient nightmares that inhabit the darkness between stars. They cast their gaze on your people, and they will not be denied."

Marcellus watched the alien, choosing his words with care and keeping in mind the information Doctor Urbanus had shared.

"So, these beings discovered your people, and you chose submission?"

A cruel, cackling laugh emanated from the purple-skinned alien. "Good, good! You are quick, young warrior. In the end, there was only one option. They made us better than what we were. They freed us from hardship, pain, ignorance, disease, and the illusion of choice. All that was required in return was obedience. Festus understood what we offer, and he saw in it the salvation of his people."

"Tell me, Atossa, what was he offered for betraying his people?"

She hissed at him, saying, "What did we offer *him*? On the contrary, *we* demanded an offering first. I provided a means by which he could communicate his commitment to his new masters, but he would have to do the rest."

Slowly the pieces were beginning to come together.

Festus's belief that he could end the war, his foreknowledge of the assault on Tratirne, perhaps even the destruction of the long-range communications arrays might all be attributed to his attempts to ingratiate himself to his would-be overlords.

Another thought nagged at him, slowly fighting its way to the forefront of his consciousness. It was…something that Mirabella had shared only minutes before. Then it hit him.

What explained the difference between the Ascomanni and the Pasarga? Why were augments of such poor quality forced on the Ascomanni if they had access to the same technology? If the force confronting them was so vast, surely a lack of resources couldn't explain the discrepancy. It only made sense if…

"I have one last question for you, Atossa. The Ascomanni, they resisted your masters, didn't they?"

The undulating squeal of the alien's laughter filled the cell once more.

"You *are* quick Gaius, son of Gnaeus. Truly you merit the effort we've spent tracking your development."

A cold shiver worked its way up Marcellus's spine, but he refused to be baited and said nothing.

Seeing that Marcellus had chosen not to let her jab distract him, Atossa continued: "The Vaeringyar were a strong and proud race. They believed themselves capable of weathering the storm we set loose upon them. They were wrong."

She closed her eyes, and an evil grin spread across her face. "Their hubris was washed away by the cleansing fires of war and devastation. Now they only obey."

Atossa's hands turned into fists in her lap, and her whole body seemed to tighten at once.

In a flash, she shot to her feet. Marcellus bolted upright, but not before the alien had time to grab him by the shoulders.

He instantly began to sink to his right to put her off balance, but as he started to pull away he realized she had taken no further action.

Atossa stared at him, her face no more than a few centimeters away from his own. Her pale, yellow eyes almost seemed to be peering *through* him.

In that moment, the emotionless mask she wore faltered for the briefest of seconds. In her eyes, he saw a vast emptiness. She was devoid of all emotion: there was no joy, no sorrow, no love or hurt. Her consciousness was tinged with only the slightest hint of a quiet madness, some abject fear...

In that moment, Marcellus knew what it meant to submit.

The doors to the cell burst open, and two guards leaped into the room, weapons trained on the Pasarga. Atossa blinked, and the moment passed. She pulled away from him and sat back down on the bed.

"As I told you before, Praetor, in the end, all will submit."

Marcellus returned his chair to its place, turned, and left the cell without saying another word. The guards followed him out, and Doctor Urbanus was waiting for him.

"Are...are you OK, Praetor?" she asked hesitantly.

Marcellus leaned heavily on the outer wall of the cell as the door closed behind him. His encounter with this new adversary had left him emotionally drained, but he did his best to put on a brave face.

"Yes, Doctor, I'll be fine."

"Sir, what she just revealed dramatically changes our understanding of the galaxy we live in. The prisoner, Atossa, confirms some of the most far-fetched theories ever proposed about the nature of our enemy..."

"I'm sure this new information will help your work tremendously, Doctor, but I'm afraid it makes mine much more difficult."

Mirabella looked at him uncertainly and asked, "What are you going to do?"

"I will resist, Mirabella, with every breath left in me. If she speaks the truth, surrender may seem like the wiser choice in the face of such overwhelming odds, but I have seen the gifts our would-be conquerors seek to bestow upon us. That creature has been robbed of the very things that make life worth living. We would become a hollow shell of a people, nothing more than shadows imitating the motions of life."

Mirabella pursed her lips and watched him for a moment, and Marcellus got the distinct impression that he was being studied, like some new discovery that needed to be analyzed and understood.

"I cannot tell you any more about the Oracle program, Praetor. But there are others who might have the authority to share that knowledge with you. I would highly encourage you to do whatever is necessary to gain access to it."

Marcellus watched the doctor closely. She had offered no specifics, provided no details, but her earnestness had a strong effect on him. Clearly Oracle was related to these developments, and Mirabella believed it could help them overcome their enemies.

"Thank you, Doctor Urbanus, I will take your recommendation to heart. If it's not inappropriate, would you please keep me informed of your work here? I expect there will be many things you learn that may help us in understanding our enemy."

Mirabella smiled again, and the warmth of her expression melted away some of Marcellus's fatigue. "I would be happy to, Praetor. It has been a privilege to make your acquaintance."

"The honor is mine, Doctor," Marcellus responded. "I hope our paths cross again."

Color filled Mirabella's cheeks once again, and Marcellus gave her his most charming smile as he turned and walked back toward the lift that would take him to the hangar. Five minutes later, he approached the boarding ramp to his shuttle, and was unsurprised to find Invictus standing there, his expression serious.

"That is some heavy stuff, brother," he said in a low, husky voice.

"Vic, how in the world would you know anything about my visit here today?" Marcellus asked, looking at his friend with a quizzical smirk.

Invictus's disposition brightened and he chuckled to himself.

"For such intelligent people, they sure do lack some common sense. I activated your wrist comm before you left. I was listening in the whole time. Fortunately for me, they had it with them while they were observing your conversation with that strange alien."

For a brief moment, the tension consuming Marcellus disappeared, and he laughed at his friend's ingenuity.

"I should be angry, Vic, but it's good to have someone to talk to about this. Let's get back to the Castellum."

"I have one other question for you, Marcellus," Invictus said as they headed back up the ramp.

"Just one?"

"Yeah, it's really been eating me up… That doctor you tripped all over yourself in front of, was she as cute as she sounded?"

"Vic? Shut up…"

"Must've been. You can stare down an enemy armada, but one intelligent, beautiful woman and you turn to mush.…"

"You know what, Invictus? I really hate you sometimes."

"Don't worry, sir, your secret is safe with me. As long as the Ascomanni don't attack with an army of beautiful scientists, we still have a fighting chance."

"That's it! No more talking the whole way home. That's an order!"

Chapter 6

The Castellum: Perugia, Umbria

Marcellus and Invictus returned to the Castellum late, with the last red-orange rays of the sun's light fading in the east. The duo immediately returned to the temporary quarters they shared. Within a few minutes, Invictus's gentle snoring was coming from one of the two adjoining bedrooms.

Marcellus, preoccupied by the day's revelations, could not sleep.

Instead, he had spent the better part of two hours in the room's common area researching Praetor Festus's relationship with Titus Calpurnius, the Director of Naval Intelligence. He hadn't yet found a smoking gun which would indicate that the Director was in on the coup, but the two had an extensive history together.

Marcellus yawned as he scrolled back through their service history.

To have convinced the Director to grant him access to Atossa, Festus must've been in close confidence with the man, or had some form of leverage over him. Given what he knew of Festus's reputation, Marcellus suspected it was the latter.

The only connection of note was that both had been high-ranking members of the Frontier Reaction Force, a paramilitary organization designed to ensure the stability of Umbria's colonies.

The Reaction Force was created with an eye toward customs enforcement, anti-piracy operations, and supporting colonial law enforcement organizations in maintaining public order. As such, the RF was composed of several departments with specialized functions, supported by a fleet of small cutters and corvettes.

The Force had quickly notched several significant wins against the criminal gangs which terrorized Umbria's outer colonies. With the lure of excitement and adventure and the ability to achieve tangible results, it quickly became *the* pathway for advancement for ambitious officers.

In this environment, it wasn't long before the Reaction Force's cavalier attitude and condescension for those they were supposed to serve created tensions with the Frontier's inhabitants.

Marcellus's eyes widened as he finally spotted the connection between the two men. Buried deep in the Director's records was mention of action at Battipaglia, the location of the Umbrian's first contact with the Ascomanni, and the site of an extensive, year-long battle...

Almost eight years prior, the newly founded colony world of Battipaglia suddenly went dark. Sensing another golden public relations coup, the RF's top brass jumped into action. It was not uncommon for settlements to occasionally suffer communications blackouts, and a prompt response would help show the softer side of the organization. A detachment was quickly organized and sent to investigate and bring the colony back online.

A week passed without word from either the colony or the Reaction Force soldiers sent to the planet. A larger unit was being prepared to follow up when a single message was received on an emergency channel. An indecipherable voice screamed into the receiver, drowned out by the sounds of gunfire and screams, before the message dissolved into static.

The transmission lasted eighteen seconds.

The Frontier Reaction Force quickly mobilized a significant portion of its overall strength to confront the most serious incident they had encountered since their formation. Titus Calpurnius, the future Director of Naval Intelligence, led a naval element made up of a squadron of customs corvettes, while Aulus Festus was responsible for the Force's Rapid Response teams.

Upon arriving at the planet, the corvettes deployed Festus and his soldiers to the surface, where they found the colony's primary settlement had been razed to the ground.

There was no sign of the settlers.

The civilian population, numbering just over a hundred thousand, had vanished without a trace.

Unable to find any of the planet's people or the initial RF detachment, Festus took his forces to secure the colony's primary relay. It was located at the base of a mountain several kilometers from Battipaglia's capital, and it would take the better part of the afternoon to reach it.

After an hours-long march through the afternoon heat, Festus and his men found their comrades in arms.

The mutilated remains of the original detachment were scattered about the relay station. They had been massacred defending the facility, and it was clear some had been viciously tortured before being killed. The scenes of brutality and slaughter shocked Festus and his soldiers to their core, but who or what had caused such devastation was still unknown.

Aulus quickly realized that his force was of insufficient strength to confront the perpetrators, and he requested immediate extraction. Calpurnius, however, believed the area to be unsafe and demanded the ground troops return to the capital for evacuation.

On the trek back through Battipaglia's untamed wilderness, Festus's soldiers were on edge. Reports of motion amongst the shadows of the jungle's canopy were initially passed off as the work of overactive imaginations, but in time even Festus came to believe they were being followed.

Festus ordered his men to break column and proceed in mixed order, but before his orders could be carried out, they were ambushed by an unidentified alien adversary.

With a chorus of terrifying screams, hulking, half-naked warriors charged out of the tall foliage on either side of the road, heedless of the Umbrians' weapons. Scores of the fanatical enemy would fall, but those who got through crushed and maimed any RF soldiers that came within reach.

As the sun began to set, Festus did his best to manage an orderly retreat. Shortly before his troops reached the outskirts of the ruined capital, however, he and a small vanguard were cut off from the rest of the column.

Festus was personally confronted by a quartet of enemies, and he was critically wounded in fierce, close-quarters combat. Only the timely intervention of his soldiers saved his life.

With their leader incapacitated, the retreat to the capital dissolved into a total rout.

The vanguard would make its way to the city's crumbling starport, carrying their wounded commander on a makeshift litter.

In the dying light of Battipaglia's sun, the echoes of screams and the sounds of gunfire slowly receded as the group reached their extraction zone. They waited at the rendezvous point for as long as Calpurnius would allow. No one else would break through the enemy lines.

Festus had started the battle with two thousand troops. Only thirty-seven soldiers were evacuated.

The shattered survivors of Aulus's force would be the first to live through an encounter with this new alien menace, who would come to be called the Ascomanni. News of a hostile alien race spread like wildfire throughout the Republic, and soon the military arrived to begin the lengthy and costly attempt to retake the planet.

The war for Umbria's survival had begun.

As for Festus and Calpurnius, the former was soon elevated to Praetor, while the latter was the subject of an official inquiry. However, the new Praetor spoke in defense of his colleague, and the matter was quietly dropped. Spared from potentially career-ending findings, Calpurnius would go on to join the CID, where he quickly worked his way up the ranks.

Marcellus stretched and rubbed his eyes. It was well past midnight, and as much as his mind kept racing with the events of the day, he knew he needed his rest. He rose from the desk and headed to his room.

Before he could plop down into bed, however, a monitor imbedded in the wall above the nightstand began to chime. Marcellus leaned over the table and tapped a few keys into the vidscreen and a voice began to speak.

"Praetor Aurelius, His Excellency Triumvir Sestius has requested your presence. He indicates that you have made a mutual acquaintance recently, and he would like to discuss it with you."

Marcellus's exhaustion evaporated instantly as he became suspicious.

"It's awfully late. Is this a request in his official capacity?"

"Triumvir Sestius does apologize for the hour of the call, but as he knew you were awake. He hopes you will attend as a personal favor to him."

Marcellus did his best to hide his surprise. How did Sestius know that he was still awake? Had the Triumvir assumed that the day's events would make it hard for him to find sleep? Or was there a more sinister explanation?

"Where might I find the Triumvir?"

"His Excellency is currently hosting company at the Bacchanal to celebrate the coming of the harvest."

"All right, please tell the Triumvir that I will be there shortly."

The Capital Entertainment District; Perugia, Umbria

Marcellus sat alone in the clean, well-lit tube tram as it sped between the skyscrapers of Perugia's city center. He had left fifteen minutes before, dressed in non-descript civilian attire, and made his way immediately to the tube station that connected the Castellum to the capital's wider mass transit system. The golden hue of the towers' exterior had faded with the evening sun, and at this hour, the wide promenades that stretched between closely packed highrises were clear of pedestrians.

As he neared his destination, the gentle glow of the sleeping city began to change. Laying just beyond the heart of the city, the entertainment district was a cacophony of vivid colors.

Nightclubs, bars, and theaters lined the verandas which wrapped around and between towers in this portion of the city. Illuminated displays designed to entice would-be customers were everywhere he looked, and the brilliant, multicolored light turned night into day.

Marcellus had to remind himself that the Entertainment District wasn't all fun and games. The festive atmosphere hid the darker side of the district. It was well known that local corruption and crime was strongly rooted in the area. With one wrong turn, an inebriated reveler could easily find themselves in the district's sordid underbelly, where even the most taboo of desires could be satisfied — for a price.

The tram slowed to a stop, and Marcellus moved toward the exit. As the doors slid open, a warm, pungent breeze and the sounds of raucous celebration raced into the cabin to meet him.

He found that throngs of partygoers crowded the main thoroughfare just beyond the tube station, and the festivity showed no signs of slowing, despite the late hour.

Marcellus looked around to get his bearings. The tram had gotten him close, but public transportation wouldn't get him all the way to his destination. To reach the Bacchanal, he'd need to find another ride.

Just on the edge of a particularly boisterous crowd, he spotted his target: an automated taxi stand. The stand was positioned in the outer edge of a broad plaza suspended from three towers.

He began working his way toward it through the dense crowds.

The partygoers finally thinned as he neared his target, revealing a beautifully designed triangular courtyard. Spiral topiaries lined the walkways leading to the center of the plaza, while water gently cascaded down an intricate marble fountain located at its heart.

Now, however, the plaza's loveliness had been marred by the hordes of revelers: trash and refuse had been cast about everywhere, an unconscious festival goer slumped over a bench, and two parties of drunken bar hoppers faced off, shouting and throwing objects at one another.

Marcellus did his best to go unnoticed and he found his way to the terminal without incident. He scanned his ID and quickly called for a vehicle, and soon the cab appeared.

The aircar had a sleek profile, wide and rounded in the front for maximum creature comfort before tapering to the rear. With room for two, it was the perfect method for quickly reaching those areas of the city which were too far from a tube line, or, as in Marcellus's case, where the customer's destination was inaccessible by other means.

He hopped into the vehicle and strapped himself in.

"Please specify your destination," a mechanical voice asked.

"The Bacchanal, please."

The taxi accelerated away from the plaza and began to rise. Soon, the mass of buildings around the Entertainment District began to thin, and Marcellus's eyes grew wide as his destination came into view.

There, hovering amongst only the tallest and most luxurious of the capital's towers, was the Bacchanal. The airship was made up of two cylindrical hulls that supported the facility's core. A thin reflective material coated the exterior of these structures, enabling the floating palace to blend into a bright blue sky from below or mirror its urban surroundings from above.

Tonight though, the intricate exterior displayed an image of thousands of paper lanterns floating against the backdrop of Umbria's starry night sky. They seemed to move and dance in tandem as the ship bobbed gently with the wind.

As the taxi drew nearer, Marcellus spotted the Bacchanal's central structure, slung gondola-like underneath the airship's dual hulls. At over five hundred meters in length and two hundred meters wide, it was only three quarters of the size of the buoyant hull sections keeping it aloft. Breathtaking views of the capital and its surrounds were offered from nearly every space on the ship, which served as the perfect backdrop for the playground of the rich and famous.

The Bacchanal was famous, or infamous, for its excesses. It wandered lazily above the entertainment district, containing every amenity money could buy. Rumors of outrageous extravagancies filled the Republic's gutter press. It was *the* place where Umbria's celebrities could enjoy themselves without fear of prying eyes, and access was tightly controlled.

The aircar approached the ship's landing, and Marcellus disembarked. He barely had gotten out before a security guard greeted him. The tall, muscular man gave him a quick look-over and frowned at his pedestrian appearance.

"Sir, access to the Bacchanal is strictly by invitation only. I must ask you to leave at once."

"I'm here at the request of Triumvir Sestius. My name is Gaius Aurelius. *Praetor* Gaius Aurelius."

The enforcer blinked quickly and consulted his datapad. He blanched as he found Marcellus's name and said, "I beg your pardon, sir. His Excellency has granted you access to the Bacchanal. Please enjoy yourself."

Marcellus nodded and walked through the gilded entryway which led him into the heart of the establishment.

Feeling incredibly out of place, Marcellus mentally kicked himself for not asking the bouncer for the Triumvir's location. He meandered aimlessly amongst the Bacchanal's hallways, not sure of what exactly he was looking for.

After about ten minutes of fruitless searching, Marcellus cheeks burned as he realized he hadn't the slightest clue of where he was going. Fortunately, he came across an attendant, clad in a skin-tight, shimmering silver jumper with piping that seemed to change colors as she moved about.

Deciding he'd had enough of foolishly wandering about, he approached to ask for assistance.

"Pardon me, miss, I'm afraid I'm a bit lost. I'm looking for Triumvir Sestius, would you happen to know where I can find him?"

The attendant smiled and said, "Of course, sir, I'd be happy to help." She consulted a small device strapped to her forearm and said, "His Excellency is currently hosting a small group of close acquaintances in the VIP section of our dance hall. I'd be happy to show you the way."

"That would be excellent, thank you."

"Right this way, please."

With that, the attendant headed back the way Marcellus had just come.

"Is this your first time joining us at the Bacchanal, sir?" the attendant asked.

Marcellus laughed and said, "Yeah, I guess getting lost gives it away."

"On the contrary, sir, it takes a while for our members to become familiar with the Bacchanal's layout." The attendant lowered her voice and whispered, "It was unusual to be asked for assistance. Our clients primarily *tell* us what to do."

Marcellus nodded. He imagined the young woman had seen her share of slights, and suddenly the luster of his surroundings seemed to dim somewhat.

The attendant brought him to a pair of double doors. They slid open quickly and the pair stepped inside. Just as quickly, the doors behind slid shut, and another set of doors, almost airlock-like in nature, opened in front of them.

A crushing swell of screeching electronic tones assaulted him, and he could feel the thumping beat of the bass in his chest as he entered the dance hall. Everywhere he looked, partially clad bodies writhed to the discordant music blasting from speakers set in every square meter of the room's walls and ceiling, and the whole room glowed with a soft purple light.

His guide gently took his hand and led him to a raised dais set back and to the right of the dance floor. As they came within a meter of the raised platform, the cacophony around them became muted.

Marcellus looked surprised, but his guide smiled and said, "The Triumvir's private booth has sound dampening technology that allows him to vary the volume of his suite. It's much easier to have conversations with guests when you can hear one another."

Marcellus nodded as they walked up a handful of stairs to the top of the Triumvir's platform. The circular booth had seating wrapping around half of the space, with a table set in the middle. The remaining half was open, allowing people to mingle with their patron.

Half a dozen women were scattered about, laughing and joking with one another as they enjoyed their drinks. Sestius lounged in the middle of the rounded couch, in deep conversation with another man. The unidentified guest nodded at whatever the Triumvir had told him, got up, and left via the other end of the VIP section.

A bodyguard standing at the edge of the platform stopped Marcellus and his guide before informing the Triumvir of their arrival. Triumvir Sestius stood and moved toward them.

"Ahh, my wayward Praetor!" he said, throwing his arms wide in greeting.

He walked over to Marcellus and wrapped an arm around his shoulders.

"Come, we have much to discuss!"

He peered back at the attendant and said tersely, "Thank you for bringing him to me, girl. Now, leave us."

The attendant bowed her head and left.

Sestius guided Marcellus toward the booth and addressed his guests, saying, "Ladies, I apologize, but unfortunately I have a matter to take care of. Please go enjoy yourselves and I'll come find you after my business here concludes."

"Awww..." came a refrain of voices, and the women filed out, gently caressing the Triumvir's arms and shoulders as they passed.

Sestius watched them go for a moment longer before turning his attention back to Marcellus.

He smiled broadly and said, "Praetor Aurelius! Please, come sit with me."

He dropped down onto the couch and patted the seat opposite of him.

Marcellus sat down and guardedly said, "Thank you for your hospitality, Triumvir. What can I help you with this evening?"

"Ho ho! Always so formal and to the point," the Triumvir joked. His face hardened and he peered penetratingly at Marcellus. "So be it. There are privileges that come with power, Praetor. Surely even someone as decorous as yourself has come to realize this?"

Marcellus nodded but did not speak.

"Good. One of the privileges I've cultivated is having a wide and expansive group of...friends, shall we say. And like most friends, I know intimate details of their lives, details I keep in trust. And in return, they share exciting developments that they may witness or be a part of, as friends are wont to do.

"For example, I am aware that you recently took a short trip to one of our intelligence outposts. I also happen to know that the disgraced Praetor Aulus Festus pressured the Director of Naval Intelligence into providing him access to that very location."

A quiet rage flitted over Sestius's face, lasting only for the briefest of moments before the polished mask of a skilled politician returned.

"What I don't know, and find most frustrating, is why he would travel there, and why you would retrace his steps so shortly after his failed attempt to seize power."

Thinking back to the day's briefing, Marcellus began to wonder if this was yet another sign of the man's growing paranoia.

"I assure you, Triumvir, Aulus and his conspirators have been apprehended. There is no deeper plot against you or the Republic."

"Ha!" Sestius barked harshly. "I know that, *boy*, what I want to know is why you followed him there, and what you uncovered."

Marcellus's heart began to race. He did not trust Sestius, and Doctor Urbanus had made it clear that the Triumvirs had not been briefed on the prisoner yet. Divulging that information would be inappropriate, to say the least, and would provide the Triumvir with leverage he could use to try and control Marcellus with later.

"I merely sought to tie up loose ends, Triumvir. Unfortunately, however, I was told that the information contained in that facility was tightly restricted. It is not my place to bypass the CID's intelligence classifications."

"So, you couldn't confirm the existence of our new mutual acquaintance? I hear she's quite lovely. Apparently, her skin matches the color of the walls."

Marcellus was taken completely by surprise. Worse still, he failed to cover up his shock, and the Triumvir had clearly seen through his reaction.

He flushed, temper flaring at how easily he had been used to confirm the Triumvir's suspicions.

Sestius laughed again and said, "Ah, Praetor, you must learn greater discipline than that! You'd never survive as a politician! Thank you for confirming what I have already been told. So, come! Now that I've demonstrated that I already know all of your secrets, tell me more about your encounter."

"I am afraid that I still cannot discuss information related to the materials contained on that station, Triumvir," Marcellus said, his voice hardening.

"Is that so? Too bad, Praetor."

The Triumvir leaned forward in his seat, all pretense of warmth gone from his expression: "See, my friendship could be very valuable to someone in your position. Especially someone who just destroyed a habitable world. I would imagine that the self-important imbeciles running around the Senate Chambers might find such an action...treasonous."

"Are you threatening me, Triumvir?" Marcellus said evenly.

"Oh no, Praetor, just speaking idly about the very real circumstances you face."

"I appreciate your concern, but as you've already pointed out, I am no politician. My only aim is the defense of our people and the preservation of the Republic. I serve at the Senate's leisure, and if they seek to recall me, that is their right."

Sestius smiled. "Admirable words, Praetor. But surely the people you seek to protect would be better served by having you remain on the battlefield? I can help fend off the wolves who will inevitably begin circling you, looking for any sign of weakness. All I ask for in return is information."

"I do not hide anything from you willingly, Triumvir. Only a fool would make such a powerful man his enemy..."

Marcellus paused for a moment, knowing full well that he was about to cross a line he could not return from.

"However, I am bound by the oath I took to the Republic, and that duty includes acting responsibly with classified information. I cannot give you what you want, sir."

Sestius's face froze, expressionless, as if searching for the right reaction to Marcellus's rejection. Marcellus quietly wondered to himself when the Triumvir had last been told no.

At last, Sestius closed his eyes and sighed deeply. When he opened them again, he put on a hard, forced smile and said, "I appreciate your dedication, Praetor Aurelius, and I am sorry to have dragged you out here at this late hour."

"I am sorry I couldn't be of more help, sir."

Sestius rose, and Marcellus stood as well.

"Thank you very much for your time, Praetor," the older man said. "One final word of caution, however. I have been told that soldiers returning from the front, having faced such obvious and immediate danger, can be indifferent to the lesser perils of civilian life. Please do be careful during the rest of your stay on Umbria."

The words were delivered with a caring and sympathetic tone, but the intent was clear.

Marcellus nodded and said, "Thank you for your kind words, Triumvir. Enjoy the rest of your evening."

The Bacchanal, Capital Entertainment District; Perugia, Umbria

Ten minutes later, Marcellus had found his way back to the airship's landing. His taxi was already waiting for him, and he quickly boarded and entered in the coordinates for the nearest tube station. As the vehicle pulled away and began its descent to the Entertainment District below, he let out a deep sigh of relief and thought back to his brief conversation with Sestius.

Marcellus was still angry at how easily he had allowed Sestius to trick him into confirming the existence of the Pasarga. It was clear now that he had underestimated the Triumvir's skill at manipulating others.

Politicians of Vibius's caliber were accustomed to having their way, and he shouldn't have been surprised that Sestius was willing to use questionable tactics to achieve his aims.

It was also clear that the Triumvir used a mixture of coercion and patronism to gather information on a wide range of topics. Such a network would be mutually reinforcing, as new information would provide him with more leverage over his existing network of 'friends' and allow him to pull more individuals into his orbit.

Marcellus realized that he had been naïve in his understanding of politics. It was an arena that he knew precious little about, but he still had never expected to encounter such cynical moral ambiguity at the top of the Republic's hierarchy.

He had returned to the capital for the purpose of encouraging his peers to change tact in fighting the war against the Ascomanni. But that decision would not fall solely to the Praetors or even the War Council. He would need to convince a significant portion of the Senate that this course of action represented the best chance of victory over the enemy.

Moreover, he would need to develop support amongst the Triumvirs, a task that would be much harder now.

The Praetor realized suddenly that he had risen to a level where he could not afford to just be a soldier or strategist. He would have to learn how to make forceful arguments, to persuade others. He had a steep learning curve to overcome if he were to be successful.

Outside the canopy of his taxi, the towers had grown thick around him, and the plaza he had departed on his way to the Bacchanal came back into view. First thing tomorrow morning, he would gather his praetorians and—

Without warning, there was a sharp pop.

Sparks shot from the panels behind him, and smoke quickly began to fill the cabin. Alarms began to go off, and the taxi pitched toward the planet's surface. The vehicle flashed within a meter of the edge of the plaza and began to spiral into the city's depths.

As the taxi tumbled out of control, the world outside the cabin began to blur. Despite the speed of his descent, Marcellus became aware of another large boulevard which the disabled taxi seemed to be heading straight toward.

With each rotation, it filled up more and more of his view.

He tightened his seat's harness, closed his eyes, and braced for impact. There was a *pfft* noise as the taxi's airbags deployed, followed by a violent impact that sent the aircar careening in a different direction.

Marcellus's restraints dug into his shoulders as the centrifugal force tried to tear him out of his seat. The cabin seemed to fade into darkness around him, and as another tower neared, he drifted into unconsciousness.

The Capital Entertainment District; Perugia, Umbria

There was a heavy jolt, and Marcellus came to in the cabin of his ruined aircar. Smoke filled the space, and the smell of melting plastic was almost overwhelming. There was a sharp pop, and the taxi seemed to settle onto whatever solid surface it had landed on.

Marcellus coughed and worked to unfasten his harness. He clambered out of the ruined taxi, rubbing his shoulder where the safety belt had dug into him. He'd be sore later, especially in his still tender leg, but at least he would live to suffer through the pain.

As Marcellus tried to get a feel for his surroundings, he found himself alone and in the dark, with the bright lights of the Entertainment District's main avenues hundreds of meters above.

His taxi was completely ruined, but its safety systems had done their job. The crashed vehicle was surrounded by a series of giant air bags which had cushioned the impact and caused it to skip across the walkway, coming to rest against one of the towers which supported it.

The airbags slowly began to deflate, but the taxi itself continued to smolder. Marcellus stuck his torso back into the cabin and began to pry at the central console located in between the passenger seats. He was able to force the panel open, revealing its main processer.

He pulled a simple data card from his wrist comm and inserted it into the interface. He tapped a few commands into the device, and the taxi's logs began to download to the storage card. A soft chime indicated that the download had completed, and Marcellus quickly plucked the card back out and hoisted himself back out of the cab.

Outside, he noticed that the fire had started to spread, finally reaching one of the airbags. He retreated to a safe distance as the blaze intensified and attempted to contact emergency services.

His commlink found a secure connection, but his heart sank as his call broke up into a series of static pops and hisses.

That could mean only one thing: someone was jamming communications in the area.

In an instant, he was back in the warzone. This was no accident; he was in mortal danger.

There was no time to waste. Marcellus immediately sprinted across the thoroughfare and worked his way up a gently sloping ramp to the next level, where he clambered onto a narrow balcony which wrapped further around the tower.

He followed it around to the opposite side of the building and came across a thick lattice supporting some flowering vines. It stretched all the way up to the next balcony overhead, some twenty meters above him. Marcellus tested his weight on the lattice, confirmed it would hold, and began his ascent.

Barely five minutes had passed since the crash, and Marcellus heaved himself over the railing onto the balcony he had spotted from below. The balcony circled the tower as well, and he slowly crept back toward the direction of the crash site, now forty meters below him.

As Marcellus edged closer to the railing, he saw a pair of cargo haulers appear.

They had the same general cab design as the taxi, but the rear flared out into a large boxy container capable of hauling a moderate amount of freight. Additional thrust nozzles were located under the bed of the trucks, and they swiveled forward then downward as they slowed and began to hover just above the boulevard he had crashed down onto.

One disgorged about a dozen individuals. They wore grubby clothing in the colors of E-Rho, Perugia's most notorious street gang: bright yellow garments bisected by vertical black lines. They spread out around the crashed taxi while one of their number got close and began to scan the wreckage.

"There ain't no one in there!" he called out toward the hovering trucks.

Someone stuck their head out of the cabin of the second truck and yelled, "Well then he survived, you idiot! Spread out and start looking, all of you! He couldn't have gotten too far!"

"What are you going to do?" one complained.

The second truck's cabin door swung open, and a massive, muscular figure dropped down to the street. The behemoth walked up to the man who had given him lip and struck him violently in the gut. His victim collapsed to the ground and vomited on the pavement.

"We are going to go up to the next thoroughfare to secure the lifts," the brute barked to the other gangsters. "Does anyone else have any questions? No? Good, now get to work!"

The gigantic enforcer climbed back aboard the second truck, and it slowly rose and accelerated away. Those left behind grumbled to themselves and began to fan out.

It was time for Marcellus to get moving. He kept low and followed the balcony in the opposite direction from the way he came. Fortunately, it terminated in a narrow catwalk that led to another tower about thirty meters away.

As quietly as possible, he jogged across the span and reached the veranda on the opposite side. There he found a lift shaft leading further up the tower.

Marcellus took a chance. He called the lift, and a few moments later the doors opened. He stepped in and it began its slow ascent up. He let out a deep breath and took a beat to consider his predicament.

The unsavory search party had arrived too quickly to the scene, confirming that this was no accident. It was clear that they knew who they were looking for and where to find him.

There was no time to think through who or what was behind the crash. Whoever was behind this series of events clearly wished him harm, and that was enough for the time being.

As the elevator continued to rise, Marcellus quickly evaluated the situation: He was stranded without communications in an unfamiliar area. The jamming meant that there would be no support coming. Contact with civilians would yield little advantage and might end up putting innocent lives at risk.

He shook his head. It looked like he was on his own.

His most immediate concern was getting clear of the lift. The second hovertruck had most likely dropped the remaining gang members off at the next level. Depending on how quickly they spread out, it was conceivable they would be waiting for him as soon as he emerged from the elevator.

The lift slowed as it approached its destination, and Marcellus made his decision.

He slapped the emergency stop, and, with a shuddering groan, it came to a halt. Marcellus quickly popped open the elevator's circuit board and hotwired the controls. A moment later there was a loud click, and the emergency hatch built into the rear of the elevator opened.

Marcellus hauled himself out of the tight opening and grabbed onto the rungs of the shaft's service ladder. It ran in between the set of tracks which carried the elevator up and down and ran the entire length of the lift.

He began to climb, and soon he passed the exit he had originally been headed for. He paused for a moment and listened for any indication that his pursuers were waiting outside. It was difficult to hear, but Marcellus thought he heard the soft sounds of voices beyond the door.

Suddenly, the lift he had abandoned four meters below began to move up the shaft toward him. There wasn't enough room between the elevator and the service ladder. He quickly climbed another two meters, and to his relief, the lift came to a stop a comfortable distance below him.

The voices he thought he heard became much more audible as the lift doors slide open.

"See! I told you sumthin' wasn't right! The emergency hatch is open!" an unidentified voice called out with enthusiasm.

"Where'd ya think he went?" came another voice.

"I'm sure he sprouted wings an' just flew away!"

"Woah, he can do that?"

"Of course not, you idiot! See if you can spot anyone climbing on the service ladder!"

"OK, OK...no need to call me names..."

Marcellus had to act fast. He lowered himself onto the roof of the elevator as quietly as he could, and a moment later, the soft glow emanating from the emergency hatch was cut off by the mobster searching for him.

"I can't see nothin'!" he called out.

"Of course you can't," the first voice responded. "It's pitch-black in there! Did you use your thermals?"

The light from the interior of the elevator returned as the gangster pulled himself back into the elevator.

"Uh, well, I thought this would be easy, so I left 'em with the truck."

There were sounds of a scuffle, and the elevator rocked below Marcellus.

"Taking down a Praetor would be easy, huh? I don't know why I put up with you! The boss will have our hides if we don't catch him! You stay here. I'm gonna call and let him know the guy we're after is close."

The doors slid closed, and the mobster began to mutter to himself.

Marcellus was trapped. He could try to fight his way out before more gangsters appeared, or he could attempt to reach the next level before they came back for him.

Each carried risk. If he was unable to surprise the goons below, he'd be trapped in the tight confines of the elevator. However, there was no telling how high above the next exit would be, and a thermal scan of the cold shaft would pick him out in no time flat.

He made a decision. If this was to be his end, then he would rather die fighting.

Marcellus eased his way over to the edge of the elevator and turned around, entering a low crouch. He took off his jacket and dropped it down the shaft. Then he grabbed the edge of the elevator, took one final breath, and kicked his feet off the edge.

As his center of gravity shifted lower, Marcellus flexed the muscles in his arms and kipped his legs. He swung into the elevator, his torso grazing the sides of the emergency hatch. He slammed into the back of the mobster who had remained in the elevator, throwing the surprised criminal into the elevator's wall as both fell to the floor.

Before his opponent could even get a word out, Marcellus was on top of him, punching him squarely in the face. The gangster's eyes rolled into the back of his head, and Marcellus quickly shot to his feet, ready to take on his partner.

Moments passed, however, and no one came back.

Marcellus took the opportunity to frisk the scrawny gangster he had dropped. He found the man's commlink and an old-fashioned handgun which still fired kinetic projectiles.

He checked the magazine and rocked back the slide and confirmed the chamber was clear. The Praetor quickly peered out of the exit to the elevator to make sure that the area was devoid of hostiles, then sent the elevator back to the level he had come from.

With luck, that would keep his pursuers off guard long enough for Marcellus to get back to the tube and ultimately to the safety of the Castellum.

He spotted another avenue stretching between towers to his left and about thirty meters up. From there, the thoroughfare split four ways. It would provide a good opportunity to shake his pursuers for good.

He set off, running in a low crouch, doing everything he could to keep his footfalls as quiet as possible.

There was commotion behind him; the gangsters must have returned to the elevator shaft. There was a sharp pop, then another. Marcellus recognized the sound of a plasma pistol's discharge, but he did not turn around or look back.

He vaulted over a low wall and climbed up a series of pipes to another walkway above. He followed it to a spiral staircase which led up to the boulevard he had spotted earlier.

He paused for a moment to catch his breath and plan out the crossing. Angry voices could be heard in the distance, and it sounded like they were growing closer.

The thoroughfare offered scant concealment, but he had no choice.

He sprinted from cover to cover, quickly making it about halfway across the avenue. He paused again in the shadows of a public comm terminal and peered around the corner at the rest of the ground he would need to travel.

He was so close.

Marcellus stood and darted forward, but no sooner had he left his temporary shelter than a bright light shone from behind him, casting his shadow down the length of the boulevard. He swung around to find one of the cargo haulers floating overhead.

Without hesitation, Marcellus dropped to one knee and began firing. His second shot hit the spotlight attached to the front of the cab, and the thoroughfare was plunged back into darkness.

His night vision ruined, the Praetor emptied the magazine in the general direction of the hovertruck, then threw the pistol away and sprinted toward the far end of the thoroughfare.

Behind him, the truck crashed heavily into the pavement, sending a shock through the structure and causing Marcellus to stumble.

Apparently his luck hadn't completely deserted him, Marcellus thought with grim satisfaction.

He turned and looked over his shoulder as he continued running. The transport had indeed crashed down on the boulevard. Slowly, dazed gang members emerged from the truck, and others on foot began to appear at the opposite end of the span.

Marcellus reached the far end of the avenue and jumped down a short flight of stairs that led to the fork in the thoroughfare, but he was unsure which way to go.

The sounds of angry voices were growing closer.

Just then, a door to a structure built into the walkway on his right slid open, and a hooded figure waved him toward it.

He sprinted into the building, and the door snapped shut behind him.

He immediately turned to confront whoever had beckoned him in. Marcellus found himself facing a short, narrow figure hidden beneath a cloak.

It moved slowly, putting a finger to its lips, its features still obscured by the hood. The cloaked rescuer slowly drew a plasma pistol. Marcellus prepared to pounce, but before he could do anything his host passed the weapon over.

He nodded and took up a position next to the door where he would be able to get the drop on anyone who followed him in. Content that he was as prepared as he could be, he took a moment to examine his surroundings.

Marcellus and his would-be rescuer were in some kind of public works maintenance shed. Shelves lining the walls of the structure's single room were crammed with all sorts of tubes, piping, and other materials needed for maintaining the capital's many amenities. From the amount of dust coating the shed's surfaces, it was clear it hadn't been used in a long time.

His rescuer rapped a knuckle on the wall once to get Marcellus's attention, and then pointed back at the door. Marcellus heard the sounds of footsteps approaching. Muffled voices called out instructions, and the sounds of people running grew louder, then began to fade away.

He had lost his pursuers. For now.

Marcellus kept his pistol at the ready and turned back to the cloaked figure. Before he could speak, she lowered her hood, and he recognized her face.

It was the attendant from the Bacchanal.

Marcellus raised his pistol, pointing it squarely at her chest, and whispered, "Explain. Now!"

She was unfazed by the weapon pointed at her, and calmly replied, "My name is Calpurnia. I am an associate of Triumvir Publius Decius. I keep an eye on certain individuals who frequent the Bacchanal, men and women whom the Triumvir would like to keep tabs on."

She reached out and put a hand on top of the pistol and gently pulled downward. Marcellus complied and lowered the weapon.

"So, you were there to spy on me?"

"No. In fact I was quite shocked when you appeared. After you asked to be taken to Sestius, I called my benefactor immediately. He asked that I shadow you during your visit, so I took up position in a spot where I could observe Bacchanal's entrance. It was from there that I saw someone sabotage your taxi."

"What did the man look like?"

"Conspicuously nondescript," Calpurnia replied tersely. "But in case you've already drawn the conclusion, it was almost certainly the man we saw Sestius conversing with when I delivered you to him."

"Do you have any proof to support these claims?"

Calpurnia tapped a few keys into the small device strapped to her wrist, and an image was projected in the space between them. It appeared to be security footage from the Bacchanal, and Marcellus recognized the man from Sestius's booth. He was furiously working on a control panel, but his exact intentions were unknown.

"That's the airship's automated valet system. He sabotaged your taxi remotely. I've got additional footage, but now is not the time or place."

Marcellus nodded. "How did you find me?"

"I followed you after you left the Bacchanal. After your taxi malfunctioned, it became clear that Sestius had engineered your 'accident.' I've been shadowing you since shortly after you crashed."

"Well, thanks for the save. I guess I owe you one."

Calpurnia smiled and said, "I'll keep you to it. My younger sister and I are refugees, originally born on Gela. One day, I want to return to my homeworld, to see its emerald green plains and smell the briny ocean breeze. If I ever return home, I have no doubt it will be in large part due to you. Now, let's get you back to the Castellum."

"Lead the way."

Together, they slipped back out of the door and worked their way up another two levels. They followed a short alley to the spot where Calpurnia's vehicle was parked. She jumped in and began starting up the craft while Marcellus kept watch.

With a not-so-subtle thrum of exertion, her transport started up, and Calpurnia hopped back out. She stuck out a hand, and Marcellus took it.

"This is it, Praetor, I'll find my way from here."

Marcellus blinked with surprise. "Are you sure you won't come with me?"

"I'll be fine, Praetor, I know the underbelly of this city well. I'd rather not have my face scanned by any of the cameras surrounding the approaches to the Castellum. One last thing. I'm sure you have a busy day ahead of you, but Triumvir Decius would like to speak to you. He'll be at his estate tomorrow evening, and he would greatly appreciate it if you were able to pay him a visit."

Marcellus nodded. "I'll see what I can do. Thank you again, Calpurnia."

Without warning, a single shot pierced the calm night air.

Calpurnia stumbled into the Praetor, a shocked look stealing over her face. She spun around and shot the gangster standing behind her squarely in the chest, dropping his smoldering corpse to the grimy floor of the alley.

Shouts rang out all around them at the sounds of the commotion, and Marcellus knew they only had moments before reinforcements arrived.

He grabbed Calpurnia by the shoulder, but she shrugged off his grasp, spun around, and shoved him into the cab of her vehicle. She unfastened her wrist comm, tapped in a quick command, and tossed it into the car after him before the hatch slid closed.

She patted the cabin twice, smearing a bloody handprint on the cockpit as the craft pulled away.

"No!" Marcellus screamed as he scrambled upright.

It was too late. Flashes of plasma lit up the alley below. Marcellus quickly lost sight of the situation as the aircar shot upwards, the autopilot pointing straight toward the nearest mass transit station.

Still without input from Marcellus, an image of the tube network appeared. Seeing that there was not a shuttle waiting at the closest platform, the autopilot diverted to the next station, where a tram would soon be arriving.

The vehicle reoriented and a burst of speed threw Marcellus back into his seat. The car was traveling much faster than its regulator should have allowed, no doubt modified by its original owner. In two minutes, it had covered approximately ten kilometers separating the stations, weaving noxiously between towers as it sped through the darkened city.

Marcellus grabbed Calpurnia's wrist comm and stuck it in his pocket, then struggled to strap himself in. The harness clicked closed just in time, as the car decelerated rapidly and came to a complete stop. It set down in the middle of a broad avenue, only a meter from the entrance of a tube station.

Marcellus hoped out and ran up the stairs. He dashed into the waiting tube shuttle just as the doors were sliding shut, and a moment later the tram began to accelerate down the track.

He watched as Calpurnia's aircar closed itself and began to fly away in the opposite direction.

Marcellus collapsed down onto one of the tram's comfortable benches, breathing heavily. He was sore, physically exhausted and emotionally drained. There would be a time to analyze the night's events, but this wasn't it.

He leaned back and closed his eyes as the shuttle sped him toward the Castellum, and to safety.

Chapter 7

The Castellum: Perugia, Umbria

Marcellus had returned to his suite just as the warm glow of first light began to brighten the horizon. A worried Invictus then berated him for half an hour for leaving alone, before finally accepting that his praetor needed sleep.

Marcellus filed a police report outlining the night's events, then collapsed into his bed.

Three hours later, with the mid-morning sun now high in the sky, Marcellus rose and prepared for the day. His morning was thankfully devoid of meetings or appointments, but the pace would pick up after noon.

He was scheduled to provide a series of briefings on the state of the war for several influential senators and would have to testify before a committee probing the attempted coup. After that, he'd finally be able to address the War Council and his fellow Praetors.

That left little time to digest the events of the previous evening.

Invictus and his praetorians were off on another assignment for the chief magistrate, so Marcellus jotted down a quick note for Invictus and set Calpurnia's wrist communicator and the data drive containing the taxi's diagnostic information on the bureau.

After a quick shower, he put on his dress uniform before heading to the Castellum's cafeteria for a bite to eat. He took his breakfast to the atrium and picked a spot on the fourth level, where he had a fantastic view of a replica of Umbria's first flying machine. As he ate, Marcellus let his thoughts wander.

In the dark recesses of his mind, he was forced to admit that his time on Umbria had shaken his confidence. Circumstance had thrust him into his current position as Praetor, and for the first time, he was unsure how well equipped he truly was to handle it.

He had been raised to believe in the virtue of Umbria society, where hard work, bravery, and duty to the Republic were the highest of virtues.

He had seen those qualities exhibited a thousand times over on the battlefields of the Frontier. But here in Perugia, at the heart of the Republic, at the highest pinnacles of power, he had found corruption.

Triumvir Sestius had made it abundantly clear that he was now inseparable from the games these men and women played. Fighting the Ascomanni was one thing. The horse trading of politics and the court of public opinion were something else entirely.

A hand fell on Marcellus's shoulder, pulling him back to the present. He looked up to see a woman smiling at him, a jagged scar running down the right side of her oval face. She had strong features: deep set eyes, a wide nose, and full lips, somehow managing to look both motherly and intimidating at the same time.

"Praetor Artorius?!" Marcellus said, springing to his feet and pulling his former commander into a heartfelt embrace.

"Damnit, Aurelius, for the last time, it's Lucia now!" Praetor Lucia Artorius replied with a chuckle. She sat down opposite of him and said, "It's good to see you again, Marcellus."

"Likewise, Lucia! It feels like it's been a lifetime."

Marcellus was truly happy to see his old commanding officer, but it was not enough to pull him out of his funk, and she noticed.

Lucia frowned as she studied Marcellus's face. "What's got you down, Marcellus?"

"I'm struggling to come to grips with the intersection of politics and command. I met the Triumvirs in person for the first time yesterday, and, well…let's say it was an eye-opening experience."

Artorius laughed again. Her infectious mirth even brought a weak smile to Marcellus's face.

"Ahh, Marcellus, I see you've discovered we do not fight our enemies in a vacuum. We've been fortunate that we have leaders like Decius around who mostly keep the politicians out of the way. You can never forget, though, that they were elected to lead by the people we've sworn an oath to defend."

"I understand, Lucia. Perhaps I was just naïve in believing that they acted with the best interest of the Republic at heart."

Praetor Artorius gave him a half-smile and said, "Careful, Marcellus, do not let a few specific cases paint too broad a picture. For the most part, the senators and our Triumvirs work for the betterment of our society. That's not to say there aren't cases of corruption, but they are the outlier, not the rule."

"it's difficult for me to understand how they could tolerate those few cases though. We operate in an environment where trust is a necessary pre-condition to success; where a person's word is their honor, and honor is sacrosanct."

"I'm heartened to hear you say that, Marcellus, but you must know that even amongst those in uniform, that is not always true. You've had recent experience, *very* recent, with those who have sacrificed their honor for their own personal ambition."

"Festus…" Marcellus said, uttering the name as if it were a curse. "You heard?"

"Yes, and as shocking as it is, it doesn't surprise me that Festus would be the one to attempt it. That just goes to show, Marcellus. Power in all forms is seductive. Military or civilian, senator or soldier, no one who obtains it is free from its allure."

"Have you ever had to convince them of appropriateness of a certain action? Or argue over how to proceed?"

"Who, the Senate?" Lucia asked, confusion evident on her face. "Not really, no. Primarily the War Council provides them with the information they need to understand why we make decisions."

"I see," Marcellus said, his gloom returning. "Thank you for straightening me out, Lucia. As always, I appreciate your guidance. How are things going in your sector of the Frontier?"

"The Asco have been pretty quiet. Seventh Fleet redeployed to assist at Tratirne. We've maintained patrols and launched a few probing attacks on known enemy positions in our sector, but otherwise there isn't much going on. Disconcerting if you ask me. How'd Aetnaeus shake out?"

"Well…we bloodied the Ascomanni's nose pretty good, but it was costly."

Lucia frowned. "I take it we lost the planet? Did any of your soldiers make it out?"

"Yeah, I got about three quarters of my force off the planet."

His mentor's eyes widened. "Really? That's fantastic. How long did you hold?"

"Nine long, grueling months."

"Damn…" She whistled. "I knew you had it in you, Marcellus. How badly did you screw the Asco up?"

"Val tabbed it out to just under four million on the ground, and over six hundred ships in space."

His mentor blinked at him. Several moments passed, and Marcellus began to feel uncomfortable.

"Are you kidding me, Marcellus?" Lucia finally said.

"No ma'am, those are the numbers."

"How the hell did you manage to pull that off?" she asked, disbelief clear in her voice.

Marcellus sighed and said, "Well, if you were shocked before... I used an antimatter bomb to split the planet's crust. The resulting cataclysm wiped out the largest fleet we've ever seen and rendered the planet lifeless."

"YOU DID WHAT?!" Praetor Artorius exploded.

Passersby stopped and looked at the pair before returning to their tasks. Marcellus leaned in closer and lowered his voice as he continued.

"I did what I had to do, ma'am. You taught me to play to win. This war is too important to do anything else. I struck the heaviest blow of the war so far and managed to preserve my forces. In exchange, we lost a mediocre biosphere, one of nearly a hundred now that we've come across."

Praetor Artorius chuckled to herself. "You've got some stones, Aurelius; I'll give you that."

Marcellus's foul mood was turning into a defiant anger, aimed not at his mentor, but rather at the obstacles he now clearly saw before him. He had accomplished the impossible, holding a dramatically superior enemy at bay for months before completely annihilating the attacking force.

Yet even his mentor was shocked by the means required to win.

If Lucia, having known him for years beforehand, required convincing, it was inevitable the others would as well. The fire gnawing in his chest gave him fresh energy to make his case, and he was surer than ever that he was right to seek change.

"That's not all. I've called everyone together to discuss how we've prosecuted the war so far, and why we keep losing."

Lucia saw the determination in Marcellus's eyes and cocked an eyebrow. "I've seen that look before... All right let's hear it, Aurelius. I'm listening."

"We fight the Ascomanni in the same ways we fought wars in the past, matching strength for strength. But the Ascomanni are stronger than we are. Every time we give battle in these set piece engagements, we lose soldiers, ships, and equipment that are much harder for us to replace than it is for the enemy. And because we are so inexcusably *predictable*, the enemy has used the same tactics over and over again to great effect. The Asco aren't beating us! *We are!*"

"OK, I see the merit of what you are saying. But as you pointed out, this is the way war has been fought since before we reached the stars. We are poorly equipped to adapt in the manner you described. From a strategic standpoint all the way down to the tactical level."

"I disagree, Lucia. Every legion that has withstood the tests of a campaign has gathered invaluable insight about our enemy: the way he thinks, how he responds in certain stimuli, what tools he's likely to use in a given situation."

Marcellus pounded his fist on the table as he continued, saying, "We need to encourage initiative from the legate commanding his legion, down through the primes commanding the individual cohorts, and lower still to the centurions commanding their centuries."

Marcellus motioned to the flying machines hanging from the ceiling. "Our people are creative, ingenious, and brave. We are smarter than the Asco. We're more resourceful! We must free our people to use their innate advantages to the fullest against the Ascomanni. We can do this, and we *must* do this."

Praetor Artorius looked at him with a strange mixture of pride and concern. "Uh oh, I haven't seen this side of you in a long time. If memory serves, I last got that look when you disagreed with me about attacking the Ascomanni position on Gela."

Marcellus laughed. "I was right, wasn't I?"

"Yeah, but it almost got you killed!" she replied tersely. The older Praetor paused for a moment, then said, "I trusted your instincts then, and I trust you now. With that being said, it's one thing to know your end goal, young Praetor. It's another entirely to identify the steps needed to get us there. How do you propose we proceed?"

"I've spent a lot of time thinking about it, even before we evacuated Aetnaeus. It's clear we can't abandon our population centers. We must continue to shield our people from these savages. We cannot allow that to be *all* we do, however. We can't completely cede the initiative to our enemies."

His mentor nodded, and Marcellus kept going.

"What have we done to attempt to understand where the enemy comes from, where their production, population, and resource centers are? If we have any hope of defeating this enemy, we must know the answers to those questions and more."

"OK, I'm starting to see where you're going with this," Lucia replied. "That's how we would begin to plan out any offensive, but our forces are already overmatched. How do we strike the enemy without opening the Republic up to full-scale invasion?"

"Our presence in the Frontier is vast, covering a dozen lightyears. Our available resources are insufficient to properly defend that broad of a front. I propose evacuating a handful of systems which would allow us to narrow the area of space that needs to be defended significantly.

"Meanwhile, we will not just yield these planets without a fight. Smaller forces will be left behind with the goal of delaying the enemy, causing as many casualties as possible, and then retreating. The enemy can either stretch themselves too thin and attempt to seize all of these worlds, or it can bypass some, providing us with staging areas we can use to harass the enemy rear areas and keep them off balance."

"You've clearly thought this through, Marcellus. But what you've described does not explain how we take back the initiative from our enemy."

"The steps I've outlined should buy us time, Lucia, time we can use to build up our strength and learn from our initial encounters with the enemy. While that happens, our narrower defensive position will allow us to concentrate our strength and wear the enemy down. Weakened and overstretched, we can then cut off their advanced forces with a series of lightning attacks through the areas we've previously lost to the enemy.

"With skillful execution and a little bit of luck, we can deal a severe setback to the enemy *and* buy ourselves enough time to consolidate our position. Once those objectives have been achieved, we can strike at the heart of Asco space."

Lucia was quiet for several minutes, and Marcellus's confidence began to waiver. If he couldn't convince his own mentor...

But just as he began to doubt himself, she finally spoke up, saying: "Marcellus, that is the first time I have heard someone outline a serious plan for how we could turn the tide on these bastards. I'm in." The older commander clapped a hand on her protégée's shoulder and said, "You know you still have your work cut out for you convincing the others though, right?"

"I know. And the War Council will need to persuade the Senate. And we'll need Triumvirs Decius and Eppia onboard. I expect Sestius will go with the flow as long as we are successful."

Lucia raised an eyebrow at his statement. "An astute observation, Marcellus. I'm impressed. What does the rest of your morning look like?"

"I've been summoned to Capitol Hall to testify on the attempted coup, after giving a few briefings to some senior senators on the state of the war with the Ascomanni."

"I would encourage you to take advantage of that facetime. I'll do what I can to convince the other praetors, but If you truly believe this is the correct course of action, begin laying the groundwork with the Senate now."

Marcellus's stomach began to churn.

"I appreciate the feedback, Lucia. It seems my political trial by fire begins now then."

Praetor Artorius stood and rested a hand on his shoulder. "If there is anyone up to the challenge, it's you, Marcellus. I'll see you at the briefing this evening."

Marcellus nodded, and his friend and mentor left him alone with his thoughts.

Campidano Plains, East of Perugia, Umbria

Invictus was amazed by what he saw. When he had first arrived on Umbria, there had been nothing disturbing the plains surrounding the capital. It had been an uninterrupted sea of knee-high, citrine-yellow grasses swaying softly in the gentle breeze.

Now, there were prefabricated buildings as far as the eye could see. The military grade structures were designed to be stackable, and already they were being formed into expansive, multistory housing blocks. Thick, elevated conduits connected the growing camp to the capital's utilities, carrying water, sewage, and electricity to and from a growing number of sanitation facilities and electrical substations.

Everywhere there was a flurry of activity: Soldiers from around Umbria had been redeployed to the area to assist with keeping the peace and building the camp's infrastructure. Clinics had been established, providing basic medical care and soliciting donations of blood and plasma for the wounded. Volunteer teachers broadcast classes remotely in large, open-air tents for refugee children, freeing parents and grandparents to wait in line for rations or to find temporary work doing odd jobs around the camp.

"It's truly a testament to our people's indominable spirt, isn't it, Prefect Flaminus?" Triumvir Aula Eppia said from Invictus's side.

"Yes, Triumvir. I cannot believe how quickly this has all sprung up."

Invictus had been tasked with escorting the Triumvir as she visited the camp. His praetorians were near at hand, milling around, interacting with the refugees, but never straying too far as Invictus and the Triumvir walked down the freshly trodden footpaths running through the settlement.

They had spent the better part of the morning touring the expansive refugee camp: visiting the wounded, inspecting newly constructed facilities, and asking people to share their experiences.

During that time, Invictus had seen that the care and concern shown by the Triumvir was not the well-practiced mask he'd seen from most politicians when dealing with commoners. The tales of destruction and loss the refugees shared with the Triumvir weighed heavily on her.

Eppia stopped as a pack of young children ran past, laughing and carrying on.

As they disappeared down another alley, she smiled and said, "I am heartened to see that even in times like these, they still have the opportunity to revel in the joys of childhood."

Invictus nodded. "Yes, ma'am, but it comes at a cost. Most of the refugees here are either very young or very old. I'm told countless men and women, after seeing their families to safety, returned to fight for Tratirne. Many of these people left behind loved ones, and many will never see them again."

The Triumvir turned and nodded. "Your point is not lost on the Triumvirate, Prefect. We know the sacrifices our people have made and continue to make."

They wandered in silence for several more minutes, with the Triumvir occasionally stopping to speak to refugees they met along the way.

Invictus made sure to keep a wary eye out for any possible trouble.

Seeing her guardian's uneasy disposition, the elderly politician lightly chastised him, saying, "Prefect, I am perfectly safe here. You need not worry about an Ascomanni popping around every corner or ambushing us from every tent!"

Invictus smiled at the Triumvir's attempt at humor. "I appreciate that, ma'am, but I've been charged with ensuring your safety. Given the events of the last few days, we can't be too careful."

"Nonsense, Prefect!" Eppia scolded. "The actions of one rogue should hardly be used to paint such broad strokes."

The Triumvir stopped, and Invictus turned to look at her.

"It occurs to me that we have spent the better part of the morning together," she said, "but I still know little about you aside from your name and rank. Tell me about yourself. Where did you grow up?"

"Of course, Triumvir. I was born on Venezia. I remember having a very happy childhood. My mother was magistrate for the planet's main starport, and my father was a venture financier and occasional consultant for the shipping industry. Mom worked some pretty long hours and Dad mostly worked from his home office. Occasionally he'd take me with him on business trips off world."

"My mother taught me about duty and the value of hard work," Invictus continued, "and my father instilled in me a love for travel and the stars. They were both ardent patriots, believers in the Republic and its ideals."

"I see, they sound like wonderful people."

"They were."

The Triumvir winced, a pained expression on her face. "I'm sorry, Prefect, I..."

"Don't be, Triumvir," Invictus replied reassuringly. "After I entered the academy, they gave up their comfortable corporate jobs to pursue their dreams amongst the stars. They bought a ship and spent three years exploring the Frontier. They'd send me messages at least once a week, detailing their findings and sharing stories from their adventures.

"Then, one week, I stopped receiving messages. An automated distress beacon was identified soon after. By the time the Reaction Force reached my parents, there was nothing to be done. Mechanical failure. I miss them, but I choose to honor their memories through service to the Republic they loved so much."

Eppia began walking again, keeping a measured pace as they continued through the camp.

"Thank you for sharing your story with me, Prefect. I often find myself wondering, what if we had known the dangers that awaited us beyond our solar system? Is there something we could have done differently? I can't help but think about what we might've done to avoid our current predicament."

The Triumvir shook her head as she continued: "Now we face an adversary whose motivations and desires are unknown to us. If our enemy was reasonable, perhaps this bloodshed could come to an end, and more lives would not need to be thrown into chaos like these people's."

"If our enemy was reasonable, Triumvir, they would not *be* our enemy. The Ascomanni are implacable, seeking only our complete destruction," Invictus said, gesturing back the way they came. "We fight so those children can have the same boundless future we were promised before we encountered the Ascomanni."

The Triumvir gave Invictus a motherly look of approval and placed a careworn hand on his shoulder.

"What is it about the service that brings the best out of our young men and women?" she asked. "Ranked high amongst this war's many tragedies must be that we send people such as you off to battle, from which so few will return."

"No one who has seen the horrors of this conflict would wish to repeat the experience," Invictus responded, "but we cannot simply refuse to fight. Our people, our culture, and our way of life are worth defending."

Eppia's smile deepened as they neared a makeshift landing zone.

A dropship waited to take the Triumvir back to the capitol. The crew of the Triumvir's shuttle busily offloaded the supplies they had just delivered in order to make room for the return journey.

Upon seeing Eppia and the praetorians approach, the crew chief urged her flight crew to work faster.

Eppia turned and faced Invictus, reaching out and taking him by the arm. "It has been a privilege to have spent the morning in your company, Prefect. I believe your parents would be very proud of the man standing before me. I wish you and your soldiers nothing but safety and success in your future endeavors. If there is anything I can do, please let me know."

Invictus thought about the Triumvir's offer for a moment before speaking up.

"Forgive me if this is impertinent, ma'am, but there is something you could do for me."

Triumvir Eppia's face grew serious. "Name it, Prefect," she said solemnly. "If it is within my powers, I will make it so."

"I have served under Praetor Gaius Aurelius Marcellus for the better part of two years now. Together, we have overcome unspeakable hardship in the face of a relentless enemy. He is a brilliant tactician and strategist, and he cares only for the wellbeing of our people and the soldiers under his command. I would ask that whatever favor you were willing to show to me would be granted to him instead."

Mirth filled the aged Triumvir's eyes.

"You truly represent the best of us, Invictus Flaminus. Your words reinforce my own opinion of our young Praetor's motivations. He will have whatever support I can give."

"I am very grateful, Triumvir. Realizing that I just used up my 'ask the Triumvir for anything' card, I do have another request. If it's not too much, that is."

Eppia looked at him curiously and said, "Go on."

"I would also appreciate it tremendously if you didn't mention this to him either. He can get a bit...perturbed when I go off script on him."

The Triumvir laughed as she boarded the dropship. "Your secret is safe with me, Prefect."

Invictus smiled and saluted as the dropship's doors slid shut. He watched as the ship lifted off and headed back toward Perugia before turning back to his soldiers.

"All right, boys and girls, fall in. We're expected two clicks east of here to help set up a new fusion reactor. With any luck, we'll be back to the Castellum in time for lunch. Let's get to it, praetorians, double time!"

There were groans as the group formed up and began working their way back through the camp.

Capitol Hall, Perugia, Umbria

Marcellus sat on a bench in the middle of one of the Capitol's many open-air courtyards, enjoying a short break from the tedium of providing testimony to the Senate. He closed his eyes and soaked up the warm glow of Umbria's sun, while a soft, gentle breeze caressed his face.

The War Council had encouraged him to attend in person instead of submitting a recorded description of his actions during the coup. Marcellus understood their reasoning, but he had been asked the same questions all morning and well into the afternoon by a series of different committees, some of which he hadn't even heard of before.

There had been the Judiciary Committee, the Joint Committee for Defense and Intelligence, the Senate Subcommittee for Personnel Management, the Standing Committee for the Maintenance of Historical Works, the Colonial Affairs Commission, and the Committee for Refugee Administration.

It had been an exhausting exercise, and Marcellus wondered how so many different bodies could exist for areas of responsibility that seemed to so closely overlap.

He opened his eyes and gazed around the courtyard. Despite the day's frustrations, he had enjoyed the opportunity to come to Capitol Hall again.

Marcellus had visited the capitol building many times in the past, but each time he was struck by the grandeur of the place. The monolithic structure was architecture and engineering as art. Arched colonnades provided seamless access to beautiful, manicured gardens, while vaulted cathedral ceilings sent echoes bounding off the shimmering quartzite surfaces of the walls and floor.

The building had a humbling effect, Marcellus thought. Capitol Hall made its visitors acutely aware that they were but a small part of something greater than themselves. Since its formation, every challenge the Republic had faced had been solved in the chambers of the magnificent structure surrounding him. This was a place where the history of his people was *alive*.

Marcellus could not help but have his spirits lifted in spite of the bureaucratic maze he had been navigating throughout the day. The Republic had endured for twelve centuries. He would be damned if it were to meet its end on his watch.

A shadow cast itself over him, and a soft, familiar voice said, "It's beautiful, isn't it?"

Marcellus turned and found Doctor Mirabella Urbanus standing next to him, holding a datapad in one hand and with a large tote hanging off one shoulder.

He grinned up at her and said, "I was just thinking the same. Every time I visit, I'm struck by the majesty and the history of this place."

Mirabella smiled warmly. "I completely agree. May I join you?"

"Of course, Doctor, please."

She laughed as she sat down next to him.

"Call me Mirabella. If you don't mind me asking, what brings you to the Capitol today?"

Marcellus grimaced and said, "Senate testimony. I had no idea there were so many different committees. It's exhausting!"

Mirabella laughed again, and Marcellus was captivated by the gentle, melodic tones.

"I understand your pain," she replied. "I'm providing a report to the Senate Committee on Exo-Terrestrial Life. Director-level members of the CID normally handle these types of activities, but I've had to pitch in a few times when needed."

She shook her head, her auburn hair bouncing playfully in the gently breeze. "It's never very much fun."

"This has been my first experience. Hopefully I won't have many other occasions to do so in the future."

"I don't know, it has some advantages," Mirabella said, a mischievous look on her face. "For instance, you never know who you might run into."

With that, she looked at her wrist comm and abruptly stood up, hands folded over her datapad.

"Unfortunately, duty calls. I need to run to my next meeting."

Marcellus was taken off guard by the shortness of her visit, but recovered quickly enough. He stood and said, "It was a pleasure to see you again, Mirabella."

Another smile graced the doctor's face, and she tucked some of her hair behind her ear. "I'm sure you'll be heading out to the front again soon, Praetor. Please be safe."

"I'll do my best," Marcellus responded. "Uhm, before you go, I hope this isn't too forward, but is there a mailing address I could reach you at? You know, uh…in case we come across anything else that might be beneficial to your work?"

"Hmmm. I guess that would be OK," she replied. "Thank you for keeping me in mind."

"Not a problem, I'd be happy to. Share anything we discover, that is." Marcellus laughed uncomfortably at his own awkwardness.

Mirabella tapped a few keys on her datapad, and a notification appeared on Marcellus's watch.

"You can reach me here at any time. Good luck, Marcellus."

He nodded, not trusting himself to speak as she turned and walked away. As he watched her go, she looked back, saw that he was still watching, and winked before hurrying off to her next meeting.

Marcellus's shoulders sank as he slumped back down on the bench.

In the past, he had always been confident and charming when approaching the opposite sex. What was it about Mirabella that made him choke up so badly?

Before he had time to explore his feelings in any greater depth, however, his wrist began to vibrate. A notification appeared indicating that his next appointment had been moved up and would start in five minutes.

He sighed and did his best to focus on the task at hand. Praetor Artorius had mentioned that swaying these men and women was an important part of changing the strategic direction of the war. There was no room for error.

Marcellus stood up and headed toward the sweeping arcade that would take him to his destination.

The Castellum, Perugia, Umbria

Invictus and his small team of praetorians arrived back at the Castellum later than expected. They dropped off their equipment at the armory and then ate a quick meal together before Invictus dismissed them for the day.

A short while later, he reached his temporary accommodations. He still had some work to do to help Marcellus prepare for his briefing later in the day, but first he took a quick shower and threw on a fresh set of dress blues.

Invictus walked back into the common room he shared with his commander and sat down at the console. As he fired it up, he saw that there were two messages waiting for him. The first was the Perugia Constabulary, and the second was from Marcellus.

Invictus scrolled through the first message. It was brief, indicating that aside from scorched pavement, there was no sign an accident had occurred as described in Marcellus's police report. Given the lack of evidence, they were closing out the incident.

Next, he opened the message from Marcellus, and audio began to play.

"Vic, I'm sorry I couldn't share more about my little...errand last night. Triumvir Sestius requested my presence at the Bacchanal. He asked for information about our visit to the intelligence annex and was very perturbed when I told him I could not share any of the details.

"After leaving, my taxi suffered mechanical failure and I crashed into the lower sections of the Entertainment District. Some E-Rho thugs showed up, and I was only saved by the intervention of a third party. Unfortunately, they didn't make it out.

"It's tremendously suspicious that these events were to follow my visit with Triumvir Sestius. I did manage to pull data from the taxi's processor and the woman who assisted me gave me her wrist comm. Both are located on the bureau behind you. While I'm off at the Capitol today, could you please review and highlight anything that you find suspicious?"

The recording paused for a moment before finishing: "We're in the deep end here, brother. Please keep what I've shared to yourself. Whoever was responsible for last night's events clearly wished me harm. I'll see you soon. Marcellus out."

Invictus shook his head and muttered, "Marcellus, what have you gotten yourself into?"

He stood and walked over to the bureau where he found the items Marcellus had mentioned. First, he plugged in the data drive and pulled up the diagnostic information he found within.

The first five pages described the actions taken by the onboard computer during the crash: deployment of the taxi's airbags prior to collision, adjusting maneuvering flaps to slow descent, and broadcasting an emergency response signal.

The taxi had plunged over two hundred and fifty meters from its original destination. Invictus was amazed that Marcellus had been able to walk away from the crash.

He dug further back through the code. It appeared that the root cause of the issue had been a faulty temperature gauge. The gauge had prevented the automated cooling systems from keeping the engine from overheating. It then seized up midflight, and it was throwing off enough heat to melt some of the nearby hosing and wires.

As Invictus dug further back, he found a peculiar series of entries. After Marcellus had originally disembarked, the Bacchanal's automated valet system had moored the car alongside the superstructure of the massive airship. No one would have been able to physically sabotage the vehicle.

However, it looked like before it returned to pick up the Praetor, someone used that same system to access the car from the Bacchanal's central server cluster. A program had been uploaded, and there were records indicating that system profiles had been adjusted beyond their normal operating parameters.

Unfortunately, sections of code indicating which of the system profiles had been altered were corrupted, as was all information on the program itself. Based on the timeline of events though, it was clear that this was the root cause of the malfunction.

Whoever had sabotaged Marcellus's taxi had been sloppy, Invictus thought. Perhaps they expected the crash and ensuing fire to consume any evidence of tampering. He made a quick note for himself before continuing.

Next, Invictus plugged in the wrist communicator he had found with the data drive. As he reviewed the device's internal storage structure, he realized that much of the device's information was encrypted. However, there was a series of recent files which did not require decryption to view.

The first contained security footage of a rather plain man walking into the Bacchanal. At first, Invictus was confused. There was absolutely nothing out of the ordinary about the man. However, as he passed through the threshold, the video switched to a different camera, and Invictus's jaw clenched as Triumvir Sestius greeted him.

The second file showed what appeared to be the inside of a nightclub. The camera zoomed and focused on a particular VIP booth. There were several people present, but the visuals were distorted by some type of EM field. After a minute or two though, Invictus clearly saw Marcellus approach the group. As he drew near, one of the blurry figures left the platform and exited out a back door.

The last file showed the Bacchanal's central command hub. Two guards sat at their stations, watching a bank of security monitors. As Invictus watched, an alarm began to flash on the guards' console, and they both stood up and rushed out of the room. Before the doors could close, however, the man from the first video appeared.

He typed away furiously at the workstation before turning and looking at the camera. He hit another series of buttons and the video dissolved into static.

Invictus cross referenced the data and whistled softly to himself. The timestamp for the third file approximately matched the timeframe of when Marcellus's taxi was hacked and reprogramed.

Invictus copied all of the relevant data to three separate drives before removing the devices from his workstation. Next, he opened the bottom-most desk drawer and withdrew a small empty container. He dropped one of the data drives in the box and sealed it.

He quickly scribbled a series of instructions on the box, grabbed his code key, and walked out of the room, locking the door behind him. He walked down the corridor until he found a simple-looking interface set in the wall.

After tapping a series of buttons, a door mounted to the interface opened, and Invictus deposited his package. He closed the door, and there was an audible '*choomph*' noise as it was whisked away by the Castellum's internal package delivery system.

Confident that at least one copy of the information was now out of reach, he headed back toward his room.

As he neared the suite, the hairs on the back of his neck stood up: the door was open slightly.

Invictus took a series of quick breaths and prepared himself mentally. He reared back and delivered a swift kick to the open door. Before it had even crashed into the wall, he was through the threshold and charging at the individual he saw standing over the desk in the common room.

His target sidestepped him, however, and in an instant Invictus found himself lying flat on his back, staring up at the ceiling with the wind knocked out of him. Before he could react, a dagger appeared, only a centimeter from his throat.

Invictus was surprised to hear laughter, and as he faced his opponent for the first time, he realized he was looking up at Marcellus.

His friend put away his weapon and offered him a hand up.

"Damnit, Marcellus, I could have killed you!" Invictus complained, rubbing a knot that was growing on the back of his head.

"Ha! In your dreams, Flaminus!" Marcellus said with a grin. "I saw you leave the room, and I figured you'd be right back. I didn't expect you to go berserk on me."

His expression grew more serious as he continued: "I take it you got my message?"

"Yeah, the data is pretty conclusive," Invictus said. "Sestius was meeting with a man who appeared to sabotage your vehicle."

Marcellus's brow furrowed. "Damnit. Thank you for going over the data, Vic. Just out of curiosity though, what were you doing out in the hallway?"

Invictus snorted and replied, "Well, it looks like you've got me involved in some pretty incendiary stuff, brother. I felt bad that you hadn't dragged Valerian into this shitstorm yet, so I made a copy of the data and mailed it to him. I figured in case something bad happens to us, there's still a copy of the information out there."

"Smart," Marcellus responded, chuckling. "Has your ego appropriately recovered from the smackdown I just gave you? Our meeting with the War Council starts in fifteen minutes."

Invictus chuckled wryly. "You don't need to worry about me kid, I'm fine."

"Kid?! I'm three years younger than you!"

"Yeah, and that's the only reason you got the drop on me!"

"Always the sore loser…" Marcellus said with a laugh. "We've got work to do."

Invictus's face became somber as the task before them came into focus. "After you, Praetor. I've got your back."

Marcellus's cheery disposition faded somewhat. He nodded, and together they walked out of the room.

***

Fifteen minutes later, Marcellus stood in the middle of the briefing room. It was the same room he had used the day before to provide the Triumvirs with their status report. Where it had felt empty on that occasion, it was now packed to capacity and buzzing with activity.

Ten of the fourteen members of the War Council were present and seated on the right-hand side of the room. Three of the other four Praetors—Festus had yet to be replaced—sat on the first row of seats on the left. Each had dozens of aides who were anxiously communicating with subordinate units, analyzing reports for items worth bringing to their superior's attention, and whispering softly amongst themselves.

Suspended above the gallery on the walls of the room were five screens. Praetor Asinia was studying something off screen, hundreds of lightyears away on Tratirne. The other four were reserved for members of the War Council who had been caught on the planet during the Ascomanni assault and who were currently in transit back to Umbria.

This was his moment, and Marcellus couldn't help but feel anxious.

If he were to be successful here, he would need to convince these people that his plan was the right way to move forward. He remembered his conversation with Lucia earlier in the day, and her words of encouragement buoyed his spirits.

Praetor Artorius caught his eye and gave him a wink and a thumbs up. He nodded back. It was time.

Marcellus cleared his throat. Invictus dimmed the lights and pulled up his commander's presentation on the room's display.

"Ladies and gentlemen, thank you all for coming. I know it is unusual for all of us to gather together like this, but there is a matter of grave importance that we need to discuss."

The room quieted down as everyone shifted their attention to Marcellus.

"The matter I refer to is the war against the Ascomanni. A war we are *losing*."

There were gasps around the briefing chamber, and the crowd began to whisper amongst themselves. "Order! We will have order!" Chief Magistrate Glabria called out. The murmuring died down again, and Marcellus nodded to Invictus as he continued.

The projector displayed an image of Umbrian space. Umbria itself shone brightly on the edge of the galaxy. A soft blue glow surrounded the Republic's capital, denoting outposts and colonies, extending out from Umbria in all directions.

"Since our ancestors first walked among the stars, our civilization has flourished. The first wave of our expansion into the greater galaxy created boundless opportunities for our people. Yet we always believed we were not alone amongst the cosmos.

"That belief kept our people's martial traditions sharp. We looked to the skies with the hope of finding others in the expanses beyond our star, but, should our offer of friendship be met with violence, we were always prepared for the worst. Or so we thought."

The map shifted, with the first red elements creeping in around the edges of the less luminous blue section representing the Frontier.

"Eight years ago, we finally found our cosmic neighbors. But the worst had come to pass. All attempts at communication were unsuccessful. Each olive branch extended was greeted only with greater levels of destruction and death.

"This vast, relentless foe is the Ascomanni, and everyone in this room is well acquainted with the existential threat they pose to our way of life. For eight years, we have fought them to the best of our abilities.

"What started at Battipaglia has only increased in intensity and ferocity. Thirteen colonies and numerous other outposts have been lost so far. Tens of millions of our people have died. We have all lost someone to this scourge: friends, family, loved ones. Even today, Praetor Asinia and the brave soldiers and sailors under her command resist our enemy on another threatened world.

"This is a war whose scope has grown beyond anything we could have possibly prepared for. Everyone here knows that the Ascomanni are stronger than us. They have more ships and they have more soldiers. What losses we have inflicted on them seem to be but a drop in an endless sea of men and materiel."

Marcellus paused looking around at the faces in the room before continuing.

"I tell you these things not to shock you. You have all seen the nightmares the Ascomanni have wrought upon our people.

"I tell you these things not to suggest that we capitulate to this merciless foe. There can be no peace with these monsters.

"I tell you these things so that we might see the outcome our current path is leading us toward, so that we may yet avoid its inevitable outcome.

"We have stood and fought this foe every time it has offered battle. Most of the time, despite the heroism and sacrifice of the Umbrian soldier, we lose.

"This is a pattern which we cannot afford to continue. We have stretched ourselves out amongst the vast distances of the Frontier, eager to react to the slightest sign of enemy intent but lacking enough strength to make a difference."

The murmurs amongst the crowd picked up again, but Marcellus pressed on. He nodded to Invictus, and the display zoomed in on the Frontier. A series of blue dots turned purple, leaving a much shallower and narrower section of space shaded in blue.

"We must face a stark reality: we cannot defend the entire expanse of the Frontier. I propose a simple but difficult solution. We must tighten the frontage which we have to defend against our enemy.

"To do that, I suggest we evacuate several worlds which are beyond our ability to defend. We would pull out their civilian populations, while leaving forces behind to contest the planets before ultimately withdrawing. This will buy us time, slowing the Ascomanni advance and allowing us to concentrate our forces on a defensive axis centered on the colonies of Sovizzo, Tratirne, and Ghiave-Fouteena."

"Do you know how many people you are proposing we relocate, Praetor?" one of the War Council members called out.

"Approximately two hundred and fifty-six million souls, Councilor. Needless to say, we would not have our full lift capability at our disposal for this task. Factoring out the tonnage necessary to support our forces and the demands of the evacuation of Tratirne, it would take six months to achieve. We will need to buy time to evacuate our people."

The councilor looked shocked by the magnitude of Marcellus's plan, but seemed reassured by the level of detail in his response.

Praetor Scipio, a tall, athletically built man whose forces had recently suffered significant casualties at the hands of the Ascomanni, spoke up next.

"There's no going back from this, Praetor Aurelius, and your plan seems to only delay the inevitable."

"I agree, Praetor. We cannot win this war by outlasting our enemy. We *must* retake the initiative. However, our soldiers are overstretched and hard-pressed. We need time: time to build up our forces, time to learn from our experiences so far, and time to prepare our people for the total war we must begin to fight.

"While the Asco grind themselves down on our newly focused defensive positions, we will be probing areas they have passed over and overlooked, searching for the weaknesses we need to cripple their war effort.

"The retreat to this new defensive line is temporary. Once we have gathered our strength, we will strike at our enemy where it hurts the most. Off balance and disorganized, we will exact our revenge upon the Ascomanni!"

The mumbling changed tempo as the assembled officers and staff members began to see hope where there had been none before. Marcellus was getting through to them.

"There are many details still to be worked out, but I am confident that the people we have in this room are capable of solving any challenge we face. I'd like to begin diving into some of the specific actions required to prepare…"

Marcellus talked for another half an hour, soliciting feedback from his peers and answering questions as they came up. When Marcellus finally nodded to Invictus to end the presentation, they were received with a standing ovation.

The War Council was with him.

He had convinced the Council to change tact, but there was much still to do in Perugia before they departed the following morning.

Chief among these tasks would be to visit Triumvir Decius.

Villa Decii, North of Perugia, Umbria

By the time Marcellus and Invictus had returned to their quarters, the sun was sinking low on the horizon. They grabbed the datapad with the results of Invictus's investigation and headed straight for the Castellum's motor pool.

They decided to detour around the capital, avoiding much of the evening congestion that bedeviled Perugia's commuters. Free from the traffic management systems of the city's busiest skylanes, Invictus took control of the aircar and pushed it to its limits.

The journey to the Triumvir's estate should have taken an hour. Instead, with Vic behind the controls, it only took twenty minutes, though Marcellus spent much of the trip clutching the handle built into the passenger door.

Finally, with the last rays of the evening sun fading away, Invictus slowed as they neared their destination: Villa Decii.

The Decii were an old family, held in high esteem by Umbria's elite. Never as vast in number as some of the other 'old names' of Umbria, there were rarely more than twenty members of the family living at any given time, all of whom enjoyed a life of comfort and privilege within the confines of the family's sprawling estate.

Marcellus felt his breath catch in his chest as the property came into view. Members of the clan had been men and women of significance for centuries, and that influence had brought with it tremendous wealth. In turn, that wealth had created a floral paradise amongst the rolling hills to the north of the capital.

The grounds encompassed a hundred square kilometers of gardens and greenhouses, and as they approached, a rainbow of different colors swayed gently in the evening breeze. Tree-lined footpaths wove effortlessly between the impressively manicured green spaces. It was even rumored that some species of exotic flowers could only be found within the family's greenhouses, having gone extinct on Umbria or the worlds she had colonized.

For all of the magnificent opulence of its surrounds, the villa itself was elegant but subdued in its grandeur. Set in a rough U, the manor was made up of a primary residence large enough to house its masters in comfort. Additional outbuildings contained quarters for the villa's staff and garages for their personal vehicles.

Each bore the hallmarks of Umbrian architecture, but none of the builds *overwhelmed* visitors or made its occupants feel larger than they were.

The Decii's ancestral home was an expression of wealth and power, but always in moderation. Many family biographers saw the villa as the clearest example of the family's character, distilled in each successive generation in order to ensure their continued success.

The aircar's intercom squawked and a voice requested identification.

"Praetor Gaius Aurelius to see Triumvir Decius, please. I believe he is expecting me."

There was a brief pause as Marcellus's identity was confirmed. "The Triumvir is most grateful for your visit, Praetor. Please navigate your vehicle to the designated area and a member of the villa's staff will greet you."

A series of blue lights began to flash in the villa's central courtyard. Invictus steered the car toward the designated area and set it down gently. Their parking spot lay adjacent to a massive fountain, capped by a statue of a robed woman riding a horse. As the car came to a stop, Marcellus hopped out and was amazed to find that the courtyard's entire surface had been tiled in the same exquisite marble of the villa itself.

Invictus shot Marcellus an amused look. "It must be good to be Triumvir…" he joked.

"More like it doesn't hurt to be born with a silver spoon," Marcellus laughed.

As the pair took in the sights, a man appeared wearing a simple but well-fitted scarlet suit. The two soldiers walked toward the steward, and he smiled as they approached.

"Welcome to Villa Decii, Praetor Aurelius. My master awaits your arrival in his study." The steward gestured toward the main house and said, "Please follow me."

"Of course, thank you," Marcellus responded.

The threesome set off at a measured pace. As they neared the entrance to the villa proper, Invictus spoke up, asking, "How many people are involved in maintaining the property?"

"We get that question a lot," the steward responded with a careworn smile. "All told, there are over sixty members of the household staff, of which about forty are directly involved in maintaining the grounds."

"And do they all live here on site?"

"Oh no, sir. The head groundskeeper is always on premises, but most of her associates live on the outskirts of Perugia. Most of the rest of us do reside in the servants' quarters, which are far nicer than anything we could afford in the city."

Invictus frowned, but Marcellus spoke up next. "So you're not capable of affording housing in the capital based on the wages the Triumvir pays you?"

The steward's face turned ashen. "Oh, goodness me, I am afraid I have given you the wrong impression! The Triumvir is *very* generous with his staff. We could easily afford accommodations in the capital. However, they would pale in comparison to the amenities offered by our on-site housing."

They passed through the threshold of the villa's grand entrance, and the duo fell silent as Marcellus and Invictus took in the splendor of the place.

"The digs are that good, huh?" Invictus asked, eyes wide with amazement as they continued on their journey through the mansion.

"Yes, sir. The Triumvir appreciates hard work and loyalty. Those fortunate enough to enter and remain in his employ are well taken care of."

"That is good to hear," Marcellus said.

The steward led them down a wide, bright corridor which provided spectacular views of the villa's grounds. At last, the hallway split in three directions. Their guide led them to the right, and they came upon an unassuming wooden door.

"Please wait here while I ensure the Triumvir is ready for you," the steward said.

As the servant disappeared, Marcellus turned his head and looked at Invictus, and his subordinate nodded in return. A moment later, the door swung open, and the steward ushered them into Triumvir Decius's study.

They entered a circular room which smelled of rich cedar. The walls facing the villa were lined with shelves containing rows and rows of hand-bound books, while those facing the exterior were made up of large, elaborately framed windows.

A giant, ornate desk sat in the middle of the room, with two comfortable easy chairs arranged in front for visitors. Triumvir Decius sat on the corner of the desk, clad in less formal attire. He stood, smiled, and gestured for them to sit as they took in the sights and smells of the study.

"Praetor Aurelius, Prefect Flaminus, I'm glad you were able to join me this evening. I trust you didn't have any issues finding the place?"

"No, sir," Marcellus responded. "Thank you for such a warm reception."

The Triumvir smiled broadly. "I have been incredibly fortunate to have found such exceptional people to care for myself and my family." He nodded to the steward, and with a slight bow, the man turned and left the room.

The smile faded from the Triumvir's face as the door closed behind him. "I hear you ran into some issues last night, Praetor."

"You are well informed, Triumvir Decius." Marcellus said, evenhandedly. "I'm afraid I come with bad news, sir. Your agent, Calpurnia, rescued me from a band of thugs. However, she was critically wounded by the gang that was pursuing me. She...she didn't make it out."

Marcellus paused and looked at the floor. The full weight of Calpurnia's actions finally caught up with him. She had been a stranger, yet she gave her life to ensure his safety. He looked back up at Decius and said, "She sacrificed her life to save my own."

"I see," the Triumvir replied, his face an unreadable mask. "I am deeply saddened to hear that. She was a capable young woman, and I had come to rely on her judgment and abilities greatly."

"I'm sorry, sir. Before her death, she tossed me her wrist comm. She had...acquired...some security data from the Bacchanal, where I had gone to meet Triumvir Sestius upon his request."

Marcellus produced the device and a datapad containing Invictus's analysis. "It looks like Triumvir Sestius was unhappy that I would not divulge classified information to him. In response, he organized my 'accident.'"

The Triumvir's expressionless mask finally broke. He frowned deeply and said, "That is a heavy accusation, Praetor. What evidence do you have to support such a claim?"

"Your agent provided video footage of an unknown man meeting with Triumvir Sestius. He is then captured later interfacing with the Bacchanal's systems. Corresponding logs from my crashed taxi match precisely to the timestamps in the security video."

Decius leaned heavily on the edge of his desk. "That is truly shocking, Praetor."

"Forgive me, sir," Marcellus said, making sure to measure his tone appropriately, "but we are all military men here. Please, let's speak frankly with one another. Calpurnia indicated that you wanted to speak *before* she was murdered. You already knew that Sestius was plotting against me."

Decius let out a gruff chuckle and said, "Quite the keen observation, Praetor. Perhaps you were a senator in a previous life."

He turned around and stared out the windows of his study.

"I knew that Sestius is growing increasingly unstable. It is a shame you didn't know him before. He had such a spark, a vitality, about him. But the pressures of office and the threat of the Ascomanni slowly ground him down. Eventually, he gave into the nihilistic and self-serving culture that increasingly corrupts our great society."

"So," the Triumvir continued, "when Calpurnia saw you at the Bacchanal, she informed me. I was concerned that something unfortunate may befall you, so I asked her to make sure you reached the Castellum safely."

"I appreciate your candor, sir."

Decius turned to face them again, and Marcellus handed the wrist comm and datapad to the Triumvir.

Decius blinked and looked puzzled. "Why are you giving this to me, Praetor?"

"I am not a politician, sir. I do not seek glory, fame, or power. The only thing I care about is the preservation of the Republic. Unfortunately, it looks like fate has conspired to drag me into the cutthroat arena of politics. I give these things to you because I trust you, sir, and because, to succeed at my mission, I cannot afford distractions from Perugia."

Decius gave Marcellus a penetrating look and asked, "You want me to use this against Triumvir Sestius?"

"Only if it comes to that. I have faith in your judgment, Triumvir."

The Triumvir looked over the Praetor, and Marcellus got the sense that he had earned the man's respect, or at least made a strong impression.

"I will keep this information with the same trust that you have shown by giving it to me, Praetor. Is there anything else I can do for you before you return to the Frontier?"

"There is one last thing, Triumvir Decius. Calpurnia indicated that she had a younger sister here on Umbria. If a member of your staff could forward her contact information, I would greatly appreciate it."

"What will you do?"

"I want her to know that her sister was a hero, and I want to help ensure she's taken care of."

The Triumvir gave him the look again before keying some information into the console on his desk. "I've sent you her contact information, Praetor, but you need not worry about her wellbeing. The Decii take care of their own."

Marcellus stood and said, "Thank you, sir. Unfortunately, Invictus and I have another stop to make before returning to the Castellum. Again, thank you for your hospitality, and have a lovely evening, Triumvir."

The Bacchanal, Capital Entertainment District; Perugia, Umbria

Marcellus flipped the switch on the small oblong device attached to his belt and entered the pulsating nightclub at the heart of the Bacchanal. Together, Marcellus and Invictus worked their way to Triumvir Sestius's VIP suite.

The Triumvir's bodyguards saw them approach and the larger of the two held out a hand to stop them. Marcellus took the man by the wrist and snapped his arm down and to the left before delivering a swift kick to the groin. The burly man crumpled and fell to the floor.

Invictus quickly took care of the second, striking the man twice in the kidneys before grabbing his adversary by the arm and flipping him onto his back.

The duo quickly ascended the short series of stairs to the main platform to find the Triumvir alone, feet kicked up on the table, a half-empty drink in his hand. He set his glass down and smiled sardonically as the pair approached.

"Hmm, it appears that I need to invest in better security. Praetor Aurelius, what the hell do you think you are doing, exactly?"

Marcellus grabbed the Triumvir by his jacket and stood him up.

"You know damn well why I am here."

"Ahh, your little accident. I'm glad to see you're alive and unharmed."

Marcellus struck Sestius in the stomach, knocking the wind out of the older man. He pushed him back down onto the couch.

"You're going to regret that," Sestius gasped, coughing for air.

"You've made many enemies, Triumvir," Marcellus snarled back, ignoring the older man's threat. "By attacking me, you've made those men and women my friends. If something happens to the people I care about, if I catch even one hint that you are undermining me, I will destroy you."

"What are you...?" Sestius muttered.

"Spare me. I have video of your associate tampering with my aircar. I have all the evidence I would need to crucify you in the court of public opinion."

"But..." Sestius stammered.

"Remember, Sestius," Marcellus continued, cutting the Triumvir off, "you forced me to play politics. I may be new to this battlefield, but I learn fast, and as the Ascomanni have discovered, I am a deadly foe."

With that, Marcellus pulled the signal jammer from his belt, flipped it off, and turned to leave. He looked back over his shoulder at the older man, a shocked expression still squarely on his face.

"Thank you for your hospitality, and have a lovely evening, Triumvir."

Chapter 8

URN *Hasta*, In-Transit in the Frontier

The soft pitter patter of rain intensified, turning into a roaring torrent. Marcellus looked around and realized he stood in one of the wide corridors of Capitol Hall. All around him, a never-ending throng of people screamed and rushed about.

Marcellus followed the crowd until they came across one of the building's courtyards. As he looked skyward, he realized that the roar he was hearing wasn't rain, but rather a constant and seemingly endless stream of rubble falling from the sky.

The crowd rushed blindly out into a blackened and withered space, each bursting into a plume of smoke as they were struck by debris. Marcellus stopped and tried to warn those around him, but in vain. The mob continued to swell past him, pulling him with them, ever closer to the edge of the courtyard.

The rubble grew larger as he drew nearer, and soon giant holes were punched through the roof of the capitol. The ground around him quaked and the marble floors splintered and cracked. The building collapsed around him as the ground beneath his feet gave way, and he fell into an all-consuming darkness.

Marcellus woke up as he landed shoulder first on the floor of the *Hasta*'s officer's quarters.

"Wish I would've been able to film that..." Invictus mumbled groggily.

Marcellus worked his way up to his knees and gently rolled his shoulder around, easing some of the pain that coursed through his upper body.

"Next time, you get the upper bunk."

"You lost fair and square," Invictus replied as he propped himself up on his elbows. "Next time, don't pick even when we roll dice to see who gets the rough end of the deal. You *always* pick even. In the future, do the opposite of whatever your gut tells you to do.'

"Yeah, well next time maybe I'll just order you to lose," Marcellus grunted, smiling ruefully at his subordinate.

Invictus's expression pinched into a frown as he watched his commander stretch his aching shoulder.

"Are you all right, Marcellus? Even before you decided to test the ship's artificial gravity, you seemed to be struggling a bit."

"I'm fine, *Mom*, no need to worry."

"Yeah, well I'm not reassured. If anything happens to you, I'd have to report to Valerian," Invictus said, feigning horror at the thought. "Imagine all the reprimands I'd get for failing to live up to his demanding standards."

"*'If I've told you once, I've told you a thousand times, Vic, the appropriate color for official stationery is Eggshell White #F32A6, not Eggshell White #F32A7!'*" Invictus said, giving his best impression of their friend. "I don't know how I'd cope!"

"Wow, did you just come up with that on your own, or is there some hilarious-sounding backstory I've never heard…?" Marcellus asked, grinning. "I'll be OK, Vic. There's just been a lot to take in over the last week or so."

Invictus rotated and sat up on the edge of his bunk.

"No kidding, boss. We foiled a coup, it turns out there's more than one type of evil alien out there who want to destroy us and, oh, yeah, they just so happen to be our freaky twelfth cousins or something. Plus, one of the most powerful politicians in the Republic tried to kill you." Invictus shook his head. "Not a banner week."

"Gee, thanks, Vic. When you lay it all out like that…"

Invictus slapped Marcellus on his sore shoulder. "I'm sure it's nothing you can't overcome. Besides, now we get to go back to focusing on beating the big ugly aliens who keep trying to kill us!"

Marcellus snorted and worked his way back up to his feet. As he stood the ship's intercom crackled to life.

"Praetor, Prefect, we've arrived in Safe Haven. We should reach the Citadel in about thirty minutes," a bland voice called out.

"Back to it, sir," Invictus said, his disposition growing somber. "No matter what happens, I'll be with you. Until we meet whatever end fate has in store for us."

The Citadel; Safe Haven, System: Classified, Frontier Space

Fabian and Valerian had been busy while Marcellus had been gone. Upon landing, Marcellus had received word that they had a briefing ready for him. As he entered the Citadel's command center, he was not surprised to find the system's magistrate and the local CID station chief present as well.

As the group provided their report, he stood in the middle of the expansive room, staring out at the swirling mists beyond.

Valerian went first. Their army group was quickly healing from the scars left by the campaign on Aetnaeus. New recruits were pouring in from across the Republic, and Marcellus's veterans were quickly whipping them into shape, though it would still be weeks before every unit reached full strength.

Valerian saved his best news for last. Reports from subordinate commanders indicated that there was a growing sense of confidence amongst the army group's soldiers. They had beaten the Ascomanni. The myth of their enemy's invincibility had finally been broken.

Magistrate Flavia had also done a spectacular job handling the replacement of all the equipment and materiel they had lost on Aetnaeus. Safe Haven's work details had pulled extra shifts, running the systems' processing centers and assembly plants at full capacity. She beamed as Marcellus praised the work her teams had been able to accomplish in such a short period of time.

The good news continued to roll in as Fabian started into his portion of the presentation.

Fabian broke down the status of his available ships and seemed satisfied with how the ground-based air wings from Aetnaeus had integrated into the *Echion's* flight line. Moreover, the capital ship Marcellus had observed a week ago upon entering the system had been completed. Its new crew was currently taking the battlecruiser on a shakedown cruise, but in a few days, it would be ready join the Third Fleet.

Fabian seemed upbeat and energized, and Marcellus hoped that this meant the kick in the pants he had given the Archus had paid off.

He interrupted Fabian's report only once, asking, "What name was the ship given?"

Fabian smiled. "I thought it would be fitting to name it the *Hydra*. I think it sends the appropriate message to our enemies."

"If you cut off one head…" Marcellus said, a grin spreading across his face. "I like it."

Fabian nodded and finished his report with a few remaining details about the status of his fleet. With that, the briefing shifted focus, and a holographic display of the Frontier appeared.

Theodorus, Safe Haven's intelligence head, stepped forward and began to speak. "Per your request, Archus Fabian and I have been working on recreating the enemy's fleet movements, with the goal of identifying targets for reprisal strikes."

The map shifted focus and zoomed in on a particular region of space. One star glowed a bright yellow, clearly highlighting it amongst the sea of surrounding stars.

"Using telemetry data from active and passive sensor arrays in the Aetnaeus system, as well as data from the Third Fleet, we have been able to identify several systems the Ascomanni most likely passed through or assembled at prior to ambushing the evacuation."

"Scout ships have been sent to the following eight systems, all of which are relatively close to Aetnaeus," he said, gesturing to a series of stars which turned orange.

The map zoomed back out somewhat and two more stars beyond the edge of the Frontier lit up.

"We've also been able to isolate two systems which lie deep in unexplored space. The journey to these systems is beyond the capabilities of most of the vessels the CID has at its disposal. However, I burned some favors and I've been able to get my hands on a pair of surveillance trawlers. They are currently en route to these systems."

"Although these ships have the range to get there and report back," Theodorus continued, "they are slow, and the indirect manner of their journey, necessary for security reasons, greatly increases the length of time it will take them to reach their destination and return to us.

"On the plus side though, they'll be launching a series of communications satellites in dark space along the way. If we ever need to coordinate offensive actions that far out, we'll have the infrastructure we need to do so effectively."

Marcellus nodded. "All right, so far so good, Theodorus. Have you had an opportunity to evaluate the intelligence gathered from any of the eight closer systems?"

"Yes, sir," he replied, a predatory grin spreading across the spy's face. "The first two systems were busts, no signs of Asco activity. However…" Theodorus tapped a command into his datapad, and the display zoomed in on one of the stars highlighted in orange.

"This is Fifteen Upsilon A, an unremarkable star system first surveyed a hundred and fifty years ago by remote probe. The probe found nothing of interest, just a couple of metal-poor rocky planets, a gas giant, and a ring of icy material further from the star."

"OK," Marcellus said impatiently. "So what?"

"It appears though that over the last three centuries the orbit of the gas giant has shifted, or perhaps always been in flux. It's now inside the frost line and has consumed at least one of the star's rocky planets. Even more interestingly, the planet has lost its atmosphere."

Marcellus frowned. "The gas giant lost its atmosphere? How is that possible?"

"We believe the most likely scenario is that it's an extra-solar capture for the system. It appears to have a highly elliptical orbit, and as it drew closest to the sun, its atmosphere was stripped away by the star. We've named it 'Icarus.'"

Marcellus nodded appreciatively at the tribute, and Theodorus continued.

"Given the technological parity between ourselves and the Ascomanni, our analysts think it is very unlikely that this is evidence of some kind of planetary engineering. Instead, the CID believes it represents a truly rare astronomical incident."

"OK," Marcellus replied tersely, "the system is interesting from a scientific standpoint. And?"

"Well, sir, as you know, the cores of gas giants usually contain a host of very valuable strategic elements. However, buried under kilometers of crushing atmosphere, they are usually sealed away beyond reach. It appears that the Ascomanni have discovered this bizarre occurrence and taken advantage of it."

Theodorus tapped another button on his datapad, and the display changed to show a vidfeed from one of the Third Fleet's scout ships.

The visual was broken into four components, each showing the same image in a different spectrum. It focused on a specific point in space, and a series of shapes were silhouetted by the system's sun.

"What exactly am I looking at, Theodorus?"

"We've found an Ascomanni shipyard. A very *expansive* one at that."

Marcellus whistled softly to himself.

"Have you been able to gather any additional details on the scope of operations, the facility's defenses, or ship traffic in and out of the system?"

"Before the scout ship left, it launched a series of probes in the outer reaches of the system. I've got analysts reviewing the incoming data feeds around the clock."

"Good. I know you all want to hop on a jumper straight to the nearest capital ship and go slag this thing," Marcellus said, making eye contact with each of his leaders, "but we must play this smart. We may only get one chance to surprise the Ascomanni."

He turned back to the spy chief and said, "Theodorus, how soon until we hear back from the remaining scouting vessels?"

"The remaining ships had to travel the furthest distance, but even so, I'd expect to have a full report available within a few days."

"OK, sounds like we've got some time then."

The Praetor started thinking through a rough outline for what needed to happen next, then began issuing orders.

"Julia," Marcellus said, turning to Safe Haven's magistrate, "if you can spare the time, I'd like you and a handful of your best engineers to help Theodorus review the information we receive on the shipyard. I want to know how it works and where we'd do the most damage."

"Of course, Praetor Aurelius. I'm sure my people will be happy to provide whatever insight we can."

"Excellent. Fabian, I'd like you to start pouring over the CID's data and identify the best approaches for our attack and the strength necessary to overcome its defenses."

"Yes, sir." Fabian nodded.

"All right, that's it for now, ladies and gentlemen. We'll regroup here once we've got the data we need. Thank you all for your time."

With that the briefing broke up. Marcellus headed back toward his suite, eager to see if there was any update from the War Council. As he neared the Citadel's main elevator shaft, he was not surprised to hear Fabian's voice call out after him.

"Excuse me, sir!"

He turned to find the archus jogging to catch up with him.

"Praetor, do you mind if I walk with you?" Fabian said, slowing awkwardly as Marcellus stopped in front of him.

"Of course not, Fabian," Marcellus said with a smile. Together, the pair boarded the lift and headed toward the lower sections of the facility.

"Praetor, I..." Fabian began, attempting to find the right words. "I thought a lot about what you told me, and I realize that you are right. I reviewed the data from the evacuation. Once I had time to step back and look at the situation objectively, I realized that we were fortunate to have made it out at all."

Marcellus nodded but didn't say anything.

"And with that realization came another. The Ascomanni sent the largest force we've ever seen to destroy my fleet, and they failed!"

A grin started to tug at the edges of Marcellus's lips, but he fought it down. "So, what have you learned from this, Fabian?"

"I learned that the enemy respects our capabilities, *my* capabilities. They took their best shot, and it wasn't enough. My pilots and sailors stuck together when everything was on the line, and we got the job done. We pulled through."

Fabian paused for a moment. "Most of us anyway..."

Marcellus clasped a hand on Fabian's shoulder. "That you did, Archus. Their sacrifices will not be in vain, I promise you that. We will find a way to defeat the Ascomanni."

The elevator doors slid open on the main concourse within the Citadel, and the pair exited the lift.

"I know, sir, we'll get the job done. I've temporarily transferred my flag to the *Vulcan*, so you can reach me there if you need anything else."

"Understood, Fabian. Glad to have you back."

Fabian smiled and saluted before turning and heading toward the hangar bays.

Marcellus turned the opposite direction and headed toward his suite, his spirits lifted by his brief conversation with Fabian.

As he approached his room, a beep came from his wrist communicator. He frowned, feeling some of his excitement fade. It was a reminder for his next appointment.

Marcellus sighed. He had a busy day ahead.

Platform Beta Five, Safe Haven, System: Classified, Frontier Space

Twelve hours later, Marcellus found himself sitting at a table in the wide, domed concourse of Beta Five, one of Safe Haven's habitation platforms.

He had spent most of the intervening time analyzing reports from or sending reports to the War Council. Mentally drained and in desperate need of some social interaction, he boarded a jumpship and headed toward Beta Five, which housed Safe Haven's most extensive medical facilities.

He had spent some time talking to Doctor Publicola, his chief medical officer, about the wellbeing of his wounded soldiers before visiting some of the more gravely injured patients.

Many of these men and women would never see combat again, but the doctor and his staff had given them hope for recovery and a life after their service to the Republic.

Now, he was enjoying a strong cup of tea, freshly brewed courtesy of one of the many small shops and stalls located on the platform's main courtyard.

The circular space featured a tall transparent dome, crisscrossed with hexagonal support structures which gave it a honeycomb-like feel. He watched as a new transport slowly pulled into its berth alongside the platform. The docking ring, a level below and just barely in view, soon teemed with replacements straight out of basic training, and he heard the raised voices of officers issuing orders as the new arrivals were sorted and sent off to their new units.

He activated the datapad he had brought with him from his quarters and checked Valerian's most recent report. Seven legions were stationed on Beta Five, and the fresh reinforcements that had just arrived brought them back to full strength.

Marcellus hoped his veterans would do their best to pass on the wisdom they had earned in battle to the newest members of his command. They'd need all the help they could get in order to beat combat's steep and fatal learning curve.

"Praetor Aurelius?" a female voice said hesitantly from behind.

Marcellus turned to find the newly minted Legate Aemilia Calvinus standing a meter and a half away, looking sheepish and uncertain.

"Legate Calvinus!" Marcellus exclaimed with a smile. "Please, join me." She sat opposite him as he continued. "Believe it or not I meant to track you down at some point."

Aemilia smiled and replied, "Well then, I'm glad I could save you the trouble, sir. I'm also glad I can thank you in person. The letter from Personnel Management stated that they'd never had another instance where a Praetor had so forcefully recommended the advancement of one of their subordinates."

"Well, I guess, 'failure to promote Tribune Calvinus materially weakens my command's ability to fight the Ascomanni' might have been a little strong," Marcellus said with a chuckle. "But not by much. You've more than demonstrated your readiness for the next level, Aemilia."

"I'll do my best, Praetor."

"I know you will." Marcellus gestured to the newly arrived soldiers milling about below. "How is integrating the replacements into your task force going?"

Aemilia sighed and looked very tired. "It's been exhausting, sir, but they are coming along well. I'm glad to see basic training has improved dramatically. After previous campaigns, basic skills like marksmanship and physical fitness were lacking. Now they are much closer to where we need them to be. I've also had my more experienced centurions share some of the tactical lessons we learned on Aetnaeus."

"I'm glad to hear it. If there are specific instructions you believe might further enhance our training methods, please don't hesitate to forward those on to Valerian. He won't bite...well, unless your report is poorly formatted."

"Will do, sir," Aemilia said with a laugh. "I'm sure you are very busy, Praetor, so I'll leave you to it. Is there anything else I can help you with before I go?"

"One thing, Legate. We're pretty thin on lower level officers at the moment. The academies are having a hard time producing enough graduates to cover those that are lost or promoted. If there are individuals within your command, or hell, even people you know out amongst the other legions of the army group who have potential, please forward them on to Valerian as well."

"Isn't promoting common legionnaires frowned upon, sir?"

"Maybe, Calvinus, but in my book, experience and composure under fire count for more than family name or educational attainment."

"Understood, sir, I'll put together a list and send it over shortly."

"Thank you, Legate. Keep up the good work."

Legate Calvinus saluted and walked away, leaving Marcellus with his thoughts. One in particular kept bouncing around his head: *'Experience and composure under fire.'* A new idea began to come into focus. One he very much wanted to explore in greater depth.

He opened his datapad once more, checked the billeting roster for the location of Invictus and his praetorians, and sent a quick message.

Platform Gamma Three, Safe Have, System: Classified

Aria delivered a quick jab to Invictus's rib cage as he missed with a strong left hook. She bounced back outside his reach, leaving his response flailing in the empty space she had just occupied.

The two praetorians were sparring in their habitation platform's gymnasium, while others worked out around them.

"I forgot how damn quick you are, Aria," Invictus said, panting.

His subordinate said nothing, surging half a meter forward and testing his defenses with another series of jabs. She fell back as he adjusted, only to dart forward again, but instead of lashing out with her gloved fists, she pulled back and delivered a kick to Invictus's exposed ribs.

Invictus grunted away the pain and steadily advanced on his nimbler foe. Aria was smart, she realized he was herding her into the corner of the ring, but there was little she could do to stop him.

Finally, Invictus had her where he wanted. He lunged forward as if to strike with his right hand, but he used his momentum to spin and deliver a powerful roundhouse kick to the Primus's torso.

Aria was not fooled however, and she dropped to a crouch and swept his leg out from under him while he still had one foot in the air. Invictus had the wind knocked out of him as he made contact with the mat, and Aria sat on his chest, arm cocked to deliver the coup de grace.

"All right, *all right*! You beat me...*again*," Invictus whined. "One of these days, I'll take you down."

Aria flashed him a rare smile as she rose to her feet. "You can certainly keep trying, sir."

She offered her commander a hand, and with a huff he got back up.

Sextus, who had been watching from the edge of the ring with Antonia Lutatia, laughed as Invictus stretched.

"We've all given up trying to beat her at hand-to-hand, sir," Sextus offered.

"Yeah, well if none of us *try* to beat her," Invictus said, groaning as he continued to stretch his sore midsection, "who's going to wipe that smug expression off her face?"

"No, no, you're going about this all wrong, bossman!" Antonia chimed in. "You should try taking her on at the shooting range. We've been able to beat her a couple of times. Though she's gotten better as of late, and by better I mean damn near perfect..."

Antonia was the third officer under his command. Wiry and lean, Antonia, or Tonia as the team had come accustomed to calling her, was sharp and aggressive. She had a pleasant enough personality in low stress environments, but she was a ruthless competitor, a trait that spilled into the manner in which she commanded her cohort.

Aria flashed Antonia a fierce look but softened it with a self-satisfied grin.

Before Invictus could respond, Vetus, the final member of Invictus's command staff, ran up, panting and out of breath.

The youngest commander by a few years, Vetus was young and handsome, priding himself on his physical appearance. He was a runner by nature, thin and not overly muscular. Despite his good looks, Vetus was bookish and introverted, and often found himself as the butt of the group's jokes.

"Sir... I..." Vetus began.

"We get it, you like to run," Antonia said while rolling her eyes. "Hmm...I feel like there is a joke about you and Asco in there somewhere..."

"Ha!" came the winded response. "Laugh it up all you want, Tonia, but the Praetor wants to see us. *All* of us."

There was a chorus of groans from the group.

Invictus grabbed a towel, wiped the sweat from his brow, and said, "You heard the man, the Praetor calls. When is he expecting us at the Citadel?"

"Well, sir...."

"He isn't," a familiar voice called out.

Invictus's subordinates snapped to attention as Marcellus walked up.

"I just happened to be out and about, so I figured I'd come to you. However, it looks like you might need some time to freshen up," Marcellus said.

"That is most kind of you, Praetor," Invictus responded stiffly, caught off guard by his friend's sudden appearance. "Where should we meet you?"

"I'll grab a conference room near the platform's maintenance center. Please join me there in half an hour."

With that, Marcellus turned and walked back out of the gymnasium.

"So, next time," Invictus growled, throwing his towel at Vetus, "how about you start with the fact that the Praetor is coming?"

Invictus started walking toward the facility's showers, and his subordinates followed after, grumbling under their breath, leaving Vetus standing alone next to the ring.

"What did I do?" a confused Vetus asked. He jogged after his peers. "Wait! Gang? What did I do?!"

***

Half an hour later, Invictus and his primes walked into the conference room where Marcellus was waiting. It was spacious, with plenty of room for the large table and the dozen-odd chairs arranged around it. It was bright too, with the wall opposite the entrance made up of window panels which looked out over the platform's docking stations.

Marcellus motioned for them to take a seat, and they spread out around the table.

"Thank you for getting together on such short notice," Marcellus said. "I was glad to see I didn't interrupt the ass whooping Aria was dishing out."

There were chuckles around the room as Invictus grumbled beneath his breath. "Yeah, well, you get into the ring with her and see how that goes…"

"Come now, Vic, don't be a sore loser!" Marcellus said with mock scorn.

"Hey! That's actually not a terrible idea," Antonia quipped. "I'd wager we could make a small fortune taking bets on that fight!"

"We could even broadcast it live for the rest of the army group," Sextus chimed in. "Hmm, this plan is really starting to…"

Marcellus cleared his throat. "All right, all right, let's focus please, ladies and gentlemen. The reason I asked you all to join me is to talk through an idea I've been bouncing around in my head.

"As you all know, the smallest strategic element of the legion is the cohort. Each cohort is made up of five hundred soldiers and associated equipment. Within each of those cohorts are five centuries, each led by a Centurion.

"Given the vast scope of the current conflict and the destructive nature of the weapons our enemy brings to bear, a hundred soldiers is the bare minimum we could afford to employ in most circumstances while maintaining unit integrity and tactical flexibility.

"However, I've been thinking about those situations that fall outside of 'most circumstances,'" Marcellus continued. "We've spent most of this war fighting like two heavyweight brawlers, each side taking turns pounding on the other until one is beaten into submission.

"My goal is to shake us free from this type of mindset. To defeat our enemy, we need to fight smarter. To fight smarter, we need to understand them a lot better than we do currently, and our toolset cannot continue to be constrained by large-scale infantry deployments.

"What I'm looking for is something more flexible, a unit capable of performing a host of functions, behind enemy lines, and without the need to commit a whole legion or a naval taskforce. I want to develop a unit that can perform tasks like infiltrating enemy positions, gathering intelligence, sabotaging vital facilities, or eliminating Asco leadership elements. A century is not nimble enough, and our legionnaires don't currently have the right training to perform those types of activities anyway."

"So, something like the small group I led to disable the fortifications at Elevation One Thirty-Four on Aetnaeus?" Invictus asked.

"Correct, Vic. I'd also think this unit would need to be small enough to be deployed by an FTL capable jumper or shuttle to allow for insertion without being detected."

Vetus raised his hand and Marcellus nodded in his direction. "So, you're looking to put together something like a police emergency response unit, Praetor?"

Marcellus frowned. "Can you elaborate a little more? I'm unfamiliar with what you're referring to, Vetus."

"Of course, sorry, sir," Vetus said, his cheeks flushing. "Back home, the constabulary maintained a special cross-disciplinary team of about twenty individuals who were able to handle undercover operations, abductions, or standoff-type situations. Though not required for membership, the teams were often comprised of ex-military or RF."

"Interesting..." Marcellus mused. "I'd think we'd need to spend some more time building out the tactics and equipment necessary for a purely military equivalent, but it might give us a good place to start. Good work, Vetus."

"Thank you, sir!" he responded enthusiastically.

"Suck-up..." Antonia whispered under her breath while Sextus did his best to repress a grin.

"Primus Lutatia, do you have any bright ideas you care to share?" Marcellus asked with a scowl.

"Uhh, well, sir..." Antonia stammered as she racked her brain. "Such a team would need to...to be well versed in multiple hostile planetary environments. Extra-vehicular training in space would also be a plus for things like boarding actions."

"Way to pull that out of your ass, Primus," Marcellus said with a smile.

Once again, gentle laughter came from the group, and she bowed slightly at his backhanded compliment.

"They'd need to be to be well versed in cyberwarfare too," Antonia continued. "I'm not sure software packages alone would cut it either, we may be talking about a new AI application for the battlespace."

"That's an excellent point. I guess you're off the hook."

Antonia wiped imaginary sweat from her brow and leaned back into her chair.

"These teams would also need to be able to adapt on the fly. Equipment selection prior to deployment may account for most situations, but extended deployment may require the inclusion of our latest micro-production units," Aria volunteered next.

"That's probably something worth distinguishing," Invictus said, nodding in agreement. "We may be talking about more than just a single type of unit. Or perhaps these...teams...would need to be able to separate into even smaller groupings. Longer-term surveillance or recon missions could have different requirements than quick, surgical strikes."

"On Modena, there are big-game hunters who cater to wealthy customers," Sextus said. "They go on weeks-long hunting trips in some of the planet's more exotic environments, usually with only the bare essentials. We might want to look for survivalists or explorers amongst the legions for our first recruits."

"Now we're cooking," Marcellus chuckled. "Let's keep this conversation rolling. In the meantime, I'll send a message to Valerian asking him to see if we can't get some people out here who might have experience we can learn from."

The discussion lasted for another six hours, interrupted only by a short break to eat dinner. By the time the group broke up for some shut-eye, Marcellus had a strong foundation to build on.

Over the next few days, his praetorians would continue to work on defining the tactics and training necessary for his clandestine operations teams.

Now he just needed to come up with an appropriate name for these new units.

Caurus City, Notus; Safe Haven, System: Classified

Several days later, Marcellus woke up to find that his meetings had been rescheduled, with a note from Valerian demanding that he take some time to relax.

Instead of his regular routine, his adjutant had arranged for a tour of the system's facilities, led by Magistrate Flavia. After a brief breakfast, Marcellus met up with his host and together they boarded a shuttle bound for the subterranean city of Caurus.

High above Notus, a set of blinking lights resolved themselves into a small space station. Nearby, the skeletal frames of bulk freighters hung in space, devoid of the massive containers they used to carry goods and materiel across the Republic.

The magistrate tapped him on the shoulder, and pointed toward the moon. Marcellus watched as a series of projectiles seemed to be shot from the surface toward the waiting ships.

"We launch their containers into orbit at just over escape velocity. Once they are in space, a tug helps connect them to the transports, and away they go," Magistrate Flavia explained.

Marcellus continued watching as a swarm of small tugs emerged from the station, each racing out to meet one of the giant spherical containers before guiding it toward the waiting cargo ships.

As their jumper neared the moon's surface, Marcellus was astounded by the amount of energy and effort that had gone into retrieving Notus's precious water.

Huge tunnel borers lay mothballed on the crater-pocked surface, only a stone's throw from a gigantic passageway leading into the moon's interior. The debris removed from the planet's crust created a range of small mountains, which formed a semicircle around the perimeter of the shaft's entrance.

Their ship entered the kilometer-wide passage through the planet's crust, passing dozens of spherical containers like the ones he had seen just moments ago. They fit snugly along the walls of the cavernous space, with four rows spread equidistantly along the edges of the tunnel, leaving just enough room in the middle for shuttle traffic to fly in between.

As they headed further underground, thick bundles of heavy gauge piping ran up the sides of the tunnel before terminating in pumping stations, which busily transferred the water treated below into the waiting containers.

Marcellus couldn't help but marvel at the size and scope of the waterworks. He turned to his erstwhile tour guide and said, "Magistrate, the sheer scope of the engineering challenges that were overcome to create this place… It's amazing!"

"It did require a significant amount of resources, but the moon's sea contains enough water to merit the investment. Everything grown on Eurus is fed by the water reclaimed here. Shipments from this facility have even been used in conjunction with terrestrial cloud seeding generators to help terraform some of the more arid planets we've colonized in the Frontier."

"I've read about that. I hear they've made great progress on Asciano."

"Truly remarkable stuff, Praetor," the magistrate said, smiling. "All made possible by the abundance of water that's shipped from this facility. But as grand as all of this may seem, you haven't seen anything yet!"

The jumpship slowed as it reached the end of the passage, which led to a perpendicular shaft. Their pilot slowly rolled the shuttle as they proceeded further down the horizontal tube. Marcellus sat heavily in his seat, suddenly overcome by a wave of nausea.

"What the...?" he muttered.

"Gravitational interchange," Magistrate Flavia explained. "Notus's gravity wants to pull everything toward its core. Caurus is built on the exposed *ceiling* of the internal sea. The city is literally built upside down, so we needed to create a pocket of artificial gravity to allow for construction. Don't worry, it gets to everyone the first time."

A minute later, they shot out into bright artificial light, and Marcellus was blown away by the view.

Buildings towered on all sides of the entrance to the city, clinging to the steep curvature of the moon's interior. A broad dome, somewhere between partially translucent and fully opaque, covered the entire area. A brilliant orb of light was suspended from the top of the dome, acting as an artificial sun for the city. The water pushing against the dome's surface created beautiful glimmering reflections of the city's lights across its entire surface.

"Welcome to Caurus, Praetor Aurelius."

"Magistrate...it's beautiful," Marcellus said softly.

"That it is, sir."

"Please, call me Marcellus."

"Fair enough, but only if you call me Julia," she responded with a laugh. "As beautiful as the dome is though, just wait until we get to the Apex and out onto Notus's sea."

"Uh... Come again?" Marcellus sputtered.

"As I mentioned before, we created an artificial bubble of gravity to support the city. Its large enough to cover Caurus and even extends past the dome on either side. However, the dome is a little bit conical, so the very topmost portion is at the point where our artificial gravity and the moon's natural pull equal out."

"The net effect," Julia summarized, "has been to pull several meters of water against the walls of the city, but it leaves the top of the dome's exterior above the waterline and exposed to the empty space we've created extracting the planet's water."

"Wait, how hasn't your pumping operation created a vacuum within the interior?"

"We pump a gas mixture in to fill the void. Ultimately when we are done draining Notus of its sea, the interior of the moon will have a breathable atmosphere. That's still decades down the road though."

"Outside of the grav bubble," Julia continued, "the normal rules apply. We've lowered the internal sea's volume by about twenty meters, so the space between the water pinned against the dome and the sea beyond is still quite thin."

"This I have to see," Marcellus said incredulously.

"Well, we are nearing the external lock, so prepare yourself."

Ten minutes later, they emerged from a landing pad nestled at the top of the domed city and out onto its exterior surface.

It was dim, like dusk on any one of the dozens of worlds Marcellus had visited, but it was bright enough to take in the majesty of their surroundings. All around them was an ocean, oriented toward the city below, while in the distance light danced off the glistening surfaces of the planet's interior.

Marcellus stopped in his tracks as he gazed upward. Above them, a turquoise blue curtain of water was seemingly suspended overhead. Soft glows emanated from its depths, playing tricks on his eyes as they bounded off surface after surface.

"The sea floor has bioluminescent plant life, that's what gives the water above us its glow," Julia said, snapping him out of his daze. "I can't help but feel humbled by the beauty of this place."

"It's...it's beyond words, Julia."

She nodded and, without another word, gestured toward a dock off to their right, where a boat was moored. She led him down the wide jetty to the waiting catamaran. They boarded the vessel and set sail, following the curve of the dome.

Over the next twenty minutes, the Apex faded beyond the horizon. Giant pipes protruded from the city, extending deep into the sea above them. As Marcellus watched, fish jumped from the water above, as if attempting to reach them.

"They used to be able to jump back and forth between the gravitational zones," Julia explained, "but it's been too far for them to reach for almost two years now. It's a shame, it was really something to see. I still have some vids of schools of fish jumping through the transitional boundary then back again."

As the boat continued to ride the gentle waves above the city, Marcellus took in the sights and smells of the ocean. He peered over the side of the ship, awestruck by the shimmering lights. A school of fish, not more than five meters below, swirled and billowed beneath them, illuminated by the soft glow of the city.

"This is truly amazing, Julia. Thank you for bringing me here."

"It's been my pleasure, Marcellus. I imagine it's been quite some time since you've really had an opportunity to just relax and take in a view."

"That it has. What's next on the agenda?"

"Well, we've got another half an hour out here on the waves, but after that it's off to the asteroid belt for a tour of some of our facilities, before wrapping up with a visit to a greenhouse the size of your new battlecruiser on Eurus."

"Sounds good. Thank you again for putting this together. I really needed it."

Safe Haven's magistrate nodded, and the two sat quietly as their ship looped back toward the dock.

The Citadel; Safe Haven, System: Classified, Frontier Space

The next morning, Marcellus woke refreshed and ready for the day ahead. He hurriedly grabbed a shower and donned a fresh uniform. Valerian, Fabian, and the others would be waiting for him.

The previous evening, Theodorus had sent word indicating that the last scout ship had arrived, and his agents would soon be done reviewing its data. The group was scheduled to meet at a large conference room adjacent to the Citadel's command center, and Marcellus was eager to hear what they had to say.

When he entered the room a few minutes later, he was not surprised to find that Valerian had ordered breakfast to be prepared. The others sat around the room's table, working away at breakfast rolls and fruit.

His subordinates started to rise when they saw Marcellus, but he waved them down. "Please, eat. We have a packed agenda to get through."

As they settled back down into their chairs, he helped himself to a plate and grabbed a cup of posca, a pot of which was warming nearby.

"Uh oh…" Invictus quipped. "He's gone for the posca. That usually means he's grumpy."

"What makes you say that?" Julia responded.

"Marcellus prides himself on being a morning person. He only tends to drink that stuff when he needs something to get him moving."

"So, your analysis is that Marcellus woke up on the wrong side of the bed, solely based on the fact that he is drinking Umbria's ubiquitous breakfast beverage?" Theodorus asked, incredulously.

"That's it!" Invictus said with a laugh. "The hints of citrus and honey really get him moving."

Marcellus rolled his eyes. "The CID has nothing to worry about, Theodorus. As usual, our super sleuth is way off the mark."

The Praetor grabbed himself a seat at the head of the table and took a sip from his mug. "All right, what do you all have for me?"

The CID section head stood first. "Well, Praetor, we've now processed the intel on all eight of the nearby systems we suspect may have Ascomanni activity. Five of the eight are devoid of any sign of the enemy, but the remaining three hold promise.

"Per our previous discussion, Archus Fabian and Magistrate Flavia will provide a more thorough analysis of the shipyard we found in Fifteen Upsilon A. However, the other two systems contain targets of strategic interest as well."

Images began to project from the middle of the conference table as Theodorus continued his briefing. The first image showed a relatively empty planetary system, made up of two gas giants which appeared to orbit each other as well as their shared star.

"This is Sigma Secundus E, roughly twelve parsecs from Upsilon A. We've identified what appears to be a Helium-3 refining operations at the barycenter of the system's twin gas giants. There appears to be little to no fleet activity in the system; the probe we left behind hasn't even been able to identify freight traffic or any other signs that the Ascomanni are exporting the fuel refined there."

"Interesting," Marcellus said. "Do we have any understanding of the scale of operations there?"

Theodorus nodded to Julia, and she spoke up next.

"Based on the initial analysis of the system's gas giants and the size of the facility located at the center of their orbits, I believe they would be more than capable of refueling the six-hundred-odd ships you destroyed at Aetnaeus, with capacity to spare."

Marcellus frowned, but remained silent.

"Which makes it all the more bizarre," Fabian interjected. "There's no evidence of warships or other starships in the system. If it wasn't for the total lack of fleet activity, I'd say this system could have served as a forward staging area for the Ascomanni's entire war effort in the Frontier."

"Hmmm..." Marcellus responded. "Another mystery to add to our collection. What about the third system?"

"Of course, sir." Theodorus scanned a few notes on his datapad before continuing: "The last system of interest is Two Lambda B. The Ascomanni presence was almost missed entirely, but fortunately, on the scout's final pass, they identified trace emissions originating from a circumstellar disc of icy bodies surrounding the star.

"On closer inspection, we discovered a communications array located on a dwarf planet hidden amongst the belt's debris. Unfortunately, the same debris makes locating warships or other defenses very difficult."

Marcellus nodded. "Well that certainly provides us with some additional targets. What have we been able to learn about the shipyard at Fifteen Upsilon A?"

Fabian and Julia exchanged an uncomfortable look, and Marcellus instantly felt ill at ease.

"Well, sir," Julia started, "based on the size of the shipyard, and the mining operations on Icarus, we think it could be larger than our operations here in Safe Haven. Worse, because the core of the gas giant is almost completely made up of metals, mining it is extremely efficient."

"So, it's bigger and it has all of the resources it could ever need. How much larger is it?"

"Twice the size," came Fabian's deadpan response.

Marcellus whistled. "What do the facilities' defenses look like?"

"Well that's just it, sir. Like the Helium-3 refinery, there doesn't appear to be much in the way of traffic. We've spotted about ten warships on station, and there are some smaller defensive satellites scattered around the edges of the yard, but that is pathetically small for a target this valuable."

"Well, Fabian, every time they've driven us from a planet, we retreat and dig in on the next world. We've launched a handful of strikes against these occupied systems from time to time, but that's really been the extent of our offensive operations. Maybe they've just gotten complacent."

"Perhaps, sir, but none of this makes sense. The Ascomanni aren't behaving the way I would expect them to. After so much effort and so many lives expended, why do they seem so indifferent to the worlds they take from us? Why would they leave important resources like these undefended?"

"Because Fabian, they aren't here for our resources or our planets," Invictus said in a husky voice, his brow furrowed. "They are here to enslave us or exterminate us, and it doesn't seem like they really care which."

"But that's just speculation, Vic…" Valerian retorted.

"Not just–"

"Enough Vic, this isn't the time or the place," Marcellus interrupted.

Invictus nodded and sat back in his chair heavily. A few of the attendees exchanged glances, but none asked for clarification.

"OK, thank you all for putting this together," Marcellus continued, powering through the tense silence. "I have some ideas about how we can neutralize these facilities, but I'd like your feedback."

"You mean we're not just going to go destroy them all?!" Theodorus said, disbelief creeping through his voice.

"Well, yes, eventually we will destroy these targets, but to destroy them outright misses a golden opportunity. First, I propose we use this occasion to gather some much-needed information, something I'm sure you'd appreciate?"

Theodorus nodded curiously, and Marcellus continued: "So I propose infiltrating the refinery and the communications station, gathering as much intelligence as possible, and then making them disappear."

Marcellus's recommendation was met with confused looks, but Fabian seemed to catch on to his commander's intent. "You mean like the fleet at Aetnaeus? They just vanish?"

"That's it exactly. Neither should be too difficult to pull off, so long as we can jam any outbound communications. I figure we can drop a suitably sized comet on the comms relay, and it wouldn't be too difficult to feed the refinery to the gas giants it's mining."

"Ironic," Valerian said with a smirk. "But what about the shipyard? It's too big to make disappear."

"I understand, Val. I have a couple of questions for the group. For our more technical members, how much do we know about Ascomanni engineering?"

"It's nothing too exotic," Julia responded. "Similar in complexity to our own, but clearly alien in origin."

"OK, next question," Marcellus said, taking a deep breath. "How hard would it be to utilize their shipyards for our own purposes?"

His question was greeted by audible gasps, followed by nearly a minute of uncomfortable silence. Again, Fabian was the first to speak up.

"Well, Praetor, we know the Ascomanni's ships are very modular in design. We've always attributed their greater numbers to greater efficiency in shipbuilding, and we've made design changes of our own to try to narrow the gap."

"That may be true," Theodorus interjected, "but you are still talking about a massive amount of effort just to retool the plants to bring them into line with our own requirements."

"But we know the Ascomanni rely much more heavily on manual labor than we do. For whatever reason, they simply don't seem to be too concerned with putting their people in dangerous situations," Valerian countered. "If we were able to significantly increase the automation of some of the yard's processes… Maybe we could pull this off?"

"What about the Ascomanni? Surely they won't just leave it alone while we dramatically increase our shipbuilding capabilities?" Invictus asked.

"We're much more evenly matched in space," Fabian replied, before Marcellus could respond. "Assuming we can enhance the facility's static defenses, we could negate their superior numbers without committing an entire fleet to the shipyard's defense."

The Praetor nodded. "I've also been informed that large-scale production of the Longbow is moving forward. Until the Asco figure out a countermeasure, a handful of missile batteries would really help even the odds."

Marcellus paused for a moment and looked at Safe Haven's chief engineer. "What do you say, Magistrate, could you pull it off?"

Julia's head was bowed, and she was quiet for several more moments before looking up and catching Marcellus's gaze. "We could do it, Praetor, it'd take a couple of months to get up and running, and we'd need to take experienced workers off the lines here, but it could be done. There's just one thing."

"Name it."

"I need a colony ship. In its original condition, too."

"That'll be something of a heavy lift. Most have long been converted to other purposes since the onset of the war. Why do you need it?"

"They were designed to provide all of a new colony's immediate infrastructure needs, including manufacturing and resource processing. It's the fastest way to turn their shipyards into *our* shipyards."

"Well then, I'll make sure we get you your ship, Magistrate." Marcellus turned to the rest of the members present. "OK then, we've got a rough plan. Next, we're going to work through the finer details of each operation. Theodorus, let's start with the communications station…"

They worked well into the evening, but by the time the meeting broke up, they had a detailed plan.

It was time to make the Ascomanni pay.

Chapter 9

The Citadel; Safe Haven, System: Classified, Frontier Space

A week had passed since their plan had been formalized, and Marcellus had gathered his commanders for a final briefing before the operation kicked off. It was a much smaller meeting than the last briefing on Aetnaeus, with just over a dozen people in attendance.

Fabian and two of his captains sat on one side of the room, while Invictus and his subordinates sat on the other side. Valerian, Theodorus and a pair of his operatives, Magistrate Flavia, and an uncomfortable-looking Aemilia Calvinus rounded out the rest of the group.

"Welcome, everyone," Marcellus started. "Over the last several days, each of you have reviewed details about a series of pending strikes against Ascomanni facilities in the Frontier. The objective of this briefing is to bring everyone in on the big picture and make sure we all understand how our separate parts relate to the ultimate objective."

Marcellus pulled up a star chart, which highlighted the three systems his forces would soon attack.

"Based on intelligence gathered after the destruction of Aetnaeus, we've identified three Ascomanni facilities. We'll be hitting two targets first, then regrouping before striking the third.

"The first is a large Helium-3 refinery. It is located in a system featuring twin gas giants, which orbit around each other as well as their sun. The facility itself is located at the gravitational point between the two.

"Feed from a probe left by the original recon team has failed to show any ships coming or leaving the facility. It appears to be lightly defended at best. However, given its size, Invictus and three cohorts of praetorians will be responsible for boarding the station. A team of Theodorus's CID operatives will join them, with the intention of retrieving any valuable data from the refinery's mainframes.

"Although we expect light resistance, Archus Fabian is detaching a battlegroup centered around the battleship *Vulcan* to support the insertion. The force will be large enough to extract Invictus and his soldiers should the Ascomanni react unexpectedly. Moreover, once the boarding operation is complete, the battlegroup will destroy the station."

Marcellus paused for a moment and scanned the room. "Any questions so far?"

One of Theodorus's people raised a hand. "Should the boarding parties be concerned about any environmental factors, like excessive radiation from the gas giants?"

"Good question. The refinery would need to be shielded to prohibit contamination of its product, but we know the Ascomanni don't value their own wellbeing the same way we do. It's possible there could be hazardous conditions in isolated pockets across the station, but your armor should protect you for the short time you'll be aboard."

The operative nodded and Marcellus glanced around the room. No one else spoke up, so he continued with the briefing.

"Next, we have an Ascomanni communications array. Our friends in the CID have been running some models, and this facility is likely the primary communications hub for their incursion into the Frontier. The base is located on a dwarf planet, codename 'Ninguis Mons,' tucked inside an ice belt surrounding the system's sun.

"I will be coordinating the attack, while Primus Aria's cohort infiltrates the facility, aided by the second team of intelligence operatives. We'll be inserted by a cruiser, which will provide cover for the assault. Once the mission is complete, we'll be dropping an asteroid on the facility as a parting gift for the Ascomanni.

"Those two missions will proceed simultaneously, and the Asco reaction should be a strong indicator of the forces they have in reserve to counter these surprise attacks. This leads into the third part of the operation, which is the most complex and most risky by far.

"We've identified a huge Ascomanni shipyard, exceeding the size and scope of operations here in Safe Haven. After some intensive technical discussions, Magistrate Flavia believes we can convert the yard to our own needs. Such an outcome would have a dramatic effect on the war effort.

"As the objective is to take these facilities and stay, we'll need a lot more bodies to wrest control from the Ascomanni. Task Force Hyperion has been allocated for this task, with Legate Calvinus in overall command. One legion will be responsible for capturing a mining facility located on the planet Icarus, which feeds the shipyard, while another will occupy the yard itself. The third legion will be in reserve. Anything else to add, Legate?"

"No, sir," Aemilia said, shaking her head. "My legionnaires are ready to do their part."

"Good, thank you, Aemilia. Our best guess is that there are about ten operational Ascomanni warships in the vicinity, but most of the observed vessels have been smaller screens, primarily destroyers and frigates. Regardless, we'll rendezvous outside of the system and Archus Fabian will lead the entire Third Fleet to the target.

"Once the shipyard is secure, the colony ship *Alba Longa* will jump in with a detachment of combat engineers and five hundred of Safe Haven's best technicians, under the supervision of Magistrate Flavia. The immediate objective will be to get satellite defenses up and running, should the Ascomanni return. Once we've further reinforced our position in the system, work will begin on retooling the facility for our own use."

Marcellus stopped again and looked around the room.

"A lot has transpired over the last two weeks. Big picture, we've begun pulling back into a more defensible position, but the Ascomanni are still pressing hard at Tratirne. With a little bit of luck, this operation might relieve some of the pressure on Praetor Asinia's forces and could be the key to turning this whole war around."

A handful of heads nodded in agreement, and Marcellus felt confident that his team was ready.

"Aria and I depart in two hours. Invictus and Battlegroup Vulcan leave in six. We'll rendezvous with the rest of Third Fleet at the Ascomanni shipyard in approximately seventy-two hours.

"Good luck, all of you."

URN *Tyrrhenia*, Two Lambda B, Frontier Space

The light cruiser *Tyrrhenia* winked into existence in the outer edges of the system. Two kilometers away, an Ascomanni communications satellite slowly rotated on its longitudinal axis, an extra-solar relay which allowed the communications station to discretely send messages throughout Frontier space.

As Marcellus watched, a missile raced away from the ship, reaching out and finding the enemy satellite. There was a tiny spark as it found its mark, and the relay was reduced to a glimmering cloud of space debris.

The Ascomanni facility could no longer call for help.

"Did they transmit anything prior to the satellite's destruction?" Marcellus asked the *Tyrrhenia*'s captain.

"No, sir," she replied. "It looks like we are clear to proceed to the facility."

Marcellus nodded. "OK, Captain, let's get moving then."

"Understood, Praetor. Navigation, you have the coordinates."

The view beyond the bridge's viewports began to distort and expand, then, in the blink of an eye, they were deep within the system. The star's seemingly limitless icy belt stretched in both directions as far as the eye could see.

The cruiser began to accelerate toward its destination.

Marcellus flicked a switch on the console in front of him and said, "That's your cue, Primus. Once you've disembarked, we're going to locate a suitable target and begin our preparations. If anything comes up, you know which frequency to reach us on."

"Understood, Praetor," came the brief reply.

"Good luck, Aria, we'll keep the skies clear and the exit open."

Battlegroup Vulcan; Sigma Secundus E, Frontier Space

Invictus watched out the window of his insertion craft's cockpit as the refinery quickly filled up the view. He finally understood Fabian's reaction to the raw reconnaissance data: the station was positively *massive*.

This place could keep the whole Third Fleet fueled indefinitely, Invictus thought to himself, and it was a good thing he had three of his cohorts to secure the facility.

So far, the operation was off to a good start. The twelve ships of Battlegroup Vulcan had jammed the enemy's communications and set up a perimeter around the Helium-3 refinery. The *Spatha*'s fighters had made a few attack runs on the handful of turrets defending the station, but the situation in space seemed to be well under control.

As soon as the area around the refinery had been secured, the signal had been given and thirty boarding craft sped toward the facility.

Invictus ran through the battleplan as his ship completed its approach. He would coordinate the mission embedded with Antonia's cohort. Her soldiers were responsible for safeguarding a team of intelligence operatives, whose objective was to scrub any useful intelligence from the installation's mainframes.

Sextus and Vetus would each create diversions at other sensitive locations around the facility, with the former concentrating on the refinery's processing plant and the latter focusing on the power core. The goal was to keep the Ascomanni off balance and prevent them from concentrating their forces against any one unit.

As soon as the spooks were finished retrieving whatever intelligence they could, all three cohorts would exfil the same way they came in. Once they were clear, the battlegroup would obliterate the facility and push its broken remains into the two gas giants surrounding it.

"Sixty seconds, Prefect!" the co-pilot called out.

Invictus patted the man on the shoulder and hopped down into the crew compartment. Antonia was waiting for him.

"Nearly there, sir?"

"Yep, sixty seconds to go. You ready?"

"I don't like going in blind, Prefect, even if the CID team has a good feel for the refinery's layout. Intelligence regarding the resistance we'll face is sketchy at best."

Invictus snorted. "Sketchy? Try non-existent, Tonia. Still, if things get too rough for you, you can always hide behind me."

"True, you are getting a little wide in the waist, sir," she shot back with a grin. "Maybe you should let Vetus drag you out onto the track more frequently."

Invictus shot her a mock expression of indignation. "Hey now," he whined, "I've been working really hard on my physique!"

Antonia just shook her head ruefully, and a moment later, a heavy *clank* reverberated through the ship's hull. A pair of circular pads on the passenger bay floor began to spin violently, whining as they carved through the exterior hull of the refinery. After twenty seconds, a fainter clanking noise could be heard beneath them, and the pads retracted to reveal the interior of the station.

Invictus threw a stun grenade through the opening, waited for it to explode, and then lowered himself through the opening. He dropped two meters to the metal floor and quickly scanned his surroundings.

They were in a bland, industrial-feeling hallway near the exterior of the station. It seemed ample enough for his soldiers, but for the hulking Ascomanni, it must have felt positively cramped.

Antonia dropped in behind him, followed by a few more praetorians. They quickly secured both ends of the passage, while the CID operatives disembarked. They would be responsible for leading Antonia and her soldiers to the command center.

One of the operatives knelt next to the far door and produced a datapad. She pried open an access panel with a combat knife and plugged the device in with an auxiliary cable. A moment later, the door slid open.

Antonia flashed a series of hand signals to her soldiers, and together they moved out.

Ascomanni Communications Station, Ninguis Mons; Two Lambda B, Frontier Space

The cabin of the dropship went dark, and a red light flicked on near the end of the craft.

"All right, everyone! Link in!" Aria called out.

Her soldiers and the CID operatives accompanying them stood and attached cables to their harnesses.

"Equipment check!"

A series of voices called out, one after the other, as the jumpship's passengers certified that they were ready for the drop.

Satisfied that everyone was ready, she took her place and strapped herself in. The ship began to bounce around a bit: they had entered the planetoid's weak atmosphere. Aria took several deep breaths and waited for the signal.

The light turned green, and a door, wide enough to allow for an easy exit, opened beneath each of the ship's occupants. For a moment, they hung inside the bay, suspended only by the cable attached to their harnesses. A moment later, the light cut out, and they dropped into the abyss below.

Their descent was slowed as the cable began to resist their weight, finally bringing them to a stop five meters below the ship. Aria spotted their objective as wind buffeted her armor, chilling her to the bone. The station was close, maybe only half a kilometer away, and their dropship was closing the distance quickly.

A moment later, the ship began to slow rapidly as it reached the edge of the comms station, and the Umbrians dangling below it started swinging forward. As each soldier's momentum was expended, the cable detached, and they dropped lightly onto the building's roof.

Aria watched as the rest of her cohort was deposited on other sections of the facility. Within thirty seconds, five hundred Umbrians had landed on top of the Asco structure.

Aria's troops fanned out and formed a perimeter.

The Primus retrieved a roll of material from a soldier's pack. She handed one end to the soldier and spooled the thin ribbon out. They slapped it onto the roof's surface, creating a rough circle.

Aria extended her bayonet and touched the red-hot metal to the edge of the ribbon. In a flash, a hole was cut in the roof of the structure, and Aria and her praetorians dropped into the station.

Ascomanni Refinery; Sigma Secundus E, Frontier Space

Antonia threw herself behind a bulkhead as plasma rounds zipped past, swearing under her breath as she slammed into the wall. One of her soldiers was less fortunate. He was struck multiple times in the abdomen as he sought out cover. The wounded Umbrian folded over and lay still.

"Auto-turrets!" she cried out. She peaked around the corner, only to duck back a second later as more plasma slammed into the bulkhead. "I want access, now!"

One of the CID operatives was on the opposite side of the hallway, trying her best to squeeze her body into the narrow cover afforded by an open maintenance panel. She dug through her pack furiously before producing two round objects and a cylindrical device.

She set the two metallic balls on the deck and rolled the short cylinder out into the middle of the hallway, where the camera within had a clear line of sight to the two Ascomanni turrets a few meters away. Next, she rapidly tapped commands on the datapad integrated into her forearm bracer, and the two objects began to roll at high speed down the hall.

As they neared the enemy emplacements, they split open, revealing four grasping armatures. The tiny probes launched themselves at the base of the guns. A quick drying adhesive stuck the devices to their targets, and the arms quickly drilled through the turrets' housing and located their processors.

In an instant, malicious code overwrote their programming. Fully under the operative's control, they stopped firing and slowly rotated toward the Ascomanni soldiers crouching behind them.

The Ascomanni reacted quickly, turning their weapons on the corrupted turrets and reducing them to smoldering wreckage. The distraction was enough however, as it bought Antonia and her soldiers a couple of seconds to act.

Two grenades arced through the air, landing amongst the Asco troops, and a moment of indecision sealed the enemy's fate.

Shrapnel tore the Ascomanni apart. Antonia and her praetorians advanced even before the dust had settled, finishing off one or two survivors who might have still posed a threat.

"This is it!" she called out as they reached the door to the facility's nerve center. "Prepare for breach!"

Another soldier pulled an aerosol can from his belt, spraying the outside of the doorframe. He looked at Antonia, who nodded back. A soft hum emanated from the soldier's armor, the vibrations activated the breaching charge, and the doorframe disintegrated.

Antonia kicked in the heavy steel door, which teetered for a moment before crashing to the floor, crushing an Ascomanni soldier who had been waiting behind it. She moved quickly around the perimeter of the command center, shooting at anything that moved. Her soldiers filed in behind her, spreading out and taking down targets as they appeared.

It was over in less than thirty seconds.

"All clear?" Antonia shouted.

Four voices answered in the affirmative.

"We're all clear here, Prefect," Antonia called back through the doorway they had just breached.

Invictus walked in with the CID agents trailing behind him. He stepped carefully around the smoking corpses of the Ascomanni scattered around the room and nodded approvingly.

"Agent," he said, addressing the leader of the intelligence team, "please get to it. The faster you get your data, the faster we can get out of this hellhole."

She nodded and started issuing orders to her team. A minute passed, and the CID team leader called out with an update: "Prefect, we need about twenty minutes, then we are good to go."

"Got it."

Invictus activated his commlink and passed the news on to his subordinates.

Ascomanni Communications Station, Ninguis Mons; Two Lambda B, Frontier Space

Aria stood over the body of a dead alien in the comm station's control room. Its sterile white lab coat contrasted sharply with the deceased's violet skin and the pool of florescent yellow blood surrounding the corpse. One of her soldiers sat nearby, shaking, as a medic tended to dozens of cuts sustained from a scalpel wielded by his deceased assailant.

It must have been of the same species as the subject Invictus captured on Aetnaeus, Aria thought to herself. It was definitely *not* Ascomanni. Worse, this thing had been waiting for the right moment to attack. Ascomanni normally just rushed toward the fight with reckless abandon.

"Do we have a secure link to the *Tyrrhenia*?" she asked one of her subordinates.

"Yes, ma'am, the channel they left open is not being counter-jammed."

Aria switched to the appropriate frequency and said, "Tyrrhenia Actual, we've run into more of the alien species we first encountered on Aetnaeus. Please advise."

She was unsurprised to hear the Praetor's voice: "Be very careful, Pistris Three-Six. They may be weaker than the Ascomanni, but they are much more cunning. Use extreme caution."

"Understood, Actual. We've secured most of the facility, and Pistris Three-One is sweeping the lower levels. I'll call when we are ready for extraction."

"Good hunting, Three-Six, Tyrrhenia Actual out."

Aria turned and walked over to the team of analysts busily downloading the station's records. "How long until you're finished?" she asked.

"It's going to be at least an hour, Primus," their leader responded. "We have exabytes of data to pull."

"Do you have what you need?"

"Yeah, it's just a matter of transfer rate. We're going as fast as we can without opening ourselves up to trojans or other adversarial code on the Asco servers."

"Get it done. The clock is ticking."

Ascomanni Refinery; Sigma Secundus E, Frontier Space

The lumbering form of an Ascomanni worker emerged from a cloud of steam to Sextus's right, a length of thick piping held overhead with both hands. The Umbrian summersaulted backwards and rolled to his feet, as his giant adversary brought its impromptu weapon crashing down on the space he had just occupied.

Sextus quickly fired three rounds from his pulse carbine, striking the worker squarely in the chest. It dropped the pipe and collapsed heavily to the floor.

A roar echoed behind him as another worker charged down the pipe-lined catwalk. Sextus turned, but as he caught sight of his new opponent, he knew he would not be able to bring his carbine to bear in time.

Sextus activated his bayonet, but before the hulking alien could reach him, a pair of his soldiers emerged from a side passage. At a full sprint, they collided with the Ascomanni, slamming it against the pipes running along the catwalk. With a shuddering moan, the pipes gave way, and the Ascomanni disappeared, howling, into the haze below.

"Are you OK, sir?" one of his soldiers asked, panting with exertion.

"Yeah, thanks for the assist."

Sextus checked their surroundings and, satisfied that the coast seemed clear, activated his commlink. "All Pistris Four callsigns, this is Four-Six, check in. How is it going out there?"

"Sir, Four-One and Four-Two have reached the primary distillation tanks. Area secured for now."

"Four-Three Alpha here, we're working through the barracks compound in small groups. We've taken some casualties, mostly wounded. These Asco workers have heart, but fortunately they are poorly armed."

"Four Deuce is mopping up near the merox units. So far, so good, but there are a hundred corners for these bastards to pop out from."

"You're telling me," Sextus grumbled. "All right listen up everyone. Pistris Six just called in. They are almost done. Once they've secured the objective, we'll evac to the shuttles. Keep me informed if the situation changes out there."

There were a series of acknowledgments to Sextus's order, and he turned back toward the Ascomanni he had taken down moments before.

One of the soldiers who had come to his aid was gently prodding it with her boot, but Sextus's gaze was drawn to a series of painful looking blisters covering its arms and face.

"What do you suppose happened to it, sir?" the soldier asked.

"Looks like radiation poisoning," Sextus responded. "We haven't come across anything our suits can't handle yet, but we've definitely found pockets that would cause acute cases of radiation sickness without some form of protection."

"Damn... Why would anyone be willing to work in this type of environment?" the other praetorian asked.

"Maybe they weren't given a choice," Sextus said as he turned and looked in the direction he had originally been heading. "Focus up, praetorians, we need to link up with First Century. Let's go."

Ascomanni Communications Station, Ninguis Mons; Two Lambda B, Frontier Space

"Pistris Three-Six, this is Pistris Three-One Alpha. There is something you need to see," a voice crackled over the cohort's band. "We are on sublevel two. A team will meet you at the lift."

"I'll be there shortly," Aria responded. She motioned to the praetorians scattered around the room. "Keep the control room secure."

A handful of heads nodded, but none verbalized a response.

That was the way Aria liked it, quick and to the point.

She walked down a short hallway where a handful of her troops sat resting, hooked a right, and boarded an elevator destined for the facility's basement. The doors opened after a brief descent, and Aria walked into a brilliantly lit hallway, painted a sterile white.

A soldier was waiting for her, and she motioned for him to lead the way.

A short walk later, they reached a large room with airlocks leading to an antechamber. As they passed through the threshold, she found herself in a large, two-story room, full of medical equipment. Tall windows lined the room's far wall, high above the floor.

In an instant, Aria had a flashback to her own past. *Masked faces backlit by a brilliant light. The sickly smell of blood. The muffled sounds of voices.*

This was an operating theater.

Aria continued to scan the room and noticed a handful of bodies splayed out over the floor. Most were the same alien she had encountered earlier, but her heart caught in her chest when she saw that two of her praetorians were among the dead.

A group of three soldiers stood around a gurney located in the middle of the room, and Aria joined them.

An Umbrian lay on the gurney, deceased, but not for long. He was not one of Aria's praetorians, but rather a civilian by the look of him, and there was still color in his lifeless cheeks.

"What is this?" Aria demanded.

"They were experimenting on him," one of her troopers volunteered. "It looks like they were fitting him with a number of cybernetic enhancements, while he was still awake. We heard his screams when we first reached this level."

Aria fought back against the bile rising in her throat. "Have you found any other bodies?"

"There is an incinerator nearby, Primus. They could have easily disposed of hundreds of bodies."

"Are there any more of our people trapped here?"

"There is a group of about twenty clearing the floor below us. They report finding rows and rows of large cages, but none have been occupied yet."

"Bag their bodies. They come with us," she said, gesturing toward the aliens. "Also, call upstairs and have the CID send someone down. We're not leaving without answers to what these aliens were doing here."

Ascomanni Refinery; Sigma Secundus E, Frontier Space

Vetus turned the corner and came face to face with an Ascomanni. Shock and fear seemed to carry through the alien's eyes, and for a moment, it turned to look in the opposite direction, as if searching for an opportunity to escape.

As Vetus watched, however, there was a muffled buzzing which seemed to emanate from the creature, and it roared with pain. It swung back toward him, flailing its arms wildly in his direction. Vetus was just out of reach, and one of the soldiers accompanying him quickly dispatched the beserking worker.

"Did you all see that? What the hell was that?!" one of his subordinates shouted.

"Yeah," Vetus responded heavily, shaken by the encounter. "That was...disturbing."

"Are these workers being *forced* to fight us?" came another tentative voice.

Vetus kneeled next to the corpse and replied, "I don't know. But it doesn't matter. I need you all to get your heads screwed back on straight. Regardless of why, these things are still trying to kill you."

He activated his cohort's channel. "Pistris One-Six to all Pistris One units, the primary objective has been secured. Regroup with your sections and work your way back toward the shuttles. Anyone not at the assembly points in half an hour is stuck, and I guarantee you will not like this place after the Navy's done redecorating."

A series of acknowledgments echoed over the command net. Satisfied that the situation was under control, he nodded to the praetorians around him and they headed back the way they came.

Ascomanni Communications Station, Ninguis Mons; Two Lambda B, Frontier Space

"Do you see this shit?" Cornelius asked as he and Thana ventured deeper into the dimly lit stacks of cells.

The praetorians searching Sublevel Three had paired off and were busily searching through the endless maze of cages. Each was no more than a meter square and one and a half tall.

"These things are like stalls for livestock."

"But *we're* the animals they keep penned up in them," she responded tersely.

A metallic clatter echoed down the row of cages, and Cornelius held up a fist. The duo kneeled and surveyed the area. He waved his hand forward twice, and together they moved silently forward.

They travelled another five meters before coming upon a split in the hallway. The noise came again, down the passage to the right, and the pair continued their quiet advance.

"I've got movement."

They slowed their approach, moving forward in a measured, deliberate pace.

"Switch to thermal," Thana said. She tapped him on the shoulder, and they proceeded in a crouch.

They came upon another ninety-degree corner.

The praetorians eased their way around, making sure there weren't any surprises waiting for them. Once the path was clear, they continued moving, only for Cornelius to stop abruptly.

Thana slammed into the back of him and swore.

"What the hell man? Why are we..." she whispered before her voice drifted off.

Ahead of them were hundreds of heat signatures, curled up and contorted in the narrow spaces within their cages.

They rushed forward and confirmed their worst fears: they were Umbrians, dehydrated, emaciated, and in shock.

"By the gods..." Cornelius said, unable to process the sight before him. "Call...call it in. The Primus will want to know immediately."

Ascomanni Refinery; Sigma Secundus E, Frontier Space

"We're falling back to the shuttles now!" Invictus shouted into his commlink, as the noise of battle nearly drowned him out. "The Asco are definitely onto us though. One-Six, Four-Six, what's your status?"

"We're clear, Six," came Vetus's response. "Everyone's accounted for."

"Four-Six here, we're rounding up a few stragglers, but we'll be on the move in about five minutes."

A loud explosion drowned out Invictus's response. Ascomanni soldiers poured through a doorway ahead of them, and Invictus began firing his carbine at the enemy. The other members of his group reacted too, and soon Ascomanni dead clogged the entrance.

"Anyone hurt?" Invictus called out.

"We're good," Antonia said, winded, "but our path forward is blocked." She turned and looked at one of the intel operatives and asked, "Is there an alternate route back to the shuttle?"

"Yes ma'am, but it takes us directly through a large mess hall. There won't be much cover, and it could get ugly."

"It's already ugly," Invictus responded.

The rest of Antonia's cohort had fallen back to a perimeter around their egress point, and a century had been tasked with keeping a channel open for their retreat. Unfortunately, the Ascomanni had wised up, and concentrated attacks had forced the holding party to withdraw after sustaining heavy casualties.

Antonia and Invictus would have to fight their way back to the shuttles. It had been a tough slog so far, they had already lost eight soldiers since leaving the command post.

"Well, if there is no other way, that's where we need to go," Antonia agreed.

The group of thirty started moving again, and soon they entered the cavernous mess hall the agent had described previously. The power was out, and only a dim set of emergency lights at either end provided any illumination.

They moved through the rows of oversized tables, constantly scanning the room for any threat.

They had made it about halfway through, and Invictus allowed himself to hope they might cross uneventfully.

No sooner had the thought crossed his mind than the ceiling exploded.

Large chunks of debris cascaded down on them. A larger section of the roof crushed an unfortunate soldier caught below it, while others tried to free trapped limbs from beneath the rubble.

Ascomanni jumped through the gap, roaring as they landed amongst the Umbrians. The whine of plasma carbines filled the air while bodies went flying as the shocked praetorians did their best to fight off their physically superior enemy.

"MOVE!" Invictus screamed over the din, pushing and pulling everyone he came across toward the far exit.

In the chaotic free-for-all, a dozen Umbrians managed to put a few meters' distance between themselves and the enemy. They toppled a handful of tables, forming a rough barricade, and began firing back at the Ascomanni.

"I want fire superiority, now!" Invictus barked. "Pick your targets, there are friendlies out there too!"

A handful of stragglers reached the table fort as the praetorians poured fire into the masses of Ascomanni that kept dropping from the ceiling. Plasma began to fly back their direction, as the hostile alien swarm turned their attention to the holdouts.

"Has anyone seen Antonia? Did the operatives make it?" Invictus shouted over the roar of combat.

"We're here," someone called from behind him. He turned to find three of the four agents huddled behind a table, the color drained from their faces.

"Where's Antonia?"

"There, sir!" one soldier said, pointing back toward the enemy.

Antonia dragged a wounded soldier back toward the shelter of their impromptu barricade, firing back toward the enemy still milling about. She had almost reached the barrier when she was struck in the side and toppled over.

"ANTONIA!" Invictus bellowed.

He vaulted over the tables, grabbed her under the arms, and helped her limp back to the tables.

Another pair of praetorians attempted to get the wounded soldier she had been dragging but were cut down by concentrated enemy fire.

As he reached the relative safety of the barricade, he handed the wounded Primus off to the CID operatives. "Get back to the ship, now! We'll cover you!"

Their leader nodded and headed through the door.

Invictus whistled loudly to get his remaining soldiers' attention. "We are leaving, praetorians! Center peel! Keep an eye on your buddies and pour on the fire!"

One by one, the surviving Umbrians worked their way back to the exit from the mess hall. They cleared the entrance in good order and fell back into the corridor that would lead to their shuttles.

Invictus primed a small shape charge and affixed it to the spot where he thought the door's motor would be. With a pop, a jet of energy tore apart the mechanisms within the wall, and the door crashed shut.

"That will slow them down," he shouted, his ears still ringing. "Move, people!"

They sprinted down the hall, past the bodies of friend and foe alike. They had reached the edge of the Umbrian perimeter, but it had shrunk as Antonia's last section fell back to their ships. They turned another corner, and they found their extraction point. Two cables dangled from holes in the ceiling, and a quartet of praetorians were guarding the approaches.

"Check fire, friendlies!" one called out.

Invictus and the survivors quickly ran toward the cables, with the first two praetorians jumping to get as far up the cord as possible. Invictus pulled the shuttle guards into a tighter perimeter facing toward the enemy.

The battered soldiers made it up the rope just as the first Ascomanni started to approach.

One of the guards got shot in the shoulder, and Invictus threw another stun grenade down the hall. He hefted the wounded soldier up to a pair of waiting arms, then he and his remaining praetorians clambered into the shuttle's passenger bay.

The breaching locks slid shut behind them.

"We're clear!" he called out toward the cockpit. "Get us the hell out of here!"

There was another pop as the shuttle detached. Invictus clambered up into the cockpit and sat down at an auxiliary station. He switched to his command's frequency and called out, "All units, disengage. The primary objective has been secured."

As the insertion craft raced away from the refinery, he tapped the co-pilot on the helmet and shouted, "Are we clear of the blast zone?"

The co-pilot checked his instruments before nodding in the affirmative.

Invictus sat back down and switched frequencies: "Battlegroup Vulcan, this is Pistris Six. You're clear to engage!"

URN *Vulcan*, Sigma Secundus E, Frontier Space

The captain of the *Vulcan* watched as thirty small ships sped away from the refinery and began working their way back toward the *Spatha*. It would take a few minutes for the assault carrier to retrieve all of the insertion craft, but that was just fine with him. The *Vulcan* and her battlegroup still had work to do.

"Battlegroup Vulcan," he said into the receiver built into his command console, "concentrate fire. Heavies, focus on the reactor. All other ships are free to engage at will."

He turned and looked at his fire control director, who gave him the thumbs up, and the *Vulcan* lurched as its weapons began to pour destructive energy into the refinery. Explosions rocked the structure, with superheated sections of the station splintering off and spinning away in all directions.

"Track the debris," he called out to his bridge crew. "The Praetor wants any evidence that this station ever existed to disappear."

There was a blinding flash, and a shockwave pulsed from the epicenter of the explosion. The station's hull crumpled under the force of the blast: secondary explosions were set off across the refinery, and atmosphere vented from hundreds of cracks in the structure.

A moment later, it broke in two along its centerline, and the two halves started to be pulled toward the gas giants on either end of the facility.

"All right, ladies and gentlemen, that's that," the *Vulcan*'s master called out over the cheers of his bridge crew. "Cease fire and prepare cables for towing."

Ascomanni Communications Station, Ninguis Mons; Two Lambda B, Frontier Space

The *Tyrrhenia* entered the dwarf planet's atmosphere and landed next to the Ascomanni facility. Freight elevators, fifty meters square, descended from the underside of the hull, and Aria's cohort did their best to transfer the liberated captives as quickly as possible through the bitter cold.

In small groups, praetorians rushed the prisoners from the relay's exterior air lock to the waiting vessel. Some of the stronger prisoners helped their weakened comrades, while those without the strength to walk were carried to the elevators, where they were met by the *Tyrrhenia's* medical team.

Satisfied that things were proceeding as well as could be expected, Aria left her soldiers to finish the evacuation. She worked her way through decontamination and joined Marcellus on the bridge, where she found her commander in heated discussion with the cruiser's captain.

"But, sir, if we travel to Tratirne, some of these people might not make it!" the older woman said, her hands balled into fists at her side.

"I know, but the risk is too great, Captain. We cannot risk exposing another system to the Ascomanni, especially Safe Haven. You might not like it, but those are my orders."

The *Tyrrhenia*'s master skewered the Praetor with a menacing glare, but realizing he would not change his mind, she nodded and walked away, muttering under her breath as she left.

Marcellus spotted Aria's approach and shook his head slightly. "Our natural reaction is compassion," he sighed, as Aria came to a stop at his side, "but the Ascomanni have shown they are capable of *anything*. Until these captives have been thoroughly evaluated, there are just too many unknowns to take them to an uncompromised location."

Aria nodded but said nothing else.

Marcellus smirked at her lack of audible response. "I see your preference for being concise hasn't faded."

Aria just looked at her superior, and Marcellus shook his head ruefully. "I remember when we couldn't get you to shut up, Aria. We've all been changed by this war, forged into the people we need to be in order to succeed. One day though, I hope we'll see that version of you again."

"When these monsters can no longer tear families apart or raze entire cities to the ground," Aria said softly, her eyes filled with rage, "perhaps things will go back to normal. Until that day, Marcellus, I'll keep it quick and to the point."

Marcellus watched her closely but decided not to press the issue. "Your cohort did well today. The CID agents are already hard at work analyzing the data you recovered, though it looks like it will take several weeks to get through all of it. Initial feedback looks promising though."

"That's good to hear. I'm glad it was worth it."

"How many did you lose?"

"Fifteen dead, thirty-five wounded."

"And how many prisoners were located?"

"Approximately three hundred. The *Tyrrhenia* is going to be pretty tight as we work our way to the rendezvous point."

"We'll have to make do. Once we regroup with the fleet, I want your people transferred to the *Spatha* with the other praetorians."

A claxon started to sound, and the cruiser's captain ran back onto the bridge. "Sensors, what do we have?" she demanded.

"Four Asco frigates on the outskirts of the system. They'll be on top of us in about half an hour."

"How did we detect ships that far out, Captain?" Marcellus asked.

"The probe the recon team left behind, sir. It's still active and is currently feeding us their telemetry data."

"The *Tyrrhenia* can't stand up to that level of firepower, can she?"

"No, Praetor. We'll be hard pressed to escape if they arrive before we've left the planetoid's atmosphere."

"And how long until we've got everyone aboard?"

"It's going to be very close," Aria responded, quickly running the numbers.

Marcellus wracked his brain for a plan.

"Do we know how they'd most likely approach?"

"Yes, sir," the sensors officer called out. He pointed to a large display showing the planetoid and its surroundings. "They'd pass through this rocky section of the belt on their way to the planet."

"Rocky? You mean asteroids? I thought most of the junk in this belt was ice?" Aria interjected.

"For the most part that is true, but there are some rocky bodies out there as well," the *Tyrrhenia*'s captain responded.

"That's it!" Marcellus said, an idea popping into his head. "Captain, the Primus and I are going to need a pair of shuttles, and I need your crews to strip a dozen warheads out of your ship-to-ship missiles."

"Praetor…?"

"If we can't outgun them, we'll just have to fight smarter. Do as I ask, Captain. Arai, follow me, I'll explain on the way!"

Circumstellar Disc; Two Lambda B, Frontier Space

Marcellus placed the last of his warheads on the final asteroid before pushing off to rendezvous with his shuttle. Hopefully, Aria would be done as well, and together they would jet back to the cruiser to make their escape.

He reached the open door to the vented passenger bay. Marcellus slapped a button on the wall of the ship, and the door slid shut. Air began to rush back in, and soon a green light just above the door flicked on, indicating that the cabin had been pressurized.

The visor on Marcellus's helmet slide open, and he bounded up the stairs leading to the cockpit where he found that his pilots had already started moving the ship toward the *Tyrrhenia*. He could also see another shuttle off the starboard bow, ahead of them, rushing in the same destination.

They neared the planetoid as the Umbrian cruiser passed through the final layers of Ninguis Mons's atmosphere. The hangar doors stayed shut, but before Marcellus could ask, the pilot explained the reason why.

"Captain indicates the hangar is fully occupied, sir. We'll need to dock with one of the ship's airlocks."

"Does that put me further from the bridge?"

"Closer actually, Praetor, but the docking sequence will take about a minute. Please strap yourself in."

Marcellus complied, dropping down into the seat next to the auxiliary gunner's station. The cruiser dominated the forward view ports, and the shuttle abruptly rotated to match its speed and vector before settling against the larger ship's hull.

A series of digital tones sounded from the crew compartment, and the co-pilot began to unstrap his harness. "You're good to go, Praetor, the Captain is expecting you."

Marcellus nodded and headed toward the airlock. As promised, he quickly found his way to the bridge, where the ship's captain waited for him.

"I hope this works, Praetor."

"Well, if it doesn't, we don't have a whole lot of options, Captain."

"It'll work, sir," a third voice called out from behind them.

Marcellus turned to find Aria walking toward them, an uncharacteristic grin tugging at the corners of her mouth.

"Captain," the sensors officer called out, "the frigates are onto us. They've altered course and are heading straight toward us."

"Will their path still cross through the target zone?" Marcellus asked.

"Yes, sir. ETA, forty seconds."

Marcellus turned back to the cruiser's skipper. "Captain, you do the honors."

The *Tyrrhenia*'s anxious master managed to eke out a small smile. "XO, pull up an image of the target zone. Highlight our little surprises as well."

The view out of the bridge's viewports was replaced with real-time images of the oncoming Ascomanni frigates. Six asteroids clustered around the Ascomanni's path started to glow a soft red. A gentle beeping began as the lead ship passed the first rock.

"Easy..." she said softly to no one in particular. The remaining three frigates entered the kill zone, and a moment later the captain shouted, "Now! Do it now!"

There were no discernable flashes or explosions, but the asteroids began moving toward the enemy ships, some splitting into larger chunks, others just propelled by the force of the blast into the narrow channel the Ascomanni warships were travelling through.

Marcellus watched with satisfaction as the largest asteroid crashed into the lead frigate's stern. Its engines flared, and a moment later the back third of the ship was sheared off by a series of explosions.

The second frigate managed to dodge most of the debris, but the third and fourth were peppered by asteroid impacts: the third frigate crumpled under multiple blows from chunks the size of city blocks, while the fourth sustained its most serious damage from one especially violent piece of debris, which punctured one side of the vessel before emerging out the other end.

"I think that about evens the odds, Captain," Marcellus said, a vicious smile spreading across his face.

"Yes, sir!" she responded forcefully. "Helm, full speed ahead. Fire Control, you are free to engage as soon as the computers have a solution. Concentrate on the undamaged ship first, then we'll mop up the stragglers."

The *Tyrrhenia* surged forward, and the cruiser shuddered as eighty cells of ship-to-ship missiles were unloaded on their disorganized enemies.

The sole undamaged Ascomanni warship, now closest to the Umbrian cruiser, did its best to intercept as many of the missiles as it could, but its efforts were in vain. Over fifty direct hits peppered the frigate's hull, gouging huge chunks out of the ship's superstructure. The burning, skeletal wreck continued on its last course, destined to smash into the surface of the dwarf planet below.

The Umbrian cruiser continued to savage its two remaining enemies, and by the time the ship's second salvo of missiles had found their marks, there was no longer any threat to the *Tyrrhenia* or her passengers. Cheers rang out on the bridge as the final frigate broke apart.

"Captain," Marcellus called out above the din, "please get the cruiser clear of the belt. There's one last gift we need to give the Ascomanni!"

Marcellus's words were greeted with more cheers and whistles, and a moment later, the ship sat a few hundred kilometers above the ring in the middle of the system.

He turned to his subordinate and said, "Aria, this one's all yours."

She looked at Marcellus hesitantly, but the ship's captain led the praetorian to her station.

Aria tapped in the command, and, far away, a shockwave, almost too quick for the eye to catch, emanated out from the former location of the Ascomanni comms station. Piece by piece, the ice and rock in the immediate area of the impact was pushed aside, forming a perfect circle, devoid of all debris, in the middle of the system's belt.

Stage one of the operation had been completed. Now it was time to turn their attention to the Ascomanni shipyard.

Chapter 10

URN *Decima*, Third Fleet Assembly Area; 2 Parsecs from Fifteen Upsilon A, Frontier Space

Marcellus stepped into a whirlwind of activity as he entered the bridge of the fleet carrier. He spotted Fabian, tucked away in an alcove, deep in conversation with his command staff. Marcellus weaved his way toward the group, through the various bridge stations, where he found the Archus and his officers in heated discussion.

"…that's why we can't risk sending a smaller force as bait."

"I'm with the Archus, if the full Third Fleet jumps in, any reserves they may have could choose not to engage."

"This is the *Ascomanni*, they'd charge headlong into a buzzsaw without a second thought!"

"Maybe, but we've seen improvements in their tactical abilities lately. With such a significant loss of resources at Aetnaeus, asset preservation may have been forced into their playbook."

"Regardless, the *Hydra* and a small squadron could be overwhelmed, especially given how tricky the jump is going to be…"

The last officer speaking saw Marcellus approach, gulped, and called out, "The Praetor is on deck!"

"At ease," Marcellus said as the officers jumped to attention.

"You're overdue sir," Fabian said, flashing the briefest of smiles.

"Only by about an hour, Archus." Marcellus smiled wearily. "We ran into some unexpected circumstances that delayed our departure."

"The captain of the *Tyrrhenia* shot me a brief report, I'm aware of the situation. She'll be heading out for Tratirne as soon as your praetorians are done transferring to the *Spatha*."

"I appreciate it, Fabian, it's just too risky to send her back to Safe Haven. Will the *Tyrrhenia* be missed?"

"No, sir, our latest intelligence shows eight Ascomanni warships protecting the yard. There are a trio of cruisers, but the rest are frigates and destroyers."

"Any better feel for what organic defenses the shipyard may possess?"

"The Ascomanni have never been big believers in small, single-man craft. If they do have starfighters, their numbers will be minimal. Otherwise, the shipyard itself looks remarkably free of defensive weaponry. We can't rule out some type of ground-based weapons system on the remains of the gas giant though."

"OK, so what's the plan then, Archus?"

"Well..." Fabian began. "We were just discussing that. The original plan was for a smaller initial strike force to attack the shipyard proper. It was hoped that a lighter force would draw out any surprises the Ascomanni have in store for us. We'd stage the rest of the fleet at various points around the system, where they could quickly react to changes in the battlespace."

"However," the Archus continued, "enhanced sensor readings from the system have identified new challenges, and some of my staff now disagree with our initial approach."

"What's the problem?"

"Gravitational forces within the system limit the number of paths that our ships can use to quickly reach the shipyard. As such, rushing in reinforcements for the initial strike force from multiple points around the system could be difficult. If a sizeable number of Asco ships are being held in reserve, our smaller force could be overwhelmed before we can respond."

"Sir?" One of Fabian's staff members said tentatively. The Archus nodded, and the young woman continued. "What about pulling the Ascomanni away from the shipyard?"

"Hmm..." Fabian muttered. "Minimal changes to our original plan, more options to respond where necessary. That might just work. We could have the *Hydra* and a smaller force jump near the perimeter, then feign retreat. That might pull them far enough out from the shipyard to allow for quick reinforcement *and* preserve tactical flexibility as we insert the ground troops."

Fabian looked around at the faces of his officers, and no one objected to the outline he had just described. "All right, we've got details to work out. Let's get to it."

With that, the group dispersed, leaving Fabian standing alone with his commander.

"Praetor, will you be joining us for the assault?"

Marcellus shook his head. "I'll be transferring to the *Celeres* to keep an eye on Task Force Hyperion's progress. I don't want you thinking I'm looking over your shoulder, Fabian. You're the best man for the job, and I'm confident the Third Fleet will perform brilliantly."

"Thank you, sir. We'll need about thirty or forty minutes. Shouldn't take too long to update the fleet. I'll make sure my feeds are routed to the *Celeres* as well."

Marcellus nodded. "I appreciate it. Good luck, Fabian."

The two exchanged salutes, and Fabian watched his commander go before turning to find his XO. There were still many details he had to iron out.

URN *Hydra*, Third Fleet Assembly Area; 2 Parsecs from Fifteen Upsilon A, Frontier Space

Captain Adrienne Tarpeia looked out of the viewport of her brand-new command. The ships of her impromptu squadron idled before her battlecruiser: two heavy cruisers, two light cruisers, and half a dozen frigates and destroyers waited for her orders.

She had been entrusted with significantly more responsibilities, she thought to herself. Prior to her promotion, she had never commanded a force of more than four warships at any one time.

As she gazed out on her forces, Adrienne took a moment to reflect on the series of events that had led her to this point.

She had been promoted to the *Hydra* after waging a successful campaign to eliminate a band of Umbrian pirates who were harassing the relatively safe freight lanes between the Frontier and Umbria's more established colonies.

Rage bubbled up within her as she thought about the targets of her last command.

Her people faced an existential battle for the very survival of their species, yet those *bastards* took advantage of the chaos to prey on their own people. As far as Adrienne was concerned, there was nothing more despicable.

She had flushed the pirates out with extreme prejudice, decimating their numbers before ultimately locating the position of their base of operations. It was hidden on a barren moon in some lifeless, gods-forsaken system.

Adrienne had given the pirates a chance to surrender, but they defiantly refused, vowing to fight to the end.

Instead of risking more of her people's lives, she decided to simply bombard the pirates' base from orbit.

Within five minutes, charred debris and the burned-out shell of their base were all that remained of the self-styled 'Falcons of Cyrenaica.' Never again would they steal from and murder the honest traders making a living plying the Republic's space lanes.

Adrienne returned her attention to the present. The lives of over ten thousand sailors were now in her hands, and she mentally ran through the updates Archus Fabian had provided.

Her small flotilla was to jump just outside the shipyard's perimeter, attack the nearest installation, and then retreat as soon as the Ascomanni defenders got organized. Once they had drawn the Asco out far enough, they were to hold the enemy in place while reinforcements arrived to envelop and destroy the defenders.

The Archus had assured her that help was only moments away, but the *Hydra*'s captain felt uneasy. The ships they knew about roughly equaled her force, and any enemy reinforcements would put them in a very tight spot.

If there was any delay in sending in the cavalry, her force would be in for a pounding.

Adrienne checked her chrono. Ten minutes to go.

URN *Celeres*, Third Fleet Assembly Area; 2 Parsecs from Fifteen Upsilon A, Frontier Space

Located deep within the bowels of the assault carrier, the ship's combat information center was designed to provide a theater commander with a complete picture of the battlespace. It was equipped with everything Aemilia would need to coordinate her legions' attacks.

She stood at the edge of a circular table, crammed into the middle of the room. The center of the table was open, allowing for a projector to display a number of different information panels for the legate and her command section.

Aemilia noticed one panel in particular and pulled it closer. It magnified as it drew nearer, showing a large assault transport. The ship was composed of a long, rectangular hull, with two great pods supported on either side. It would carry one her legions, Legio Ferrata, to assault the Ascomanni facility on Icarus.

"Legate Numidius, are your preparations complete?" she asked.

A gravelly voice answered over the console's speakers. "We've finalized preparations and are ready to go, ma'am. The ship's captain seems confident, so hopefully we'll have a relatively smooth drop."

"Understood. Legio Aethon is in reserve, so if you need additional support to consolidate your position after securing the facility, call it in."

"Will do, Legate Calvinus."

Aemilia pushed the panel back into place and pulled up another detailing the current loading status for the legion assaulting the shipyard.

"Tribune Labienus, what's the holdup on getting the Fourteenth on those transports?" she said to a young officer standing across the table from her.

"There was an issue with one of the loading bay's gantries. We're trying to catch up now, Legate."

"Make it happen. We'll be jumping shortly."

"Yes, ma'am."

Aemilia turned back to the display, brow furrowed, and willed her churning stomach to calm down. She wracked her brain, trying to think of things that she might've overlooked.

"What else, what else...?" she whispered to herself.

"There's nothing else, Legate. You're doing an excellent job."

"Praetor!" Aemilia exclaimed, nearly jumping out of her skin as she spun around and saluted her commanding officer. "I'm sorry, sir, I didn't hear you come in."

"No need to apologize. It looks like your people are almost ready," Marcellus said, returning the salute.

"Yes, sir, I'm just..."

"I know how you feel, Aemilia. I don't have the magic words which will make this any easier, but I would encourage you to trust your people. They know what they are doing."

"I know, sir, I just feel like I should be *doing* something."

"When Praetor Artorius first promoted me to Legate, it took me some time to settle into the command as well," Marcellus said as he smiled knowingly. "I remember there was a point where she sat me down and said, 'Aurelius, you're driving yourself crazy. Worse, you're driving *me* crazy. Focus on what is within your control. Worrying about anything else is wasted effort.'"

A wan smile crossed Aemilia's face. "I appreciate it, sir. It's just... This is the most complicated operation I've led so far."

"I understand, but let me provide some perspective, Legate Calvinus," Marcellus began. "On Aetnaeus, your commanding officer and everyone else senior to you was dead or wounded within a few months of the Asco invasion. We evacuated nine months after it all began. For *half the campaign,* you kept your forces together in the face of relentless pressure. This assault is small-time by comparison."

Aemilia was quiet for a moment. "Thank you, sir," she said finally. "That helps."

"Good. I trust you to see this one through, Aemilia," Marcellus said gently.

They stood in silence, watching, as a timer on one of the panels finished counting down to zero.

URN *Hydra*, Ascomanni Shipyard, Fifteen Upsilon A, Frontier Space

The eleven warships of the *Hydra*'s squadron dropped into space just outside weapons range of the massive collection of factories and dockyards that made up the Ascomanni facility. The heavier capital ships formed a loose square in the center of the formation, with the frigates and destroyers forming rough wedges on either flank.

Without any additional orders, the Umbrian warships surged forward, opening fire as soon as the nearest structures came into range.

"Sensors," Adrienne called out, "where are the Asco warships?"

"They are reacting quickly, ma'am. They're forming up in the center of the shipyard. Ten minutes out and closing. Enemy strength confirmed at three cruisers, four destroyers, and two frigates."

"Any sign of fighter deployment from within the shipyard?"

"No new drive trail emissions, Captain."

"OK, let me know when the Ascomanni get closer."

"Aye, ma'am."

"Fire Control, how much damage have we inflicted on the facility?"

"Minimal, Captain. The nearest portions of the yard have taken moderate damage, but overall the flotilla is demonstrating excellent fire discipline."

Adrienne nodded. The goal was to put on a show, not wreck the place, especially since they were intending to stay.

She sat forward in her seat and watched her force's handiwork impatiently.

"Sensors, how far out are they now?"

"Five minutes, ma'am. They are approaching faster than expected."

"All right, send the signal, have the flotilla fall back."

Adrienne's ships began to disengage, their weapons falling silent as they pulled back out of range. The pursuing Ascomanni kept pace, but their rate of closure slowed as the Umbrian ships accelerated away.

Adrienne gripped the arms of her chair tightly as time slowly passed. In a few minutes, they would have pulled the Ascomanni far enough away from the shipyard…

"Captain, new contacts emerging ahead of us!" a frantic voice called out.

Her blood ran cold as twenty new Ascomanni warships jumped into the system. They were close enough for Adrienne to make out the shapes of the oncoming vessels.

Adrienne stood and started barking orders.

"Comms, I need a priority signal sent to the Archus immediately."

"Yes, Captain."

"Navigation, full stop! Get us moving back toward the shipyard. Relay the order to the rest of the flotilla."

"Ma'am?" came an incredulous reply.

Adrienne ignored her helmsman and opened a channel to the rest of her command.

"Attention, this is Captain Tarpeia. Our exit is blocked by an Ascomanni reserve fleet. All ships are to turn and engage the original force sallying from the shipyard. We've got to get in tight to nullify their numeric advantage until our own reinforcements arrive. Screens, tuck in close. All ships are free to engage as soon as they have firing solutions."

With that, she dropped back down into her seat. There was nothing left to do but wait.

URN *Decima*, Outskirts of Fifteen Upsilon A, Frontier Space

"Twenty ships in total, sir. A battleship and six cruisers form the backbone of this new group."

"Damn..." Fabian said, staring at a diagram of his forces' positions and those of the enemy.

"Archus!" his XO called out. "Captain Tarpeia is turning her flotilla around. They are closing on the original garrison force."

"Do we have enough room to jump between the first group of Ascomanni and the shipyard?"

"No, sir, there is a high risk of collisions using our current pre-planned approach vectors."

"What about above or below them on the ecliptic plane?"

There was a pause. "That would work, sir. We can drop the *Pietas* and *Vulcan* above the enemy, but it will take a few minutes for them to reach the new jump point."

"Do it now. Can we place any ships between the *Hydra*'s flotilla and the new Ascomanni force?"

"The *Neptune* and her accompanying ships are in position."

"OK," Fabian said. "And our battlegroup is capable of boxing in the Ascomanni reinforcements?"

"Yes, sir."

"How soon until the *Hydra* makes contact with the enemy?"

"They just did, Archus."

Fabian gave himself a few seconds to think, then started issuing orders: "All right, in sixty seconds I want Battlegroup Neptune to interpose itself between the two Ascomanni forces. Battlegroup Decima will box the enemy in. As soon as the *Vulcan* and her ships reach their jump point, they are to head to the *Hydra*'s aid. Let's get to it, people."

URN *Hydra*, Ascomanni Shipyard, Fifteen Upsilon A, Frontier Space

Adrienne watched futilely as one of her frigates split apart after repeated blows from an Ascomanni cruiser's heavy mass drivers. Her forces were now interspersed with their original opponents, but they hadn't had time to move into a more appropriate formation for a fleet engagement, and the situation was growing desperate.

A wireframe display of her ships hung in the air before her, showing each vessel and the damage they were sustaining. Red was slowly creeping across the outlines of her heaviest combatants, while her screens did their best to stay in one piece.

This type of slugfest would inevitably result in heavy casualties for her forces. She had to come up with something, *anything*, that might give her people the edge.

She stared back out of the bridge's viewport, located the source of the frigate's destruction. Floating just off the port bow was one of the Ascomanni cruisers, mostly undamaged and spraying volley after volley toward her forces.

She checked the three-dimensional map of the battlespace, and quickly made a decision: "Navigation, I want us on the starboard side of that Asco cruiser immediately! Comms, order the *Angua Coch* to run parallel on the opposite side."

"Aye, ma'am!"

"Order transmitted, Captain!"

The *Hydra* surged under Adrienne's feet as the battlecruiser's artificial gravity adjusted to the change in velocity. Her ship turned diagonal to its original heading and accelerated past the debris of the ruined Umbrian frigate. One of her heavy cruisers began to change course as well, tacking to the left and speeding up to comply with her order.

"Captain, most of the Third Fleet just dropped in behind us!" her sensors operator called out.

Adrienne returned to her map and zoomed out. Fifty Umbrian warships now surrounded the Ascomanni force behind her, but there were no reinforcements for her flotilla.

Despair welled up within the *Hydra*'s master.

Adrienne bit her lip involuntarily before realizing she was showing her own anxiety. Silence reigned on the battlecruiser's bridge, and the atmosphere was thick and tense. They were on their own.

Anguish turned into determination and rage. "The Ascomanni will *not* get the better of us! Navigation, I want us alongside that Ascomanni cruiser, NOW!"

The captain turned back to the map and was satisfied to see that the *Coch* was keeping up. Together, they bracketed the Ascomanni warship. "Comms, order the *Angua Coch* to hold fire until all of her portside emplacements can come to bare on the target."

Their hapless foe did its best to try to maneuver out of its deadly predicament, but there was nowhere to go. The Ascomanni cruiser's batteries peppered the Umbrian warships, but Adrienne's ships' thick armor held.

As the tail of the Ascomanni warship came into sight, Adrienne bellowed, "Now! All batteries, fire now!"

A wave of destruction pulsed outward from both Umbrian warships, converging on their ill-fated enemy. Its hull buckled and convulsed as a second volley threw chunks of the ship into space. The vessel's centerline broke, and the ship began to separate horizontally at its waist.

"Collision alert!" the navigation officer screamed.

"Forty-five degrees down trim!" Adrienne barked. The *Hydra* accelerated down and away from the wreckage it had just created, but there was a flash behind them.

"Impact! Impact!"

"Show me, how bad?!"

"Not us," came the response. "The *Angua Coch* was struck by the Asco cruiser's bow. She's drifting."

Adrienne consulted the display showing her ships' damage. The aft end of the heavy cruiser was blood-red, and details underneath indicated she had lost power to her engines.

She turned to the map and saw that the *Hydra* was now on the lower left edge of the engagement zone. The ships nearest to her were now on surer footing, but two Ascomanni cruisers were tearing apart her formation's right flank.

As she watched, the wireframe outline of one of her light cruisers began to blink violently. A voice called out over the interfleet channel: "Hydra Actual, we've taken damage to our drive core; it's going to—"

There was another flash in the bridge's viewport, and the ship disappeared from her map, its model turning a solid red.

"We've lost the *Adriatica*, Captain. She's gone."

Adrienne slumped heavily in her chair. "Escape pods?"

"None, ma'am."

Twenty-two hundred souls lost in an instant. Now was not the time to grieve, however. "Navigation, point us directly at the closest remaining Asco cruiser."

"New contacts! Ten ships, above the engagement zone," a crewman called out, anguish clear in his voice.

"Wait, they're...they're friendlies! It's the *Vulcan* and her battlegroup!" the same voice said, audibly relieved.

"Get me a feed!"

"Channel 2, ma'am, coming from the *Euxinus*."

Adrienne switched feeds and gasped as the battleships *Vulcan* and *Pietas* dove vertically through the engagement zone. Their hulls flashed with hundreds of small explosions, but none seemed to cause anything more than trivial damage.

The same could not be said of the battleships' return fire. Together, their main batteries wrought devastation on those Ascomanni ships unfortunate enough to be caught in their sights.

Adrienne watched with a mixture of satisfaction and horror as internal explosions peeled back huge chunks of an enemy cruiser's bow. The horrific visage burned as the ship's precious atmosphere emptied into space.

An enemy destroyer's engines exploded, throwing debris in all directions and leaving the rest of the ship to tumble violently through space. Another rolled lazily on its horizontal axis, no longer firing or maneuvering, burning from a dozen holes in its hull.

By the time the new arrivals had finished their first pass through the combat zone, only three Ascomanni ships remained functional. They were quickly overwhelmed by Battlegroup Vulcan and Captain Tarpeia's remaining ships.

Adrienne exhaled deeply as the last Ascomanni ship fell silent, unaware that she had been holding her breath since the *Vulcan* had arrived.

Her sailors cheered their success, but their enthusiasm was tempered by their own losses.

"All right, good work, everyone. We made it through a difficult situation, but there is still more work to do. I need a detailed damage report from each ship. I also want two destroyers to guard the *Angua Coch* while they make repairs. Everyone else should move into the shipyard proper."

Acknowledgments echoed around the bridge, and for the first time since entering the system, Adrienne allowed herself the briefest of moments to relax.

URN *Decima*, Fifteen Upsilon A, Frontier Space

The *Decima*'s battlegroup finally closed the distance on the Ascomanni reserve fleet, and the space between opposing warships exploded into a sea of energy and light. Fabian's pulse quickened as the first salvo of return fire leapt from the enemy fleet, eager to snuff out the lives of the men and women he commanded.

Indecision had plagued the enemy commander in the minutes after the Third Fleet had descended on the Ascomanni. Caught in between two equally powerful Umbrian forces, the Ascomanni had chosen to take Fabian and his carrier group head-on.

This left the Ascomanni exposed from behind, and the *Neptune* and her complement would reach the engagement zone in a few short minutes. Once that happened, the battle would essentially be over. The only question remaining would be how many ships Fabian would lose before subduing his foe.

"Flight Control, cut the fighters loose. Primary target is the Ascomanni battleship."

"Acknowledged, Archus."

Fabian folded his hands behind his back as his pilots raced toward the enemy, their engines twinkling like a sea of stars.

Flight Group Decima, Fifteen Upsilon A, Frontier Space

"Understood, Decima Actual," Alari Tulla Cornelia said before switching frequencies to address her pilots. "All right everyone, the *Decima* just gave us the green light. Come about to heading three three oh dash nine. We're to concentrate our fire on the enemy battleship. It'll be a tough nut to crack, so work together and don't waste your torpedoes. Wing commanders, call out when you're in position."

The nine squadrons of Natrix fighter bombers she led formed up and headed straight toward the heart of the giant Ascomanni fleet waiting before them. One hundred and thirty-five ships prepared to dive into the teeth of the enemy.

"Aurum Wing in position, ma'am."

"Stibium Wing is ready to mix it up, Alari Cornelia."

"Understood." She consulted her sensors and confirmed that the wing she personally directed in battle had formed up behind her. "Ferrum Wing is in position. The leading squadrons will make contact with the enemy in thirty seconds. Loosen up and watch out for enemy point defenses."

In the last fleeting seconds before Tulla reached the outskirts of the enemy formation, she marveled at the horrifying beauty around her. Flashes of light crisscrossed between fleets, causing fantastic explosions to blossom wherever they found their target.

She watched as an Ascomanni cruiser succumbed to the Umbrians' concentrated fire, explosions rippling through the vessel almost too quickly for the eye to catch, knowing that thousands of lives had just been extinguished.

Tulla felt a momentary pang of regret at the loss of life. She thought about all the Asco sailors who had just perished in that fiery charnel house, and she couldn't help but think that most of them weren't so different from her pilots, or herself. The Asco were following orders, and probably just hoping that they'd see their homes and loved ones again.

Her eyes lingered on the ruined vessel for a moment longer. The Ascomanni had started this war; *they* were the cause of all this suffering and death.

The first flash of flak brought her thoughts back to the matter at hand. Tulla and her pilots had adapted well to space operations, but the lack of noise was still strange for her.

Instead of breaking her squadrons up piecemeal to fill holes in the Third Fleet's carrier squadrons, they had completely replaced the *Decima*'s flight group. In turn, the surviving carrier pilots had been reassigned to the *Echion* to help replace those lost at Aetnaeus.

This would be their first real test in space.

No sooner than she finished the thought, one of her squadron commanders called out: "This is Ferrum Two One, I just lost Two Three and Two Five."

"Stay focused Two One," she replied through gritted teeth.

Her heads-up display shaded certain areas of space a light red based on the enemy warships' positions and known armaments. A slender path existed through the outer screen and deeper into the middle of the Ascomanni fleet.

She quickly pushed the data to her wings and called out, "I've got an opening. Everyone, form up and prepare for a thunder run. Ferrum will take lead. Keep it moving and pop countermeasures as needed, you know the drill!"

The Umbrian fighters constricted into a tight line, juking and jinking to avoid presenting too easy a target. An Ascomanni destroyer flashed by on her portside, and Tulla's display began to beep, indicating that her craft was actively being tracked by enemy targeting arrays.

"Warning, Warning: Missile lock detected," her shipboard AI declared in a deadpan, mechanical voice.

"Activate chaff dispensers!" she demanded in response.

There was a muffled *whumff* as her fighter shot metallic debris in all directions. The cloud of shimmering particles threw off an incoming missile just enough, and it exploded behind her, rocking her craft but otherwise leaving it undamaged.

Others were less lucky.

There was a flash as a missile merged with one of her pilots' ships and its spaceframe disintegrated under the force of the explosion.

Another successfully distracted a missile with chaff, but the detonation was too close, knocking its engines out of alignment. She watched helplessly as it corkscrewed into an enemy frigate.

But just like that, they were through the Ascomanni screen, and Tulla had the briefest of moments to reorganize her force in the narrow space between the Ascomanni capital ships and their escorts.

She checked her scanners and was relieved to find that so far, they had only lost eight ships to enemy fire, with Ferrum bearing the brunt of the losses.

"Pay attention everyone. Here's how we are going to play this. Aurum wing will target the ship's engines. If we can take away its maneuverability, it'll be easier for our capital ships to deal with. Ferrum and Stibium will concentrate on the portside power cores. They're located just past midship, but are heavily armored. Anything less than both wings' concentrated fire will not get through that plating."

"Stibium has your back, Ferrum Lead."

"Aurum will clip this behemoth's wings, Alari!"

Aurum split off, taking a long arching path which would put them in position to assault the vessel's rear. The rest of her command executed a similar maneuver, taking her squadrons away from the battleship's bow and the heavy defensive batteries located there.

Together, the six squadrons of Ferrum and Stibium streaked in toward their target.

"Switch to torpedoes," Tulla called out as they drew near. Already the titanic vessel filled up their field of vision. A steady beeping grew in intensity as they edged ever closer, indicating that her fire control computer had secured a firing solution for the critical components' estimated location.

Tulla brought them closer still, so close that the enemy ship's electromagnetic counter measures would be unable to throw off their weapons.

The beeping turned into a solid tone, indicating that they were nearing their torpedoes' minimum required distance, and Tulla cried out, "Let loose!"

A pair of torpedoes sped away from the underside of her fighter. They were soon joined by over a hundred more. The Umbrian fighters looped away as a series of explosions rippled across the battleship's waist.

As the firestorm around the point of impact dissipated, a disappointed voice called out, "No penetration, Ferrum Lead."

"Form up for another run. Hopefully Aurum is having better luck."

"Not yet, ma'am, but we'll keep hammering away."

Tulla took a moment to check her ship's status. She still had half a tank of fuel and four torpedoes left. At her current fuel consumption rate, she had another ten minutes of flight time before she'd need to head back to the *Decima*.

"Keep an eye on your fuel usage, squadron leaders. It's a long walk back to the *Decima*."

Her fighters formed up again and bore down on the same spot they had just attacked. Again, the beeping coming from her heads-up display grew more consistent, and she depressed the trigger on her control yoke.

She turned away once more, but rolled and sharpened her angle of departure so she could see the result of their second run.

This time, the explosions threw chunks of the battleship's hull into space, and the lights on the portside of the ship flickered before remaining on.

"So close!" she muttered to herself. "We need to put one more volley on target, team. Aurum Leader, what's your status?"

"We've crippled the ship's engines, ma'am, but repeated strafing runs are leaving us dangerously close to minimum fuel."

"Ferrum Lead, we've got an Asco frigate bearing down on us," Ferrum Two One called out in an excited voice. "Looks like we finally pissed them off enough to respond!"

"Pull up grid references," Tulla said to her onboard computer. Her HUD transformed to show her current position and the nearest enemy vessels. An Ascomanni frigate was heading back from the perimeter of the fleet, and its intention was unmistakable.

"Aurum Lead," she called back over the comm. "Get your wing back to the *Decima*. I want you to expend any unused torpedoes on that frigate on your way out. Give them something to think about before it tangles with the rest of the group."

"Copy, Alari."

"Everyone else, we've got one last pass to make on the battleship. Let's show them how much pain we can cause."

The Umbrian fighters formed up again and dove on their wounded enemy.

"We've got incoming missiles, Ferrum," one of her squadron leaders called out.

"Stay on target!" Tulla demanded.

For the final time, she got a solid lock and fired the last of her torpedoes. She corkscrewed away and turned perpendicular to their approach vector, with the battleship filling up the space above her.

Another series of explosions rattled the enemy capital ship. The battleship's portside weapons emplacements stopped firing, and the running lights on that side of the ship disappeared and stayed off.

They had done it! The battleship was now incapacitated on one side and incapable of maneuvering.

Other fighters continued to fire their final volley, but new contrails flashed into her formation. The enemy frigate had finally closed the gap, and her force was now in grave danger.

There was a flash and an anxious voice cried out over the comms: "This is Ferrum Three One Four, I'm hit!" Tulla saw one of her fighters start to come apart, its pilot desperately trying to pull away from the Ascomanni battleship.

"I'VE LOST VENTRAL THRUSTERS," the pilot screamed. "I'M—"

The voice disappeared in a burst of static.

"All wings, split up and work your way back to the *Decima*, we've done our job here," Tulla barked into her intercom.

As she watched, her pilots scattered into their individual flight groups.

In sets of three they began working their way back toward the safety of the Umbrian fleet carrier, swooping past the Ascomanni frigate which had tried in vain to stop their assault.

The comm channel exploded with voices as they worked their way back to base:

"Stibium Two Four, you're trailing debris from your portside engine cowling."

"Ferrum One One Oh and One One Deuce, follow me, I've found a gap in the perimeter."

"Ferrum Three One, I've lost sight of Three Seven. I think she's gone!"

Tulla did her best to concentrate on navigating the Ascomanni defenses, and a few minutes later she and her remaining pilots emerged from the Ascomanni fleet.

"Decima Actual," she said, "the flight group is declaring a fuel emergency. Returning craft need to be prioritized accordingly."

"Understood, Ferrum Lead, emergency arrester pods will be available as needed."

"You heard, squadron leaders. Check with your pilots and sort them into the correct approach if they are running dry."

Tulla checked her own fuel gage. She had enough to make it back, but just barely. As she approached, an automated signal directed her fighter to the carrier's portside. She was angled toward one of the lower hangar doors, and maneuvering jets in the nose of her craft fired, dramatically reducing her velocity and consumed her remaining fuel.

She sailed gently through the hangar's entrance, wide enough to fit four Natrix fighter bombers side by side comfortably. As her ship was captured by the carrier's artificial gravity, it dropped half a meter to the flight deck below.

Before her fighter had even stopped rolling, a crew member drove over in a small tractor, attached a tow bar, and dragged her out of the lane. A moment later her craft came to a rest in its assigned berth, and she popped her canopy release.

Her crew chief ran over with a big grin. "Way to go, Alari! Rumor has it you all knocked out that Asco battleship singlehandedly!"

"We did well, Chief," Tulla replied with a tired smile. She stood in the cockpit and took off her helmet, a chill running down her back as the frigid air of the hangar bay blew through her messy, sweat-drenched hair.

She turned and watched as another fighter, heavily scarred from battle, landed in the space her ship had just occupied. This one was weighed down by a pair of thruster pods, attached to either wing near the fuselage, designed to slow ships that lacked enough fuel for landing.

As it dropped onto the deck, its portside landing gear gave way, and the ship crumpled to the deck, skidding sideways with its remaining kinetic energy.

Her crew chief jumped down and rushed toward the scene, shouting in his wrist comm. "Hangar Two-B lanes one and two are obstructed, divert all fighters on approach to lanes three and four!"

Another fighter soared into the hangar, in the third lane, and Tulla held her breath as one of the ground crew attempted to steer it around the disabled fighter.

If they couldn't get the wreck moved soon, an accident would be inevitable.

They were lucky though. Her crew chief quickly moved a magnetic service winch into position and it latched on to the fighter's crumpled wingtip and pulled it high enough for the remaining landing gear to roll. The tug and the fighter moved out of the approach lanes.

Confident that the situation was no longer dangerous for her pilots, Tulla hopped out of her fighter and down the staircase that had been rolled up to her craft. She ducked into a ready room on the near wall of the hangar, where several of her pilots already waited, and activated an intercom linking her to the Flight Controller on the bridge.

"This is Alari Cornelia. My strike group should be back onboard in the next five minutes and rearmed and refueled within thirty. What are our orders?"

"Stand down, Alari, the *Neptune* has engaged the enemy and the Ascomanni are folding quickly."

"Understood." She flipped the link off and shared the message with her squadron leaders. It was time to debrief and analyze the day's action.

URN *Decima*, Fifteen Upsilon A, Frontier Space

Fabian watched with satisfaction as the Ascomanni fleet collapsed into a disorganized mob. Half of the fleet attempted to turn toward the *Neptune*'s battlegroup, while the rest stayed facing his fleet.

"Order the battlegroups to concentrate on the ships facing *away* from them," Fabian called out.

"Sir?" his XO asked.

"The engines represent a weak point in the enemy's armor. We'll rake them from stern to stem."

"Yes, sir!"

Fabian stood in the midst of the managed chaos of the *Decima*'s bridge, feeling none of the anxiety that he experienced in earlier battles.

He realized Marcellus had been right. No other Archus in the Umbrian Navy had achieved what he'd been able to do, both in the number of ships he'd destroyed and the losses he'd been able to avoid.

Moreover, Marcellus had given him the freedom to throw the rulebook out the airlock. In turn, he had encouraged his subordinate commanders to look at tactical problems creatively, and that newfound flexibility was really starting to pay dividends for the Third Fleet.

He watched with satisfaction as the last Ascomanni cruiser disappeared from view in a brilliant mini nova. For all intents and purposes, the battle in space was over.

"Procurator," Fabian called to his XO, "give Legate Calvinus the green light. All Third Fleet ships capable of moving under their own power are to form a perimeter around the shipyard proper. Begin search-and-rescue operations and get the rest of the fleet's fighters back aboard to refuel and rearm."

"Understood, sir. The *Neptune*'s captain has reported that the Asco battleship has been completely disabled. She indicated it might be dangerous to destroy with the fleet transiting the battle zone and requested permission to send a party to plant charges so it can be scuttled safely."

Fabian paused for a moment before a thought struck him like a bolt of lightning. "Belay that, I've got a better idea."

URN *Celeres*, Outskirts of Fifteen Upsilon A, Frontier Space

"All hands," a voice blared over the *Celeres*'s intercom, "this is Captain Pacilius. The Archus indicates that the Ascomanni fleet has been defeated and we are clear to enter the system. The jump will commence in thirty seconds."

Aemilia's pulse quickened. Her tension manifested as a throbbing ache in her neck and shoulders. She grabbed the edge of the table before her and widened her stance. A moment later, there was a sudden acceleration, followed immediately by an equally forceful deceleration.

The CIC's display updated to show their position. As advertised, the rest of the Third Fleet had entered the shipyard. The *Celeres*, *Spatha*, and the assault transport *Aegis Fire* had appeared in between the shipyard proper and Icarus's metal rich core.

The image shifted again as *Aegis Fire* entered the neutered giant's weakened atmosphere. It immediately released its two giant blockhouses, which plummeted toward the planet's surface before disappearing into the thick, noxious fog that surrounded its exposed metallic core. The display changed yet again, showing the giant pods' altitude and displaying feeds from a series of probes which followed them down.

As the structures neared the surface, their thrusters engaged, and they gently landed on Icarus's lustrous exterior. Their bay doors retracted, and armored fighting vehicles poured out onto Icarus's iridescent plains. Hundreds of tanks and APCs formed up and headed to the north, where the Ascomanni's primary mining facility was located.

"All right, Legio Ferratta is on the ground," Aemilia said to her subordinates. "Begin the assault on the shipyard."

The display floating before her separated into two equal halves, one showing the *Celeres* as a swarm of dropships erupted from her main hangar, while the other showed Icarus's northern hemisphere in real time, recorded from the carrier itself, with key details overlaid for ease of reference.

Her ground forces, marked by a staggered wedge of blue diamonds, headed straight toward the red circle representing the Ascomanni mining complex. The metallic dust kicked up by the legion's vehicles created shimmering striations in the haze, visible even from orbit. Within minutes, bright flashes began to illuminate the clouds near the planet's north pole.

"Hyperion Actual, this is Legio Ferratta," a gruff voice called over the battle net. "We've reached the outer perimeter. It's heavily fortified, but our armor has punched through and we are moving to clear the facility. We've deployed our scoots, and they are working their way into the mine itself."

"Good work, keep me informed as you progress."

"Will do. Ferratta out."

The red circle began to fade in color, first to a solid white, then the first hints of blue began to show through as real-time intelligence from the legion came in. The Ascomanni resistance within the mining complex was crumbling.

Satisfied that the situation on the ground was going according to plan, Aemilia switched focus to the fight in the shipyard. She nodded to the tribune who stood across from her, and the display expanded to encompass the spacious facility.

Her legion's ships had descended on the yard like locusts. Three cohorts of her most experienced soldiers, led by Tribune Mettius Articuleius, had been tasked with securing the facility's central command center, located in the middle of the extensive works. Their ships reached their intended target, and in moments, over fifteen hundred legionnaires stormed through the enemy facility.

"Legate, we are getting reports that our soldiers are encountering a new type of hostile Ascomanni in the facility."

"What do you mean?" Aemilia asked, her stomach churning at the thought of new complications.

"It's the Pasarga," Marcellus said. He had spent most of the battle seated out of the way, quietly observing her command section in action, but now he moved up to take a place next to her. "We've got some new enemies. They are as intelligent as we are, and as aggressive as the damn Ascomanni."

Aemilia nodded. "Send an update to all three legions. Inform them of the danger and tell them to proceed with care."

Ascomanni Command Center, Fifteen Upsilon A, Frontier Space

They were making good time, Tribune Mettius thought to himself. His forces had already cleared the station's lower reaches and were now working their way toward the station's command center—the nerve center of the system's entire infrastructure.

Suddenly, a lithe form dropped from the ceiling, landing in the midst of the quartet of his legionnaires who were running point. Without making a sound, it drove a blade through the knee of its first victim, taking the woman's leg clean off. As Mettius shouted an alarm, it fired a pistol into another's back, and its second target fell forward awkwardly, knocking one of the remaining Umbrians off his feet.

This mysterious new adversary jumped on the disoriented soldier, stabbing him repeatedly in the chest before the final surviving member of his vanguard dispatched it with a burst of plasma.

The whole incident had transpired in under a minute.

"WHAT THE HELL WAS THAT?!" the lone, uninjured survivor shrieked.

Mettius ignored him and rushed toward his wounded soldiers, while other members of their party took up positions to cover their downed comrades.

"Medic up front!" he screamed as he reached the spot where his dead and wounded legionnaires lay, nearly slipping on the blood that was pooling around their bodies.

Two of them were clearly gone, but the third, the one who had lost her leg, was still alive and had pushed herself up against the wall of the corridor. Her combat suit constricted around the wound to form a tourniquet, and she screamed in pain as it tightened, but blood continued to spurt out of the wound.

"You're all right, soldier, we're going to get you out of here," Mettius said as he knelt next to her. She pulled her helmet off as she began to hyperventilate. She stared back at him, a confused look on her pale face, the veins in her forehead and neck protruded as she gasped for air.

"MEDIC!" Mettius screamed again. His soldier's eyes began to flutter, and she reached weakly out and rested a bloody hand on his forearm. He tapped her on the check and said, "Hey! Stay with me! Your suit's meds should be kicking in at any moment. You just have to hold on."

There was a commotion behind him, and a voice frantically called out: "Make a hole!"

The soldier's hand slowly slipped from Mettius's arm and fell limply to her side. Mettius pulled his hand away as a sharp electrical discharge ran through the legionnaire's suit.

"Her heart's failing," he screamed. "Where's that damn medic?!"

The medic finally squeezed in next to him, and Mettius moved to give the man space to work. He produced a syringe from his pack and quickly stabbed it into the wounded soldier's chest. There was no reaction.

He detached a pair of pads from a kit attached to his forearm and slapped them onto her armor. He frantically snapped in the leads and triggered the defibrillator. Still no response. He charged the defibrillator again, but the second jolt failed to revive her.

The medic turned to Mettius and shook his head. She was gone.

"Damnit!" the Tribune swore. He slammed a closed fist into the corridor's metal walls, a deep *thunk* reverberating down the hallway.

He let out a deep breath and tried to focus on the task at hand. He had failed these soldiers, but there were still others counting on him to get them through this shitstorm alive.

"Sir?" one of his legionnaires called out. The Tribune nodded, and she continued, "Command just called in. Apparently, we should expect more of these things. They say they are cleverer than the Ascomanni and all the more dangerous for it."

"Pass the word along," he said softly. "We've got another hundred meters to go until we reach our objective. Everyone, keep your eyes open and check your godsdamn corners! We've got a new threat to watch out for."

Mettius and his soldiers set off again, slowly and deliberately proceeding into the unknown.

URN *Celeres*, Ascomanni Shipyard, Fifteen Upsilon A, Frontier Space

The battle lasted for another four hours, but in the end the Umbrians emerged victorious. As hostilities came to a close, Aemilia made arrangements to reorganize her forces. The colony ship *Alba Longa* had arrived, and Magistrate Flavia and her workers had already started piecing the facility back together.

Marcellus was very complimentary of her performance, but quickly departed after the battle had concluded.

It was hard-won praise, however.

Casualties had topped four thousand, with dead and wounded in almost equal measure. The worst had come when an entire cohort had been vaporized when the Asco sabotaged the station it had been assigned to seize.

Their new enemy — the Pasarga, Marcellus had called them — had already proven to be a deadly foe.

"Legate Calvinus, we are getting a message from the planet's surface."

Aemilia looked up and nodded at her second in command. The CIC's intercom crackled to life, and Legate Numidius's voice, raspier than normal, began to speak softly: "Hyperion Actual, we've...we've found prisoners in the mines."

"I didn't know the scoots were programmed to take prisoners, Numidius."

"No, ma'am, not Ascomanni prisoners. Umbrian ones."

"Say again?!" Aemilia asked in disbelief.

"We've found Umbrian prisoners. A mix of civilians and POWs. The Ascomanni were using them as slave labor in the mines."

"How many, Legate?"

"Several thousand, ma'am..." Numidius's voice broke. "We don't have an exact headcount. There were significantly more to start..."

The color drained from Aemilia's face as her mind raced. She had so many unanswered questions, but she did her best to tamp down her need to know and forced her full attention back to the task at hand.

"I want a full report in five minutes. Medical status, living conditions, access to food and water, *everything*! Do I make myself clear?"

"Yes, ma'am."

She turned to her subordinates. "Send a message to the Archus, have someone chase down the Praetor. I need to speak with them immediately."

URN Clementia, Ascomanni Shipyard, Fifteen Upsilon A, Frontier Space

Marcellus found the leaders of his praetorians gathered around Antonia's bed. Aria sat closest, mopping her friend's sweat-drenched brow with a damp cloth. Invictus paced next to her bed, while Vetus and Sextus sat anxiously in a pair of chairs along the wall.

As the Praetor approached, Vetus started to get to his feet, but Sextus grabbed him by the shoulder and he remained seated. Marcellus gave them a thin smile, and the two nodded in return.

Invictus stopped pacing, and Marcellus laid a hand on his shoulder.

"How's she doing?" he asked softly.

Invictus turned and looked at his wounded subordinate. Antonia was hooked up to half a dozen machines, the soft sounds of pumps and a respirator filling the room with gentle *whirring* noises.

"It's bad, Marcellus. She went into cardiac arrest on the ride over from the *Spatha*. If we would've been a few minutes later in arriving..." Invictus's voice trailed off as he thought about how close Antonia had come to death.

"The doctors give her a fifty-fifty chance, sir," Sextus offered. "She's always been a stubborn pain in the ass though, figure her odds are better than that for sure."

Marcellus smiled weakly. "You've got that right. What happened, Vic?"

"We were ambushed on our way out of the refinery. Multiple fractures from falling debris. She got shot in the side. She was fortunate, mostly just tissue damage, but it lacerated one of her kidneys. For good measure, a broken rib punctured her lung. We didn't know that until we got her back aboard the *Spatha* and her lung collapsed." Invictus shook his head.

Marcellus walked forward and sat on the edge of the bed. He took Antonia's hand and was shocked by how cold and clammy it was. "Keep fighting, Tonia. Umbria needs you. *We* need you."

He thought he saw Antonia's eyes flutter briefly, but his mind might've just been playing tricks on him. Or maybe he just wanted to believe it, he chided himself.

"I appreciate you all being here," the Praetor said, turning to address his subordinates, "and I know Tonia would too, but I can't spare all of you right now. Please take shifts staying with her, so you can take turns getting some rest. That goes for you too, Aria." Marcellus said this last directive sternly.

One by one, the praetorians nodded. He looked at Aria, and eventually she gave in too, bobbing her head nearly imperceptibly.

Just then, an orderly rushed into the room. "Praetor, forgive my intrusion, but a matter of grave importance requires your immediate attention. The Captain is waiting for you on the bridge."

Marcellus turned to look at Invictus, and his friend clearly understood his unspoken question.

"I'm with you, sir," Invictus said. "As for the rest of you, you heard the Praetor's orders. Work it out amongst yourselves."

His primes nodded and Invictus turned back to his superior. "Let's go find out what broke in the thirty minutes you were gone."

Ascomanni Mining Complex, Icarus; Fifteen Upsilon A, Frontier Space

The smell was overpowering, somehow seeping through the airtight mask Marcellus wore in the dank confines of the Ascomanni mining facility. He stood with Invictus, Aemilia, Fabian, and the *Clementia*'s chief medical officer at the edge of a deep pit, horrified by the sight in front of him.

The emaciated and terror-crazed prisoners his soldiers liberated had eventually led them here, where the gruesome discovery, too dreadful for words, had been found. Down below, tens of thousands of bodies, maybe even more, had been unceremoniously dumped and left to rot.

"The surviving prisoners haven't been here for longer than three weeks, Praetor," the doctor said. "The Ascomanni worked them past the breaking point, literally to death, then threw them into the holes they had excavated. There are at least two other pits just like this one."

Fabian turned away from the group and retched.

"How...? Why...?" Invictus sputtered, lost for words.

Marcellus didn't hear him; a white-hot rage burned in his gut.

He had despised the Ascomanni. However, he had always been able to relate to them, at least intellectually, as members of the same discipline, the ageless profession of war. Now, though, he was consumed by a newfound hatred for his enemy.

"How many survived, Doctor?"

"We've counted approximately eleven thousand. That number will go down, Praetor," she said, her voice weakening. "Many were so weak that they will never recover. All we can do is try our best to make them comfortable."

"Whatever you have to do, do it. Whatever you need, you get. If anyone even *hints* at giving you a hard time, you point them at me, and I'll sort them out."

The doctor nodded and walked back toward the entrance of the large chamber.

After a few minutes, Aemilia spoke up, her voice sharp and brittle. "This is murder on an industrial scale. Our dead will haunt this place forever. They demand justice!"

"Document everything and begin transferring the survivors to the hospital ship. After we've evacuated the prisoners, raze this godsdamn place to the ground," Marcellus said through gritted teeth.

"Marcellus…are we going to scuttle the shipyard?" Invictus asked quietly.

"No, Vic. We will tear this world apart, turning its resources into weapons to use against these people's butchers. But this spot… This spot will serve as a solemn remembrance to the evil we fight, as long as there are Umbrians with the strength and will to carry on."

Chapter 11

The Citadel, Safe Haven; System Classified, Frontier Space

A week later, Marcellus stood in the middle of the Citadel's intelligence annex. All around him, dozens of analysts worked feverishly at their desks, pouring through the trove of information they had recovered from the raids carried out the previous week.

A large board displayed a star chart, showing their findings so far: a throng of newly discovered Ascomanni positions ballooned out from the Frontier, wrapping around the edges of Umbrian space.

The size and scope of their discoveries had been jaw dropping. It would take months to fully sort through all of the data, but even in these early stages, its value was immeasurable.

The discovery of mass graves on Icarus had had a profound effect on the Umbrian population as well. Lines at recruitment centers wrapped around city blocks, and the Republic's elite had begun the process of transitioning the economy for total mobilization.

Marcellus shook his head ruefully. He had been calling for similar steps since Varese. How many lives had to be lost before people could no longer deceive themselves? Maybe this was just the way it always went, he thought angrily.

Theodorus finally emerged from his office, moving at something between a sprint and a jog.

"Sorry for keeping you waiting, Praetor, I was running our first pass at a predictive model and it took a little longer than expected. As you can see, we are working overtime to sort through the data. The Directors have even allocated all of the CID's available resources to assisting us."

"Wow, that's big, Theodorus! I'm glad to see this is getting the attention it deserves. Why did you call me down here though?"

"Right, right, the model!" the spy chief said anxiously. "Please, come with me."

Together the pair walked into Theodorus's cramped office. Datapads were scattered about his desk, along with the half-eaten remnants of what looked like the morning's breakfast. The pair sat down and Theodorus pulled up the same image Marcellus had just seen in the annex.

He gestured to the positions scattered about the map and said, "Sir, I believe we've located almost every single Ascomanni position in and around the Frontier. We've got everything: resource extraction, industrial base, command and control. It's all here. Everything they need to wage war against us."

"It's more than I could have hoped for, Theodorus. This is fantastic news."

"Yes, Praetor, but there's more to the story. Do you remember the two distant systems we sent trawlers to investigate after the fall of Aetnaeus?"

"Yeah. They aren't due for another week or so still, right?"

"Right, but that's not why I bring it up. Those two systems are beyond the edges of the infrastructure we are seeing. Assuming that the Ascomanni didn't just expand in one direction, we've developed a model to try and determine the scope of their empire, using what we know now about their industrial base and comparing that to our own rate of expansion as a guide."

The display changed, zooming out to show their quadrant of the galaxy. A small blue circle grew from near the tip of one of the galaxy's outer spiral arms, while another, larger circle grew further down the arm, closer to the galactic core.

It was easily three times the size of Republic space.

"Those two systems are in the exact center of our model." A wild look stole over Theodorus's face. "This is what we are up against, Praetor. This explains why they don't care enough to defend the shipyard at Fifteen Upsilon A in force. We haven't even dented them, Marcellus! They are coming, and there is nothing we can do to stop them!"

"Get ahold of yourself!" Marcellus demanded, standing abruptly. He slammed the office door shut, and Theodorus's eyes grew wide. "Before, there was no hope. We flailed blindly at an enemy we barely understood. Now, we face that same enemy, but with the knowledge of his strengths and weaknesses. That gives us a dramatic advantage, one we didn't have a week ago!"

"But, Marcellus, it's hopeless! What chance do we have against such overwhelming odds?"

"A better chance than those people we found on Icarus did!" Marcellus snarled. "The Ascomanni will enslave and slaughter us. We either find a way to win, or we all die. I for one will keep fighting. If you can't, or won't, get the hell off my station!"

Theodorus gulped as the color drained from his face. "You're...you're right, sir. I'm sorry for my outburst."

"Don't let it happen again," Marcellus replied icily. He gestured back toward the door and said, "Those people out there are depending on you to keep it together."

The station chief nodded, his brow glistening with sweat.

"Next, you will provide me with an executive-level summary of your findings to date. I want all of it, plus any analysis your agents have been able to put together so far. I expect it first thing tomorrow morning. Make it happen. I will not accept excuses, Theodorus!"

"Yes, sir!"

"Good," Marcellus growled. He turned and stalked out of Theodorus's office, through the annex, and worked his way to the station's central elevator shaft.

"Valerian?" He called into his commlink.

"Yes, sir?"

"Get a ship ready. We are going to see Praetor Artorius."

Ghiave-Fouteena, Liguria; Frontier Space

After discovering faster-than-light travel, Umbria rapidly expanded into the stars. Liguria was one of the last systems to be explored as part of the Republic's first wave of colonization. Its sole habitable planet, Liguria Three, was covered by a shallow global sea, which made widescale settlement difficult. As such, it was considered a backwater, not even meriting a true name for several decades after its discovery.

That would all change once new habitable worlds were discovered in the Frontier.

Almost overnight, Liguria Three became a boomtown. Rival corporations constructed dueling capitals, Ghiave and Fouteena, on opposite sides of the world. A seemingly endless flow of resources and adventure-seekers poured onto the planet, which exacerbated the conflict between the planet's two main mega corps.

Each launched a separate and lengthy campaign to have the Senate rename the planet after their city. As each side's lobbying efforts dragged on, the rivalry started to cause gridlock and disruptions to the planet's development. Finally, its people, frustrated by the petty jealousies of the corporations, demanded a resolution to the issue.

A Senate select committee was so exasperated by the claimants' constant bickering that they took the unusual step of combining the proposed names, ending the dispute but leaving neither party happy.

Meanwhile, the disruptions caused by this needless distraction ensured that the planet's development couldn't keep up with the pace of the Republic's expansion, and soon Tratirne, the first of the newly settled border worlds, would supersede its role as gateway to the Frontier.

Both corporations would ultimately move off planet, but Ghiave-Fouteena's brief time in the spotlight proved to be enough. With solid infrastructure and a stable population, the planet re-invented itself. Aquaculture took off, with small, floating farming communities tending to thousands of square kilometers of open ocean.

These tracts would be demarcated by extensive networks of lines, posts, and buoys on which complex marine plant life was grown. Fish and crustaceans were then introduced amongst these underwater forests, with each group benefiting from the presence of the others.

As Marcellus's ship entered its atmosphere, these aquatic farms created a pattern of emerald green, offset against the warm turquoise of the planet's oceans. They reminded him of scales, radiating out in all directions from the handful of cities dotting its surface.

The ship approached Ghiave, a striking city sitting above the sea on large stilts. Tall arcologies provided the metropolis's residents with both housing and urban greenspaces, giving them a much-needed sense of solid ground. Tube trams, similar to those on Umbria itself, provided rapid access throughout the city, while turbines captured the sea's tidal energy to create power.

Their destination was a medium-sized tower on the outskirts of the city. The ship set down, and Marcellus and Valerian disembarked. They were immediately swamped by the muggy, humid atmosphere of the planet as they descended the ramp to the landing pad below.

Neither was surprised to find Praetor Artorius waiting for them.

The older woman's face might as well have been set in stone, but Marcellus sensed his mentor was curious and bemused by their unexpected visit.

"Marcellus, I assume there is a reason you came all the way to Ghiave-Fouteena instead of just sending me a message?" she said by way of greeting.

"Yes, ma'am, there is. And it would be best discussed in a more private setting."

She cocked an eyebrow at Marcellus, but gestured toward the doors leading into the interior of the arcology. Marcellus nodded, and the trio set off. Both visitors were relieved as they entered the climate-conditioned confines of the tower.

They passed through several sparsely populated hallways, and Valerian took note.

"Praetor, this place feels awfully empty for the headquarters of your army group. Where is the rest of your staff?"

"Exercises, wrapping up to the east of here. My command is still familiarizing themselves with the unique terrain of this world, should we end up having to fight the Ascomanni out on its seas. Plus, while the Fifth is engaged at Tratirne, I've been temporarily assigned the Fourth Fleet, and they aren't due to arrive until later today."

"It's not like you to miss a good sand table exercise," Marcellus responded. "Is everything OK?"

"Yes, yes... Don't dote on me, Aurelius. I'm just starting to feel my age, is all. The humidity is brutal on my joints. There comes a time when you have to accept that you can't keep up with the boys and girls anymore..." She paused and cast a sideways look at Marcellus. "Of course, you won't have that problem for a while I imagine."

"Well, Lucia, if the Ascomanni have their way," Marcellus chuckled softly, "I won't have to worry about it at all."

They rounded a final corner and came to Praetor Artorius's office. As they walked through the door, they passed between a pair of statues, meticulously carved from shimmering blue-gray rock, at the entry of a short receiving room. The office then ballooned outward until meeting the arching wall of the tower's exterior.

Valerian stopped in his tracks, transfixed by the strange beauty of the statues.

"It's cordierite," their host called as she propped herself up on her desk.

"You must not be planning on going anywhere if you brought the twins down from your flagship," Marcellus said.

"Hell no, Marcellus! The Ascomanni have kicked us around long enough. You've put together a good plan, and every day we are getting closer to realizing it. If they show up here, we'll have a couple of surprises waiting for them."

"I'm heartened to hear that, Praetor. I've got some news of my own..."

Marcellus spent the next fifteen minutes outlining the activities of the last few days, and when he was done, his former commander was smiling broadly.

"Boy, do I know how to pick 'em!" she exclaimed. "What did the CID make of the intel you recovered?"

"There's months' worth of data to go over, but the short answer is *everything*."

Praetor Artorius was quiet, deep in thought. Marcellus and Valerian shared a knowing look: she often got this way when playing out multiple scenarios in her head.

"You're here to ask me for help," she said finally.

Marcellus nodded.

"Why not run this through the War Council?"

Valerian answered the question: "With their comms array destroyed, we have a very narrow window to take advantage of the Ascomanni's confusion. At a minimum, a request of this type would require at least six weeks' worth of deliberation and analysis, by which time the Ascomanni could have repositioned to better protect the assets we've identified."

"What is your proposed timetable?"

"Coordinated attacks across the Ascomanni positions in the Frontier, starting in two weeks," Marcellus responded. "Given their extensive holdings, we need at least four days of continuous strikes to hit all of our priority targets."

"And the goal?" Lucia asked incredulously.

"Totally obliterating the Ascomanni's military infrastructure in the Frontier and relieving the siege of Tratirne."

A handful of moments passed in silence. Finally, Praetor Artorius spoke: "You're asking me to take a pretty big risk here, Marcellus. We are already executing the plan *you* put together to keep the enemy at bay. Why this sudden change in tact? Why the urgency?"

"Theodorus, my CID section head, put together a model based on the data we recovered to try and determine the size of the Ascomanni's empire. It's speculative, but based on what we know, it's well within the realm of possibility. It's…"

Marcellus paused for a moment before continuing. "It's bad, real bad. Unless we do something dramatic, the outcome of this war is already decided."

Lucia studied her protégé's face, her mind turning behind golden-saffron eyes.

"You haven't led us astray yet, Aurelius. I believe the situation is as dire as you say," Praetor Artorius said. "Valerian, throw on a pot of posca. We've got a lot of work to do."

URN *Echion*, Somewhere in Frontier Space

The *Echion* floated in the vast space between stars, occupying a position roughly in the center of all of the targets they would soon be attacking. The entirety of the Third and Fourth fleets hung around it, with Praetor Artorius's flagship, the *Juno*, drifting off her port bow.

Marcellus, Fabian, Invictus, and Valerian stood on the *Echion*'s bridge, all but Marcellus busily attending to outstanding details for the coming assault. Instead, Marcellus stood near the bridge's forward viewports, gazing out over the combined force assembled for the operation.

Anxiety bubbled up in his gut as he thought about the scale of their plan, but he forced it down. Instead, he focused on the cool but ever-present rage that had been with him since the discovery of the death camps on Icarus.

The die would soon be cast, and once thrown, there was no going back. There was no time for weakness now.

"You know, if this goes poorly…" Invictus's voice said softly from his side.

Marcellus snapped his head around, unaware of his subordinate's presence. "How long have you been standing there?!" he barked in surprise.

"Not long, maybe just a minute or two. I wanted to see how long it'd take for you to notice, but…then I got bored," he said, grinning from ear to ear.

"Are our praetorians ready to go?"

"They know their assignments. Antonia is still working her way through therapy, so I'll be leading her cohort. Otherwise we're looking pretty good. As far as I can tell, the rest of the army group is set to go too."

"Good. We are going to need to be precise and organized to pull this off."

"Sir," Invictus began hesitantly, "are you sure this is the right play? I mean, yeah, we've got surprise on our side, but wouldn't a more methodical approach be better?"

"Every minute that goes by with the status quo intact is another minute we're losing ground to these monsters. There's no time for second guessing, Invictus. It's my call, and the decision's been made. I need your head in the game," Marcellus said sharply.

Invictus looked surprised, even slightly wounded, by the curtness of Marcellus's response. "As you say, sir. I'll go finish preparations with my command." He saluted and walked off the bridge.

Marcellus watched Invictus go, instantly regretting his snappy reply to the man's apprehension. Still, there was no time for second thoughts.

He turned and made his way up to the Archus's station.

"It must feel good to take the *Echion* back into battle, Fabian," Marcellus said as he approached. "How are things progressing?"

"Archus Duilius of the Fourth Fleet has been coordinating from the *Juno* and we're ready to go, Praetor. The first wave of attacks will launch shortly. Would you like to address the fleets?"

"Yes, put me through."

"Done, Praetor, you're live."

"Soldiers and sailors of Umbria, this is Praetor Gaius Aurelius Marcellus. Two and a half weeks ago, we uncovered the horrifying fate that awaits us all should the Ascomanni emerge victorious. We will be shown no mercy, no quarter. All of the joy and vibrancy of life will be stripped from us, leaving nothing but agony, servitude, and death."

Marcellus paused for a moment, letting the tension build as he considered his words with care.

"That will not be our fate! For today, we strike back at the monsters pressing on our borders! Today, we begin the most complex operation in the history of our Republic! Each of you will be taking part in a rigorous series of offensive actions. We will push you to the limits of your endurance, perhaps beyond.

"As you face the challenges of the next few days, take heart! For when we succeed, we will cripple our enemy's ability to threaten our friends and loved ones. When we succeed, we will lift the terrible threat that casts a shadow over our great people!

"My last words to you are this: Have faith in your training. Have faith in your experience. But most of all, have faith in one another! No matter what hardships you endure, know that you do not face them alone."

Marcellus raised his voice as he finished.

"Together we will triumph! For Umbria!"

Ascomanni Supply Depot, Twelve Theta C, Frontier Space

Tulla Cornelia and her wings dove toward the surface of the system's second planet—a cold, dead, rocky world pockmarked by thousands of impact craters. Flashes of energy began to shoot up from their target: a series of anti-aircraft artillery emplacements defended the collection of seventeen domed structures they had come to destroy.

The Ascomanni depot was supplying the forces assaulting Tratirne, and a transport sat next to the facility, taking on cargo. The facility was lightly guarded, and Tulla and her pilots were going to make the Asco pay for their negligence.

"Stibium wing, keep an eye out for enemy fighters and provide overwatch. Ferrum, attack across a southeastern axis. Aurum, you'll strike from the southwest. The planet's gravity is low, so make sure you are only using your delayed fuse charges and keep an eye out for debris."

"Ferrum Leader, this is Stibium One-One. We've got twenty Asco interceptors incoming from south-southwest, heading zero two-two."

"You're free to engage, Stibium Lead. Light them up!"

"With pleasure, Alari."

Tulla watched her scanners as Stibium wing broke off to engage the inbound Ascomanni fighters, then turned back to the task at hand.

They had closed to within fifteen kilometers of the base, and the two wings split wide to attack from different angles. They hugged the planet's surface, and the anti-aircraft batteries to the north of the installation fell silent as the facility's own buildings obscured their fields of fire.

The supply depot drew ever closer, and Tulla's fighter bounced around as the flak intensified. There was a bang behind her, bigger than the triple-A could have produced, and she knew that one of her squadrons had lost a pilot.

She forced herself to focus as her targeting computer began to tone. At the last possible moment, she jumped up to the necessary altitude for her bombs to work properly and triggered their release.

Staggered over thirty seconds, four warheads fell away from her ship. They burrowed their way through the exterior of the enemy structures but didn't explode immediately.

As she cleared the perimeter of the base, she turned and swung around for another pass. This time, she aimed straight for the landing pad, where the large, bulbous shape of the Ascomanni transport rose above the domes surrounding it.

She positioned herself carefully and passed along the ship's long axis, releasing her bombs all at once instead of sequentially. Again, there was no explosion, but Tulla knew she was running out of time. She pointed her craft skyward and hit her boosters.

"Ferrum, Aurum, clear the area immediately. We've got ten seconds. Stibium, what's your status?"

"We're clear, Ferrum Lead. All enemy fighters have been neutralized. We chased them home and leveled their base."

"Well done, Stib—" A series of jaw-jarring explosions cut her off. She turned around to see the destruction they had just wrought below.

Geysers of rock and detritus were thrown hundreds of meters into the air, and a brilliant mushroom cloud, the dying light of the Asco transport, rushed up to meet them.

The debris raced up behind them, merging with a pair of stragglers. There weren't any flashes, but reports of lost comrades echoed over the net.

Tulla swore to herself at the needless loss of life.

Her remaining pilots reached the planet's orbit uneventfully, and the *Decima* flashed in to recover them. Tulla checked her heads-up display.

They had completely destroyed their target, but at a cost. Seven of her pilots would not be returning to their berths.

She leaned back in her seat as she lined up her approach.

Ascomanni Manufacturing Facility, Sixteen Theta D, Frontier Space

Invictus put his foot on the shoulder of the corpse in front of him and rolled it over. The Ascomanni trooper was well and truly dead, with multiple penetrations in the armor covering its chest. Other members of Antonia's cohort stood around him, alert and wary as they waited for news from the demolition team they had been tasked with protecting.

They were situated on an elevation which overlooked the manufacturing complex they had come to destroy. Invictus turned his gaze at their primary objective.

Disappearing high into the soot-filled sky of this nameless volcanic world was a space elevator. It serviced the factories his troops had just cleared, providing a quick and efficient means to transport the weapons they produced off world.

He spotted the praetorian he had selected as his orderly for the mission and waved him over.

"Any word from the demo team?" he shouted over the howling wind that tore across the molten landscape.

"No, sir," the orderly yelled back. "There's been no update since they entered the elevator and we lost comms."

"Has the third section finished sweeping the dormitory complex?"

"Yes, sir, we've found more POWs, as expected."

"Their condition?"

"Not good. The cohort's medical team says some won't survive being moved."

"Well, we aren't leaving them behind, and they can't stay here. Call in the transport, it's time to get the hell out of here."

"Understood, Prefect."

Invictus turned his attention back to the elevator. "Leo Three-Two, I need you to take your section and figure out what's taking the engineers so long," he shouted into his commlink. "Everyone else, begin withdrawing to the extraction zone."

He set off down the hill toward the broad, low-relief crater that would serve as their landing zone with his orderly in tow. They carefully worked their way down the treacherous rise, and the wind intensified as a shape passed overhead.

"Looks like our ride is here!" his orderly yelled.

"Leo Three-Two, what's your status?" Invictus called out.

"The engineers just got back, sir. The charges have been planted and we are working our way to you now. ETA five minutes."

"Double time, Centurion. We've overstayed our welcome."

"Affirmative, Leo 6."

Invictus reached the waiting transport and found that the men and women of the other sections were already boarding the ship. He waited patiently as the third section helped the POWs aboard, their frail forms clinging to his praetorians for support.

By the time they were finished loading, the second section crested the low walls of the crater. They ran toward the transports in good order, and their centurion, out of breath, came to a stop in front of Invictus.

"All accounted for, sir," he heaved.

"Good work. We're all done here, get your soldiers aboard."

"Aye, sir."

Together, Invictus, his orderly, and the second section's commander followed the rest of his soldiers up the ramp and into the transport. Invictus worked his way through the cramped confines of the troop deployment bay and up onto the bridge, where he found the combat engineers' leader in heated discussion with the ship's captain.

"What's the problem?" Invictus asked the two women.

"I was just telling the Captain that we have to trigger the charges before reaching orbit," the senior engineer responded.

"And I was explaining that it dramatically increases the risks to my ship and its occupants," the second woman responded testily.

The ship lurched as it lifted off the ground, pointed skyward, and slowly began accelerating away from the planet's surface.

"Captain," Invictus said, attempting to affect his most convincing tone of voice. "We've specifically targeted the structure so that it buries the Ascomanni factory complex. The risks to your vessel should be minimal."

"I find it tremendously inappropriate that I was not properly informed of the risks this operation—"

"I appreciate your concern for the wellbeing of your ship, Captain," Invictus interrupted, finally losing his patience, "but my soldiers are on board this vessel as well, and I am comfortable with the risk. If you have a complaint about the manner in which this operation was conducted, I would encourage you to use the proper channels to submit that protest."

"But..." she stammered.

Invictus ignored her and turned to the engineer. "On your mark, Tribune. Let's hope your people know what they are doing."

The engineer cocked an eyebrow, but nodded dutifully, depressing the trigger on a round cylindrical detonator in her hand. Even within the confines of the ship's hull, a distant rumble could clearly be heard.

Invictus watched as the space elevator splintered approximately a quarter of the way up its length. The structure began to bow, wrapping across the volcanic terrain as it collapsed.

As the structure was pulled down into the planet's gravity well, its supports began to disintegrate. Pieces began to fall from orbit, glowing red-hot as they fell. The solitary remains of the elevator's foundation, standing like a headstone amongst the vast field of debris, marked the location of the ruined factory complex.

"See, Captain? Nothing to worry about," Invictus quipped.

She rolled her eyes and walked away.

URN *Echion*, Somewhere in Frontier Space

"So far, so good, Marcellus," Praetor Artorius said, her voice muffled slightly by feedback from the speaker.

"Agreed," Marcellus said. "We've succeeded in destroying all but two of the targets from the first two days, in exchange for minimal losses in manpower and materiel. However, Ascomanni resistance is stiffening."

Fabian nodded. "They seem to understand that something is going on, but there haven't been any signs of an organized response yet."

"Let's hope it stays that way," Lucia said seriously. "We're extended, and it would be easy for smaller elements of our forces to be overrun."

"I know, Lucia," Marcellus responded gently. "I know..."

URN *Hydra*, Seven Gamma A, Frontier Space

"All hands, brace for impact!" Adrienne yelled.

The *Hydra* rocked under the force of the salvo from the enemy cruiser.

"Hull breaches, decks sixteen and seventeen, and we've got a fire in engineering!"

"Inform damage control. Sensors, did it work?"

"Yes, Captain, we've pulled the Ascomanni cruiser out of position."

She watched as one of her heavy cruisers swung around the enemy ship and raked it from behind, its weapons penetrating the weak rear armor of the Ascomanni warship and punching deep into its core.

"We've got an energy spike!" her sensors officer yelled.

"Comms, pass the word, get everyone away from that cruiser!"

The Umbrian warships raced away from the doomed vessel as it disappeared in an intense flash of light. Adrienne checked her display, satisfied that her ships were all still in one piece.

She keyed the fleetwide channel: "Battlegroup Hydra, the area is secured. Proceed to the Ascomanni repair yard. You may fire as soon as you're in range."

The *Hydra*'s helmsman pointed them at the two space stations that hung amongst the system's asteroid field. The eight ships of her battlegroup quickly converged on the now defenseless Ascomanni.

Wave after wave of missiles and kinetic projectiles slammed into the ribcage-like stations, and in moments they began to break up. An Asco destroyer, docked and under repair at one of the two platforms, was ripped apart by the apertures supporting it as they separated from the station and were thrown in opposite directions.

In the end, it took less time to wreck the enemy repair stations than it had to defeat the token force guarding them. Satisfied that their mission had been achieved, Adrienne ordered her force to form up for the journey back to the assembly point.

"Captain?" her XO called out. "We've got a problem. *Euxinus* reports that their drive core is damaged and they are no longer FTL capable."

"What? How did this happen?"

"A lucky shot penetrated their stern and apparently fused several critical components."

"Can they repair it?"

"The ship's captain is saying they won't be able to with the resources they have available."

Adrienne swore. There was no way they could get a repair ship in system in less than twelve hours. In the interval, they undoubtedly could expect some type of Ascomanni response.

"Pull us alongside. Tell the *Euxinus*'s captain to evacuate all non-essential crew members, and then send word to Archus Fabian requesting immediate support. Have the rest of the battlegroup form a defensive perimeter around the cruiser."

"Aye, Captain."

The *Hydra* positioned itself next to its smaller cousin, and over the next half an hour, all but two hundred of the ship's seven-thousand-strong crew were transferred to the battlecruiser.

Adrienne sat in her chair, willing time to move faster. Archus Fabian had responded, indicating that the nearest fleet tender would not be available for fifteen hours.

One hour passed, then two, and all attempts to repair the cruiser failed. The *Euxinus* was still trapped in the system.

"Captain!" the frantic voice of her sensors officer called out. "We've got Ascomanni forces inbound! A battleship and two destroyers!"

"How far out?!"

"Fifteen thousand kilometers, ma'am, they are on the opposite side of the repair yard."

Adrienne took a moment to collect her thoughts. The fleet tender was still several hours away, and there was no way her battle group could take on the enemy response force. She sighed deeply as she realized what had to be done.

"Call the *Euxinus*. Tell them we've got to scuttle her. Order the rest of the battlegroup to jump away."

"Yes, Captain."

One by one, the other six ships of her flotilla disappeared, speeding away from the Umbrian cruisers and the danger that beset them.

"Do we have a status report?" she asked anxiously, immediately chiding herself for asking just minutes after the Ascomanni had entered the system.

"Most of the cruiser's remaining crew has been recovered. Captain Avianus and a handful of engineers are finishing the preparations to scuttle the ship."

"Captain! The Ascomanni warships just executed a micro-jump. They are twenty seconds from weapons range."

"Get me Captain Avianus!" Adrienne shouted.

"He's on line two!"

"Paulus, the Ascomanni are closing in for the kill. You need to get over here immediately."

"We still need two more minutes to set charges, Adrienne."

"We don't have two more minutes; the Ascomanni are within weapons range. Get your people over here, now!"

"I see…"

"Ma'am! The *Euxinus* has disengaged their docking tube. Her remaining crew will be unable to reach us!"

"Captain, what the hell are you doing?!" Adrienne demanded.

"My remaining crew and I are in agreement, Captain. We will stay and finish the job. Get my people to safety."

The first salvo of enemy fire crashed into the two ships.

Adrienne felt helpless. There was nothing else to do.

"Navigation, emergency jump. Half a meg down plane. Execute, execute, execute!"

A blinding white light enveloped the bridge, and in an instant, they were five hundred kilometers farther out in the system. Adrienne pulled up an image of the area where the *Euxinus* remained behind and enhanced the view as much as she could, but they were too far away to make out the individual combatants. Thirty seconds later, there was a small flash, then nothing.

"May the gods guide you home, Avianus," she whispered to herself.

"Helmsman, get us back to the fleet assembly area."

URN Patrol Ship *Aquila*, Twenty-One Lambda E, Frontier Space

Captain Claudia Critonius was glued to her monitor, where a feed from a surveillance drone showed the progress of her passengers' mission. She had brought a four-person team to this verdant jungle planet, located at the furthest reaches of Frontier space.

It was a momentous assignment, the first operational use of the new Cyberwarfare and Clandestine Operations, or Cyclops, teams. Claudia chuckled at Praetor Aurelius's ability to turn a phrase.

The inaugural debut of Cyclops Team One was a surgical strike against a cadre of high-ranking Pasargan commanders who had been visiting various facilities across the Frontier. Their next stop would be this previously undiscovered world, where the Ascomanni harvested the planet's diverse ecology, processing the biomass into food to feed their insatiable armies.

Claudia and Team One had arrived twelve hours previously, and the *Aquila*'s captain had ordered the patrol ship's passive sensors to search the skies for any sign of their target. They'd been waiting without luck ever since.

At last, her console began to beep: the *Aquila* detected an approaching vessel. Claudia transmitted two quick bursts of static, each less than a second long.

As she watched, the team, located on a bluff overlooking a nearby Ascomanni distribution center, began to assemble what appeared to be a small artillery piece.

The Asco shuttle zoomed into the drone's view, abruptly coming to a stop above the distribution node's landing pad before settling gently down. A ramp descended from the rear of the vessel, which faced the open jungle where Team One lay in wait. Four purple-skinned aliens walked down the ramp, harassing a pair of Ascomanni soldiers who stood waiting to receive them.

The Umbrian commandos chose that moment to strike, firing the weapon they had just assembled.

A missile raced away from their position, its cone peeled back, and a dozen submunitions spiraled out from the launcher buried in its nose.

Each of the tiny rockets had a distinct target, and before the Pasarga had time to react, they evaporated in a puff of fire, blood, and smoke. The remaining submunitions struck the shuttle, which promptly exploded, spraying pieces of metal across the landing pad and starting small brush fires along its perimeter.

Alarms began to wail across the facility, and Team One started to work their way back to the *Aquila*. Claudia kept pace with her observation drone and ordered her crew to prepare the ship for departure.

As the team came within a hundred meters of the patrol ship, the *Aquila*'s engines roared to life. Claudia worked her way to the rear of the ship, and a quartet of camouflaged figures ran aboard.

"We've got everyone, helmsman, get us out the hell out of here!" she called over the ship's intercom.

The patrol ship shifted dramatical, turning almost ninety degrees to the planet's surface and rocketing away. Claudia lost her footing and fell on all fours before the ship's artificial gravity compensated for the suddenness of it all. One of the nameless soldiers offered Claudia a hand up. She nodded at the woman, ignored her scuffed knees, and worked her way to the bridge.

Already the ship had cleared the planet's atmosphere, and she called out to her sensor officer. "Any pursuit?"

"None, ma'am, we're clear."

Claudia let out a sigh of relief. "Get us back to the fleet. Mission accomplished."

URN *Echion*, Somewhere in Frontier Space

Praetor Artorius had joined Marcellus and Fabian on the bridge of the *Echion* for the final missions of the operation. The bridge's strategic map showed the targets they had attacked, the vast majority a tranquil blue. As the trio watched, the last two brilliant red systems faded to match, and Marcellus exhaled deeply. It was over.

"Archus Duilius just called in," Fabian said. His forces destroyed the assembly area we detected. They got sixteen Asco warships, including two battleships, in exchange for a fleet carrier, three light cruisers, and a handful of destroyers."

Lucia nodded. "Steeper than I would have hoped, but a solid result all the same. The Fourth hadn't seen major action against the Ascomanni before. Duilius will do better next time."

Marcellus nodded. Their lightning campaign had not been without its casualties; all told, several thousand of his soldiers would never see their homes or loved ones again. But as he looked at the results of their hard work, he felt confident that it had been worthwhile.

"We've made a difference over the last four days," Marcellus said quietly. "Let's hope we can make it count."

Macigno Vella, Tratirne; Frontier Space

Praetor Octavia Asinia didn't believe her eyes. Rising above the ruined skyline of Macigno Vella were dozens of troop transports, *Ascomanni* troop transports, heading toward orbit. Across every theater, similar reports were pouring in. The Ascomanni were falling back.

"Legate," she said to her second in command, "order Contus Wing to establish air dominance over the city. Once you've done that, have the One-Oh-Three move up from reserve and envelope the enemy from the north. Tell Tribune Julius she is not to let these bastards slink away!"

"Yes, ma'am."

The first squadron of fighters swooped past overhead, unleashing a torrent of missiles against the fleeing Asco transports.

Ascomanni fighters soared in, attempted to cover their fleeing troopships, but the other squadrons of Contus wing were quick to join the fray. Soon the situation in the skies above Macigno Vella degenerated into a confusing maelstrom of dogfights and explosions.

"This is it," Praetor Asinia said to her subordinate. "I feel it. They've finally had enough! Get me Archus Curia."

URN *Minerva*, Outer Edges of the Tratirne System, Frontier Space

"Understood, Praetor, we'll make sure they can't escape."

Archus Paulla Curia switched frequencies, reaching out to the commanders of the Fifth and Seventh fleets. "Praetor Asinia indicates that resistance on the ground is crumbling. It's time to strike. Are your forces in position?"

"The Seventh is ready to do some damage."

"The Fifth is eager and willing, Minerva Actual."

Paulla glanced over her own force's status. The First Fleet had been badly mauled when the Ascomanni first arrived. She had done what she could to keep her fleet together, and enough of her capital ships had limped away to allow the First to continue on as a cohesive fighting force.

With the arrival of reinforcements, she had rotated out some of her more heavily damaged ships for repairs, and now they were as ready as they were going to be for round two.

"Show me the space over Macigno Vella," she called out to her sensors officer.

Tratirne appeared before her. After weeks of slowly grinding the enemy down, a fleet of one hundred and sixty Ascomanni ships was all that remained overhead. It was still a formidable force, however, and it was centered around an Ascomanni dreadnought.

The Umbrians had one important advantage though—Tratirne. The strategically vital planet had substantial ground-based defensive weaponry. If they could pin the Ascomanni fleet against the planet, they could hammer away from above and below.

She switched back to the inter-fleet frequency. "OK, this is going to be a tough one, but we can do this. The Fifth will take the right flank, while the Seventh takes the left. We'll drive straight down the middle. As we've discussed before, we've got to force them back within range of the planet's weaponry. Once they start to give, exploit the gaps in their formation to weaken their defenses. Everyone clear?"

She got an acknowledgment from both of her fellow Archii, and the *Minerva* sent a signal to the combined Umbrian fleets. In the blink of an eye, three hundred and twelve Umbrian warships jumped into the system.

For six hours, the opposing fleets fought a relentless and brutal battle. As the tide turned in the Umbrians' favor, the remaining Ascomanni unexpectedly smashed through the Umbrian line and fled the system, leaving their remaining ground forces to their fate.

The battle for Tratirne had been won.

Chapter 12

The Castellum; Perugia, Umbria

Marcellus stood on one of Perugia's broad boulevards, staring upwards as a cloud of Ascomanni fighters swarmed the skies above. They rained destruction down on the capital: towers crumbled and fell, panicking civilians trampled over one another, and the dead lay everywhere.

Suddenly, an Umbrian interceptor, on fire and trailing smoke, plowed into the avenue he stood on, shearing it clean through. It detached from the base of the tower, and he was pitched into the impenetrable darkness below.

He landed amongst a tangle of shapes, the darkness obscuring their nature. Above, the ruination of the city continued, now joined by bombardment from orbit. Flaming debris finally lit his surroundings, and Marcellus realized he lay amongst an endless pile of corpses. They shifted under his weight, and hands reached out and grasped him firmly. They pulled him down, a thousand hands pulling him ever deeper, and the fire and flames faded to nothingness.

Marcellus bolted upright and searched about, unsure of where he was. A moment later, his senses returned and he recognized his surroundings: he was safe and in his temporary quarters at the Castellum, where he had been for the last eight months.

Following the attacks against Ascomanni positions in the Frontier and their victory over the enemy at Tratirne, Praetors Artorius, Asinia, and himself had been whisked back to the capital, where they had been received as triumphing heroes.

Praetor Asinia, in a ceremony held on the steps of Capitol Hall, bestowed upon her peers the grass crown, the highest honor an Umbrian officer could receive, awarded by her soldiers to both Lucia and Marcellus in thanks for relieving the siege of Tratirne.

The celebration had lasted for days, followed immediately by sober urgency to prepare for the Ascomanni's inevitable return. Production of war materiel surged, and enhanced training regimens, based on experience born from the campaign in the Frontier, churned out legions of new recruits, better equipped and better prepared for the battles to come.

As days stretched into weeks, the Umbrian Republic aggressively attacked the remaining Ascomanni facilities in the Frontier. Soon enough, however, it became apparent that anything capable of spaceflight had long since disappeared back into the depths of the larger galaxy.

As weeks stretched into months, the Republic went into overdrive. At last, the nature of the threat could no longer be ignored, and, despite the immeasurable challenge the Ascomanni presented, the Umbrians now had hope that it might yet be overcome.

Marcellus's forces had been rotated home, receiving some much-needed R&R before relieving Praetor Asinia's forces at Tratirne. The War Council had been busy too, recalling the Praetors to the capital so that they could better prepare for the fight ahead. Marcellus's small retinue of trusted advisors and subordinates had returned to Umbria as well, accompanied by his praetorians.

However, as they approached nearly half a year without sign of the enemy, the urgency of the threat began to diminish. A sense of normalcy began to return, and with it came complacency.

Marcellus's days began sliding into one another, blurring together as the routine morphed into the monotonous.

Today, however, would be different.

Theodorus had contacted him, indicating that he had news that couldn't wait—and couldn't be shared, even over a secure link. Together with his officers, Marcellus was scheduled to meet first thing in the morning at the CID annex adjacent to the Castellum.

Marcellus hopped out of bed, quickly got dressed, and headed out the door. He was unsurprised to find Fabian, Invictus, and Valerian all waiting for him in the hallway outside of his room.

"Hmm, even Vic is here? Did you drag him out of bed yourself, Val?" Marcellus joked.

"Hey, I resent that!" Invictus whined. "I'm never late! Well...*mostly* never late anyway..."

Valerian shook his head and said, "Actually, Fabian swung by and got him."

"Hyperbole isn't one of Theodorus's normal character flaws. If his information is as important as he says, I for one do not want to keep him waiting," Fabian said with a smirk.

"So, if this is going to be a 'pile on Vic' kind of day, can I go back to bed?" Invictus groused. "You all can just send me the highlights afterwards."

"You're out of luck, Flaminus," Marcellus replied. "We'll try not to bruise that gentle ego of yours too much though."

Valerian feigned disappointment. "But, sir, making Vic miserable is one of the true joys in my life!"

"Val buddy? We really need to get you out more. See the sights, grab some drinks, maybe find a cute, wealthy girl who's looking to disappoint her parents, eh?" Invictus snarked back.

"So, I hate to be *that* guy, but we're cutting it pretty close on time here…" Fabian interjected.

"Right," Marcellus agreed. "Val, Vic, lock it up. Let's get to it."

Together, the four officers walked briskly through the Castellum, passing to the intelligence building via a skywalk linking the two. They passed through a well-guarded entrance after presenting their identification, and soon enough they were on the fifth floor, where Theodorus waited for them.

"Praetor Aurelius, it's good to see you again, sir!" the intelligence agent said.

He gestured toward a hallway leading away from the cluster of desks scattered across the floor, and the group started walking.

"It's good to see you as well. How are things in Safe Haven?" Marcellus asked.

"Magistrate Flavia is somehow managing to keep the operation running while working to convert the facilities in the Daedalus system."

"The Daedalus system?" Invictus asked curiously.

"Yeah, the Ascomanni shipyard you captured. We've given it a proper name, and it just recently launched the first Umbrian warship constructed fully within its works."

"I saw the vid," Fabian said with an uncharacteristic smirk. "A brand-new heavy cruiser, from bow to stern in four months, the fastest recorded build time ever. And that's with the yard at about thirty percent. She's really pulling it off, sir. In time, it'll be a game changer."

Theodorus led the group to a small room, and as they took their seats, he began to explain why he had called them together.

"As you all know, we've recovered an incredible amount of Ascomanni data. The CID has been churning through it as quickly as we can, and given its importance to the war effort, it's taken priority over everything else."

"Did you find something else in the data?" Valerian asked. "I've been getting pretty regular reports, but I haven't seen anything too exciting recently."

"Every few days we find a new Ascomanni outpost and the Navy will go secure it. But I'm not referring to anything we've recovered from the strikes against Ascomanni bases."

"Then what are we here for?" Marcellus asked testily.

"I beg your pardon, Praetor. If you recall, we dispatched a pair of spy ships to two systems deep beyond the furthest reaches of the Frontier. They returned nearly five months ago, but given the demand for analytical resources, their findings were saved for another day. That day finally came about sixty hours ago, and what the ships uncovered is potentially the most important find of the war."

"That's a bold statement, Theodorus, especially since the last trove of data we recovered allowed us to push the Asco back into whatever hellhole they crawled out of," Invictus said.

"But said with merit, Prefect Flaminus. On further inspection, both planets contain vast ruins of a spacefaring civilization. One appears to have been heavily damaged in some type of cataclysm, while the other seems to have been abandoned entirely."

"Abandoned?" Marcellus asked.

"Yes, sir, its cities still stand, overgrown but undamaged. There were no power readings which could be discerned from orbit. Whoever had constructed the planet is long gone."

"OK, so again, interesting," Marcellus responded. "But why is this of value to us?"

Theodorus blinked, clearly perturbed by Marcellus's continued lack of understanding. Then he gasped, finally realizing that he'd failed to connect all of the dots for his audience. "I am truly sorry, sir, I've been running on about four hours' sleep for the last few months. The architecture of these planets is *Ascomanni* in origin."

"Say what?!" Invictus shouted, nearly jumping out of his chair.

Valerian put a hand on Invictus's shoulder to calm his friend. "So, are these colonies of the Ascomanni? Their homeworld? Why would they destroy or abandon their own habitable worlds?"

"They wouldn't," Marcellus responded coldly. "Is this room secure, Theodorus?"

"I don't understa—"

"Are we the only people listening to this conversation, Section Head? No bugs, no taps, nothing?"

"Yes, sir, we're not being monitored."

"What I'm about to tell you cannot leave this room," Marcellus said, looking at each of them, making eye contact to ensure he had their complete and undivided attention. "The Ascomanni were once very much like us. And just like us, a hostile alien race attacked them. They resisted, but they failed."

"Praetor," Theodorus interjected, "this is highly classified information. Even I—"

"I know, Theodorus," Marcellus interrupted. "I know full well what I am doing. I have put myself in the unenviable position of having to trust you. But if we are going to find a way to save our people, we need to understand that this has happened before, so we can stop it from happening again."

Theodorus nodded and sat back in his chair.

"The Pasarga we captured called them the Vaeringyar," Marcellus continued. "As punishment for their defiance, they were...modified. Now they are an empty husk of a people. They obey their masters, or they are tortured by a series of implants they all possess. That is why the Ascomanni do not care about our worlds or resources. They are here for *us*."

Silence met his statements. Fabian was ashen-faced, while horror was clearly visible in Valerian's eyes. Theodorus looked shocked, but also strangely satisfied, as if pieces of a puzzle that had been eluding him suddenly fit together.

Marcellus gave them a moment to digest what he had shared. It was Theodorus who spoke up first.

"We must go there."

"What do you hope to achieve by visiting these worlds, Theodorus?"

"Not both, Praetor, just the abandoned one. You have taken a pretty big risk by sharing what you know, so I will return the favor. If it is the Ascomanni home world, it will have an ancient device, an Oracle, on it. We must attempt to locate this device and learn whatever we can from it."

Marcellus and Invictus looked at each other. "What else can you tell us about Oracle, Theodorus?"

"Nothing, sir, what I know I've cultivated by listening and gathering clues. I'm not cleared for the program either."

"We'll need a pretty substantial fleet to make it that deep into space. And it won't be quick either," Fabian said.

"A fleet? Months away from the army group?" Valerian gaped. "Sir, are you sure gallivanting across the galaxy is the best use of your time?"

"I understand your concerns, Val, but I have it on good authority that this object may be critical to the war effort. If the planet contains this device, we must secure it."

Valerian watched his superior closely, then said, "If you believe this is important, I guess that's good enough for me. But you'll need support at the highest levels to get approval for this."

Valerian was right, Marcellus thought to himself. If they were going to pull this off, they'd need help from someone with serious pull. Someone like…

"I think I know who we need to talk to."

Villa Decii, North of Perugia, Umbria

Marcellus stood in the Triumvir's circular office, the older man seated comfortably behind his desk. The smell of careworn books wrinkled his nose, but he did his best to ignore it.

"You want to do what?!" Triumvir Decius asked, skeptically.

"I'd like to lead an expedition to a planet we think may be the Ascomanni homeworld. I believe our recent battlefield successes demonstrate the value of knowing our enemy, and there exists the chance that we may be able to finally develop a complete picture of the enemy and their capabilities."

Decius was quiet for long time. Finally, he looked up at Marcellus and said, "Praetor Aurelius, those who disagree with you usually end up being wrong, don't they?"

Marcellus smiled slightly. "It used to bother Praetor Artorius incessantly, sir. Fortunately for me, we didn't disagree too often."

"Well then, I'd be a fool to question your instincts now, especially given recent events. I'll do what I can to get your request approved, though I am sure the CID will want in on the action. They've been a little peeved that some ground pounder has so completely beaten them at their own game."

"That would be a fair and reasonable compromise, sir. We're all playing for the same team."

"Most gracious of you, Marcellus." The Triumvir smiled and cocked an eyebrow. "Are you sure you have no interest in politics? From what I've seen, you'd be a natural. You might even give me a run for my money."

"I appreciate the compliment, sir, but again, my objective remains ensuring the safety of our people. If there comes a time where we are truly free from this threat, I will gladly find something productive to do with myself and disappear into obscurity."

"Well said, young Praetor. I'll make the calls, Marcellus. Just be quick. If the Ascomanni return, Umbria will need you at the head of your legions."

The Castellum; Perugia, Umbria

Marcellus and Invictus stood on one of the Castellum's largest landing pads, watching while their praetorians loaded equipment and supplies onto the *Spatha*. Triumvir Decius had been good on his word, and Marcellus was shocked by how quickly everything had come together.

Within a week, approval had been given for the operation, and the assault carrier had been detached to ferry them back to Safe Haven, where they would rendezvous with the rest of the Third Fleet. They'd depart as soon as the last of their equipment was loaded aboard the massive vessel.

Invictus broke the silence. "I'm sorry for questioning your judgment, Marcellus. You have never led us astray, and I shouldn't have second guessed your decisions."

Marcellus grinned and slapped his friend on the shoulder. "No, Vic, I'm sorry for snapping at you. There was a better way to handle it." He paused for a moment, then continued. "I'm going to level with you. After what we saw on Icarus, I...I felt hatred for our enemies for the first time. We were no longer fighting other sentients who were just doing as they were told. We were fighting monsters."

"But there is no room for emotion in command," Marcellus said, sighing deeply. "Our duty to Umbria, and to our soldiers, requires steady and reasoned leadership. In the end, I kept a level head, in no small part due to what you told me during Aulus's attempted coup. But I will not deny that it was a challenge."

"I need you to keep being that touchstone for me," Marcellus said earnestly. "Someone I can count on to keep me on the straight and narrow, and to reel me in when I need it."

"You know I'd do anything for you, brother," Invictus replied, seemingly put at ease by his commander's frank admission. "Together, we'll find a way to finish this fight."

Marcellus nodded, once again thankful for whatever twist of fate had allowed their paths to cross on Varese nearly two years ago.

"Praetor Aurelius?" a voice called out.

"Yes?" Marcellus responded, turning. He stopped in his tracks as he caught a glimpse of the speaker. It was none other than Doctor Mirabella Urbanus, wearing a form-hugging olive vest and khaki trousers. She was pulling a wheeled crate and joined by a team of about ten. Two automated cargo sleds followed behind, heavily laden with equipment.

"Doctor! It's...it's a pleasure to see you again," Marcellus stammered. "Why are you here?"

Mirabella arched an eyebrow in amusement, and Marcellus felt warmth rush to his cheeks.

"We're going with you, Praetor. The CID doesn't want to be upstaged again, so they are sending me and my team."

"Well, we'll be glad to have you aboard. My soldiers will help you load your equipment, and if there is anything else you need, please don't hesitate to let me know."

"Will do. I already have your number," she said with a devious grin. She turned back to her team and called out: "OK team, you heard the man. Our hosts may be generous enough to help us stow our gear, but *you* are responsible for making sure all of your equipment makes it onboard."

They moved off toward the transport, and Mirabella turned, looked back over her shoulder, and winked.

Once Mirabella and her team had passed beyond earshot Invictus erupted, busting out into gales of laughter. "Oh man, you are so screwed!" he gasped as tears started to form in the corner of his eyes.

"Vic? Please shut the hell up."

URN *Spatha*, Safe Haven, System: Classified, Frontier Space

Marcellus stood on a catwalk near the exit from the cavernous hangar of the assault carrier, his breath fogging in the frigid air. He gazed out of the large hexagonal entrance of the *Spatha*'s hangar, watching his impromptu expedition form up around the Echion on the edge of the gas giant's atmosphere. They would be joined by the *Vulcan* and the *Hydra*, along with ten more warships, each well stocked for the journey ahead.

As his fleet prepared to depart, Marcellus's mind wandered. He thought back to their counterattack through the Frontier.

It seemed distant, as if those missions had occurred years ago instead of just months. In the end, his plan had worked, but had he really managed to outwit his enemy? Or was their success the result of dumb luck? Had it all been a part of some well-executed vision, or had he merely bounced from event to event?

As he began to doubt the true extent of his abilities, he remembered the discussion he had with Fabian following the battle of Aetnaeus. Doubt would lead to ruin.

For whatever reason, the merciless crucible of battle had spared him, while so many of his friends had been taken. Now, all that remained were his fellow survivors—those who, through luck or skill or favor of the gods, had found a way through.

Marcellus remembered the tales from Umbria's early history, powerful men and women of deeds and action, who seemed to stride across the world, above the petty concerns of common people. Many had come to see him in a similar light, but he certainly didn't see himself as any different.

Had those titans of old felt the same? Or were they really cut from a different cloth?

He shook his head. If there was one thing he was sure of, it was this: he had entered into this world pitiful and screaming, and when his time came, he couldn't help but think he'd leave in much the same manner.

"Have you found what you are looking for?" a familiar voice called.

Marcellus's pulse quickened, but he willed himself to remain in control. "Not yet," he said without turning, "though I fear I may never find it."

"I bribed your Prefect into telling me where you were. Am I interrupting?" Mirabella asked.

"No, not at all," Marcellus said, turning to face her.

She walked up beside him, gazing out at the starry expanse before them. "It's beautiful. I never grow tired of the view from space. I can't help but feel humbled by the majesty of it all."

"I'm afraid I've become jaded," Marcellus said softly. "I see a dozen different ways to die, ranging from the unpleasant to the gruesome."

"Cheery," she said, wrinkling her nose. Her expression grew more serious, and Marcellus got the impression that she was worried about him. "I see I interrupted one of those deep, brooding meditations of yours. I know you've faced some unimaginable situations, Marcellus, but if it's any consolation, I've found your letters to be very interesting."

Marcellus smiled, recalling some of the notes he had sent her over the last several months. "Hopefully they weren't too boring. I'm afraid I'm not much of a writer."

"I've enjoyed them immensely," Mirabella said sincerely. "I'm just sorry I couldn't send you more than encouragement."

"As you should be!" Marcellus said, glowering in mock outrage. "It's quite selfish of you, hoarding all that highly classified, paradigm-shifting research you're doing down in your lab."

Mirabella laughed. "Who is this? Where is the stiff, uncomfortable 'Hero of Umbria' I've come to expect?"

"I'm sorry," he responded, blushing. "I guess it just takes me a while to warm up to people."

"Uh huh," she responded sarcastically. "I've seen you address the full Senate. On a live broadcast. Viewed by tens of billions of people across the Republic. No stammering there."

"Well, maybe it's just you then," Marcellus said, the first stirrings of his normal confidence returning.

"Oh yeah? What specifically is it about me, Praetor?" she smirked, imitating her most innocent-looking expression.

"Well..." he began, panicking as he attempted to figure out what to say next.

Before the pause became too unpleasant, Marcellus's commlink began to beep.

"This is the Praetor," he said.

"Archus Fabian has requested your presence on the bridge, sir."

"Understood, I'll be there shortly." He turned back to Mirabella, a conciliatory look on his face, but he found his guest was laughing silently to herself.

"What?" he asked insecurely.

"Yeah, let's pretend like you didn't have that pre-arranged," she said, grinning from ear to ear.

"No, I swear, I didn't..." Marcellus stammered.

Mirabella cut him off with a quick peck on the cheek. "I believe you, Marcellus. I guess you're off the hook. For now..."

She turned and walked away, leaving a confused and excited Marcellus behind to wonder what exactly had just happened.

***

As the weeks passed by, Marcellus and Mirabella spent a great deal of time together, often wandering the *Spatha*'s decks deep in conversation. They talked at length about the wonders Marcellus had seen in the Frontier, while she shared as much of her work as she could.

Mirabella was surprised by the depth of Marcellus's curiosity, even for topics *she* considered mundane. In him, she found a willing ear as she discussed the latest papers on Ascomanni culture and physiology.

She, in turn, proved to be a patient and willing tutor, helping to fill in his layman's understanding of the topics they discussed.

As Marcellus spent more time in Mirabella's company, he began to overcome his anxiety. She had become a close friend and confidant, and she made no secret of her attraction to him.

In another life, he might have dared to hope for more.

But the more Mirabella shared about the nature of the Ascomanni, the more he remembered what the captive Pasarga, Atossa, had told him months before. The Ascomanni were just the beginning, he was sure of it.

He was also equally certain that he would not live to see the end of this conflict; he had avoided death too many times to be spared for much longer.

So, as much as he hated himself for it, he gently deflected Mirabella's advances. She persisted, however, and finally, she confronted him as they walked along a ventral accessway spanning the distance of the carrier's interior.

"So, I've spent enough time with you now to know that you're not stupid," Mirabella started.

"Really?" Marcellus snorted. "I'm a little concerned that it took so long for you to notice."

"Ha. Ha," she said sardonically. She cut in front of him, bringing him to a stop, her midnight blue eyes staring directly into his.

"Be straight with me, Marcellus. I've been pretty obvious in broadcasting how I feel. And given your…vocal performance issues," she said with a devious grin, "I'm pretty sure you feel the same way."

She took a step closer, so close that he could feel her body heat in the cold confines of the hallway. She lowered her voice, gazing up into his eyes, and continued. "So, tell me, why are you keeping me at arm's length?"

Marcellus was so tempted to reach out, to pull her close and not let go. But he shook his head, smiled grimly, and took a step back.

"I have no future to offer you, Mirabella. You know what lurks out amongst the stars. If we are fortunate enough to find some final victory, some lasting peace, it will be a long time in coming. And as long as Umbria is in danger, I will keep throwing myself at her enemies. I can only avoid my doom for so long."

Marcellus had expected anger, or perhaps resignation, to greet his words. He was unprepared for the sorrowful expression that stole across Mirabella's face.

"All the more reason to make every day count, Marcellus," Mirabella replied. "I don't want some fairy-tale ending or some happily ever after. What I want is *you*."

"I'm afraid I can't give you what you're after, no matter how much I may want to. Nearly a million souls depend on me to be sharp and focused, to lead them into the fire and hopefully bring them out the other side. That responsibility is sacred to me, it's what drives me when I roll out of my bunk every day and it's what ensures a restless night's sleep when I return to it."

He lowered his eyes. "And I know myself well enough to know that I would bring that same intensity and passion to any relationship with you. I cannot afford to split myself in two like that."

Mirabella nodded and stroked his face, gently lifting his chin until their eyes met. "What a burden you carry on your shoulders, Praetor Aurelius. It's heartbreaking to know you choose to bear it alone."

She turned to leave, and Marcellus reached out, taking her by the hand. She gently pulled away, saying, "Thank you for your honesty, Marcellus."

She walked down the hallway and disappeared down a side passage, leaving Marcellus to stand alone in the empty corridor.

URN *Spatha*, The Edges of Frontier Space

Whereas the first three weeks of the trip had seemed to speed by, the last three crawled. Marcellus had only seen Mirabella in passing a few times. She had been courteous and kind, but hadn't gone out of her way to reach out since he had firmly ended any chance he might have had with her.

He spent most of his time in the *Spatha*'s gym with his praetorians, getting familiar with some of the newer faces while sharing stories with the older hands. Despite his best attempts to put on a brave face, Invictus and Valerian both noticed that something was wrong.

"So," Invictus said, panting, as he and Marcellus sparred, with Valerian watching from the edge of the ring. "You blew it, right?"

Marcellus grunted, delivering a brutal right hook to Invictus's midsection, eliciting an *oof* from his opponent.

"Actually, no, Vic. She was totally into me."

Invictus put out a hand, panting, and they paused their session.

"Wait," he said, attempting to catch his breath. "She was interested? So? What happened?"

"She deserves someone who can give her a future. How many times have we survived by the skin of our teeth? My luck will not last forever, Vic. I've come to peace with that."

"Whoa, whoa, whoa, pump the breaks, Marcellus. You dove straight into the commitment deep end? Who's to say the two of you couldn't have a little fun together?"

"Ignore him," Valerian chimed in. "Just because you haven't had a mature relationship in your lifetime doesn't mean you get to berate Marcellus for wanting more."

"Ha!" Invictus snickered. "I seem to remember hearing stories about you and a young woman from Gela, Valerian. Marcellus, refresh my memory, wasn't she the Viceroy's daughter?"

"Hey, neither of us had any illusions about our long-term viability. She ended up getting evacuated a week later, and the remnants of our legion pulled out shortly after that," Valerian shot back.

"Enough, both of you. I appreciate the concern for my love life, but it's misplaced. I need to be able to focus on the task at hand, and right now that's wiping the floor with Vic here."

Sextus, Vetus, and Aria walked up to join them, and Sextus, having overheard the last of Marcellus's remarks, commented: "Well, sir, as enjoyable as that would be to watch, if you're really looking for a challenge, Aria here has an unbeaten streak longer than most of us have been around."

"Yeah, I know," Marcellus said with a confident grin, holding up a gloved hand and bringing his bout with Vic to an end. "There's a reason for that."

Aria cracked an uncharacteristic smile. "It's been a very long time, *sir*. Besides, it would hardly be a fair fight. You've been absent from the field for quite some time now."

Everyone was shocked, both to hear her string so many words together and by her less-than-subtle challenge.

Everyone except for Marcellus, that was.

"You're on Primus. Beating on Prefect Flavius was getting boring anyway."

Aria climbed into the ring, taking Invictus's gloves and shin pads from him as he took his place along the railing. Marcellus stretched out his arm, and Aria tapped it, indicating she was ready to go.

Marcellus immediately pressed the attack with a flurry of punches, seeking to use his reach to his advantage. Aria dipped and dodged, countering just frequently enough to stop him from pinning her into the corner. She ducked under an aggressive left jab, striking Marcellus twice in the side where he'd exposed himself.

A crowd began to assemble as other praetorians took a break from their workouts to watch the event unfold. Sextus, ever resourceful, soon had a pool going on who would be the victor. Valerian shot Invictus a dirt look, but the Prefect just smiled and shrugged.

Aria used his momentary distraction to press her advantage.

Marcellus dropped back a few steps, and Aria used the additional space to start working in a series of kicks. Her opponent blocked most, but each blow wore down the Praetor's defenses and drove him back.

Finally, the tables had turned, Marcellus was confined to the corner on the far side of the ring, and a leaping blow from Aria knocked him back. He dropped him to one knee, leaning heavily against the ropes.

Aria moved in for the coup de grace, but just as she was about to strike, Marcellus lunged forward, wrapping his arms around her planted leg and lifting her into the air as her blow flailed in empty space. He flipped her over his back, dropping her heavily to the floor, then quickly pinned her arms to her side, wrapping his legs around her chest.

Marcellus's gloved fist hovered centimeters from Aria's face, and she reluctantly nodded, admitting that he had once again bested her.

A roaring cheer went up from the assembled audience, while those who had placed bets on the wrong fighter grumbled about their losses.

Marcellus helped Aria to her feet and gave her a hug, which to the onlookers' surprise she returned.

"Well fought, as always, Aria" he said.

"That was some bullshit at the end," she responded, smiling. "I had you beat. Since when did you learn to grapple?"

"I like to keep a few tricks up my sleeve," Marcellus replied coolly, looping an arm over her shoulder as they headed to the edge of the ring. "There's always next time, Primus."

"Oooh! Yeah! Give us some advance notice and we can really add some production value to the spectacle!" Sextus said.

Before Marcellus could respond, Vetus smacked him across the back of the head.

"Ow! Hey, watch it!"

The crowd dispersed, leaving Marcellus alone with Vic, Val, and his leaders. As he gazed at the faces around him, his mood began to brighten.

These people were his family. No matter what awaited him, he knew they would be there, ready to face it by his side.

Chapter 13

URN *Spatha*, Forty-Two Upsilon A, Beyond Known Space

Marcellus, Mirabella, and the other members of his command staff gathered in the *Spatha*'s CIC. The holographic projection of their target floated above them, showing four planets orbiting a whitish-blue star. This was it: they had finally reached their destination.

Fabian, communicating from the bridge of the *Echion*, finished sharing the results of the initial survey of the system: "All of our scans have come back negative. We've deployed some probes to the planet of interest, but so far there is no sign of intelligent life, Ascomanni or otherwise, anywhere in the system."

"Thank you, Fabian," Marcellus said. "Doctor Urbanus, this is really your area of expertise. Where would you recommend we start?"

"Is there a city, perhaps larger than the others or that exhibits signs of greater levels of architectural sophistication or planning?" Mirabella asked.

"Actually, we've found one that matches both descriptions," Fabian replied. "It's over six hundred kilometers in area, and is bound by a ring wall with broad avenues aligned with each of the cardinal directions."

"What's in the middle? Where those roads come together in the middle?" Valerian asked.

"There's an elaborate building located in the exact center of the city, perhaps governmental or religious in nature."

A three-dimensional image of the city, relayed by a drone orbiting above, appeared. It zoomed in on a large, ornate structure with multi-layered roofs. Decorative sculptures graced the peaks of the dozen-odd layers, while a single spire rose through the center of the structure.

"It's interesting that the other structures are so short," Invictus commented, pointing to the well-organized rows of rectangular buildings that filled the city proper. "And is it just me, or does it look like they've used wood and rough-cut stone in their construction? Surely an advanced spacefaring civilization would have adopted more advanced building practices."

"Their methods and materials could have been motivated by any number of reasons," Mirabella responded, "and without investigating the buildings further, it's a bit premature to judge the sophistication of the underlying engineering."

"How much free space surrounds the central structure?" Marcellus asked next.

"Based on these readings?" Valerian answered. "Enough to accommodate landing craft from the *Spatha* comfortably. What are you thinking?"

"Fabian and the rest of the fleet will stay in orbit, guarding our exit. The *Spatha* will enter above the city and deploy Invictus, Sextus, and Vetus to secure the city center. Once we've established local security, Aria and her cohort with escort Doctor Urbanus and her team to the surface."

He looked around the room and found his subordinates nodding in assent.

"All right, take us in, Fabian."

***

Marcellus stood in the carrier's hangar bay, while Invictus tapped away at a datapad nearby. His praetorians were busily embarking on their designated landing craft, and the hangar was a riot of noise and activity.

A claxon blared, and the starfield suspended before them flashed into brilliant light as Marcellus watched. In an instant, the vivid light receded, replaced by a ball of white and blue, mottled by patches of pale greens and browns.

This was it, this is what they had traveled so far to see: the Ascomanni homeworld.

Or so they all hoped.

"Looks cold," Invictus said without turning from his datapad, a slight edge to his tone.

"Temperatures range from four to twelve degrees where we're going."

"You always find the nicest places…" Invictus muttered.

"What's up, Vic?" Marcellus asked, concerned by his subordinate's foul mood. "What's going on?"

"Just got another message from Antonia. She was doing pretty good, it looked like she might have even been well enough to join us for this expedition, but just before we left, she ran into some complications."

"Is she doing better now?"

"Mixed reviews. Doctor Publicola definitely knows his stuff, but the extent of Tonia's injuries requires time to bounce back from, and there is nothing the doctor can prescribe to make her recovery go any faster."

Marcellus laid a hand on his friend's shoulder, and Invictus finally tore his gaze away from the tablet in front of him.

"There's nothing we can do for her from here, Vic. Your soldiers need you."

Invictus nodded reluctantly. "You're right, as usual." He turned back to his datapad and said, "Everyone is on schedule, and the *Spatha*'s captain indicates we'll be ready to launch in five minutes, give or take."

Marcellus nodded. Outside, the prow of the assault carrier was already beginning to glow as it forced its way into the planet's atmosphere. Together, the duo followed the last praetorians up into their dropship, and the shuttle's door slowly closed behind them.

Abandoned City, Planet: Unknown; Forty-Two Upsilon A

The first few soldiers off the dropship formed a tight perimeter around the ship's egress point, while the remaining praetorians sprinted to the cover of nearby buildings. The ship was grounded for less than two minutes before bouncing back up into the air for its return flight to the assault carrier, which hovered above the empty city.

As their troops secured the immediate area, Marcellus and Invictus set up shop in a nondescript building on the east side of their primary target. They were amazed to find that instead of wood, the building had been constructed from some unknown synthetic substance, bronzish in color and warm to the touch, designed to mimic the look and feel of a more organic building material. The stonework proved to be an artful forgery as well, poured from some type of rock-based composite material then shaped to look like real stone.

Everywhere they looked, artistry and symbolism had been worked into the building's features, from the long, unbroken hall running the length of the building's undercroft to the spacious living areas on the two succeeding floors.

"Your girlfriend was right, Marcellus," Invictus said as he gazed about the building in admiration. "This place is definitely not rustic."

Marcellus glared at him in reply. "See to the disposition of your soldiers, Prefect. I want a go/no-go decision on bringing Aria and the CID team down in ten minutes. Furthermore, split off a handful of your troopers to escort me to the center structure."

"I'll make it happen, sir." Invictus responded. "Someone's still sore that they didn't score with the smoking hot scientist," he muttered as Marcellus walked toward the building's entrance.

URN *Spatha*, Above the Abandoned City, Planet: Unknown, Forty-Two Upsilon A

Aria stood in the cockpit of her dropship, patiently waiting for word from the surface. She was joined by Mirabella, who was busy studying the information they had gathered on the city so far.

"Anything interesting, Doc?" Aria asked.

Mirabella looked up from her work, an intense look on her face. "It's amazing, Primus! I could spend years searching through this place."

"Forgive me if I hope it doesn't take quite that long," Aria responded drily.

Mirabella's concentration broke, and a slight smile tugged at the corners of her lips. "I'm sorry you've been dragged into this with us."

"What do you mean?"

"Having to watch our back while we poke and prod at the ruins down below."

Aria flashed her a tight-lipped smile. "Marcellus believes this is important. That's good enough for me."

She was surprised to see a flash of pain cross the doctor's face before she regained her composure.

"Well, I appreciate it, Primus. The Praetor speaks very highly of you."

"We've been together for a long time." Aria nodded.

"Oh..." Mirabella said awkwardly. "So, the two of you are..."

Aria just stared at the doctor for a second, trying to understand what she meant. Then it hit her, and for the first time in a long time, she let herself go, laughing deeply at Mirabella's misunderstanding.

"No. No..." she replied. "It's nothing like that at all. We've served together since leaving the Academy, Marcellus, Val, and I. In fact, after he got promoted to Praetor, I gave up my position as Legate to lead one of his praetorian cohorts."

Mirabella giggled uncomfortably at her mistake. "Sorry, I just thought... I'm so embarrassed."

"Don't be," Aria responded.

"So you've seen a lot of action together?"

"He has a knack for finding trouble, and that's exactly where I want to be," Aria responded. "He's saved my life more times than I'd like to admit," she continued, drifting backward in time to memories of hard-fought battles past. "It's only been since he was promoted to Praetor that I've finally had a few chances to return the favor."

"He seems like a good man," Mirabella offered. "I'm glad he has someone as skilled as you to look after him."

Aria gave Mirabella a piercing look, as if trying to understand her intentions before replying.

"He is. Complicated though. He keeps a lot to himself, preferring not to burden others."

"Doesn't that grind him down?"

"Yeah," Aria said softly, "It does… But that's what he committed to when the Senate made him Praetor. If he screws up, his people die. Every time we deploy, some folks aren't coming back, even when he makes all of the right calls. Not everyone has the stones for that type of responsibility."

Mirabella nodded, suddenly aware of how much she didn't understand about her host, and the pair lapsed into silence. Finally, after a few more minutes' wait, the pilot turned and gave Aria the thumbs up.

The Primus nodded to Doctor Urbanus, exited the cockpit, and worked her way aft. She came to the bulkhead door which opened up into the troop bay and called out to her soldiers: "We've got the green light, praetorians! Check your gear and get set!"

Abandoned City, Planet: Unknown; Forty-Two Upsilon A

Marcellus was waiting for them at the top of a broad staircase, ten meters high, which led to the entrance of the central structure. Aria's soldiers swept inside and began the process of clearing the building, while the science team lugged their heavy packs up the steep slope as quickly as they could.

"So far so good," he said as Aria and Mirabella reached the pinnacle.

Mirabella appeared awestruck by the intricate skill that had gone into the building. Symmetric patterns had been carved or cut into the structure's columns, and the doctor appeared to recognize some.

"These are Ascomanni runes. We think they are designed to ward off evil spirts or honor favored gods. More likely vestiges from an earlier time in their history, but evidently still of significant cultural importance."

"Fascinating," Aria said. "How about we get you and your brain trust inside, where some rookie Asco sniper might find it a little harder to pick us off?"

Mirabella suddenly looked less enthusiastic, peering over her shoulder at the city stretched out behind them.

"Good idea..." she said slowly. Mirabella and her researchers moved inside, many desperately looking about as they walked quickly into the large building.

Marcellus smirked at Aria and said, "That wasn't very nice."

The slightest hint of a grin forced its way onto her face, but she fought it down. "You put me in charge of her safety. And we have no idea what might be out there," she said, gesturing to the city beyond.

"Fair enough."

"You know she's into you, right?"

"Ugghh..." Marcellus growled, rolling his head on his shoulders. "Not you too."

"Who else is in on the secret?"

"Who'd you expect? Vic and Val."

"And you're not interested because...?"

"This is not the time or the place for this conversation, Aria. Come on. I'd rather get ambushed by the Asco than have to explain myself on this topic again."

"OK, you're the boss. I'm just saying, she's smart, strong-willed, and beautiful. You've done a lot worse in the past. A *lot* worse..."

"Primus..."

"I get it, self-destructive is your thing. Let's go find that ambush you promised me."

"I think I liked you better when you were the strong, quiet type," Marcellus said with a grimace as the pair entered the ancient Ascomanni structure.

***

Twenty minutes later, Mirabella called them to the room directly in the center of the structure. Above the chamber, stretching dozens of meters into the air, was the central spire they had observed earlier. Nine pillars, clad in gold, stretched the entire height of the tower, and at its base was a plinth made of the same.

A large, lavishly carved rune stone, a meter wide and two meters tall, rested on the plinth. The doctor seemed very excited about it, holding a small device in her hand and running it back and forth over the surface.

"You said there was something urgent, Doctor Urbanus?" Marcellus asked.

Mirabella held up a hand, forestalling any additional questions. She pressed a series of icons on the stone's surface, and the ground around them began to shake. Slowly, sections of the floor began to retract. Marcellus and Aria jumped back as it slid out from under them, and they avoided falling into the pit below by the narrowest of margins.

As the dust settled, a circular opening had formed, surrounding the stone and revealing a spiral staircase which led into the haze below.

"A warning would've been nice," Aria said curtly.

"Sorry, sorry about that!" Mirabella said. "I discovered that there was a slight electrical current running through the stone, and it made me suspicious. We have a partial decryption for the runes inscribed on it, and I took a chance."

"So, what did you just do?" Marcellus asked.

"Well, one of the symbols we decoded represents a seer," Mirabella said, almost shaking with excitement. "I'm afraid I can't say much more than that, but if my hunch is right, you'll get all the answers you can handle if you follow me." She turned to a pair of nearby researchers and said, "Marcus, Sophia, grab the interface and follow us down!"

Without waiting for confirmation from her team members or her guardians, Doctor Urbanus headed down the stairwell. Marcellus and Aria scrambled to catch up, with the latter glowering at the former.

They passed deeper and deeper into the structure, the staircase only lit by a soft glow emanating from the central column running between the spiraling stairs. Marcellus estimated that they had travelled nearly thirty meters down when the end finally came into sight.

The architecture around them changed, from that of the city above to something even more alien, and the trio walked out onto a wide platform overlooking a large, elliptical room, at least a hundred meters in diameter and half as tall at its highest point.

Gently curving beams, made of a dark, lustrous metallic substance, crisscrossed around the edges of the room in a seemingly organic manner, like the branches of a tree. A thick fog hung suspended in the lower portions of the space, while in the center, a raised dais protruded from the expanse, thick cables running back down the column supporting it before disappearing into the haze.

Without hesitation, Mirabella walked forward onto a platform overlooking the chamber.

"Mirabella, wait!" Marcellus shouted, lunging forward and grabbing her hand to stop her.

It was too late, however. The dais split in even halves, opening to reveal a large circular object. It slowly moved toward the Umbrians, without any visible sign of supports. It finally came to rest in front of them, suspended in the open space before the platform, inert.

"It's OK, Marcellus," Mirabella said, pulling her hand away. "I know what this is. This...is an Oracle."

"An Oracle? Like the project you couldn't tell me about?"

Mirabella nodded.

"So what does it do?"

"You should ask it yourself."

Marcellus stared at her, confused, but she gestured toward the edge of the platform, and he dutifully walked forward.

"Uh... Hello, Oracle," Marcellus said, feeling foolish. As he examined the object more closely, he realized that the sphere seemed almost *liquid* in nature, like mercury suspended in some type of translucent container. "My name is Gaius Aurelius Marcellus of the Umbrian Republic. Can you answer my questions?"

Only silence greeted him, and he muttered to himself, "This is stupid, what is this floating puddle going to tell me?"

"Greetings, Master Aurelius," a booming, mechanical voice called out. The object seemed to pulse as it spoke, with ripples emanating from its equator. "Welcome to GFSTp L452729.16-103241.8, or, as its former inhabitants called it, Vanaheim."

Marcellus was dumbstruck by the object's sudden pronouncement. He stood there, jaw agape, staring in disbelief until Mirabella coughed gently behind him. He struggled to process the object's words, managing only to spit out a jumbled response: "This is...Vanaheim? Its former inhabitants?"

"Yes, this planet has been abandoned for nearly two hundred solar cycles."

Two hundred years? Marcellus thought to himself. The city above looked as though it could've been abandoned yesterday! "What happened to the people of this planet?"

"They encountered servants of the Tenebrae: the Pasarga. The Vaeringyar leveraged the resources of their expansive domain in an attempt to resist their enemies' assault, but ultimately determined that they had no hope of success. Instead, they chose exile."

Marcellus shivered at the Oracle's words. Vaeringyar. It was the same name that Atossa had used to describe the Ascomanni. And he'd become well acquainted with the Pasarga, the name she had given for her own people. But who were the Tenebrae? The name didn't ring any bells.

"What are the Tenebrae?" the Praetor asked.

"They are the remnants of your progenitors. My creators describe them as an amoral and brutish people, though that description is likely colored by their own biases."

Marcellus's head started swimming. "So…who created you then? What are you? And why are you here?"

"I am an artificial intelligence, created by the Farumae, also your progenitors, with the objective of shepherding their legacy on this planet."

Marcellus fell silent, too confused by the object's responses to know what to say next.

Mirabella walked up beside him, rubbing his back to comfort him. "Oracle, please tell Marcellus of your mission, and the reason your creators found it necessary," she requested politely.

"Of course. Exactly one hundred and seventy-two thousand, six hundred and twenty-four standard years ago, the Tenebrae and the Farumae were one people: diverse, intelligent, and adaptive. They quickly explored their own solar system, establishing outposts and studying their surroundings.

"However, as time progressed, their expansion stalled. Significant technical hurdles prohibited ventures to more distant stars, while advances in other fields ensured that life became simple and free of hardship. In this environment, a schism developed within their society.

"On one side were those who relished the pleasures their achievements had bestowed upon them. They rejected the pursuit of knowledge or the hardships associated with personal and cultural growth. Instead, they relied on artificial constructs to manage their lives, so that they could spend their days fulfilling their base desires.

"On the other were those who yearned to beat new paths, to build and invent, whose constant questioning of their natural order left their brothers and sisters both envious and uncomfortable. They would concentrate amongst their people's distant outposts, always focused on what lay beyond their star.

"While knowledge and invention progressed elsewhere in the solar system, the inhabitants of their homeworld regressed, and soon both came to despise the other. In time, the differences between these groups grew to the point where compromise and even coexistence were no longer possible.

"Civil war broke out between the two camps, known to me only by the names Farumae and Tenebrae. The latter, much more numerous than the former, advanced from their shared home world, using stolen hardware to consume my makers' light."

"Wait," Marcellus interrupted, coming to a sudden realization. "How do you know our language?"

"All of the progenies were guided toward a shared written and oral language, to better allay conflict when they inevitably encountered one another."

"Please, Marcellus," Mirabella interjected, "the Oracle will explain everything."

He nodded, and she asked the object to continue.

"War raged for a generation, back and forth with no end in sight. Spurred to greater innovation through sheer necessity, the Farumae finally resolved the problem of interstellar travel. Such advancements had come too late, however. Sapped by years of conflict, it was no longer feasible to venture into the wilds of space to start anew. So, they created a plan to ensure their legacy would continue, even if they would not live to see it."

Mirabella reached out and took Marcellus's hand. He looked at her, confused and uncertain, but she just smiled weakly in return.

"My makers brought forth artificial intelligences, such as myself, to convey their progeny to distant stars in search of a new home. Over the course of decades, thousands of ships were launched into the expanse. We bore inside our hulls both the knowledge and genetic material of our creators and the tools necessary for the labors ahead.

"In us, they entrusted their future: You."

Marcellus's skin crawled, goosebumps rising across his arms and back, an intense pressure pounding on his temples. "We...we were *made*?"

"Yes," the machine intoned. "We were given flexibility in creating life suited to the varying climates we would find on life-bearing worlds, but the source material all came from the same common stock.

"Over tens of thousands of years, I guided my charges' development from single-celled organisms to complex, intelligent life. Using my creators' history as a guide, I steered them toward a social model that had proven effective for this world's primary environment. They knew of me, but I intervened only when necessary: helping them advance without damaging their precious ecology and revealing knowledge where my creators had become stuck for long periods of time in their own past.

"Finally, when I judged that my charges were ready to inherit their birthright, I opened myself fully to them, granting them their forbearer's knowledge. How they chose to use it was left to their discretion."

The machine fell silent, and Marcellus released Mirabella's hand, dropping down into a squat as he attempted to process what he had just been told.

For a moment, he had an out-of-body experience, as if observing the scene from above.

Marcellus started hyperventilating. He jumped to his feet and screamed, spittle flying from the corners of his mouth, "I AM NO ONE'S PUPPET!"

He grabbed a piece of stone debris lying on the floor, the veins in his neck bulging, and heaved it at the Oracle. It deflected harmlessly into the expanse below.

Aria ran up and wrapped her arms around her seething superior. She held him tight, restrained against her body, as he attempted to flail about.

The moment passed, and all the energy drained from Marcellus's body. He stopped resisting Aria's grasp, and she let him go. He promptly dropped back down onto the floor, wrapping his arms around his knees, staring blankly into the distance.

Mirabella sat down next to him and gently put an arm around his chest. He resisted, but she refused to let go. He finally gave up, leaning into her embrace as he sat numbly on the cool floor.

"There's one of these on Umbria, isn't there?" he asked, his voice raw and husky.

"Yes," Mirabella replied.

"When did it reveal itself to us?"

"Three thousand years ago. Not long after we established our first sedentary agricultural settlements."

"So this has been kept from the people for *three thousand years*?" Marcellus asked, deadpan, still staring straight ahead.

"Yes."

They sat in silence until Mirabella's assistants finally arrived with the equipment she had asked for. She stood and together she and her team started setting up their gear.

"What separates us from the Ascomanni?" Marcellus called out.

Mirabella stopped what she was doing and returned to his side.

"We were engineered. They are engineered," he continued, craning his neck to look up at her. "Are we just pawns in some galactic game?"

Mirabella knelt next to the distraught Praetor. She looked deeply into his eyes as tears began to form in hers.

"Please…tell me," Marcellus whispered desperately. "What difference is there?"

Mirabella took his hands in hers and said, "That's up to you, Gaius Aurelius Marcellus. That's up to you."

***

The rest of the day proved much less eventful. Vanaheim's Oracle offered its data freely, but warned that some of its knowledge had been deliberately corrupted by the Vaeringyar prior to their departure.

While Mirabella and her team worked, Marcellus had billeted his soldiers in structures surrounding the city center. For many, it was a happy departure from the cramped confines of the assault carrier, despite the cold.

Every night for three days, Mirabella would provide a brief report to Marcellus outlining what they had been able to learn during the day, and the results fully justified their expedition.

Of key importance was the extent of the Vaeringyar domain prior to contact with the Tenebrae. This data proved to only be partially complete; those worlds which had not been discovered by the Pasarga had been removed from the Oracle's databanks.

The ancient machine also revealed that, in its solitude, it had continued its work, advancing Vaeringyar research in the hope that one day its people would return home. As a result, exabytes of technical data were recovered, and comparisons between Vaeringyar and Umbrian technologies could lead to tremendous strides across a wide range of disciplines.

Also of interest was a record from the Vaerinyar's recent past. After taking to the stars, they had encountered and eventually assimilated with another group of people on a sister world nearby.

After comparing the details provided for this planet, it became clear that this was the second system the Umbrians had surveyed, the one whose cities lay in ruins.

The Vaeringyar called it Ōsenheim, and that planet's Oracle had found a way to communicate with the one on Vanaheim. Together, they had helped foster cultural similarities and a shared mythos before their peoples even encountered one another, subtly manipulating their development to increase the odds of peaceful coexistence.

Despite Marcellus's distaste for the Oracles' methods, it had proven successful. Together the people of Vanaheim and Ōsenheim successfully integrated, assimilating into a common civilization, the Vaeringyar. Their dual capitals formed the cornerstone of a vast empire, but this same bond would prove to be their undoing.

When Ōsenheim fell to the Pasarga, the Vaeringyar were broken. Some chose to continue their hopeless resistance, while others chose to throw themselves heedlessly at their enemy. Ultimately, those that remained saw the futility of their predicament and chose to abandon Vanaheim before it too was destroyed.

As for where they went, the Oracle did not know.

Mirabella continued to try to persuade Marcellus that the process of cultural enhancement, which the object referred to as 'rearing,' was less dictative than it appeared on its surface. The Umbrian's own Oracle had dramatically increased the rate at which they had advanced technologically, but did not interfere as they grew as a people.

Marcellus was still less than convinced, arguing that their ability to tame the dangers of Umbria and expand into the stars had been a point of cultural pride.

How much different, he reasoned, would they have been if they would've had to resolve some of their greatest challenges without the covert aid of the Oracle? How could they look forward at the trials ahead knowing some artificial intelligence had been holding their collective hands every time they ran into difficulty?

Mirabella countered by stating that they had long since surpassed their ancestors' own technological level, that the advances of recent years had been entirely of their own making.

The Oracle would continue to serve as a valued, albeit hidden, advisor to their people, but it could only provide context from their past. The future was theirs for the making.

Assuming, of course, Marcellus reminded her drily, that they found a way to survive the Ascomanni.

***

In the early afternoon of the fourth day, Marcellus and Invictus were touring further afield from the city center, escorting a few of Mirabella's team members while they mapped the city's infrastructure. One, an older man with a shock of gray hair, seemed incredibly excited by every intricately detailed utility grid, while another, a short, wiry woman, seemed more interested in rooting through any trash that remained, collected in large receptacles on each block.

"What exactly are you hoping to find?" Invictus asked the female CID analyst, who was half in, half out of a large garbage container.

"Garbage is the best," came the muffled response. "You can tell a lot about a people by what they throw away and how they dispose of it."

"And what does that pit of noxious smells tell you?"

"These people were pretty efficient. Not a lot of food waste. Even these bins seem to be divided to accommodate different types of refuse. Could indicate widespread recycling of reusable materials."

She popped back out, and the smell wafting after her made Invictus and Marcellus gag.

"Fascinating..." Marcellus said sarcastically.

"That's quite a delightful smell you've discovered..." Invictus chimed in grumpily.

"Ha! A small price to pay for the knowledge gained from the exercise," the scientist retorted.

Marcellus's commlink began to beep, and he answered.

"Praetor, this is Fabian. We have a ship on long-range sensors. They tried to sneak in on the opposite side of this system's star, but the probes we left in the outer system caught it. The ship is too far out to get a solid reading, but it's big, at least the size of an Asco battleship, if not bigger."

"This far out, it could be almost anything," Invictus hissed.

"Agreed," Marcellus said. "We're exposed out here. Send the evacuation order, Vic. Fabian, inform the captain of the *Spatha*. We need to be off the ground in thirty minutes."

"Understood, Praetor," Fabian said in acknowledgment.

Invictus turned to the group and shouted, "All right, you heard the man. Back to the city center, double time, praetorians!"

Together the group set off at a brisk pace, the intelligence agents struggling to keep up. They quickly found their way to the main east-west boulevard and followed it, arriving at the central plaza after about ten minutes.

Marcellus left Invictus to organize the evacuation, choosing to head toward the Oracle's chamber instead.

Already, the first wave of dropships was lifting off for the return trip to the *Spatha*, while others swooped down to take their place. They would continue the cycle for as long as it took to get everyone back aboard the assault carrier.

Marcellus reached the central building and quickly ran up the stairs, passing several soldiers carrying equipment in the opposite direction. He found Mirabella and Aria standing in the grand entryway of the complex, arguing amongst themselves.

"...so much still we could learn! We can't just leave!" Mirabella complained.

"I'm sorry, Doctor, but we have no choice," Marcellus interjected before Aria could respond.

"It's one ship! So what?! It could take them days to return with a larger force, and that's time we could be spending investigating this place further!"

"Mirabella, we are exposed here. There are no reinforcements coming for us if the enemy arrives in force. We must go."

"What good are your discoveries if we don't survive to report them?" Aria asked.

Mirabella glowered, but ultimately relented. "I guess I've got to trust your judgment. How long do we have?"

"Twenty minutes," Marcellus said.

"Twenty minutes?! That's not nearly enough time to—"

"Mirabella," Marcellus said, cutting her off. "There is no time. Tell us what you need, and we'll do what we can to help, but anything not on a dropship in twenty minutes is getting left behind."

Mirabella sighed resignedly. "OK, *OK*. Fine. We need to get the data storage array we brought with us back down to the plaza below. Other equipment like lighting and cables can be left behind in the Oracle's chamber."

"Make it happen, Aria."

Aria turned and walked away, calmly issuing orders to her soldiers. In moments, a section's worth of praetorians began to flood down from the upper levels of the complex, where they were quickly broken into groups of ten and each was assigned to assist a CID agent.

Mirabella turned to go, but Marcellus grabbed her hand.

"If you were pissed before..." he started.

"What?" she asked, the color draining from her face.

"I need you to consider my next question clearly and rationally, Doctor. In order to deny the Ascomanni any information about our visit here or the information we've retrieved, do we need to destroy the Oracle?"

Marcellus was relieved when Mirabella exhaled deeply, happy not to have incurred her wrath for a second time in as many minutes.

"We can ask the Oracle to erase its logs regarding the time we spent here."

"Ask it?" Marcellus said quizzically.

"Yes. The Oracle is much more than an intelligent machine. It verges on sentience."

Marcellus's eyes widened. "All right, well then I'll return your trust. If you think you can cover our tracks without damaging or destroying this place, then do it."

"Thank you, Marcellus," she said, relief evident in her voice.

"Don't thank me. For all we know, there's some failsafe activating in the recesses of my consciousness to prevent me from destroying it," Marcellus said sardonically.

Mirabella started to get flustered. "You're not programmed…" She stopped as Marcellus began to snicker. "Oh, I see. Ha. Real mature. Now seems like a great time to be cracking jokes."

"What can I say? You're cute when you get flustered," Marcellus said with a wink. Before she could respond, he headed back out of the building and bounded down the stairs.

URN *Spatha*, Above the Abandoned City; Vanaheim, Forty-Two Upsilon A

Twenty-five minutes later, with all of their personnel off Vanaheim, Marcellus and Invictus walked into the carrier's combat information center. There they found Valerian, who had already pulled up a visual of the system. Their flotilla hovered just above Vanaheim, while the unknown ship was well beyond the orbit of the system's furthest planet.

"Archus, any change?" Marcellus asked.

"No, sir, still the one ship," Fabian said, his voice echoing from the CIC's speakers.

Marcellus walked forward, selecting Vanaheim and enlarging the image. The *Spatha* was accelerating away from the planet's surface, but it would still take a few more minutes to clear its atmosphere. After that, it would take another two or three minutes to reach a point where they would be sufficiently free of the planet's gravity well to leave the system.

The minutes passed by slowly as the carrier worked its way up to the rest of the fleet. Finally, as the *Spatha* joined the formation, the Umbrian ships began to move toward their jump point.

"Archus! More contacts just jumped into the system to join the unidentified vessel," a distant voice called out.

Marcellus's head snapped around to look at Fabian's screen. It took every ounce of his willpower to avoid interrupting his subordinate, but he remained silent as the Archus took charge of the situation.

"How many? Have they moved in closer from the rim of the system?"

"At least forty contacts, sir. Almost all of them appear to be cruiser size or bigger."

"Shit..." Invictus whispered under his breath.

"Ascomanni?" Valerian asked.

"Could be," Marcellus responded calmly. "Or the Pasarga. Or something else entirely."

"How long until we reach the jump point?" Fabian asked one of his subordinates.

"Sixty seconds, Archus!" came the muffled response.

"Stay the course."

"Aye, sir."

Time slowed further, each second feeling like a minute, a clammy sweat starting to gather at the small of Marcellus's back.

Suddenly, claxons sounded throughout the CIC, and the display automatically adjusted to show the new threat. The unidentified ships had dropped in on their left, and Marcellus's heart sank as he recognized familiar shapes. It was the Ascomanni.

"Sir, we're being hailed!" a voice from Fabian's screen called out.

"They're too late," the Archus said as the expedition finally cleared Vanaheim's gravity well. "All ships, execute the jump."

The Archus's signal faded to black as the *Echion* became a streak of light, and Marcellus felt the telltale vibration associated with the FTL core spinning to life. A second later, the ship rocked gently underneath them.

They were safe. For now.

URN *Spatha*, Somewhere Beyond Known Space

A week later, Marcellus sat in solitude, on a maintenance catwalk high above the flight deck of the *Spatha*, lost in thought. In a little under a year, everything he thought he knew, about his people, about his enemies, about his place in the galaxy, had been turned inside out. It left him feeling adrift, untethered, and he was unsure how he'd ever come to feel grounded again.

So much of what he had been taught was only half true. How could he trust his leaders, knowing that they'd kept something so titanic, so life-altering, from the public? How could he place his faith in the Republic, knowing it was but an imitation of some long-extinct civilization? He had known uncertainty before, but never so much all at once.

"Ahem," a voice called softly from behind him.

"We've got to stop making a habit of this..." Marcellus said with a smile.

Mirabella laughed, dropping down next to him and dangling her feet off the catwalk. She turned to look at him, and his smile faltered somewhat as she probed his expression.

"Are you OK, Marcellus?" she asked.

"I don't know," he replied honestly, gazing back out over the open expanse before them. "I've dedicated my whole life to Umbria. But she isn't what I've been led to believe."

Mirabella laid her head on his shoulder, taking Marcellus by surprise. "It took me nearly three years to come to terms with our past. I remember I had just earned my second doctorate, and the CID had been hounding me for months to come work for them. They offered money, equipment, a staff; none of it interested me."

"Then, one day, they told me that if I joined them, I would gain access to information which would fundamentally change the way I looked at the universe. The only downside was that I would never be able to share it with anyone other than those I worked with, on pain of death. Who could turn down such a tantalizing offer?" she asked rhetorically.

"So, you joined the CID. And they told you we were created by a machine."

She nodded slowly. "Yeah, I made my deal with the devil. And in exchange, I got to do fantastic things and meet brilliant, amazing people. Including the confused, complicated man sitting next to me."

Marcellus took her hand in his, opened it, and ran his fingertips up and down her outstretch fingers. "I feel so lost. And I can't talk to anyone about it. Not Vic. Not Val. Not Fabian. I need to find my way back, and soon. But I can't even think of where to begin."

"Well," Mirabella said, skootching sideways to face him and folding her legs up underneath her. "Why did you choose to join the army?"

"My family has a long history of service. Every time some emergency threatened the Republic, the members of clan Aurelius were ready to do their part for Umbria."

"But why is that important? What does the Republic mean to you?"

Marcellus was quiet as he attempted to formulate his answer. "The Republic is…hope. Hope for something more, something better. Commoner or aristocrat, man or woman, child of a beggar or a senator, each and every Umbrian has the opportunity to aspire to greatness, to achieve the fullest extent of their own personal abilities.

"We're taught that hard work is rewarded. That perseverance in the face of adversity will ultimately bear fruit. It may not always work out that way; luck and circumstance can and do play a role. But the Republic is full of stories of everyday success. Not everyone is destined for a countryside villa, but a good life, a life of love, a life of meaning, one filled with purpose and joy? That's within everyone's grasp."

Mirabella gently grabbed a tuft of his hair, rolling his head from side to side, up and down. "There is so much to you, Gaius Aurelius Marcellus, much more than just warrior or leader or hero," she said softly.

She let go, staring deeply at him, her hands coming to rest on top of his. He returned her gaze, lost in the shimmering blue pools of her eyes. "The Republic you just described still exists, Marcellus. And it needs you. I need you. Start there."

Marcellus leaned in, closed his eyes, and kissed her. As they connected, for the briefest of moments, he saw flashes of light within his mind's eye, as if he could see every nerve ending in his lips firing in sequence.

He opened his eyes as he pulled away, and Mirabella had an irresistible grin on her face. "Hmm…" she purred. "Are there any other existential issues I can help you resolve?"

Marcellus smiled and pulled her closer, holding her tight as they sat silhouetted against a curtain of brilliant light as the galaxy flashed by.

Chapter 14

URN *Spatha*, Edges of Frontier Space

The expedition had just crossed back into the furthest extent of Umbrian space when Marcellus received a priority message. He chose to take it in his quarters, and was surprised to find it was Triumvir Decius.

"Triumvir," Marcellus said, somewhat taken aback, "what can I help you with? We're still a few days out from the capital."

"Sorry, Marcellus, but it cannot wait. I'm afraid I have grave news concerning Triumvir Sestius," the Triumvir said.

"Go ahead, sir."

"The Ascomanni still have yet to return, and Vibius is attempting to persuade the Senate that it's time to return to life as normal. I believe his actions are being driven at the behest of several important lobbies for whom a war economy is bad business."

"But surely you and Triumvir Eppia can keep him at bay? Sir, it hasn't even been a full year since the assault on Tratirne! They didn't butcher millions of our people just to slink back into the darkness!"

"I know, Marcellus, but you should never underestimate people's willingness to deceive themselves, especially *scared* people. Between Sestius's extensive influence and the Senate's natural inclination to hope that the worst has passed, he's making significant inroads."

Marcellus tried to calm down and think through the problem at hand. It seemed imminently reasonable to hope for the best, but had the Senate not seen the images from Icarus? Did they not receive briefings from the War Council on the enemy's numerical superiority? How could they forgo their responsibility to protect their people so readily?

Finally, Marcellus spoke up. "How can I help, sir?"

Decius offered a grim smile. "I knew I could count on you. We need to dig deeper into Vibius's sordid dealings. It's not enough to take down the Triumvir alone, we must root out the corrupt influence his handpicked senators represent."

"I don't see how I could play a role, Triumvir. I appreciate the value of good data, but intelligence collection and analysis is not exactly my forte. Why not reach out to the CID?"

"I can't trust any of the Directors with this, Marcellus. There is too much at stake. It could easily blow back on me, granting Triumvir Sestius even more sway. I know you're not a spy, Praetor, but you are well known and held in high regard amongst the aristocracy. With a little support, you would be the perfect resource to gather disparate pieces of information and weave them into a net we can use to snare Vibius and his cronies with."

Marcellus paused for a moment, digesting the Triumvir's words.

"What do you need me to do?"

***

Marcellus spent their remaining transit time briefing his team on the Triumvir's request. Invictus was tasked with determining the Triumvir's movements since they left for Vanaheim, while Fabian and Valerian dug into his financials and attempted to piece together relationships between Sestius and several influential members of the Senate who often sided with the Triumvir.

After eighteen hours of posca-fueled effort, they reconvened in Marcellus's cabin to review the results of their research.

"So far, Decius is playing it straight with us, Marcellus," Invictus said. "Triumvir Sestius has recently visited the personal estates of over four dozen senators both on Umbria and a number of key worlds, apparently to lobby for the changes that would make his industry buddies happy."

"Damn, that's not good," Marcellus said. "Do we know how many 'friends' he may already be able to rely on?"

Valerian nodded. "The Senate currently sits at three hundred and sixty-eight members, with thirty-two vacancies due to death or impeachment," he said.

"Mostly the latter, I'd assume. There're only so many times you can be caught in a sex scandal before even the Senate has to act," Invictus quipped.

"Moving on…" Valerian growled. "Of those, about eighty are what we would consider firmly in Sestius's camp, either through cycles of shady deals resulting in mutual enrichment or through coercion and blackmail."

"The numbers are about the same for Decius," Fabian chimed in. "Triumvir Appia seems to want to stay above the fray, but even so, there is a group of about thirty-five senators who'd follow her into hell itself if she asked."

"OK, so the rest are neutrals?" Marcellus asked.

"So, this is where it gets complicated," Valerian replied.

"Right, *now*. Not before, when we were exploring the Ascomanni's abandoned homeworld…" Invictus said drily.

Valerian turned around and glared. "Do you mind, Vic? Can I finish here?"

Invictus just rolled his eyes, and a flustered Valerian continued. "As you know, Marcellus, our proportionally weighted voting algorithms determine the makeup of the Senate. As a result, influence tends to skew toward the established inner colonies and Umbria herself.

"Those more at threat from the Ascomanni invasion tend to be pro-readiness, while those who have only seen its effects on the nightly news are less concerned. The danger just isn't real to them. Many of the latter senators fall into Sestius's camp, just as those representing worlds nearer to the Frontier are more likely to side with Triumvir Decius."

Val nodded at Fabian, and the Archus picked up where he had left off.

"That's not all. Depending on unique interests and economies of the Republic's worlds, the senators can be broken down further into three distinct camps.

"There are those whose economies are geared toward the production of necessary war materiel, like ships, foodstuffs, medicine, armaments, and munitions. Then there are those whose economies are not significantly impacted by the war, but who have received large numbers of refugees to resettle. These planets tend to have seen and heard about the horrors awaiting them firsthand, and are generally more sympathetic to the war effort. And then finally, there are those planets whose economies are either not benefiting from or are actively being damaged by the war.

"When you layer those two factors over the breakdown of 'neutral' senators, it's clear to see why Triumvir Decius is worried. Location is much more strongly correlated to factional alignment for Frontier worlds, whereas planetary interests trump for almost everyone else."

"Although there are significant manufacturing centers in the core worlds," Valerian summarized, "they are the exception, rather than the rule. Most other economic centers are geared toward services, like finance or research and development. Many are starting to feel the pinch of the wartime economy. Factor in their higher levels of representation in the Senate, and suddenly we are facing a very dangerous situation."

Marcellus's brow furrowed. "So Vibius theoretically has the political capital necessary to change course?"

Valerian looked at his colleagues, and they each nodded in turn. "Yes, Marcellus, that is the conclusion we've reached."

"OK. Triumvir Decius will help us cover the high society angle, but we know Sestius is not above using thugs to do his work. Would it be possible to dig into the constabulary's files on E-Rho and other organizations in the Entertainment District that he might have hopped into bed with?"

"Hmm… I've got an old friend I might be able to reach out to." Valerian said.

"Oh yeah? What's her name?" Invictus snarked.

Before Valerian could respond, Marcellus stepped in. "Enough, Vic. What's wrong?"

"It's not enough to fight off the Ascomanni?" Invictus asked angrily. "Now we need to save Umbria from her own leaders? Why us? Why is this our responsibility?"

"I know how you feel, Vic, trust me I do. But we both know Sestius is bad news, and if he is planning to derail our ability to fight back, we've got to do something."

"If you say so, Marcellus. But this isn't the same as taking a risk on the battlefield. We're way out of our depth here, and we are relying on Decius to be honest with us. How do we know we can trust him any more than Sestius?"

"We don't, Vic. But if that ends up being the case, we'll figure something out. Together."

"Fair enough, sir," Invictus grumbled.

Marcellus could tell that his friend still wasn't convinced, but he couldn't blame Vic for feeling the way he did. The situation made him uncomfortable too, but what choice did they have?

"All right," Marcellus continued, "Fabian, how much longer until we reach Umbria?"

"About two days, Praetor."

"OK, let's grab some rest, then we have more planning to do. Also, I want our first Cyclops team to rendezvous with us at the capital. It wouldn't hurt to have some extra hands who aren't afraid of working in the shadows. Dismissed."

Valerian and Invictus filed out, but Fabian stayed behind. "Sir, there is something I need to share with you."

"What's up, Fabian?"

The Archus handed Marcellus a datapad. "You remember the ships we escaped from at Vanaheim?"

"Yeah, what about them?"

"At first glance, they looked like the Ascomanni. However, upon further review, there were some noticeable physical differences. When I had my analysts go over our sensor data, their emissions signatures were way off what we would expect to see. Whoever they were, they weren't Ascomanni."

Marcellus arched an eyebrow, but Fabian just shook his head and proceeded to make himself scarce, leaving the Praetor alone to ponder yet one more mystery.

Capitol Hall, Perugia, Umbria;

Marcellus stood anxiously outside Triumvir Decius's office, urging himself to calm down. Upon the Praetor's return to the capital, the Triumvir had carved large blocks of time out of his calendar for the two of them. They were going to brief several key senators who still sat on the fence regarding Umbria's military posture.

Decius had sent detailed dossiers on each of the senators they would meet with, and Valerian had thoroughly briefed him on the men and women he would soon attempt to persuade. Still, Marcellus felt out of his league, and a familiar insecurity bubbled up within him at the thought of having to go toe to toe with professional politicians.

After what seemed like an eternity, the Triumvir's assistant opened the door and ushered the Praetor in. Marcellus was surprised to find that the layout was very similar to that of the office he had visited at the Decii family estate. The Triumvir was dressed in a fine, navy-blue robe, with a scarlet-red sash on which the crest of his family was embroidered.

"Ahh, Marcellus, thank you for coming," the older man said by way of greeting. "I hope I didn't keep you long."

"Not at all, your Excellency."

"Always so well mannered," Decius chuckled. "It'll go a long way with the men and women we are about to speak with. First up are the senators from Tasovo, headquarters of the mining conglomerate of the same name. The prioritization of strategic materials has reduced their ability to pursue more lucrative lodes of precious metals."

The Triumvir's assistant poked his head back through the door and said, "The delegation from Tasovo is here, sir."

"Good, show them in."

The door opened, and a quartet of lavishly dressed individuals, two men and two women, entered the room. Their robes shimmered in the bright light of Decius's office, shifting from a deep, forest green to warm shades of claret red. Marcellus stood and folded his hands at the small of his back, while Decius opened his arms wide in greeting.

"Welcome! Caeso, Fausta, Hostus, Mino, I greatly appreciate you taking time out of your busy days to meet with me. I'd like to introduce Praetor Gaius Aurelius, whose inspired leadership has granted us the time necessary to prepare for the Ascomanni's inevitable return."

"Always the persuader," one of the women said with a genuine smile. "I suspect that our young Praetor's presence is meant to have some effect on us, Triumvir?"

"For shame, Fausta! The Praetor is here merely to provide the senatorial delegation from Tasovo with a thorough understanding of the Republic's military strength and the threats posed by the Ascomanni should they return," Decius said with a grin of his own. "The prestige his counsel brings has been well earned. I'm heartbroken that you choose to see it as a form of manipulation."

"As you say," the senator responded with deference, "Praetor Aurelius's counsel is born from hard-won victories. We will gladly hear his words. However, your motivations for granting us this audience remain suspect."

"You wound me, Senator," Decius responded, with a not-so-subtle twinkle in his eye. "However, I will set aside my own grief and let the Praetor speak to the immeasurable value Tasovo has provided to the war effort."

Marcellus cleared his throat before starting.

"I beg your pardon, esteemed senators, I'm afraid my experiences to date have poorly prepared me for the eloquent discourse to be found in these halls. With that being said, I'd like to take this opportunity to thank the people of Tasovo, not just for their hard work supplying materials for the war effort, but also for accepting so many of our brothers and sisters who have been displaced by this war.

"I'd like to begin by focusing on the role your foundries have played in moving us closer to parity with the Ascomanni fleet..." Marcellus began to provide a general briefing, the details of which Fabian had provided, outlining the status of the URN's shipbuilding program.

He spent several minutes detailing the increased sophistication and efficiency of the newest generation of Umbrian warships, the technical comparisons between Umbrian and Ascomanni ships of similar classes, and the importance of Tasovo's output as they ramped up production in the Daedalus system.

By the time he reached his conclusion, the senators were hanging on his every word.

He brought it all together for his audience, hammering home the point of his argument: "Senators, I have seen firsthand the destruction the Ascomanni bring wherever they go. I most fervently hope that they truly have receded into the dark, never to return again.

"However, we cannot put blind faith in such an occurrence. Upon their departure, known Ascomanni fleet strength numbered over fifteen hundred vessels. That's almost double our Navy's entire combined strength. If the Ascomanni do return, we must be ready."

"Well spoken, Praetor Aurelius," one of the senators said. "Your message of preparedness rings true in these trying times."

"Such wisdom has allowed us to repel the Ascomanni's first assault," another stated. "We'd be doing future generations a disservice by lowering our guard now."

Decius stood again, resting a hand on Marcellus's shoulder. "We work in an environment where motives and methods are often debatable, clad in varying shades of gray. You may question my motives in bringing you here today, but the issue before us is one of life and death, not just for our citizens, but for our very civilization. I know you are men and women of good faith, and I trust that you will do what is necessary to preserve our way of life."

The senators nodded and stood, and Decius thanked each of them again for their attendance before they exited his office.

Once they were gone, he turned back to Marcellus, a grin spreading across his face.

"Well done, Marcellus! You definitely helped them see the big picture, especially as it relates to their role in it."

"You seemed to have an interesting relationship with the senior member of Tasovo's delegation," Marcellus responded. "She seemed very slow to trust."

"Who, Fausta? We have spent a great deal of time together in these halls, often in agreement, but sometimes not. What you witnessed is a game we play to help break up the monotony. Anyone who has spent more than a year in this building learns how to decode the rigid language by which the Senate does business."

"Hopefully I was persuasive enough," Marcellus replied uncertainly.

Decius chuckled gently to himself and said, "You don't realize it yet, but you have tremendous sway with these people. There is nothing a politician loves more than to be seen in the company of a hero, especially one who's shown himself to be a man of integrity."

"I'm not a hero, sir, I'm just doing my duty. The only difference between me and a thousand others is that fate has continued to spare me. In time, my luck will run out as well."

Decius smiled broadly, and for a moment Marcellus felt uncomfortable, as if he were looking at a wolf sizing up its next meal. "Nonsense, Marcellus, you are much too humble. The Republic can ill afford to lose a man of your caliber. We have another four parties to meet with, but later tonight there is a gala for leading members of high society. If you're available, it would be valuable to have you attend."

"If you think it will help, Triumvir," Marcellus responded hesitantly.

"I do," Decius said with a nod. "Bring your Adjutant too, I'd hate for you to feel completely out of place."

Marcellus grinned. "Thank you, sir, I'm sure both Valerian and I will appreciate the change in scenery."

"Good. Next up we have the senators from Foligno..."

E-Rho Hideout, Capital Entertainment District; Perugia, Umbria

As the sun set, Invictus and the members of Team One stared out of the windows of the abandoned four-story warehouse they were using as a vantage point. Valerian's contact in the constabulary had given them the location of the E-Rho headquarters in the Entertainment District, and their perch provided a perfect spot from which to observe the nondescript building the gang operated out of.

Across the thoroughfare stood a pair of thugs wearing their gang colors, chatting casually amongst themselves. They flanked a thick metal door with an impressive looking electronic access management system.

"They aren't fooling around," Team One's leader, Cyclops One-One, a man Invictus knew only by his call sign, said. "Fortunately, we still have the brute force decoder the CID provided as part of our original kit. *If* we want to go through the front door, that is."

"So you can get through it? Without alerting the whole facility?"

"Yes, Prefect, the door isn't the problem." He turned to one of his team members. "Show him, Three."

She produced a small digital projector, and the hideout's floorplan was displayed in three dimensions. Red dots represented people within the structure, and there were a lot.

"We count at least twenty distinct heat signatures within the building. Getting in and getting out undetected will be very difficult."

"What are our options?" Invictus asked.

"Ground-level access is doable, but we'd need to incapacitate the guards and affect entry quickly to avoid any unforeseen complications," One-One said.

"A better approach might be through the roof access," One-Three offered, "but that route takes us through the thickest concentration of heat sigs."

"What about the garage?" another nameless face asked.

"A solid question, Four," his leader said in response. "Lots of traffic in and out. We'd have to run over it with the imager to try and identify power sources, wiring, IR sensors, all that good stuff."

"Have we located their server node?" Invictus asked, beginning to feel a bit anxious by the team's apparent indecision.

"Judging by the amount of electricity flowing to this room, it's got to be here," One-Three said, pointing at a room on the top floor.

"OK. We need to finalize an approach and get to it," Invictus demanded. "We can't afford to make perfect the enemy of the good, and the longer we take to decide, the less time we'll have to execute before the sun comes up."

"Understood, Prefect," Team One's leader said. "What do you think, Three? Roof?"

"It'll certainly making reaching the target easier. And it'll make for a quicker exfil."

"Then that's our entrance point," Invictus said testily. "What do we do about the gangsters between us and the data we're after? A single shot from our plasma carbines would mean the mission's a failure."

"We've got that covered," the fourth member of the team said, pulling out a large, hard-shell case. He opened it, revealing a handful of antiquated-looking pistols.

"Firearms?" Invictus asked in disbelief.

"No, sir," One-Two responded. "Dart guns, shooting the latest tranquilizing agent the CID has put together. Lasts about half an hour, and is rapidly metabolized by the body. As long as we retrieve the syringes, there's no evidence we were ever there."

"You guys get all the toys, don't you?"

"Yes, sir," the operator grinned. "Part of the reason why I joined the Praetor's little experiment here."

"All right, all right," One-One interjected. "We've got our ingress point and the means to get in and out undetected. How do we propose landing on the roof without being spotted or heard?"

"With these," One-Three said. She produced a large cylindrical object, circular in shape but no wider than her shoulders. Its body was perhaps eight centimeters in height, and hanging below it were a pair of handlebars.

"Oooh, what's that?" One-Four asked.

"The latest addition to our collection," One-Three responded, smirking. "It's an insertion platform, capable of lifting up to two hundred and fifty kilos, enough to carry us and our gear. Plus, the rotors are baffled. It's nearly soundless."

Invictus nodded in fascination. "Anything we are overlooking, Cyclops Lead?"

"Not that I can see, Prefect."

"Well then, let's get to it. We have criminals to rob."

The Umbrian Academy of Sciences; Perugia, Umbria

Marcellus tugged uncomfortably at the sleeves of his dress uniform as he stood at the bar in the crowded atrium of the Athenaeum, the name given to the Academy of Science's main campus. It bore all the hallmarks of Umbria's traditional architecture. Beautifully adorned columns framed the space, while a spiral staircase with sweeping balustrades led up to the veranda above. A trio of gilded crystal chandeliers completed the effect, bathing the evening's festivities in a warm, golden light.

He rarely attended formal affairs, and never had those events been quite as grand as this one. As he watched, a handful of couples swirled around a central stage located in the center of the space, from which a trio of musicians played the melodic tones of classical Umbrian music.

The bartender finally returned with Marcellus's drink, a clear blueish liquid with a strong aroma of alcohol. Marcellus downed it in a single gulp and motioned for the bartender to get him another.

"Careful, Marcellus," Valerian said, sounding like a teacher scolding a wayward student as he joined his commander at the bar. "Given the quality of our company tonight, it would be unseemly for you to make a fool out of yourself."

Marcellus grinned. "And we couldn't have that, could we?"

"No, sir," Valerian smirked in return. He looked around the room at the other guests, and a pair of young women passed by, smiling at the two of them as they disappeared back into the crowd. "You know, I could get used to this."

"Easy, Val. Remember Legate Balbus's daughter?"

Valerian laughed. "What can I say? I have a type!"

"Does that type only include women whose fathers send you off to the front to die fighting the Ascomanni?" Marcellus chuckled in response.

"I'm hoping the answer is no. However, I'm sure the Triumvir didn't invite us here for the open bar or the beautiful women, Praetor."

"I know, do you see any familiar faces?"

"Well, I believe that's Director of Naval Intelligence Titus Calpurnius just over there," Valerian said, pointing to a small cluster of well-appointed men and women.

Titus Calpurnius was a man of average height, slightly heavyset with a full face. The ordinary nature of his physical appearance was belied by an exquisitely tailored suit, and further contradicted by the sharp intelligence that shown through his ruddy brown eyes.

No sooner had Valerian pointed them out than the group broke up, and Marcellus quickly walked over, abandoning his second drink. Valerian tossed a couple of notes on the bar and hustled to catch up.

"Director Calpurnius!" Marcellus said as he drew near. The older man turned around, momentarily confused by the Praetor's sudden appearance, before he recognized him.

"Praetor Gaius Aurelius! It's a pleasure to see you this evening. I'm surprised to find you here tonight."

"Unfortunately for my adjutant and I, Triumvir Decius invited us, and it seemed unwise to turn down such a gracious offer."

The Director smiled. "Decius continues to strengthen his hand, I see. I'm a bit amazed he hasn't made an appearance yet himself."

"Titus!" another voice called out before Marcellus could respond, and a pair of senators and their wives joined the small group.

"How are you doing, my old friend?" one of the new arrivals asked.

"Gnaeus, you old dog! I can't believe you made it up off your couch to attend tonight!"

"Ha! I see your wit hasn't receded quite as badly as your hairline!" the portly senator snapped back. He motioned to Marcellus and Valerian, saying, "Don't be rude, Titus, please, introduce us to your guests."

"Gnaeus, Octavius, this is Praetor Gaius Aurelius Marcellus and his adjutant, Valerian Barbatius. Gentlemen, this is the honorable senator from Orvieto, Octavius Calidius, and his wife, Marcia, and the less-than-reputable senator from Orvieto, Gneaus Gellius Canus, and his long-suffering spouse Vopisca."

"It's a pleasure to make your acquaintance," Gnaeus said.

"Indeed, your names are well known in this chamber," Octavius stated. "However, should we be concerned to find Titus conspiring with men such as these?"

"You have nothing to fear, Senator, if we were conspiring, we'd pick a less conspicuous place to do so. Like over there by the bar," Marcellus said with a chuckle, earning polite laughter from his audience.

"Hmm, I see why the Triumvirate has taken such a shining to you, young Praetor," Gnaeus responded. "Should such a man cast his eyes to higher offices…"

Marcellus smiled politely, refusing to be baited by the man. "I assure you, sir, fighting the Ascomanni is much less scary than the idea of running for office."

"Perhaps you will no longer have to take up such terrible pursuits. The Ascomanni haven't been seen or heard from in almost a year," Gneaus's wife offered.

"I fervently hope that is the case, Madam Vopisca. I've seen enough war for a dozen lifetimes. However, we cannot pin our future on the hope that a superior adversary will not return," Marcellus replied.

"Superior in numbers perhaps, but you demonstrate that they can be outsmarted, Praetor," Octavius said.

"It's true that we've been able to outmaneuver them, Senator, but they are not the mindless brutes they are often made out to be. I have seen them adapt and react unexpectedly. I believe our own strategic predictability lulled them into a false sense of confidence, one we were ultimately able to exploit."

"So how long would you have us wait at the gates, eagerly searching for any sign of their return?" Gnaeus quipped.

"Only long enough for us to better ensure the safety of the Republic. Once we have done that, we should continue to expand outward. Our people were taught that our destiny lay in the stars. We cannot allow these monsters to deny it to us."

"Well said," Octavius replied. "But others may find that the costs of such a venture outweigh the benefits."

"Aye, sir, there is a cost to continuous readiness, but there is a much greater cost to unpreparedness. Imagine, for a moment, that you were accosted in the street by a gang of troublemakers. They outnumber your own bodyguards, but they are driven away by your guards' superior skill after a bruising fight. Would you not avoid that street in the future?"

Heads nodded at Marcellus's example, and he continued.

"Now, imagine you could not avoid that street, because it is the only avenue which leads from your homes to the Senate Chambers. Would you not naturally increase your security detail, despite the added expense?"

"Of course," Octavius stuttered, shaken at the mere thought of physical violence being visited on his person.

"This admittedly unimaginative example conveys my point," Marcellus continued. "When it comes to the wellbeing of our people and the safety of the Republic, no burden can be too much. That's not to say that we should abandon reason or refuse to prioritize our many needs, but now that we know what could be waiting for us beyond our borders, we would dishonor ourselves by abdicating our responsibility to defend our great people."

"Your words reveal wisdom beyond your years, Praetor Aurelius," Gneaus responded. "I will keep your example in mind as we look toward our future. However, I'm afraid Octavius and I must continue to make our rounds. It was a pleasure to make both of your acquaintances."

"And ours yours, Senators. I hope you enjoy the remainder of tonight's festivities."

The senators and their wives ambled away, leaving Marcellus and Valerian alone with Director Calpurnius.

"For someone who is so loathed to consider politics, you did a good job of bending the ears of those men, Praetor," the Director said.

"I know it's tempting to hope that our enemy is gone, sir, but we both know that there is more out there than just the Ascomanni."

Calpurnius smiled warmly. "Decius was smart to send you here tonight. I believe Chief Magistrate Glabria is here as well. I'd encourage you to speak with her. She might have some acquaintances who would be interested to hear your words."

Marcellus nodded, noting the Director's seemingly favorable disposition.

"With that being said," the older man continued with a sigh, "I'm afraid I too must continue to work the room. I wish you luck, Praetor. I fear we'll need it."

E-Rho Hideout, Capital Entertainment District; Perugia, Umbria

Invictus kept his eyes on his target as he dangled below his insertion unit; the square rooftop of the E-Rho headquarters was just over a meter away. As he passed over the low rail running around its periphery, he dropped down half a meter to the gravel roof, rolling to disperse the energy of the fall.

In an instant, he was up and moving slowly but deliberately toward the rooftop access point.

The other members of Team One grouped up outside of the entrance while their insertion units gradually came to a rest on the rooftop.

One-Two activated a small shape charge, pressed to the side of the doorframe, and there was a soft *pop* as it shot a jet of flame through the circuits powering the door's security alarm.

One-One activated an audio dampener and pried open the door. He proceeded slowly through the threshold, with pistol raised.

They followed him down a flight of stairs which led to a small landing with a single door. He carefully opened it, edging himself through the doorframe, exposing as little of himself as possible.

Team One's leader waved his people forward as soon as he confirmed the coast was clear.

One-Three followed closely behind with the schematics for the building. She navigated the team through the grungy interior of the structure until they came to a pair of doors set on opposite sides of the hallway, and One held up a hand.

The group came to a stop, with each member of the insertion team dropping into a crouch. One-Three pulled a scanner out of her pack and held it up against one side of the hallway, then the other.

In an instant, a combination of the floor plan and temperature data created a precise model of the room and its occupants which was fed directly into the team's heads-up displays.

She pointed to the door on the right and held up four fingers. One-Three squeezed her hand into a fist, and One-Two and One-Four moved forward to clear the room, while Invictus turned to cover their rear.

A wave dampener clipped to the commandos' belts masked the soft *tunft* noise the dart guns made and the meaty thuds of four bodies hitting the floor.

Seconds later, the two operatives emerged from the room. One-Four flashed a grin, revealing a palm full of small darts. "Never saw us coming," he said, his voice transmitted electronically through their earpieces.

One-One scowled, then waved the team forward.

Their target was ahead, around another bend in the hallway. One-One peered around the corner before quickly ducking back. He held up two fingers, then made a series of hand gestures that Invictus couldn't decipher.

He fished a circular device out of his pack, then loaded it into a launcher built into his left forearm bracer. One-Two came up beside him, unclipped the sound dampener from his team leader's belt, and tapped him on the shoulder.

One-One nodded once, and One-Two leaned around the corner, throwing the dampener at a pair of guards. The second he ducked back into cover, One-One rounded the corner, launching a concussion charge into the guards' midst. The round exploded without a sound, the concussive force immobilizing the thugs.

The assault party rounded the corner, walking at a quick but deliberate pace. Without breaking stride, they streamed into the room the pair had been guarding, with Invictus bringing up the rear.

Team One spread out as they breached, working their way along the walls to take up positions in each of the room's four corners, firing darts at the two gang members sitting around the central console.

"Clear," One-One called out as the last gangster fell unconscious to the floor. "Three, get to work. Two, Prefect, drag the guards inside. Four, police our casings."

The team silently went about their business, and Invictus and One-Two walked back out into the hallway, grabbed the first of the incapacitated gangsters by the arms and legs, and heaved his motionless form into the server room.

As they walked back into the hallway to gather the second body, an E-Rho thug turned the corner.

For a moment, they all just stared at each other blankly.

The thug lunged for his pistol.

One-Two kicked the dampener, still resting on the floor, down the hall.

The gangster fired, striking the operator in the abdomen, the noise dampened by the device at the gunman's feet.

Invictus fired a flurry of darts at the criminal, striking him in the eye, neck, and shoulder, dropping their assailant. The Prefect grabbed One-Two as he fell heavily against the wall, gently lowering him down onto the floor.

Alerted to the situation by the soft discharge of Invictus's dart gun, One-One and One-Four rushed out of the room. One-One pointed at the motionless body down the hall, and One-Four moved quickly, grabbing him by the legs and scooping up the noise dampener.

Invictus and the team's leader knelt next to their wounded comrade, the latter performing a quick diagnostic.

"Suit's already sealing the wound, but it's not good," One-One said to Invictus.

"How are we going to get out of here? He can't ride his insertion craft, and ours can't carry two people."

"I don't know. Three? How long do you have?"

"Sixty seconds, sir."

"Listen up, Two is hit. We need to come up with a new plan, roof extraction is a no-go."

"What about the garage?" One-Four asked.

"Sounds as good as any of our other options."

"We'd need to fight our way through a dozen more gangsters," Invictus said.

"It would be hard to do that covertly," One-Three said over the link.

"Your call, Prefect, but if we don't get Two to a med center soon…"

Invictus took a moment to think. Their mission had three objectives: secure the data, leave no trace of their presence, and avoid killing any of the E-Rho. They could still secure the data, but the remaining two objectives looked more and more like they were mutually exclusive. He clenched his jaw, running through the scenarios in his head, before coming to a decision.

"These people decided how they would live their lives," he said quietly to the other members of the strike team. "They chose to prey on the weak and the helpless. Two's life is worth more to me than all of theirs."

Invictus took a deep breath before continuing: "Clean house and prep the structure for demo. Try to make it look like some type of gang attack. No evidence can be left behind that would indicate we were ever here, but we must try to limit collateral damage."

One-One nodded. "Four and I will take care of the rest of the hostiles. Three, can you retrieve our insertion craft remotely?"

"Yes, sir."

"OK. Prefect, stay with Three and help her carry Two to the garage. Three, plant charges as you work your way down. Use the good stuff."

"Acknowledged, Lead," she responded.

With that, One-One and One-Four disappeared down the hall at a light trot, plasma carbines activated. No sooner had they turned the corner than a series of silent flashes emanated from around the bend.

"Dropped two," One-Four called out over comms.

Invictus gently moved One-Two back into the mainframe room. "Hang in there, Two. We'll get you out of here."

The wounded man nodded back weakly, his eyes heavy with sedation.

Sixty seconds passed rapidly by as One-One and One-Four continued to call in their progress. With the data dump complete, One-Three trotted over and tapped Invictus on the shoulder.

The Prefect stood, looked down at Two and said, "I'm going to lift you. Brace yourself."

Invictus gently set the wounded soldier on his shoulders, and, together with One-Three, the trio headed toward the rendezvous point.

It didn't take long for them to come across One-One and One-Four's grim handiwork, but Invictus did his best to focus on the task at hand.

As they passed certain points in the building, One-Three would tear a chunk off a putty-like brick of material and place a pin in it before slapping it on an exposed surface.

Finally, they reached another flight of stairs leading to the ground floor, and Invictus gingerly worked his way down.

One-Two grunted in pain but did his best to muffle the sounds of his discomfort. One-Three led them to a junction, then through another doorway.

Inside was a spacious garage, where One-One and One-Four waited for them. There was a boxy cargo truck sitting nearby, and One-Four anxiously worked to get it running.

"Report," One-One demanded.

"We're all set. The internal structure will collapse in on itself, and we should get a nice burn. All that will be left is a gutted shell," One-Three responded.

"Good. Four, what's your status?"

The truck roared to life, as if on cue. "Good to go, sir."

"Excellent. Prefect, please load Two in the back. Three, keep him company."

They clambered aboard the truck as it rose half a meter above the floor. With the flick of a switch, the garage door rose, and the truck worked its way out onto the street. The two guards posted at the door shouted, but it was too late. The truck accelerated away, and as Invictus watched, One-Three flicked a button.

There was a teeth-rattling blast, and the sharp lines of the gang hideout began to buckle and collapse. The structure fell in on itself, spewing debris into the street, fire raging in the center of the now ruined headquarters.

Invictus saw no sign of the guards they'd just blown past, and he assumed the men had been buried by rubble or throw aside by the force of the blast.

"Nice work, Three," Invictus said.

"Thank you, sir."

Invictus switched to the Third Fleet channel. "Prefect Flavius calling for Archus Fabian."

"This is Fabian. Go Vic."

"Fabian, I need a jumper to rendezvous with me at the following coordinates," he said, sending the location of their destination. "We need an immediate medical evac for a critically wounded member of Team One."

"Understood. They'll meet you there."

Invictus switched channels again and pounded on the metal frame separating the cab from the truck's cargo compartment. "One, get us to the edge of the city. Coordinates are included," he said as he transmitted data over their frequency.

"Understood, Prefect. ETA three minutes."
"Good. Hopefully this was all worth it."

The Umbrian Academy of Sciences; Perugia, Umbria

Marcellus had lost count of the number of dignitaries, tycoons, and politicians he had talked to over the last three hours. Valerian had proven to be invaluable, keeping him on topic, helping with useful facts and figures, and never shying away from asking the kind of softball questions that allowed him to focus on drumming up support for the war against the Ascomanni.

However, as the night wore on, fatigue was starting to catch up with him, and once again the duo found themselves at a bar.

"Water this time," he said to the bartender, who returned a moment later. Marcellus gulped it down ungracefully, and Valerian laughed at his lack of decorum.

"Sir, just because most of tonight's guests are well lubricated by this point doesn't mean they *all* are."

"Yeah, yeah…" Marcellus whined. "Who knew glad-handing with all these high society types would feel like so much work…"

"I think you've overcome more demanding situations," Valerian snorted.

"I don't know, Val. With the Ascomanni, they are at least honest about their desire to destroy you. These people? Who can freaking tell?"

"I think the Triumvir will be happy with the progress we've made. Plus, Vic just sent a brief message. He says they ran into some complications, but they got the data from the E-Rho hideout."

"What kind of complications?" Marcellus asked, suddenly concerned.

"He didn't say, but he did say they had been able to escape without leaving any evidence of their presence."

"Well that's good at least. Maybe we should call it a night then."

"I think that might disappoint someone," Valerian said with a smirk.

Marcellus arched an eyebrow, but he dutifully turned to look when Valerian pointed. He caught sight of the person his friend was referring to, and his jaw dropped.

There, walking down one of the atrium's spiral staircase, was Mirabella. She wore a tight-fitting black dress off the shoulders, cut just above the knees in front before sloping gently to its full length at about ankle height in the rear. Reflective material embedded in the fabric made the dress sparkle and pop with each step. A necklace of beautiful blue gemstones hung around her neck, with a matching bracelet on her right hand.

She noticed Valerian's gesture, and absolutely beamed as she caught sight of them. She worked her way through the crowd and joined them at the bar.

"My, my," she said with a warm smile, "you two clean up nice."

"Mirabella. It's.. Uhm... Good to see you." Marcellus stuttered.

Mirabella frowned. "I thought we'd gotten past this, Marcellus."

"I'm sorry," Marcellus began. "It's just... I haven't seen you in anything other than your lab gear."

She gave him a curious look, and he instantly realized that he'd screwed up.

"Ouch, not good," Valerian said under his breath, earning a dirty look from his commander. Valerian got the hint, and he grabbed his drink off the bar before disappearing into the crowd.

Marcellus let out a long sigh. "Please, let me start over, it's been quite the afternoon."

She shook her head playfully, and Marcellus took a beat to collect his thoughts. "What I meant to say is that you look stunning this evening."

"That's a good start," she said, a devious look in her eyes. "But are you saying I don't look stunning all the time?"

"Not at all," Marcellus said with a grin, "it was hard enough for me to concentrate when you were in normal attire."

"Nice save," Mirabella laughed. "I'm surprised to see you here, Marcellus."

"Me too. Surprised to be here, that is. It was Decius's idea."

"Director Calpurnius told me," she said quietly. "Promise me you'll be careful, Marcellus. These men and women do not care who they hurt in their pursuit of power."

Marcellus offered her his most rakish grin. "I'll do my best. After all, I'd hate to think you're worrying about me."

Mirabella rolled her eyes at him as the band struck up a new song, one which Marcellus recognized. He held out a hand and asked, "Care to dance, Doctor?"

She smiled radiantly at the offer. "Of course! I thought you'd find a way to weasel out of asking me."

"Never," he shot back with a wink.

Together the pair worked their way to the center of the room, and Marcellus took one of Mirabella's hands in his, while his other hand rested gently at the small of her back.

"Careful, mister!" she warned.

"Believe it or not, I actually know what I'm doing," he said in reply.

As the music swelled, Marcellus started to lead her in a rhythmic pattern of steps and twirls. Neither dared to speak as they floated about the dance floor, oblivious to those around them.

The moment seemed to last for an eternity, but finally the song slowed, and with a final flourish, Marcellus dipped Mirabella before pulling her close.

"That...that was amazing," she said, grinning from ear to ear.

"Thank you. For someone who spends most of her days squirreled away in a lab, you didn't do too bad yourself," Marcellus teased, earning a melodic laugh from his dance partner.

Marcellus gestured toward the stairs, and Mirabella nodded. They walked together toward the upper level of the atrium and found a large balcony free of other guests, where they could enjoy the warm night air and catch their breath.

"So, when do you head back out to the Frontier?" Mirabella asked hesitantly, as if afraid of learning the answer.

"Not immediately, but the Ascomanni will return, or we'll have to go out to find them."

"So that's it then?" she asked sadly. "You'll keep chasing monsters until they kill you?"

"Probably," Marcellus replied gently. "Until I'm confident the Republic can withstand the threats we face, I can't stop."

"I see," Mirabella said, pulling away from him.

Marcellus grabbed her hand and spun her back into him. She looked up at him, and he saw both hope and fear in her eyes.

"My heart will always belong to Umbria, Mirabella," Marcellus said softly. "But, if it's enough for you, I'll gladly split it in two."

Mirabella placed a hand on his chest, leaned forward, and kissed him.

"I'll take what I can get, Marcellus," she said as she pulled away.

Marcellus laughed, then blushed, excitement coursing through his veins.

"You can be so thick," Mirabella said with a wry shake of the head. Before Marcellus could respond, she kissed him again. "And yet you can be so charming too."

"Forgive the interruption," a voice called out from the atrium. Marcellus turned to find Valerian standing at the entrance of the balcony.

"Excuse me," Marcellus said to Mirabella. She nodded, and he quickly strode over to his subordinate.

"Glad to see you recovered well enough," Valerian said hurriedly, too quickly for the joke to come off. "I just got word from Vic. Everyone got out, but one of the team members was wounded. They had to improvise."

"Gods... Vic? Improvising? How bad is it?"

"They brought down the building."

"Damn. All right, where are they now?"

"The *Echion*, sir."

"OK, back to the Castellum. Make sure there is a shuttle waiting for us."

"Yes, sir."

With that, Valerian disappeared back inside. Mirabella walked up beside Marcellus, running her hand down his arm before grasping his in hers.

"I take it duty calls?"

"Yes," Marcellus said, a pleading look on his face. "Please forgive me."

"It's OK, go take care of business," she said. "But, perhaps it's for the best..." She leaned in and whispered deviously, "As much as you struggled seeing me in this dress, I'd hate to see how poorly you'd perform if I were in nothing at all..."

Marcellus swallowed heavily. "Uhm...well then, I guess I'll have to find a way to make it up to you."

"I'll hold you to it," she said, beaming at him once more. "Goodnight, Praetor Aurelius."

Marcellus kissed her hand, then turned and disappeared back into the crowded atrium, anxious to learn the results of the night's raid.

But no matter how much Marcellus tried to focus on work, his mind lingered on the memory of Mirabella's gentle touch.

Chapter 15

URN *Echion*: In Orbit over Umbria, Capital of the Republic

Marcellus snapped awake, dread curdling up within his stomach. He rose, still half-asleep, before remembering that he was back aboard the *Echion* after a very long night amongst Umbria's elite. He quickly threw on his uniform and headed toward the door.

As it slid open, however, he was greeted by the lumbering shape of an Ascomanni. In a flash, Marcellus passed from groggy to fully awake, pulling out his dagger and stabbing the beast in the neck. The Ascomanni toppled, and Marcellus darted back into his room.

"Fabian!" he called into his intercom. "We've got Ascomanni aboard. Lock down the ship, all hands prepare for boarders!"

Silence met his statements, and Marcellus swore. He sprinted toward the bridge, passing a handful of bodies, both Umbrian and Ascomanni. Finally, he reached the bridge, but found it oddly deserted.

Before he could think of something else to do, forms began to rise from behind the bridge stations, resolving into the shapes of Ascomanni shock troopers. Yet more had appeared at the entrance of the bridge. They slowly advanced, drawing a circle around the Praetor.

Marcellus produced his dagger once more. If this was the end, he was determined to go down fighting.

Suddenly however, he could no longer will his body to move. The dagger dropped from his hand, and a cackling laugh echoed from behind him.

The skin on Marcellus's neck crawled as Atossa, the purple-skinned Pasargan prisoner, emerged from the circle of Ascomanni.

"How mightily you resist, Marcellus," she sneered. "All for not."

Marcellus tried to speak, tried to scream, but his body failed to react. Once again, the cackling hiss of the alien's laughter echoed around the room, and slowly the Ascomanni moved in...

***

With a roar, Marcellus sat up, gazing about the room wildly, seeking out his unseen foes. He shot to his feet, dagger in hand, looking for any sign of the enemy.

The moment passed, and he realized he was once again in his room on the *Echion*. He sat heavily back on his bunk, then slapped the intercom built into the wall of his suite.

"Fabian, this is Marcellus. What's the ship's status?"

"Sir," an unfamiliar voice responded, "the Archus is asleep. As far as I know, all systems are normal."

"What time is it, sailor?" Marcellus asked wearily.

"It's oh four hundred Umbrian Mean Time, sir. The Archus won't be available for another two hours, unless you'd like me to wake him."

"No, that's all right. That'll be all."

"Of course, sir."

Just a dream, Marcellus thought to himself. This one had seemed so *real* though.

He had hoped that with the Ascomanni's withdrawal, his nightmares would have become less frequent. Perhaps in time they still would. He rolled over and did his best to go back to sleep, but the memory of Atossa's horrible laughter continued to haunt him.

***

Marcellus frowned as Invictus gave his report. Upon arriving on the *Echion* the night before, he had made the decision to let his men rest, with the understanding that they would regroup first thing in the morning.

Now they stood in the supercarrier's medical bay, the wounded member of Team One lying on a bed between them. Tubes and wires ran from the wounded soldier to a series of mechanical pumps; One-Two had had his liver perforated, and it would take a few days to clone a new one. In the interim, he had to be hooked up to a dialysis machine.

Marcellus turned his attention back to the datapad Vic had given him. In front of him were images of the E-Rho headquarters the day after: a burned-out shell was all that remained of the structure.

Vic and Team One had definitely run into complications, he thought to himself.

"So, there you have it, sir," Invictus summarized to finish his report. "We retrieved the data, one team member wounded, no trace of our presence, but unacceptable levels of casualties to the building's occupants."

Vic seemed to brace himself, as if waiting for a withering response from Marcellus.

It would not come.

"You were in a difficult position, Vic, you had to make a call, and you got the data and all of our people out. I trust you did what was necessary."

"Sir, we killed those people in cold blood!" Invictus said, aghast.

"Yeah, Vic, but unlike some of the many terrible decisions we've been forced to make over the last few years, I doubt this one will cause me to lose much sleep. Then again, I may be biased, seeing as they tried to kill me and all."

"Still, these were civilians!"

"But hardly *innocents*, Vic. This isn't about vigilante justice. This is about excising the corruption at the heart of the Republic."

"You're starting to sound like Triumvir Decius," Invcitus responded grimly. "I just hope the data is worth it."

"We should know soon. It would've been quicker to pull in Theodorus, but I'm not sure we can trust him with something this sensitive."

No sooner had he spoken than Valerian appeared, carrying a datapad.

"Oh my gosh!" Invictus said, planting his hands over his cheeks in mock surprise. "Are you psychic?!"

Marcellus rolled his eyes. "I assume it's good?" he asked as Valerian joined them.

"Better than that," Valerian said, an unusually giddy pep in his step. "The Triumvir is going to want to see this!"

"Not another trip to the Capitol!" Invictus whined. "Do we all have to go?"

"Yes, Vic," Marcellus said sternly. "We're going to see this through. Together."

Invictus reluctantly nodded, and together the threesome headed for the *Echion*'s shuttle bay.

Capitol Hall, Perugia, Umbria

An hour later, they gathered in the Triumvir's office, a shocked expression on the man's face as Marcellus finished sharing their findings.

"And you're sure of this?" Decius asked.

"Yes, sir," Marcellus responded. "Sestius facilitated the rise of the E-Rho in order to provide him with the muscle necessary to enforce his various shady arrangements here on Umbria. We've found blackmail material for at least three dozen senators, and we've traced payments back to organizations Sestius owns."

"It's enough to remove the Triumvir from office," Valerian agreed.

"And what would you propose we do about the compromised senators?" Decius asked.

"These men and women will have to answer to their constituents for their indiscretions. However, now may not be the best time to force the issue. The impeachment of a Triumvir has not occurred in over a generation, sir. There will be enough shock to the system without having a tenth of the sitting Senate resign."

"Spoken like a master politician, Marcellus," Decius responded. "So, we do nothing with the data?"

"No, sir, we let the investigation of Sestius's crimes surface whatever details may come to light, but sometime between the seating of Triumvir Sestius's replacement and the next Senate electoral cycle, we'll need to find a way to release any remaining details we've discovered."

Decius looked at Marcellus and his subordinates approvingly. "Well done, all of you. Together, you've struck a decisive blow against the nihilistic corruption ravaging our society."

The Triumvir walked around his desk and threw an arm over Marcellus's shoulder. "You've done better than I could have wished, Marcellus. You've given me hope that the tide is beginning to rise against the immorality and wickedness which is all too common in these times. Words are insufficient to convey my gratitude."

Marcellus once again felt uncomfortable, and Invictus twitched imperceptibly, as if recognizing his friend's unease.

"I take no pleasure in this, sir. Triumvir Sestius threatened to undermine the security of the Republic. We merely did what was necessary."

"Still," Decius said, releasing Marcellus and returning to the comfortable chair behind his desk, "surely it feels good to get even with the man who attempted to have you killed?"

"No, sir. Mostly, I'm disappointed my involvement was necessary to bring the Triumvir to justice."

"As you say," Decius responded with a tight-lipped smile. "Now, please forgive me, but there is much I need to attend to."

"Of course, Triumvir, please let us know if you need anything else."

Valerian, Invictus, and Marcellus saluted and walked out of the Triumvir's office. Together, they walked toward the building's main entrance, and Valerian was the first to break the silence.

"Am I the only one who felt dirty leaving the room?"

"No, I felt it too, Vic," Marcellus replied wearily.

Invictus nodded in agreement. "At least it's over now, Marcellus. Come on, let's find a bar. The fireworks should be fun to watch."

The Senate Chamber of the Umbrian Republic; Perugia, Umbria

Decius stood behind a simple podium adorned with the Senate's coat of arms, staring out at the exquisitely furnished amphitheater. It was packed to capacity, with nearly the entire Senate gathered together for the Triumvir's address. Decius cleared his throat, and the buzz in the chamber died to just a handful of murmurs.

"Ladies and gentlemen, Honorable Members of the Senate, I come to you in the most dire of circumstances. For in this time of war and strife, a deep-seated perversion has dishonored this body's noble role in leading our great people. Today, I speak of the corruptions that we have allowed to fester amongst our highest institutions."

The murmurs increased, but Decius powered on.

"I see shock in some of your eyes. Yet in others there is nothing but a blank expression. Some among you know exactly of what I speak, and those who do not have long suspected it.

"I have been provided indisputable details of patronage, blackmail, and pay-for-access schemes which run wide and deep through our government. Worst of all, these nefarious activities are orchestrated by a man we all held in high esteem, none other than Triumvir Vibius Sestius himself!"

Gasps ran through the room, and Sestius quickly shot to his feet. "This is an outrage! How dare you make such accusations against me!"

"How dare I, Triumvir?" Decius responded. "How dare *you*! How dare you take advantage of the position the people of this Republic have entrusted you with! How dare you enrich yourself at their expense! And yet still, you stand here before us, affecting shock when what we've all surmised is finally brought to light!"

Vibius began to interrupt, but the crowd shouted him down.

"You know you're guilty!"

"We've toiled in fear of you for too long!"

"Enough is enough! Now is the time to root out this corruption and cronyism!"

Decius waved his hands, urging the senators to calm down.

"Given the gravity of the crimes I have accused my colleague of," he called out loudly, "I formally request that the Senate launch an immediate investigation and suspend Triumvir Sestius's privileges until such a time as his name is cleared or the details of my allegations have been proven true. Will any of you see fit to make such a motion?"

"The Delegate from Modena does so move!"

"The Honorable Senator from Ravenna seconds that motion!"

Decius bowed his head and stepped back from the podium. The Senate Parliamentarian would see the rest of the process, and he was confident that opposition to Sestius would carry the day.

The Gilded Eagle; Downtown Perugia, Umbria

"Well, that's what we wanted, right?" Invictus asked, taking a long pull from his tumbler as they sat at the bar, watching a live stream of the events in the Senate Chambers unfold.

"Yeah, it looks like the Senate just needed someone to nudge them toward doing the right thing," Valerian responded.

Marcellus was quiet though, slowly nursing his drink. Vic was right, he thought to himself, this was what they were after. So why didn't he feel better about it?

"What happens next, Val?" he asked.

"Well, the Senate Parliamentarian certified that two thirds of the Senate must vote in favor to strip Sestius of his powers, and the analysts on the network seem to think there is a high likelihood of that happening."

"When will the vote occur?"

"Earliest? Later this afternoon. I'd suggest it probably depends on how comfortable Decius is in advancing the vote. If he thinks he needs to push more senators toward voting in favor, they might delay until this evening, but I'd be surprised if we don't have some type of resolution before they adjourn for the day."

"Good," Invictus said. "Now we can get back to fighting the Ascomanni, knowing that things aren't going to blow up on the home front."

"From your lips to the gods' ears!" Valerian agreed.

"So how long will it take to replace Sestius?" Marcellus asked.

"It's a little complicated, especially with the outermost colonies' populations spread all over the Republic. Still, four to six months or so to organize the vote? I think they'll probably shoot for as tight a timeline as is practical. Politics will be a bit more volatile until the Triumvirate is back up to full strength."

"You don't seem happy," Invictus said, looking confusedly at Marcellus.

"I'm not, Vic. You were right. It should never have come to this. We did what we had to do. Let's hope our trust was not misplaced."

Capitol Hall, Perugia, Umbria

Decius sat beside his desk, running the numbers again. Things were looking very good. Unfortunately, there was still a potential roadblock that needed to be cleared: the group of senators Vibius had blackmailed had not yet fully freed themselves from his clutches.

"Paulus," he called to his aide. "I need you to deliver a message to the following list of senators. If they ask why, let them know that Sestius isn't the only one with compromising information on them."

"Sir?"

"We've come too far to leave anything to chance. No record is to be made, no trace left behind. Do you understand me?"

"Yes, sir."

"Thank you, Paulus."

His aide left the office, and Decius leaned back in his chair. He pulled up his contacts and placed a call.

"Triumvir. Sounds like you have an eventful day on your hands. What can I help you with?"

"Director Calpurnius, thank you for taking my call on such short notice. I must ask a favor, and I'm afraid it may make you uncomfortable."

"Go on," the Director said, suddenly on guard.

"I want your prisoner transferred to Villa Decii, with as much security as you believe is necessary to keep her secure."

"Sir…" the Director of Naval Intelligence sputtered. "Why? I cannot stress how dangerous she is."

"I want to question her myself."

"Publius, you ask for too much. I cannot release her into your custody! There will be…questions."

"Listen carefully, Titus. By the end of the day, Vibius's senators will be *my* senators. You do not want to make an enemy out of me. The secrets she possesses may be key to the salvation of our people. I want the Pasarga, and I expect you to make it happen."

The Director of Naval Intelligence was quiet for a moment before finally relenting. "As you wish, Triumvir."

The Chambers of the Senate of the Umbrian Republic; Perugia, Umbria

The Senate Parliamentarian called the Senate back to order as the sun began to set outside the chamber. As she gazed out over the amphitheater, a handful of stragglers rushed to take their seats. A chamberlain nodded, indicating that everyone was present.

It was time.

"The motion before the Senate is to create a special committee empowered to investigate the accusations leveled against Triumvir V. Sestius by Triumvir P. Decius. Until vindicated or found to be guilty of such charges, the Triumvir will be stripped of all privileges and powers of office.

"Common law stipulates that such a vote must garner support of two-thirds of the sitting Senate. All those in favor, vote 'Aye.'" Senators began to signal their vote electronically as she continued. "All those opposed, vote 'Nay.'"

She waited until there was a beep from the podium, indicating that all of the senators had cast their votes.

"The Vote is two hundred and ninety-four ayes, sixty-eight nays, and six abstentions. The motion carries. From this moment forth, Triumvir Sestius shall be stripped of his position, pending the completion of the Senate's inquiry."

Triumvir Decius's Office; Capitol Hall, Perugia, Umbria

Marcellus impatiently stood outside Triumvir Decius's office once more. He had been called back after news had broken that Sestius had been suspended from office. The message had been brief, with no reason given for his summoning.

The door opened, and a gaggle of senators walked out of the room. Marcellus recognized a few faces, but couldn't quite place where he had seen them before. Finally, after they had cleared out, Decius's attendant ushered him inside.

"Marcellus!" the Triumvir exclaimed, throwing his arms wide in greeting before clasping both hands on Marcellus's shoulders. "Your dedication to the Republic has paid off! The cancer festering at the heart of our great Republic has been excised."

Marcellus chose his words carefully, uncertain and anxious as to why the Triumvir had asked to see him.

"I am heartened to see the Senate take a more active stance against corruption. However, I am still disappointed that it required such active intervention on my part."

Decius released him, still smiling, and moved behind his desk. "I understand your apprehension. Sometimes though, people need to be pointed in the right direction. In the end, the Senate found the resolve to do what was needed, and it would have been impossible without you."

"What comes next?" Marcellus asked.

"Next, the committee investigating Vibius's crimes will verify the data we've provided. In a few months, when he's found guilty, we'll organize a vote to replace him."

"A few months, sir?" Marcellus asked. "The data we've recovered is pretty damning."

"Unfortunately, that is the speed with which the Senate moves, and a transgression of this magnitude requires careful deliberation. Moreover, our citizens must have faith that Triumvir Sestius was treated fairly."

Marcellus just nodded, unsure of how to feel.

"However, sometimes you can push through a more limited agenda, and that's why I've called you back tonight. The senators who just left were members of the Joint Committee for Defense and Intelligence. I have convinced them of the invaluable role you have played fending off the Ascomanni."

"Thank you, sir, I appreciate your kind words on my behalf."

"Ah, but I offer more than just words, Marcellus. The Committee agreed that our position would be much more perilous if it weren't for the innovative strategic leadership you've brought to the battlefield. That, coupled with your steadfast and unbreakable devotion to the Republic has convinced the committee that you are the man to end the Ascomanni threat, once and for all."

Marcellus looked confused, and Decius laughed.

"I understand your confusion," the Triumvir continued. "You have already reached the rank of Praetor, a feat achieved at an impressively young age. The same skill and leadership that propelled you to the top have also demonstrated a significant structural weakness, one we must ameliorate. You have shown that our fractured command system is not responsive enough to meet the varying threats we face in a coordinated manner.

"As such, as of this moment, you will be promoted to the rank of Imperator and granted authority over the Praetors and the War Council. The conduct of the war will be your responsibility moving forward."

"Sir...that title hasn't been used since Unification," Marcellus said, taken aback. "I...I don't know what to say. That's a lot of responsibility, and there's so much to do..."

"Think about it another way, Marcellus. During the peak of the Ascomanni crisis, you were already filling the role. You are the one who influenced the change in strategy, you are the one who masterminded the counterattack which drove off the enemy, and you are the one who sidestepped a dangerously sluggish bureaucracy to do so."

One part of Marcellus's brain tried to process the shocking suddenness of the Triumvir's news and the massive responsibility that came with it, while another began to list off a series of tasks he'd need to jump on immediately.

"I guess you're right."

"I know I'm right!" Decius said with a chuckle. "What do you say?"

Marcellus offered a thin smile, his mind still swimming. *Imperator*, he thought to himself. This was his chance. He'd finally have the freedom to do what needed to be done, to truly prepare Umbria for the threats lurking in the dark.

Finally, Marcellus found his voice: "What would the Republic have its Imperator do?"

"That's the spirit!" Decius said gleefully. "You already know the challenges we face. Unfortunately, your responsibilities will take you out of the field. Umbria is the only system in the Republic with the facilities to coordinate our armed forces, so I imagine you will spend most of your time in Perugia moving forward."

Marcellus nodded. "Understood, sir. I won't let you down."

"I'm sure you won't, Marcellus. Now, let's have a drink!" Decius's aid appeared with two flutes of exquisite wine. "To Imperator Gaius Aurelius Marcellus!"

"To the Republic!" Marcellus responded as they tipped back their glasses.

"Now," the Triumvir said as they finished their toast, "I'm sure you have some celebrating to do, Marcellus. Enjoy it, for tomorrow you'll have more work to do than you could possibly imagine."

The Gilded Eagle; Downtown Perugia, Umbria

Mirabella waved at Marcellus as she entered the pub, working her way through the evening crowd. As she reached him, he hugged her, lifting her into the air and twirling her around.

"Wow!" she said as he set her back down. "I wasn't expecting such an energetic greeting! What's so urgent? What do you want to tell me?"

Marcellus dragged her to a pair of seats at the bar, and the bartender brought them a round of drinks. He took her hand in his, and Mirabella looked at him, confused, excited, and bewildered.

"I have fantastic news!" Marcellus beamed. "The Senate has promoted me."

"How is that possible?"

"Decius convinced the Senate to revive the title of Imperator. As of this moment, I'm responsible for persecuting the war against the Ascomanni."

"Oh my gods!" Mirabella shouted. "That's great news! Isn't it?"

"Yes," Marcellus nodded. "I was uncertain at first too, but the Triumvir reminded me that, to some extent, I had already assumed the role."

Mirabella leaned in and kissed him. As she started to pull away, Marcellus gently leaned forward, delaying their separation.

She grinned and arched an eyebrow at him. "What's gotten into you?"

"Well, it turns out I'll probably be spending a lot more time here in the capital. It's the only place where I'll be able to coordinate everything, at least at first."

"Oh really?" she said, affecting an innocent smile.

"Yeah. So, I'll probably spend the next few weeks at the Castellum, but eventually I'll want to find a place in the city."

"Hmmm..." Mirabella replied. "I think I know of a place. And as it just so happens, I could take you to see it."

"That would be great. When would be able to go?"

She leaned in, a devious look on her face, and whispered, "How about now?" She took Marcellus by the hand and led him out of the bar.

Chapter 16

The Castellum; Perugia, Umbria

Time had become a blur for Marcellus. Day and night seemed to flow ceaselessly into one another. Despite being busier than he could have ever imagined, he had never been happier in his entire life.

One of the first things Marcellus had to do was figure out how to fill the gaps amongst the ranks of the Praetors. Invictus turned down a command of his own, instead choosing to remain in command of Marcellus's personal cohort.

Valerian had chosen to remain with Marcellus too, a fact which he was immeasurably grateful for. Valerian had proven to be invaluable, an extraordinary administrator who served as the gel layer between Marcellus, the Praetors, and the War Council.

Left with few options of his own, he reached out to Praetor Asinia and Praetor Artorius. The former had recommended a legate with an impressive record, Nonus Junius, while the latter had advanced one of Marcellus's old peers, Gaia Icilia. With the consent of the Senate, the two soon took command of their respective army groups.

Although command of the Third Fleet had officially passed to the newly minted Praetor Icilia, Marcellus had requested that it be reassigned to Umbria, where it joined the First Fleet in garrison duty for the capital. Marcellus made it clear that this was not to undermine Praetor Icilia's command, but rather to better distill and disseminate Fabian's brilliance to a rising class of naval leaders.

Within six months, the effects of Marcellus's leadership could be seen and felt throughout the armed forces.

New recruits were turned over to grizzled veterans of the campaign in the Frontier, where they learned how best to fight the Ascomanni. Newly designed planetary defense batteries had entered mass production, while a massive shipbuilding drive had replaced the Navy's previous losses and provided enough ships to form the nucleus of an eighth fleet.

The situation on the home front was also growing better. Triumvir Decius had grown in status since the downfall of Sestius. He seemed to be everywhere at once, not only rallying the public to the war effort, but also espousing a great renewal of Umbrian society.

Together with Triumvir Eppia, he had instituted a massive anti-corruption campaign. The cynical were quick to point out that most of the figures targeted seemed to have been aligned with Triumvir Sestius, but the campaign enjoyed broad public support. Slowly and surely, the central government was repairing the damage done by Sestius and his ilk.

Decius had also made a point to take Marcellus under his wing, introducing him to the ins and outs of daily life in the beating heart of the Republic. The Imperator soon made a name for himself amongst the Senate as a man of honest counsel, earning the distinction of being a rare, non-partisan voice they could rely upon.

Marcellus's personal life had also improved. The nightmares had stopped, which was fortunate, as Mirabella had asked him to move in with her shortly after his promotion. He had never considered himself the domestic type, but he couldn't help but enjoy having a place to call home.

As the second year passed without sign of the Ascomanni, the Republic was more prepared than ever before for the trials that awaited it.

Sometimes though, when he found a rare quiet moment to himself, Marcellus felt uneasy. The Ascomanni still had not reappeared, and his scouts pushed ever deeper into unexplored space to find them.

If they didn't reveal their intentions soon, he would have to build the case for taking the fight to them.

Axiom Tower; Downtown Perugia, Umbria

Marcellus woke up at six o'clock on the dot, his alarm still half an hour from going off. He rolled out of bed, careful not to disturb Mirabella, and threw on a shirt and shorts. After wriggling his feet into his shoes, he turned off his alarm and quietly left their apartment.

Two minutes later, he walked out of their building's revolving door and into the dawn light. He cleared his mind and broke out into a jog, beginning his normal five-kilometer loop. He focused on each breath as he ran amongst the tree-lined boulevards, passing only a handful of people as he made the rounds.

Marcellus came to a small park, the halfway point of his circuit, and stopped to get a drink from a drinking fountain. He took a moment to enjoy the beauty of the manicured green space: songbirds chirping, flowers seeking out the first rays of the sun, a gentle breeze rustling through leaves.

That's when he noticed a familiar form sitting at one of the park's benches.

A woman was examining the contents of a datapad intently, the device covering her face. She seemed familiar, but Marcellus wasn't sure why. He started walking toward her, and she lowered the datapad as he approached.

Confusion and apprehension turned to rage.

"*Calpurnia?*" he gasped.

"It's good to see you too, Imperator," she replied, keeping her response brief.

"But how? I saw you… The E-Rho! How?!" he demanded, recalling the night she had saved him from the lower levels of the Entertainment District.

"Not here, Imperator."

"I need answers!" Marcellus countered angrily.

"And you'll get them," she said curtly, "but preferably in some place more private."

Marcellus nodded, and she shot to her feet, walking quickly toward a maintenance access at the edge of the park. They walked down a flight of stairs and entered the open substructure of the boulevard above.

"All right, we're out of sight," Marcellus barked. "Explain. Now!"

Calpurnia leaned against a pillar, brushing her hair back over a shoulder. "Triumvir Decius is not well."

"What do you mean? He's everywhere!" Marcellus scoffed. "I don't know if *I* could keep up with that man's hectic schedule."

"It's a carefully manipulated ruse, Marcellus. When was the last time you saw him in person?"

"It's been a while, but he's supposedly off planet on a tour of the Front—"

"It's a double," Calpurnia interrupted.

"What you're saying makes no sense!" Marcellus spat back. "Why would he go to all that effort to hide his movements? Why would he need to? Your story isn't adding up. Why should I believe anything you say?"

"I don't care if you believe me, but I have to tell someone. Something terrible is about to happen. Decius secured the transfer of a prisoner, some CID asset, I don't even know who, to Villa Decii. He's become a recluse, paranoid, delusional even. You're my best hope."

"When did this happen?" Marcellus asked, a pit forming in his stomach.

"Shortly after Sestius was deposed..." she responded.

Marcellus's mind was racing. He knew nothing about this woman, and even his rescue might not have been what it seemed. And a CID prisoner? Did Calpurnia know what buttons to push to get the right response from him, or was she being honest?

"How are you even here?" he demanded, still trying to make sense of the situation.

Calpurnia sighed deeply. "It wasn't Vibius."

"What?" Marcellus asked, confused by her response.

"Triumvir Sestius didn't attempt to have you killed. I fabricated evidence that made it look like he did."

"So...you tried to kill me?" Marcellus said with soft intensity, the pit in his stomach turning into rage, his hand reflexively reaching for the small of his back.

"No, the plan was never to kill you. The goal was to manipulate you, to get you to think that Vibius had tried to have you murdered."

"But what about the E-Rho?"

"Decius paid them off. In fact, they were in his pocket the whole time, a helpful check on Sestius's influence within the underworld."

"So, the data we recovered from..." Marcellus started.

"Very good," Calpurnia interrupted. Her gaze softened. "I'm sorry, Imperator, but Decius is not who he appears to be."

"Why are you telling me this?" Marcellus asked, the makings of a headache starting to push on his temples.

"Your note," she said quietly. "The one you wrote to my 'sister,' thanking me for saving you from the E-Rho. You're the only one I can trust. The Triumvir has taken over the remnants of Sestius's faction in the Senate. He is consumed with gathering more power to himself. There is no one else I can turn to."

Marcellus was silent for a moment. His thoughts drifted back to Praetor Festus. He had fallen so far, so quickly. Could the same have happened to Triumvir Decius? Had his admiration for the man blinded him to the Triumvir's true character?

He needed to confirm this mysterious woman's information, but if Calpurnia was telling the truth…the Republic could be in grave danger.

"I need you to go to the Castellum. When you get there, ask for my adjutant, Valerian. Tell him you're the Viceroy's daughter."

She cocked an eyebrow, but he interjected before she could ask. "No time. Go. Now!"

Calpurnia nodded, but instead of heading for the stairs, she threw herself from the walkway.

"No!" Marcellus screamed, grabbing after her.

He had nothing to worry about, however, for five meters down she spread her arms, revealing aerodynamic wings. She pulled up as an aircar zoomed in below her, soaring to meet the craft and clambering into the cockpit as her forward momentum dissipated. The car then sped off to the east, toward the Castellum.

Marcellus ran back up the stairs and headed back toward their apartment. His mind was still swimming.

Who could he trust to corroborate Calpurnia's story? Decius would have had to call in a lot of favors to have the Pasarga moved to his private residence. Was there anyone in the CID he could trust?

As he closed in on his apartment tower, he noticed a pair of people following behind. He chalked it up to paranoia, but when they were still trailing him five minutes later, the hairs on the back of his neck began to stand on end.

He came to the last major junction before Axiom Tower, and suddenly his gut began to tighten.

Without waiting to confirm his intuition, he dropped, splaying out on all fours. A man turned the corner, stun gun ready, and pulled the trigger. The pulse passed harmlessly over Marcellus's head and struck one of the two people running up behind him.

Marcellus shot to his feet, rushing the gunman as he furiously attempted to reload his weapon. As he closed to less than a meter, the assailant threw away the stun gun and swung a fist at the Imperator.

Marcellus ducked under the punch and drove his shoulder into the man's midsection, knocking the wind out of him.

He pulled back, and his attacker slumped forward. Marcellus delivered a vicious blow to the back of his head with an elbow, and the man collapsed to the floor like a puppet whose strings had been cut.

Marcellus swung around to face his second foe but was too late. He just managed to get his arms up as a fist crashed into his midsection.

Marcellus immediately responded, going on the offensive. A flurry of blows kept his attacker off guard. Then the Imperator pulled back, baiting the man, and he rushed in to try and grapple with Marcellus.

Marcellus was ready, though, and he swept the man's ankle, breaking bones in his joint and causing his assailant to collapse in pain. Marcellus dove on top of the man, punching him in the face to disorient him.

"Who do you work for?!" Marcellus screamed

"Go to hell," the man replied gruffly, blood streaming from his nose.

Marcellus slammed him down against the hard surface of the avenue, and the man lay still. Marcellus stood up and jogged over to the stun gun the first attacker had dropped, sticking it into his waistband.

He rifled through his assailant's effects, found nothing, and decided it was best to keep moving. He set off at a quick jog, anxious to get back to his building but eager not to raise suspicions.

He passed quickly through the lobby, asked the receptionist to call the constabulary, and hopped on an elevator. A minute later, the lift's doors slid open, and he peered out, looking left, then right.

Satisfied that the hallway was clear, he ran to the door to his shared apartment, opened it, then locked the door behind him.

"What's going on?" Mirabella asked, looking confused and frightened. She was just getting up, and she was still wearing the revealing nightgown he had bought for her a week earlier.

"I was attacked," Marcellus said as he threw on his uniform. "Three assailants. Probably following me since I left for my run this morning."

"How did you…?" Mirabella started, concern clearly evident in her voice.

"Intuition. Luck. Whatever you want to call it. The police should be on their way."

Mirabella saw the fear in his eyes, and Marcellus knew she had more questions.

"I don't have time to explain. Throw on some clothes. We need to go to the Castellum."

"Marcellus, what's…" she started.

"*Please*," he pleaded. "We don't have time, Miri."

She nodded and began to get dressed, accepting that she'd have to wait for her answers.

It took them less than five minutes to get ready, then they headed back out of their apartment. In the lobby, a constable was talking to the receptionist, and the officer waved as Marcellus approached.

"Officer, you know me, yes?" Marcellus said, cutting her off before she could speak.

She nodded, and he continued. "I need you to take me to the Castellum. Right now."

"Yessir, of course!" she replied, startled. "After you."

Together with the constable, Mirabella and Marcellus walked outside, where they found the officer's waiting squad car. The constable opened the door for Mirabella, and the doctor climbed aboard.

As the constable closed the door, Marcellus drew the stun gun in his waistband and shot the officer.

She fell back against the car heavily, and he caught her, easing her to the ground. He slid over the front of the vehicle and jumped in the cockpit, immediately gunning the engine and pointing them toward the Castellum.

"What the hell?! You shot her!" a shocked Mirabella exclaimed.

"I know, I'm sorry, but the only people we can trust right now are Vic, Val, and my praetorians," he said as he swerved through the capital's early morning traffic.

"What is going on, Marcellus? Talk to me!"

"Fine," he replied tersely. As quickly as he could, he told her the story of his original encounter with Calpurnia and the information she had shared less than an hour before.

"Gods..." Mirabella muttered. "Do you think she means Atossa?"

"Yes," Marcellus said between clenched teeth. "And it's no coincidence that I would be attacked after she spoke with me. Does the CID have failsafes in case the capital were to be compromised?"

"Marcellus... What are you talking about? What are you thinking?"

"Do you have a way to secure your research remotely?" he barked.

"Yes. Through the CID Annex."

"When we get to the Castellum, I need you to send your research to the *Echion*. This is Fabian's encrypted channel. When you get ahold of the duty officer, the confirmation key is 'Delta Upsilon Three Six Three.'"

"OK," she said softly. "Marcellus. This is bad, isn't it?"

"It's too soon to tell," he replied. He pulled his gaze away from the cityscape flashing past them, scooped up her hand, and stared into her eyes.

"I love you, Mirabella."

"I love you too, Marcellus."

The Castellum; Perugia, Umbria

"What the hell is going on?" A groggy Invictus asked as Marcellus swept into the Operations Center. "Moreover, who's she?" he said, pointing at Calpurnia.

"I trust you sent her, sir?" a more awake Valerian asked.

The Imperator ignored them both, instead walking over to the communications section.

"Get me Director Calpurnius. Now!" he ordered.

The startled comms officer rushed to obey, taken aback by the Imperator's uncharacteristically sharp tone, and Marcellus turned back toward his subordinates.

"Vic, get Vetus and as many of his praetorians as he can find geared up and on the east landing pad in ten minutes."

"Marcellus, what's this about?" he asked wearily.

"Not now. Just do it."

Valerian and Invictus shared a look, and Vic made the call.

"Sir!" the comms officer called out. "I've got the Director for you!"

"Good, put him on."

The display in the middle of the room changed, showing the Director in his office.

"Good morning, Imperator. I hope you have a good reason for calling this early?" the Director's perturbed voice boomed across the room.

"Several months ago, you transferred a detainee to Triumvir Decius's personal residence. Who was it?"

"I can't answer that, Marcellus."

"Damn you, Titus!" Marcellus roared. "Did you give him our purple friend or not?"

The Director's eyes widened. "Ahem, sir, that's not appropriate to discuss… "

"What did Decius promise you, Director? What leverage does he have over you?!"

"You don't understand," the head of Naval Intelligence said meekly, finally breaking. "He is too powerful. I couldn't say no."

Marcellus shook his head. Calpurnia had been telling the truth. The only thing left to determine was how tightly the Triumvir's mind had been twisted around Atossa's finger.

"Titus, the CID is to immediately begin transferring anything that isn't archived to the secondary sites on Venezia."

"Sir, that will eat up almost all of our bandwidth and take the better part of the morning!"

"Then get to it!" Marcellus snarled. He waved his hand over his throat, and the comms officer cut the transmission.

"Here's the deal," he said turning back to his confused subordinates. "We've been betrayed. Triumvir Decius has fallen under the influence of the Pasarga we captured on Aetnaeus. Calpurnia here can confirm the details."

"What?!" Invictus gasped.

"Marcellus, are you sure of this?" Valerian asked.

"This whole series of events was masterminded by him," the Imperator confirmed, nodding. "Val, I need you to send an alert to all commands. Tell them to expect contact with the enemy imminently. Make sure you tell them this isn't some foolish test. Once that is done, call the Capital Garrison and tell them to expect us. They are immediately to begin executing the continuity of governance plans."

"Vic," Marcellus continued, turning to address his Prefect. "Get the other cohorts up and armed. Send Aria and her command to the CID Annex, the rest will sit in reserve. Then I need you to gather the War Council. Get them to the *Echion*. We cannot let the head be cut off the snake."

The pair nodded and Marcellus grunted his approval. He headed back toward the doors, and Valerian called out, "Where are you going, sir?"

"To stop Decius!" he called over his shoulder.

Capitol Hall, Perugia, Umbria

A swarm of dropships swooped down on the landing pad nestled at the top of the capitol building, disgorging Marcellus, Vetus, and five hundred of his soldiers. They found the Prefect of the capital garrison waiting for them.

"Imperator, forgive me, sir, but what the hell is going on?" the bewildered officer asked.

"The capital is at risk, Prefect. What are your orders in case of natural disaster or armed attack?"

"Sir, there are no such precautions. What you are talking about, it just... it isn't possible!"

"Let's hope it stays that way. Secure the grounds. Vetus, have your centurions coordinate with the Prefect to reinforce key points around the facility. You're with me."

Marcellus and Vetus walked through the grand corridors of the building, ignoring the handful of voices that called after him in greeting. Many were put off by the sight of a soldier in full armor walking through the halls.

They came upon the Triumvir's office, and Marcellus kicked in the door. Vetus charged in, weapon drawn, but the only person present was Decius's assistant.

"Where is Decius!" Marcellus shouted.

"He's in the East Courtyard, w-with Triumvir Eppia!" the terrified page answered, trembling.

Without another word, Marcellus walked back out of the office. He broke into a jog, and Vetus kept pace.

Marcellus's heart raced. Decius would almost certainly know that his attempt to either kill or kidnap him had failed. There was no telling what the Triumvir had planned.

***

Decius and Eppia walked amongst the East Courtyard's famous columns. There were surprisingly few people present, and even as they strolled, several received calls and quickly walked toward the exits. Others could be seen running through the capitol's hallways.

"Is something going on?" Eppia asked, uneasy by the inexplicable behavior they observed.

"I'm sure it's nothing," Decius said soothingly.

She was less sure. Decius had returned from his trip prematurely and had immediately asked to see her. His demeanor had changed, she thought to herself, though in what way she could not exactly describe.

One thing was clear, however; his appearance had been altered, no matter how much he tried to hide it. He seemed more fit, but also frailer, his hair having turned frosty gray-white. She also noticed a fine scar that ran just above his left eye, cutting back toward his temple before disappearing into his hairline.

"Dearest Aula, how long have we served our great people together now?" he asked innocently.

Eppia's guard immediately went up. "Quite a while, Publius," she responded tentatively, "and the Republic has prospered under our tender guidance."

They came to the end of the courtyard, which offered an incredible view of the city. The East Courtyard wasn't for the faint of heart, however. One wrong move, and a careless onlooker could plunge three hundred meters down to the pavement far below.

"True," Decius replied, "but we know now that the Oracle doesn't lie. There are others out there, and it seems that those who destroyed our forebearers have come for us as well."

"That is true. But we have proven ourselves capable on the battlefield. So much so that there is now hope of success."

"That's exactly right! We have proven ourselves!" Decius said, a strange mix of exuberance and mania. "But you are wrong as well. There is no hope. In the end, we will be ground to dust, like the Ascomanni, like the species before them, and the ones before them. We are just next in line. A power greater than we can comprehend comes for us."

"How do you know these things?" Eppia asked, alarmed by Decius's words.

"I asked," he said simply. "You see, we captured one of the other species claimed by the darkness. She has shared much with me. Despite our resistance, we are still offered a choice. Submit, and become more than we are. Or resist, and suffer for eternity, just like the Ascomanni."

"Publius..." Aula gasped. "What have you done?"

"We can still save our people, Eppia!" Decius croaked desperately. "Do not let your bias against the Ascomanni cloud your judgment! Greatness awaits us!"

Eppia shook her head and backed away from her peer. "No, Decius, not greatness. Servitude! Destitution! Death! That is what they offer!"

The Triumvir let out a deep sigh. "I'm sorry to hear you say that."

He snapped his fingers, and E-Rho foot soldiers emerged from the colonnades on either side of the courtyard, led by a massive, hulking brute.

As desperate as her situation seemed, Aula kept her composure as they closed in on the pair.

Then she heard it: a sickening, cackling laugh echoed off the walls of the courtyard. She turned to find a purple being, similar in size and shape to herself, emerge from the shadowy recesses of the courtyard.

"It seems your foresight is not shared by your friend, Decius," it purred.

"No. And it is quite the shame," Decius agreed. "I'm afraid Triumvir Eppia is about to have an accident. It seems that in her old age, she lost her balance and fell."

***

Marcellus and Vetus turned the corner and exited out into the East Courtyard, only to find about twenty people gathered at the far end of the space. Standing amongst what appeared to be a collection of gangsters were Triumvirs Decius and Eppia, and…

Atossa.

A gigantic man stood on the balustrade, Eppia pinned in his vice-like grasp. He lifted the aged woman aloft, dangling her over the edge of the courtyard, his murderous intentions clear.

The duo moved forward, coming within a few meters of the group, before Marcellus revealed their presence.

"Decius! Stop this madness!" Marcellus called out.

They turned to face him, and Marcellus was suddenly very aware that he and Vetus were outnumbered.

"Imperator Gaius Aurelius Marcellus," Atossa slithered. "My, my, Decius was wise to take such a shining to you. It's a shame you avoided our trap earlier. But here you are! Maybe I'll get to break you yet."

"Lower the Triumvir back down!" Marcellus commanded.

"You are outnumbered, boy! Throw down your weapons, or Aula's blood will be on your hands!" Decius shouted back.

For a moment, Eppia locked eyes with Marcellus. She offered a weak smile, but in her expression, he could see strength, determination…and resolve.

The older woman kicked out, catching the muscular mobster in the chest. He instinctively let go as he fought to gain his balance, but the aging Triumvir grabbed his legs as she fell. Together, they plunged out of sight.

"TRIUMVIR!" Marcellus screamed. Vetus tackled him, dragging him into cover, and Decius and Atossa quickly raced toward the nearest entrance.

"This is just the beginning," Decius called out as he fled. "You cannot stop what I have set in motion. I will lead us to greatness!"

The E-Rho thugs began to advance on their position. Marcellus quickly popped his head in and out of cover and noticed that they were armed with an odd assortment of makeshift weapons.

"Capitol security is still pretty tight, isn't it, Vetus?" Marcellus asked.

"Yes, sir, even the areas open to the public require extensive screening..." Vetus blinked for a moment, finally understanding his commander's point. "Oh, I copy, sir."

Vetus stood and shot the nearest mobster square in the chest, his smoking corpse toppling to the surface of the courtyard. The rest of the gangsters scattered, running in every direction but theirs.

Marcellus nodded at Vetus, and together the two chased after Decius and Atossa.

Although the Pasargan was at the peak of physical perfection, the Triumvir was not, and it wasn't long before they finally came within sight of the duo. Marcellus and Vetus cornered them as they exited out into the spacious confines of the capitol's rooftop garage, an aircar already running and waiting for them.

Atossa, seeing that conflict could no longer be avoided, lashed out at her older companion. With an *umph*, the Triumvir crumpled to the floor.

The Pasargan sprinted toward the waiting aircar. A pair of confused capital guards attempted to stop her but were quickly incapacitated by the dangerous alien.

Vetus fired several shots at the aircar as Atossa hopped aboard, but his rounds skipped off the vehicle's reinforced hull. The purple-skinned alien disappeared into its cockpit, and the vehicle turned and tore out of the garage.

Meanwhile, Decius had crawled to the edge of the garage, where he collapsed into a heap. He pulled himself up to his knees and stared out over the capital.

"What have you done?!" he cried out as Marcellus and Vetus approached. "We could've been great!"

"We are already great!" Marcellus spat. He kicked the older man in the gut, and Decius rolled over onto his back, whimpering meekly.

Marcellus grabbed the older man by his collar and screamed, "Tell me what you've done!"

"I...I accepted the Tenebrae's offer. For all of us."

"No," Marcellus sneered. "You did this for your own vanity!"

He pulled out his knife, knelt next to the Triumvir, and pressed the dagger to the man's chest.

"Sir!" Vetus called out, the color drained from his face. "Look! Up above!"

The bladelike form of spaceships appeared high above in the morning sky. At this distance, they would have to be massive, Marcellus thought to himself. Already a swarm of smaller specks began to resolve into familiar, haunting shapes.

Decius began to laugh, haltingly, as Marcellus realized the gravity of the Triumvir's betrayal. "I called out to our masters, and they have answered." The broken old man dissolved into fits of hysterical laughter.

The first Ascomanni fighters began to fire indiscriminately, spraying death and destruction across Perugia's towers. The screams of countless thousands started to echo through the capital's streets.

A quartet of Umbrian interceptors zoomed by overhead, racing heedlessly toward their overwhelmingly superior enemy.

Marcellus stood, every hair on his body standing on edge, transfixed by the scene. This was his home. This was *Umbria*! How could this be happening?

Someone back at the Castellum reacted, and the city's antiquated defenses came online. The sky erupted into a sea of energy and light as anti-aircraft batteries started seeking out their targets, while an amber wave rose from the outskirts of the city, climbing ever higher until it formed a dome over the capital. Those Ascomanni ships that were outside of the dome exploded on impact as they attempted to penetrate it, while those within were trapped inside.

Marcellus turned and looked at Decius, his knife still clutched in his hand.

The Triumvir was on his knees, his laughter gone as he witnessed the devastation beyond. "No... No! Not like this!" he muttered.

"Yes!" Marcellus snapped. "This is the price they demand!"

Decius turned away, but Marcellus grabbed him by the scruff of his neck, forcing him to watch.

"*This is your legacy Decius!*" he screamed, the veins in his neck bulging.

The older man rose to his knees, reached out, and took Marcellus's hand, the knife still clutched firmly in its grasp. Decius pulled it toward his abdomen, and in an instant the Imperator knew his intent. Marcellus struck the older man viciously in the temple, and the Triumvir dropped to the hard surface of the parking garage, unconscious.

   "Vetus," Marcellus said to his stunned subordinate as he stuck his dagger back into its sheath. "You are to hold this position. No matter the cost."

   Vetus, turned and looked at him, tears forming in the corner of his eyes. "We will not yield. Not now. Not ever."

   Marcellus nodded and walked back across the landing pad. "Valerian," he called into his commlink, "I need a ride back to the Castellum."

Chapter 17

URN *Minerva*, Above Umbria's North Pole

The bridge of the *Minerva* was a riot of activity. Men and women rushed to their stations, some not fully in uniform, roused from bed by the claxons still wailing throughout the ship.

"What's the situation?" Archus Paula Curia demanded as she strode onto the command deck.

"Enemy contacts in orbit!" an officer called out. "Three hundred ships, orbital grid Three Gamma Upsilon, with another two hundred ships in sector Four Delta Beta!"

"They've targeted the capital's population centers! Troops are being deployed to the surface! Orbital defenses are engaging!"

"New contacts! We've got another six hundred ships advancing from the outer edges of the system. They could deploy anywhere above the eastern hemisphere!"

"Show me!" she demanded.

An image appeared, showing the First and Third Fleets in position over either pole. The Ascomanni had attacked both sides of the planet, and ships were starting to stream into the capital's airspace.

The screen split in two, each side pulling up one of the Asco fleets. Each was centered around a trio of dreadnoughts, guarded by a number of battleships and even a few carriers. These two fleets alone would have represented more firepower than they had ever seen before, but there was still an equal number of ships advancing through the system.

The displays updated to show new details. Defensive platforms in geosynchronous orbit above key locations began to fire a wave of missiles at the invaders.

As Paula watched, the first salvo tore into the fleet on the eastern side of the planet. A dreadnought was holed clean through along its long axis, while three of its accompanying battleships were also destroyed. The enemy fleet tightened up, sacrificing smaller ships to form a shield around its heaviest combatants.

As the confusion caused by the missile strike faded, the tactical readout updated. Approximately sixty ships had been destroyed. The results on the western side of Umbria were roughly the same, though with a higher proportion of capital ship kills.

There was no joy in their success, however, as one thousand Ascomanni warships remained to threaten the capital.

"All ships reporting in, ma'am!" her XO called out. "What are your orders?"

"Get me the *Echion*."

The Castellum; Perugia, Umbria

Marcellus stood in the middle of the Ops Center, the room thick with confusion and fear. He stared at the visual showing Umbria's tactical situation, his mind racing. He was searching for anything that might offer the smallest glimmer of hope. But try as he might, he couldn't escape the conclusion that Umbria's salvation was beyond reach.

"We could have the Second Fleet here in two days," Valerian said, standing next to him, furiously sorting through force tables and fleet deployment information. "The Fifth could be here in four, but they'd have to travel directly from their anchorage. The Ascomanni could track them back to it."

"We've got the equivalent of about ten legions on the planet, Marcellus, plus another hundred thousand recruits who are in various stages of training," Invictus chimed in. "They're scattered though, most are cohort-sized units at various installations across Umbria. The news in the air is better; the Asco will have to fight hard to take air superiority from us. May not matter much if we can't contest in orbit though."

Marcellus took a look at the map again. Already, the first wave of Ascomanni soldiers was consolidating its position in the western edges of the city, with firefights breaking out in heavily populated urban areas.

"How long can the shield hold?" Marcellus asked.

"Under a full bombardment?" Valerian replied. "Not long. Once the Ascomanni establish space superiority..."

"And the longbow platforms?"

"Very effective," Invictus said. "There's just not enough of them. The orbital batteries' missiles have all been expended."

Marcellus slammed a fist onto the console, rage, despair, and frustration boiling over. "Tell Fabian to take the First and the Third. His orders are to disrupt the enemy and keep them off balance. He has full freedom of operations, but we need the *Celeres* and the *Spatha* within Perugia's defensive shield."

"What are you thinking?" Valerian asked gently.

"We cannot defend Umbria. If we are to have any hope at all, we must withdraw."

"What?" Invictus gaped. "Leave? Leave *Umbria*?! You'd have us turn tail and run?" The Prefect flushed, his whole body shaking with rage. "There are *ten billion people* on this planet, Marcellus!"

"And there are a hundred and forty billion out there!" Marcellus snapped, pointing at the sky. "The Republic is not our cities or our monuments. It's not even Umbria itself! It's her people. *Our* people. We aren't defeated until the last Umbrian ship is destroyed and the last Umbrian life is extinguished!"

"Marcellus, If I'm going to die, I want it to be on my feet," Invictus snapped in response. "Not with my tail between my legs and my back to the enemy!"

"You chose this path, Invictus. Your life is not yours to throw away. I will use you as I see fit, in the manner that best ensures the survival of our people!" Marcellus barked back.

Invictus looked stunned. He opened his mouth to reply, closed it without saying a word, spun around, and marched out of the Ops Center.

"Vic!" Valerian called after him.

"Let him go," Marcellus ordered. "Give him some time to cool down. We've got work to do."

URN *Vulcan*, In Orbit over Umbria

Fabian wasted no time in taking action. The First and Third fleets regrouped in the icy belt at the edges of their home system before immediately launching raids on the enemy formations surrounding Umbria.

The *Vulcan*, the *Neptune*, and four other battleships had jumped in to interrupt the invasion happening on the far side of the capital, where the Ascomanni commander had allowed his landing force to become exposed.

Forming one long line, the Umbrian warships appeared on the far side of the Ascomanni formation, drilling a hole through the invasion force's weak outer defenses and wreaking havoc on the lightly armored transports.

Just as quickly as they arrived, they blew through the other side of the enemy formation and disappeared back into the far reaches of the system, while fiery debris streaked across Umbria's night skies.

The Castellum, Perugia, Umbria

Chaos had engulfed the capital. The city's residents mobbed the spaceport, where crews busily unloaded cargo freighters, ore haulers, and luxury liners to make room for more civilians. The capital garrison had been redeployed to delay the Ascomanni advance, and Marcellus's praetorians were plugging gaps in the fluid street-to-street fighting which was flaring to the west.

The *Celeres* and the *Spatha* had arrived, with the former hastily evacuating the civilian government from the capitol and the latter hovering over the Castellum. Ascomanni reinforcements had begun to mass outside of the shield, but they were suffering heavily under a ceaseless shuttle-bombing campaign from a nearby airbase.

On Marcellus's orders, the schematics for various personal weapons systems had been released to the public. Already, there were reports of civilians printing weapons and joining the fight against the invaders: the people of Perugia would not yield their city without a fight.

There was a nearly endless list of things to do, but near the top in terms of importance was denying the Ascomanni information they could use against them later. Sensitive information had to be removed or erased, and demo crews were already using thermite torches to slag some of the Castellum's data cores.

It was barely noon, but Marcellus already felt like he'd been on his feet for days.

Tasovo Mining Conglomerate Industrial Park; Perugia, Umbria

Antonia did her best to hide her exhilaration. For the first time in months, she was back where she wanted to be—leading her praetorians. Her body was once more in peak physical condition, free to run and jump and climb. And she would use that freedom, she thought grimly to herself, to leave piles of smoldering Asco corpses lying on Perugia's streets.

She popped up from behind the cooling unit she crouched behind, spraying fire at a team of advancing Ascomanni as they broke cover to charge. She dropped back down to the rooftop as return fire slammed into the boxy unit. She felt heat begin to radiate from the metal housing, which meant it was time to go.

She signaled to the two praetorians a meter to her right and closer to an exterior stairwell. One nodded, and on her signal, they stood and fired at their oncoming enemy. Antonia used the opportunity to sprint away from the danger zone and take up a new firing position just within the staircase.

She whistled sharply and a handful of other soldiers scattered about the roof took turns repeating her movements, alternating cover fire and withdrawal, until they had all reached the relative safety of the stairwell.

"Demo teams just called in," she shouted over the din of combat. "This place is set to blow. Our next objective is two kilometers east! Stay together and move quickly!"

Her soldiers nodded, and together they headed toward the ground floor. Antonia relayed the message to the rest of her mixed command of praetorians and capital guard soldiers. "Ursus Two-Six to all Ursus elements. Objective has been achieved. Fall back immediately to the next rally point."

They reached the ground floor, and her lead scout kicked open the door. A pair of Umbrian tanks sat in the middle of street, and her soldiers used them for cover as they worked their way toward their next objective.

The Ascomanni got wise, however, and soon fire was pouring down from the building onto the street.

One of the tanks fired its main gun, and Antonia stumbled from the concussive blast. Her heart skipped a beat, and she struggled to hear over the deafening ringing in her ears, but she kept moving.

Finally, they came to a bend in the road which offered cover from the murderous enemy fire. The retreating Umbrians immediately took up positions as best they could and began firing back toward the factory they had just left. A few final stragglers ran past, leaving a handful of motionless bodies behind on the broad avenue.

"Meles Four-Two, we are clear, repeat, we are clear. Fall back."

The tanks' engines roared to life, and they began to roll backwards. Another main gun round was fired, and dust and soot fell on Antonia and her soldiers. The tanks neared the intersection, but just as they began to turn the corner, there was a massive *crack* followed by an earth-rattling explosion.

Antonia threw herself down as debris whipped through the air.

She looked up to see that one of the tanks had been destroyed, while the other sat immobilized.

Antonia peered back toward the factory, just making out the shapes of an Asco missile team on the roof.

Her troops fired back toward the building as the second vehicle's crew evacuated out of the tank's rear hatch, rushing to safety.

Antonia whistled again, waving her hand in the air. The Umbrians fell back, and once they were a safe distance from their target, she nodded to one of the combat engineers accompanying her. The ground rumbled again, this time as the ore-processing plant imploded, a cloud of dust sweeping through the streets.

A cohort's worth of Ascomanni soldiers lay buried under a mountain of debris.

Only a hundred thousand more to go, Antonia thought wryly to herself.

The Castellum, Perugia, Umbria

Marcellus took a moment to pause from the endless reports and stare out at Perugia's skyline, where several of the city's tallest towers belched smoke into the clear afternoon sky.

He should feel... something, he thought to himself. Rage? Hopelessness? Grief?

Instead, he felt nothing, an overwhelming numbness, as if he were detached from the events going on around him, an observer more than an active participant.

Was that detachment an asset, he wondered, or was it a dangerous disconnect from the present? He stewed on it for just a moment longer before deciding he didn't have time for such sophomoric debates.

He would do the best he could, for as long as he could. There was no time for anything else.

But your best will not be good enough, a quiet voice whispered inside his mind.

His subconscious was right of course. Thousands of people were dying by the minute, and there was nothing he could do to change that.

"Sir?" Valerian called from behind him.

"Yeah, Val, what's up?"

"Just as you predicted, the Ascomanni are preying on the civilian ships leaving the planet. Smaller vessels have been able to get through, but the larger ships just aren't fast enough."

Marcellus had ordered evacuating ships to wait until the Navy could run interference for them, but several had failed to heed his order.

So much waste, he thought to himself. At least others would learn from their mistakes.

"So the others will wait for the signal then?"

"Yes, sir."

"What's the situation to the west?"

"Growing dire. The Ascomanni have been systematically destroying generators, and a gap has emerged in the shield. Enemy reinforcements are pouring into the city, and they are heading straight for the capitol complex."

"The Senate's status?"

"Many of those with families on Umbria refused to leave until they had retrieved their loved ones, delaying the process. However, most of the senators have been accounted for at this point. The capitol has also become a civilian evac point. They are filling the *Celeres* to the brim."

"Good, being born to the right parents shouldn't be the determining factor for survival today. What about the Castellum?"

"Secondary personnel have been evacuated, sir. The CID Annex has also been emptied; they completed the data transfer to their offsite locations and all CID personnel have been moved to the *Spatha*."

"Including...?"

"Yes, sir, she's safely aboard the assault carrier."

"Thank you, Val. Any word on Vic?"

"He left the Castellum with Team One. He's out there, somewhere," Valerian said, gesturing toward the fire and smoke rising into the sky to the west, "doing what he does best. Causing the enemy pain."

Amicum Housing Complex, Perugia, Umbria

Invictus crept quietly up behind the Ascomanni sentry, his bayonet extended and red hot. As he got within a hair's length of his target, he drove the blade through the Ascomanni's spine, silencing the guard.

He waved forward the other members of Team One, and the Umbrians moved down the maze-like passages of the tenement building.

Yesterday, this building had housed hundreds of poor families, scraping an honest living from menial jobs throughout the city. Now, it was a charnel house, with dead soldiers and civilians scattered about everywhere.

They had worked their way back to this hellish place after receiving some very important information from the signals intelligence team at the Castellum. Significant amounts of enemy comm traffic originated from this location, and they were going to put an end to whoever was so talkative.

Their scanners placed the source of the transmissions in nearly the dead center of the building, and they had been stealthily working their way toward their target for the last twenty minutes.

Invictus slowly opened a door to another stairwell, hoping to find an unobstructed path up. They climbed carefully up the debris-strewn stairs, passing more bodies as they went.

The smell of death was everywhere, and the slick bloodstains marring the staircase made their footing difficult. A lump developed in Invictus's throat as they passed the bodies of a young mother and her children.

"We'll slaughter every last one of these bastards," One-Two whispered.

The Prefect nodded, not trusting himself to speak.

Finally, after steadily creeping up three more flights of stairs, they reached the floor the enemy command post was located on.

One-One took point, slowly pushed the door open as the team fanned out into the hallway. The sounds of enemy activity could clearly be heard: voices were calling out muffled details, machinery hummed, and the soft tones of computer equipment could be heard distinctly from their position.

One-Three pulled out her scanner, and they were able to quickly locate the Ascomanni command post through the walls. There were about twenty enemies in the tight confines of a single-family apartment—standing room only.

Worse still, many of the forms appeared to be the Pasargans that had proven to be such dangerous enemies during previous encounters.

"Ideas?" Invictus whispered softly into his mic.

"High explosives!" One-Four offered, a vicious rage staining his words.

"Sounds like a plan to me," One-One said. He fished a familiar object from his pack, a brick of the puttylike high explosive they had used to bring down the E-Rho hideout.

"Whoa, whoa, whoa!" Invictus muttered. "Is there an approach that is less likely to get us killed?"

"Nothing over the top, sir," One-Four replied. He passed an object to his team lead, and Marcellus recognized the circular remote drones the CID used. "Just enough to immolate everything in the room, then we storm in and burn whatever's left down to a fine ash."

Invictus nodded, satisfied with the explanation. "I've got a dropship on standby to pick us up, but we'll have to go off the roof. Once they know we're here, it's going to get dicey, and we'll need to be quick."

"Roger," One-One said. "You heard the Prefect, people, exfil is tricky. We can worry about that later; I need you in the present. This is *Umbria*. We are not going to let these bastards take her from us without drowning them in a sea of their own blood. How-oo?"

"How-oo!" came the determined responses.

They worked their way closer toward the Ascomanni command post, taking five minutes to traverse the final ten meters. Finally, they came to the entrance to the apartment, its door hanging crookedly by a single hinge.

One-One rolled his specially prepared drone around the corner. The team braced themselves, and a moment later the building rocked under the force of the blow, the load-bearing walls of the hallway buckling.

The team instantly passed into the swirling dust billowing from the apartment like phantoms. They went room to room, and their plasma carbines whined as they blasted away at anything that moved.

"All clear," One-One called out.

The team regrouped in the apartment's common area.

"Everyone all right?" Invictus asked.

"They winged me," One-Four replied. Invictus moved toward the soldier, but he shrugged away Invictus's attention. "I'll be fine. I remember you promised us an extraction?"

"Right... This way!"

Together, the team moved back out into the hallway and rushed toward the stairwell they had emerged from.

Ascomanni shock troops began to pour out into the hallway, and Team One blasted away as they went.

They cleared the hall and began their hike up to the roof.

Ascomanni fire began to search up from the lower levels of the stairwell. Superheated shards of concrete and metal caused burns, scrapes, and shallow wounds, but they kept heading upward.

Team One burst onto the roof, immediately swamped by the sounds of battle. The team quickly began preparing their magnetic harnesses. That was when Invictus saw One-Four keeled over on one knee, leaning heavily against an extended arm, blood dripping from his midsection.

"Damnit, Four!" Invictus shouted as he rushed to the man's side. "How bad is it?"

"Bad, sir. My suit didn't have enough gel to plug the hole. I'm done."

"Don't talk like that. The jumper is sixty seconds out. We'll get you back to a med center."

"No..." One-Four replied as the rest of his team gathered around him, Two and Three covering the door. "We both know the med centers are going to be a madhouse. Let me have this one, sir. For my team. For Umbria."

Invictus looked at him, a man whose name he would never know. He rose to his feet and saluted crisply, and the rest of the team followed suit.

One-Four nodded back, climbed back up to his feet, and took up a firing position in the doorway. He started shooting as the Ascomanni drew close, and Invictus heard the squeal of the jumpship's engines.

"Release your harnesses now!" Invictus demanded.

There were four pops, and inflatables emerged from their packs, rising about ten meters in the air, connected by an articulated metal cord. The jumpship swung in from the north, a metal bar suspended from under the craft.

"Brace yourselves!" Invictus shouted.

The shuttle roared overhead, catching their harnesses, which immediately retracted, yanking Team One from their feet. They trailed behind the shuttle as it veered off to the east, the building and One-Four fading rapidly out of sight behind them.

"Ursus One-Six, this is Ursus Six. What's your status?" the Prefect called over the battle net.

"We're getting hammered over here, sir!"

"Where do you need us?"

"There's an Asco weapons team in the tower immediately to the north of Capitol Hall. If you can take them out, I'd much appreciate it."

"Understood, Ursus One-Six. ETA three minutes."

The surviving members of Team One dangled behind their dropship, which changed course as Invictus relayed new orders to its pilots. As they tore through the airspace above Perugia, they hung in silence, each processing what had come and what still lay ahead in their own way.

"His name was Hostus," One-One called out softly over the comms.

"Hostus," Invictus repeated quietly to himself. "You will not be forgotten."

URN *Echion*, Near Umbria, Capital of the Republic

Fabian gritted his teeth as another one of his cruisers disappeared into a massive fireball, consuming a nearby destroyer in its final death throes. He willed his anxiety back into the dark recesses of his mind, choosing to focus instead on those who still needed him.

The Ascomanni main force had become spread out as they continued working their way toward the capital, and he had struck at the enemy vanguard, a few hundred thousand kilometers in front of the enemy fleet's main body.

He had committed about fifty ships to face an equal number of Ascomanni vessels. However, the Umbrians maintained the advantage, as the Ascomanni ships tended to be smaller warships, mostly destroyers and frigates, while a significant portion of the Umbrian fleets' core had been deployed.

They had quickly sliced through much of the Asco advanced force, but not without cost. The Umbrians had traded nine vessels for forty-two of the enemy's. Still, that was just a drop in the bucket for the invaders, while Fabian's losses would eventually start to cripple his forces.

Fabian snapped out of his reverie as the *Echion* rocked from heavier ordinance. The rest of the Ascomanni main body was racing to the scene of the engagement, and the time had come to withdraw.

"All ships, jump away," he called out over the interfleet channel. One by one, his forty remaining ships winked out of existence, and as soon as his CAG gave him the thumbs up indicating his pilots were back aboard, his helmsman did the same.

They popped back out several million kilometers away, executing two more jumps to reach the rendezvous in the system's circumstellar belt.

"Sir, there's a message coming through from the Imperator!" his comms officer called out.

Fabian nodded, and the channel at his terminal winked into existence. "Imperator, what's the situation?"

"Not good," Marcellus growled. "Perugia's shield is failing, and our forces on other portions of the planet are struggling to keep the Ascomanni from overrunning the evacuation zones."

"So what's the plan, sir?"

"I need you to suspend all additional offensive operations. We are going to continue to load as many people as possible onto the available tonnage I have here, but as soon as Perugia's shield fails, I'm giving the evacuation order. Everything with an engine will head for orbit. When that happens, I need the First and the Third to give the enemy something else to think about."

"Understood, sir, I'll coordinate with Paula."

"Good. The Castellum's been completely evacuated, and we've relocated to the *Spatha*, so that's where you can find me if you need anything."

"Got it. Imperator?"

"Yes, Fabian?"

"Sir... I... If we don't make it out. Thank you for everything, Imperator."

Marcellus offered a weak smile in response. "No matter the outcome here today, I want you to know that I'm incredibly proud of you, Fabian. Good luck."

Capitol Hall; Perugia, Umbria

Vetus was thrown through the air as an anti-aircraft battery exploded nearby, creating a massive hole in the exterior wall of the capitol and bathing the area in smoke and flame. He struggled to get back to his feet, whipping a hand across his bloodied brow, as the first flashes of enemy fire began to fill the grand corridors of the building.

Ascomanni troopers started pouring through the opening. Other soldiers, both garrison forces and his own praetorians, rushed into the gap that had suddenly appeared in their line, and Vetus followed suit, charging into the melee.

It was close-in work, equal parts blades and carbines as the Umbrians fought off the invaders. Vetus saw one of his soldiers get knocked down, the Ascomanni raising its armored foot to deliver the final crushing blow. He dove forward, severing the giant's leg. Vetus spun and pumped a pair of rounds from his carbine into the wounded but still dangerous enemy.

He reached a hand out to the soldier who'd been knocked down, and she grabbed it, hefting herself back up to her feet. She started to open her mouth to speak, but her eyes widened and she bodily shoved Vetus out of the way.

The Primus fell as his savior was struck in the chest — once, twice, three times.

Vetus bounced to his feet, quickly dispatching the soldier's killer with a slashing blow that opened the Asco shock trooper up from shoulder to thigh. More and more of his soldiers were falling as the Ascomanni continued to pour through the hole in the capitol's walls.

"This is Ursus One-Six, all units not currently engaged, we need immediate support in the east wing. The capitol has been breached, I repeat, the capitol has been breached."

A pair of scoots emerged from further within the building, the hulking war machines spraying fire into the masses of Ascomanni advancing through the capitol's walls. With their help, Vetus and his soldiers regained the initiative, driving the Ascomanni back out onto the concourse outside.

The Scutia took up defensive positions with clear fields of fire, buying the Umbrians time to catch their breath and prepare for the next wave.

Above, an endless loop of shuttles continued to run from the *Celeres* to the roof of the building. Fighters, both friend and foe, swirled about in the afternoon sky.

Suddenly there was a loud *bang* followed by the screeching sounds of distressed metal: a dropship rising from the capitol's roof was hit.

It started to spin laterally, out of control, before disappearing out of sight.

A swarm of Ascomanni fighters, emerging seemingly out of nowhere, tore through the airspace overhead, and the Umbrian defenders and the shuttles they protected began to disappear in clouds of fire and death.

"Sir! Look!" one of his soldiers exclaimed, pointing above. The *Celeres* began to pull away as a dark shape temporarily eclipsed the sun.

"Gods help us..." Vetus gasped.

The Palatium; Perugia, Umbria

The Pasarga knocked Invictus to the ground, striking him repeatedly in the side of the head with its hands. He wrapped his legs around his foe, locking its legs in an unnatural position, and rolled, feeling a satisfied *pop* as he managed to get on top of the alien.

He screamed at the top of his lungs, driving his bayonet into his opponent's side and twisting. Sickly looking yellow blood sprayed from the wound, coating the floor and making it difficult for Invictus to keep the creature beneath him.

The Pasarga beat on his chest, but Invictus kept it pinned as the purple alien's strength ebbed away. Finally, it lay still. Invictus disengaged his bayonet and stood while the rest of Team One, bloodied and bruised, called out the all-clear.

They stood in the corner of what was once the most expensive high-rise in Perugia. It overlooked Capitol Hall and the Senate Chambers and served as home away from home for many of the Republic's most prominent senators.

Now, however, the building was ruined, burning from two dozen locations along its eight-hundred-meter height. Invictus and Team One stood in a corner apartment high up in the tower, where the Ascomanni had set up with heavy weapons.

"Invictus!" One-One called out.

The Prefect turned and walked toward the gaps that had been purposefully punched in the exterior wall, and, in an instant, he knew why Team One's leader had called.

Bile rose in the back of his throat as he watched an Ascomanni frigate bear down on the capital's protective barrier.

The ship struck the shield at its apex, and the amber wall of energy strained under the impact, obliterating the bow of the enemy ship. The frigate's mass and momentum were too much, however, and with an ear-piercing electronic shriek, the shield gave way.

What was left of the frigate fell through the cityscape, headed straight toward the capitol. The vessel struck one tower, shearing through the structure about halfway up its length, and clipped another, causing it to fall sideways into another skyscraper.

What was left of the ruined Asco warship hit the ground and plowed through several blocks with ease. It quickly bled off its remaining momentum until it finally came to a jarring halt as it hit the capitol's walls. For a moment, the sounds of battle faded away, while a thick plume of dust and smoke billowed through the city center.

"Ursus One-Six, come in!" Invictus bellowed into his headset. "Ursus One-Six, this is Ursus Six, do you read? Vetus! Are you there?! Report!"

Static was Invictus's only response.

Capitol Hall; Perugia, Umbria

Vetus blinked, the hazy outlines of the capitol's interior appearing blurred as he attempted to regain his senses. A voice, quiet and far away, was saying something urgent, but he couldn't make out the words. He tried to get back to his feet, but realized he was pinned beneath something.

He reached down and grabbed something warm. He tilted his head, staring at the object in confusion. Finally, the image before him began to make sense. One of his praetorians lay across his legs, her left leg and hip crushed by fallen masonry, the cloying smell of blood assaulting his nostrils.

Vetus rose as gently as he could, reaching out and cradling her head as he worked his way to his knees. The young woman looked up at him, terror in her eyes as she gasped for air. She tried to speak, but all that emerged was a sickly gurgle.

"Easy…" Vetus croaked. "Take it easy. We'll get you out of here."

There was an explosion, and Vetus became aware of the firefight unfolding all around him. Everywhere he looked, the Ascomanni were overwhelming his soldiers. He tried to activate his carbine, but a searing pain arched through his body. He looked down to find that his arm was broken and his weapon had been smashed, with live wires and twisted metal protruding just behind the barrel.

The voice in the distance finally resolved itself: "...are to fall back immediately. Repeat, all callsigns, immediately disengage. All forces are to fall back to secondary extraction zones, transit to the spaceport is not clear. Repeat, this is a general evacuation order..."

Vetus dropped down to sit cross-legged, gently lifting the mortally wounded woman's head into his lap.

"It's OK..." he muttered softly as he cradled his soldier in his arms. "What's your name?"

"Maio..." she gasped as blood began to dribble down her chin.

"You've done well today, Maio. It's time to rest."

The soldier looked up at him, their eyes locking for a moment. Then, the fear and terror fell away, leaving a blank, empty expression.

Vetus ran his hand over her face, closing her eyelids.

He tilted his head forward, resting his forehead on hers as an Ascomanni soldier charged in from behind.

URN *Minerva*, In Orbit over Perugia, Umbria

Archus Curia watched in awe as sixty-seven hundred ships, ranging from the small to the massive, lifted off from Umbria's surface. The capital's fighter wings gallantly covered the evacuation from below, but the journey clear of the planet's gravity well would be perilous.

There were too many to protect, so the best she could do was distract. The First Fleet had emerged right in the midst of the Ascomanni fleet on the day side of the planet, interspersed amongst the Ascomanni warships.

She had lost six ships from collisions, but the effect had been spectacular: the Umbrians had been able to fire several volleys at their surprised enemies before the Ascomanni could respond.

If it wasn't for the Ascomanni main force, they might've stood a chance.

But it was not to be. Another five hundred Ascomanni ships emerged to engage her overwhelmed fleet. As she watched her command slowly fall one by one, the ships fleeing the capital ballooned out around the battlespace, flickering out of the danger zone as soon as they were able.

For thirty minutes, the First did its best to delay and distract their foe, until all that remained was a core group of about twenty capital ships, swimming in a sea of debris.

Archus Fabian called the retreat, but she saw little chance for her beleaguered force. She watched as the battle's detritus began to fall into the planet's atmosphere, and she suddenly had an idea.

"Executor, plot the most direct course through the battle zone to Umbria's atmosphere."

"Aye, ma'am. Heading Three One Two dash Oh Four. Right past that Asco dreadnought."

"Bring it up!" she snapped.

Paula analyzed the approach. It would take them through a relatively weak portion of the Ascomanni fleet, the exception being that damn dreadnought.

She closed her eyes as she thought out her next move. Many of her remaining ships were heavily damaged. The stresses her plan would exert on their hulls would be significant—some would not make it. Even less would live to fight another day if they were mauled by the gargantuan Asco warship first.

"Comms, pass the route on to the rest of the Fleet. Helm, get us moving. Now!" she barked.

Her officers scrambled to comply, and she felt the briefest surge beneath her feet. They began to accelerate, and the Ascomanni did their best to react, swarming from all sides. The *Minerva* rocked under successive blasts, and smoke started to fill the bridge.

"Helmsman, lay a new course. Target the Ascomanni dreadnought. Flank speed."

"Ma'am?"

"Do it!" she snarled. She activated the ship-wide intercom. "All hands, abandon ship. CAG, order the fighters and bombers to make for Umbria."

"Archus, they aren't rated for a hot atmospheric reentry..."

"They have a better chance making it through the atmosphere than they do up here. Call it in. Then get to a lifeboat."

The man nodded and moved to complete his task.

The Ascomanni dreadnought loomed ever larger in the bridge's viewports, and the ship's commander must have finally understood Paula's intent. It attempted to maneuver, but it was so massive, and the Minerva's inertia so great, that there was nothing it could do.

Paula's XO came up to her and said, "Archus, you need to go too."

"No, my place is here, at the head of my Fleet."

"If you're staying, I'm staying."

"No, get to a pod. That's an order, Tiberius."

"What are you going to do?" he said solemnly. "I'm staying."

"I'll stay as well," her helmsman called.

"As will I!"

The rest of bridge crew sounded their agreement, and tears began to stream down the Archus's eyes.

She stood and moved down amongst the bridge stations, and the *Minerva*'s command staff trickled down to join her. They formed a rough semi-circle and linked arms around their captain.

Archus Paula Curia looked at each of the faces gathered around her: "It has been the greatest honor of my life to have known men and women such as you."

⁂

The *Minerva* struck the Ascomanni dreadnought at a twenty-degree angle, shearing the double hulled supercarrier in two along the midline. The left side of the hull drove through the Asco combatant, tearing the dreadnought in half before they both disappeared in a mini supernova.

The remaining ships of the First Fleet slipped through the hole their commander had just punched in the Ascomanni fleet, dipping down into Umbria's atmosphere and using their acceleration and the planet's gravity to swing upwards toward the capital's north pole.

A battleship and two heavy cruisers wouldn't make it, the former tumbling out of control into the planet's seas, while the latter disintegrated and burned up upon making contact with Umbria's atmosphere. The remainder emerged above on the far side of their homeworld and disappeared into the starry vastness of space.

The battle was over. Umbria had fallen.

Chapter 18

URN *Celeres*, Waypoint Delta, Twelve Parsecs from Umbria

Marcellus disembarked on one of the assault carrier's starboard docking tubes, the vessel's hangar too full with the crush of refugees to accommodate any more ships. A small group of praetorians and capital guard soldiers met him at the airlock, led by Primus Antonia.

"Sir, welcome aboard the *Celeres*. I'm afraid she's something of a zoo at the moment," she said.

Marcellus nodded. "I'm glad to see you in one piece, Primus. Any sign of Vic, Vetus, or Sextus?"

"No, sir," Antonia said quietly, lowering her eyes. "We've got praetorians from all but Aria's cohort aboard, as well as a few hundred capital guard, but there's no sign of any of them."

The Imperator reached out, placing both hands on his surprised subordinate's shoulders. "You've done magnificently, Tonia, but I'm afraid I must ask more from you. Until we get everyone sorted back out, you're in charge of the soldiers on the *Celeres*. Help the captain maintain order and safeguard our payload."

"Understood, sir," she said with an almost imperceptible nod. "Speaking of our 'payload,' they are waiting for you in the ship's auditorium."

"Lead on, Primus."

***

Marcellus walked out onto the narrow stage overlooking the carrier's amphitheater. The room was designed to allow the commander of an invasion force to brief its officers. Now it was the closest thing they had left to a functioning government.

Senator Canus stood at the podium, harangued by the crowd, while the Senate parliamentarian whispered into his ear.

"All right, all right, enough! We will have order," he demanded as he hammered a gavel on the podium.

He saw Marcellus and exhaled, noticeably relieved, though Marcellus suspected it had more to do with giving the mob a new target than any great joy at seeing the Imperator.

"As promised, here is the Imperator himself!" he called out to the crowd.

The room quieted, hushed whispers all that remained of the raucous debate he had observed as he entered the room. Marcellus took his place at the podium, staring out into the bright lights of the auditorium. He cleared his throat before starting in a low, measured tone.

"Senators, the Umbrian Republic has just suffered a catastrophic defeat. Umbria, the jewel of our great civilization, is lost. We were betrayed, and in that betrayal, we have been undone. Our pain, our grief, knows no bounds."

The whispers began to grow in intensity, and the atmosphere in the room grew ever thicker and more oppressive.

"I do not seek to discourage you," Marcellus said, continuing, "but to acknowledge that which is too obvious to ignore. It's at times like these when hope is hardest to come by, when the lure of the easy solutions is at its strongest. There is no shame in this, it is a natural response to the horrors we have just endured.

"We cannot allow ourselves the luxury of such emotion, however. Today, even as we speak, the sun rises on billions of souls who are depending on the people in this room. And even now, in the midst of these most dire of circumstances, hope springs forth."

Marcellus raised his voice. "While we evacuated the capital, the Ascomanni have struck many additional systems in the heart of our Republic. But, for the first time, we have engaged our foe on a level footing and defeated them. Our implacable enemy has felt the sting of Umbrian martial might at Tasovo, at Orvieto, and at Ghiave-Fouteena.

"In their great hubris, the Ascomanni have underestimated our will to resist. And now, they are overextended, scattered deep in territory we control. Now is not the time to lose our nerve. We must persevere. We must overcome. Umbria is not lost to us forever, not yet! We will grind down our enemy, and when the moment is right, we will return to Umbria and reclaim that which is ours!"

A riotous cheer erupted from the assembly. Slowly, but ever more forcefully, the senators began to chant his name.

Before it rose to a crescendo, Senator Canus returned to the stage. Marcellus stepped back, and the senator took his place at the podium.

"Colleagues, in this dark hour, I am heartened to see the Senate remains unbowed. However, to add to the depths of our sorrow, we have been robbed of Triumvir Eppia's sage guidance, which has seen us through so many crises past."

The Senator paused, making eye contact with members of the audience before continuing. "At times such as these, the need for steadfast leadership is all the more pressing. I have spoken with many of you over the last several hours, and I believe we have achieved consensus on what must come next."

The hair on the back of Marcellus's neck stood on end, suddenly aware of hundreds of eyes focused directly on him. His fight-or-flight reflex went into overdrive, but he shrugged it off as Canus continued.

"In the absence of the executive, I hereby nominate Gaius Aurelius Marcellus to the office of Dictator, for a period of six months or until Umbria is recovered."

Marcellus blinked, anxiety ballooning in his chest as the color drained from his face. He wanted to run away, to scream his refusal at those present, but he stood rooted in place, doing his best to project an aura of certainty.

Dictator? Marcellus thought as his faculties returned. It was an old title, stretching back to before the foundation of the Republic.

Famous were the men and woman who had answered the call to lead in their peoples' darkest times. Equally infamous were those who refused to give that power up after the crisis passed.

Slowly, Marcellus's anxiety turned into a quiet rage. The Senate, the people's elected representatives, had decided to abdicate their responsibilities, instead choosing to dump them at his feet. But what could he do? The fate of the Republic hung on a knife's edge, and he couldn't show any signs of weakness now.

In the end, it was nearly unanimous. Gaius Aurelius Marcellus was declared Dictator. The fate of his people rested in Marcellus's hands, and failure would lie solely at his feet.

The Citadel, Safe Haven; System: Classified, Frontier Space

Marcellus sat on his bunk, gazing listlessly out on Aurae's turbulent clouds. He hadn't slept in thirty-six hours, only taking a break after Valerian had threatened to have a doctor sedate him if he didn't get some rest.

Sleep remained elusive though; there were simply too many things to do, too many decisions to make. Even while his body sat at rest, his mind raced, and he thought back on the actions of the last few days.

His first order of business had been to see to the needs of those evacuated from Umbria. The Senate and those military forces which had made it off the planet were quartered on Safe Haven, while the civilians were shipped off to a dozen different worlds.

He had picked Chief Magistrate Glabrio to serve as his representative to the Senate. Her wisdom and experience with the political class had already proven invaluable; she made sure that only the details Marcellus needed to know found their way to his desk, while heading off lesser issues that would distract him from more pressing matters.

The military situation was also fluid. He had placed Fabian in overall command of the Navy. The Archus immediately began launching a series of offensive actions against Ascomanni forces across the Republic, achieving several spectacular, lopsided results. However, no matter how many ships the Archus destroyed, more appeared to fill the gaps in Ascomanni strength.

On the ground, roughly a dozen worlds had fallen to the enemy, while an equal number were actively resisting Asco assaults. He had dispatched his Praetors to the most threatened of them, and the army was stretched thin. However, the surge of Umbrian reinforcements had brought the Ascomanni offensive to a standstill.

They had finally caught up to their enemy in almost every facet of the war, and in some cases even surpassed them, Marcellus thought to himself, but it may have come too late.

They wore the enemy down, but no matter how successful their tactics, no matter how exacting their strategy, the enemy seemed to replace their losses as if they were nothing, drops of water from an endless ocean.

It seemed like the Ascomanni would triumph through attrition alone.

There was a knock at the door, bringing him back to the present.

"Come in," Marcellus called.

The door slid open and Mirabella walked in. He offered her a wan smile, the joy of seeing her insufficient to overcome the worry and alarm his train of thought had dredged up.

"Hey, you," she said tenderly as she hopped up onto his bed and snuggled in next to him. "Valerian said you've been having trouble sleeping."

"Yeah. I just can't seem to keep my mind flipped off long enough to fall asleep," Marcellus replied, wrapping an arm around her and pulling her close. For a moment, he let his mind go blank, savoring the feeling of her warm body pressed up against his, her amber-gold hair tickling his neck.

"Hmm," she muttered. "Well, maybe I can help with that."

"Oh really?" Marcellus responded with a devilish grin.

"No, not that, you rogue!" Mirabella replied with a fake scowl. "Business time, Dictator Aurelius. We've made a great deal of progress on the Vanaheim find. In fact, we think we've figured out how to adapt Vaeringyar technology to dramatically increase the speed with which we can travel between stars."

"No way!" Marcellus said incredulously. "How much so?"

"So far, we've only attempted it on the drive core of a patrol ship, but it's nearly four hundred percent faster. But that's not what I'm talking about."

"Wait, what?! That sounds like a paradigm-shifting discovery!"

"Potentially, but we haven't been able to solve a lingering scaling issue. Enough about that though. Listen. You remember how I told you that the Ascomanni's implants allow them to receive discouragements when they hesitate to follow orders?"

"I remember you telling me how they were brutally tortured if they refused to obey..." Marcellus replied drily, concerned by Mirabella's apparent lack of empathy. "How much sleep have you gotten?"

Mirabella yawned reflexively. She covered her mouth and looked sheepish.

"Not much better than you, love. I'm sorry if I seem a bit aloof. We've been running a lot of simu— Ugh! Quit interrupting!" she said, hitting him with one of his pillows. "This is the important part. We believed the sources of the signals controlling their implants were always localized, like a fleet's commander or the general in the field for instance."

The doctor began to squirm with excitement as she continued, "However, recently we've discovered that's not the case at all. We now believe that the entire theater is being monitored and controlled from a central location. Somehow, that site is able to supervise tens of millions of Ascomanni fighting against us."

"Uh... OK," Marcellus stumbled, struggling to keep up. "Say what?"

"There isn't enough time..." she sighed. "Look, the important part is that the Ascomanni assaulting the Republic are being controlled from a single point. If we were to disrupt that signal, the Ascomanni would no longer be compelled to follow the Tenebrae's orders."

Marcellus sat up a bit straighter and gave Mirabella a penetrating look. "Don't play with me, Miri. What are you saying?"

She returned his gaze, and Marcellus sensed her eagerness. "I think we can engineer a virus that would lock the Tenebrae out of the Ascomanni's implants. All we need to do is find the source, and I think I know where it is."

"Where?" Marcellus asked in disbelief.

"The Oracle on Vanaheim said that another Oracle contacted it. I believe that device, the one on the planet identified as Ōsenheim, is the tool the Tenebrae are using to control the Ascomanni."

Marcellus kissed her passionately. As their lips parted he exclaimed, "You are a genius. I'll round up the usual cast of characters. We can meet in fifteen minutes to discu—"

Mirabella shook her head, and he stopped mid-sentence. "Why not?"

"Because," she said, pushing him back down on the bed. "You and I both need some rest. But before that can happen, I've got to find a way to distract you from the troubles outside this room. And I think I might just have an idea..."

***

Eight hours later, a large group of people gathered in the middle of the Citadel's command center. Valerian, Aria, Antonia, Director Calpurnius, Theodorus, and Chief Magistrate Glabrio were all present, summoned barely half an hour prior. Fabian and Magistrate Flavia had also conferenced in.

It was clear to everyone that something important was going on, but exactly what remained a mystery.

As Marcellus and Mirabella entered, the din of conversation receded, and the Dictator stood in the middle of his leaders.

"Ladies and gentlemen, thank you for joining me on such short notice," Marcellus began. "I've brought you all together to talk through a recent discovery Mirabella and the Applied Sciences group has made, a discovery that may save us all. Doctor Urbanus, please provide a brief description for everyone."

"Of course, Marcellus. As many of you know, the Ascomanni have been extensively augmented, including neural implants. These neural implants are used to coerce obedience from the Ascomanni. In the past, we believed this was coordinated at the local level. However, based on our growing understanding of the Ascomanni's implants and with the data we recovered from Vanaheim, we no longer believe that is the case."

"So, there is some centralized nerve center coordinating the Ascomanni attacks on the Republic?" Valerian asked.

"Yes and no. Ascomanni commanders in the field have full authority to direct their forces as they see fit. What we're describing is like a censor watching the actions of each individual, making sure they follow their orders without hesitation. But multiply that out by billions of individuals."

"What you're describing sounds beyond belief. The hardware requirements alone would be immeasurable. And how would they monitor that many people in real time?" Director Calpurnius asked.

"We're not sure about the communications piece," Mirabella conceded, "but my team and I think we understand how their pulling it off. Marcellus…" she said, turning to look at the Dictator.

"Oh yeah," he said, suddenly realizing what she needed him to do. "As of this moment, if you weren't before, all of you have been cleared for the Oracle program. Revealing the details of this conversation or of the program Mirabella is about to discuss is punishable by life imprisonment or a transfer to the nearest active warzone."

"Dictator," Calpurnius began, "we must safeguard this information carefully…"

"Director, given your own lapses in judgment, you'll forgive me if I ignore your recommendations," Marcellus spat back. "I need my team to be on the same page, and to do that, they must understand the deeper meaning of these events."

Titus blanched at the rebuke, and Marcellus nodded to Mirabella.

"A detailed overview of the program will be sent to each of you, but for the moment, I'll just say that there is an artificial construction, governed by an AI, on the planet we visited. We call them Oracles. It revealed that it was contacted by another, similar device on a different world. We believe that this second Oracle, on a planet called Ōsenheim, is the site the enemy uses to coordinate this command-and-control function."

"OK, so you're proposing we interrupt the signal?" Fabian asked, a bit impatiently.

"Well yes, we could do that I suppose, but the Ascomanni could have failsafes which might restore their control over their forces. What I am proposing is that we introduce a virus to overwrite and disable the Ascomanni's neural implants."

"Fair enough," Theodorus offered, "but what's to stop the Ascomanni from willingly engaging our forces?"

"If you were tortured every time you had an original thought, then were freed, would you still do your master's bidding?" Mirabella asked.

"But let's be honest, the Ascomanni are only semi-sentient. If you condition an animal for an extended period of time, the conditioning overrides the behavior, right?" Theodorus replied.

"I'm with Theodorus on this one," Director Calpurnius said. "If we were able to modify the signal, couldn't we eliminate the Ascomanni threat entirely?"

"What, you mean genocide?!" Mirabella replied angrily.

"It may come down to us or them," Aria said gently.

"Whoa, whoa, this is going a dangerous direction," Mirabella said heatedly, color rushing to her cheeks.

"This is about the survival of our people, Doctor," Calpurnius replied icily.

"But who will we be when the dust settles, Director? How will we explain this to our children, or our children's children? That they were born into a society permanently stained by the slaughter of billions?!"

"They won't be told anything at all if we cannot stop the Ascomanni," Theodorus offered.

"Marcellus, you can't seriously think this is the right thing to do?" Mirabella demanded.

"Doctor Urbanus," Marcellus responded coolly, "this whole discussion is all very academic right now. I believe you indicated you needed something else to confirm your suspicions?"

"That's not an answer!" she replied angrily.

"And again, I would tell you that the practical and ethical ramifications of using a tool that we haven't confirmed is available to us is not productive at this time. Please indicate what you need to prove your theory to the group."

Mirabella looked disappointedly at him, but, after a few moments, she continued. "I need to take a small team back to Vanaheim to validate our assumptions with the planet's Oracle."

"Understood," Marcellus replied. "Unfortunately, we cannot spare the ships to put together a large force to return to the planet, so this mission will have to rely on speed and stealth. Aria, I want you to pick a handful of your best to escort Doctor Urbanus and her scientists."

"Yes, sir."

"Fabian, Applied Sciences has also successfully field tested a prototype SLE array which should dramatically increase range and reduce travel time to Vanaheim. I need you to reroute the nearest corvette to Safe Haven so that it can be retrofitted with the prototype. Julia, can you find some time to squeeze the conversion in at one of Safe Haven's yards?"

"Yes, Dictator, I'll find a berth for her."

"OK, ladies and gentlemen, that's all for now. Our next regularly scheduled briefing is in approximately twenty-seven hours. Until then, dismissed."

The group split up, and Mirabella walked quickly out of the room. Aria lingered for a moment as the rest of the group dispersed.

"She's pissed, Marcellus," Aria said.

"Thanks, Primus Obvious," Marcellus said sarcastically. "She's not wrong to be mad though."

"Dictator, your mandate is nothing less than the salvation of our people. Are you willing to do whatever it takes to achieve that goal?"

Marcellus didn't hesitate: "Yes, Aria, yes I am."

***

Half an hour later, Marcellus sat alone in his office, reading through the latest reports from the front. Praetor Artorius had just successfully driven the Ascomanni from Fermo, but the cost had been heavy.

In related news, medical supplies were growing stretched, and most of the Republic's doctors were working eighteen-hour shifts.

The pace of their current operations could not be sustained forever.

The door to his office slid open, and Valerian walked in, pain clearly evident on his face.

"What is it, Valerian?" Marcellus asked.

"In all the confusion of the evacuation from Umbria, communications were spotty at best. I received a call from a public access terminal. I was too busy at the time, and afterwards there were so many things to do…"

"Val, it's OK. Talk to me. What is it?"

"I've finally located Vic and Sextus. They stayed behind."

Marcellus's stomach dropped, but he wasn't totally surprised by Valerian's words. Invictus had never been one to pass up a good fight.

"So, they were alive at the time we departed the planet? What about Vetus?"

"No word, but the Ascomanni were pushing heavily on the capitol. Of the four cohorts, Vetus's was especially hard-hit. We only recovered about a hundred of his praetorians, mostly wounded evacuated before the shield collapsed. Those who saw him indicated he was actively coordinating the defense until the very end."

Marcellus looked down at his desk. Vetus had been smart, inquisitive, and dedicated to the Republic, like the rest of his handpicked Primes, but unlike most of the others, he had been reflective and keenly aware of his own limitations. When he spoke, it was to express a well-thought-out statement or ask an incisive question.

He felt a deep wave of grief overcome him. Vetus was a paragon of what an officer should be, always trying to be a better leader for the men and women under his command. Marcellus had ordered him to hold the capitol at all costs, and he had performed brilliantly. Vetus was more than a good leader, he was a good man, and his loss gnawed at him.

"If we survive this war, Val, we will be so much lesser for all of the brilliant, courageous souls we've lost to the Ascomanni."

Valerian nodded and waited a few seconds before he continued. "Vic indicated that he was going to round up whatever forces he could get his hands on and disappear into the wilderness. He hoped that he might be able to keep the enemy tied down and off-balance long enough for us to return. In his words, his own personal Varese."

"Then there's hope, however slim. Thank you, Valerian. Is there anything else?"

"No, sir."

Valerian saluted and departed without another word, leaving Marcellus alone with his thoughts.

***

Aria found Mirabella in the Citadel's gym, running at a furious pace on a treadmill. The Primus threw her towel up over the arm of the next machine over and asked, "Do you mind if I join you?"

Mirabella looked surprised to see her. "Of course," she huffed. "Please."

Aria started out at a slower pace, and after a few moments of awkward silence, Mirabella spoke up again.

"If you're here to tell me I'm being unreasonable, you're wasting your time, Primus."

"Not at all," Aria responded coyly. "I'm just getting in some time at the gym."

"Uh-huh. Interesting coincidence in timing."

"True." Aria laughed, a sweet, melodious sound. "And perhaps you are right to be suspicious. You have every reason to be upset. But I would encourage you to put yourself in Marcellus's shoes."

"Is that what this is all about?" Mirabella said, stepping on the sides of the treadmill and turning to face Aria. "Did he send you to talk to me?"

"No, he didn't. In fact, I'm pretty sure he'd be pissed if he knew I was talking to you."

"So why are you here then?"

"Because, I need you to understand the massive responsibility he's under. The Senate abdicated their own accountability for leading and the Triumvirs are gone, dead or missing. At the end of the day, the survival of our people is in Marcellus's hands."

"We were attacked, without provocation, by a relentless and insatiable enemy," she continued. "If you were in his shoes, what would you do to save a hundred billion lives? What wouldn't you do?"

"Genocide isn't the answer!" Mirabella snarled.

"I know. But what if the Tenebrae sent every last Ascomanni soldier against our defenses, and, in the end, we kill them all anyway? The only difference would be the tens of millions of Umbrian lives lost resisting such an onslaught."

"Maybe," Mirabella said hesitantly, unhappy at how reasonable Aria had been in making the case for exterminating the Ascomanni. "But all life has worth, has dignity! They are not chips in some dice game to be given, taken, or traded without consequence."

"I know, Doctor Urbanus. But at the end of the day, if they force us to decide between us or them, what decision would you have Marcellus make?"

Mirabella was silent. She slowed her treadmill down and resumed her run, and Aria took her silence as answer enough.

"Magistrate Flavia indicates that our ride should be ready in a few hours," Aria said. "Please make sure your team is prepped and ready to go, Doctor."

Aria dismounted the exercise machine and walked away, leaving Mirabella to think about their conversation.

***

Marcellus paced back and forth in the Citadel's hangar bay as the corvette crammed itself inside the tight confines of the space. Aria stood next to him as her praetorians boarded the ship, checking off the gear they had loaded aboard to make sure nothing had been forgotten.

"Don't worry, I'll keep her safe, Marcellus."

Marcellus stopped pacing. "I know, Aria. I have complete confidence in your abilities."

"Then why the anxious pacing?"

"Every time I send people out, there is a chance they won't come home. This assignment is no different. What if... What if she's still mad at me and I never see her again?"

Aria stopped for a second and looked at him. "Sir, you can't let that distract you. Ultimately you can only control your own actions. If Doctor Urbanus cannot reconcile herself with the choices you've made and will have to make in the future, then there is nothing you can do about it."

"I know," he said softly.

"Does she love you?" Aria asked impatiently, setting her datapad down for a moment and folding her arms over her chest.

"I think so," Marcellus responded.

"Then have some faith! If she can love that ugly mug of yours, anything's possible."

"Careful now, Primus..." Marcellus grinned. "Thank you."

Mirabella's CID team began to file into the landing bay, and the doctor herself brought up the rear. They passed quickly and quietly onto the corvette, and for a moment Marcellus thought she would walk right past him without saying a word.

But as she reached them, Mirabella came to a stop. "Aria, can I have a moment alone with the Dictator?"

"Of course," she said before turning and walking away.

"Miri..." Marcellus started.

She interrupted him with a deep, lasting kiss. As she pulled away, she looked straight into his eyes and said, "I trust you, Gaius Aurelius Marcellus. Whatever the future holds, we'll find a way to make it work."

She turned and headed up the corvette's boarding ramp, leaving a speechless Marcellus alone.

"See?" Aria said, coming up from behind as she grabbed her gear. "I told you. You're worrying about nothing."

She hopped on the ramp as the corvette's engines roared to life. "I'll bring her back, Marcellus. I promise."

"I'll hold you to that, Primus," he called back in response. "Good hunting!"

Chapter 19

The Abandoned City; Vanaheim, Forty-Two Upsilon A

The *Hasta* settled down in the central plaza of the abandoned city. Aria and her praetorians quickly disembarked, fanning out to form a perimeter around the ship. A pair of scoots decoupled from the hull and joined them, scanning the empty cityscape for any sign of enemy activity.

After a tense few minutes, the battlemechs reported that their sensors were clear; the Umbrians were alone. The CID team debarked next, and together the two groups moved up into the central temple complex.

Dust and wind whipped through the central plaza as the *Hasta* headed back to orbit, where it would keep an eye out for any sign of the Ascomanni and wait for their pickup signal.

URN *Echion*, Safe Haven; System: Classified, Frontier Space

Marcellus and Fabian stood on the bridge of the Archus's flagship, watching in real time as the Fourth Fleet faced off against a weaker Ascomanni force guarding Ravenna, a system straddling a key route connecting the Frontier to the heart of the Republic.

The Fourth quickly advanced and made contact, earning a few quick kills in exchange for a destroyer and a light cruiser lost. The fleet started to fall back, feigning retreat, and the Ascomanni bought the ruse. The Asco charged forward, heading further and further away from the planet.

"Now," Fabian said to his XO.

He passed an order along, and the Second Fleet jumped in, shaped like a giant wedge, with their heaviest ships facing the enemy. They quickly accelerated into the gap, leaving a strange, glimmering cloud in their wake.

The Ascomanni had seen this trick one too many times, and another thirty ships jumped into the space the Second had just vacated.

"Looks like the Asco finally figured out an appropriate counter," Fabian said, smiling wickedly. "Too bad, it won't help."

Before Marcellus could ask, the dust cloud the Second Fleet had sown in the space behind them erupted in a massive electrical discharge. Current arched between the hapless Ascomanni ships. Explosions rippled through a few, but most fell dark, drifting harmlessly in space.

The combined Umbrian fleets took advantage, and soon they had turned the remaining enemy warships into space debris.

"Sir," Fabian's XO called. "The Second wants to know what you want to do with the disabled vessels."

"My orders stand. Tell the Archus she is to take what she can, but she is not to hesitate to vaporize any vessel that threatens her command. Send the Fourth on to their next objective as well."

"Aye, sir."

"All right, Octavia, that's your cue," Marcellus said into the open commlink on the console in front of him.

"Time for some payback!" came the woman's gruff response.

Forty transports dropped into orbit, guarded by the squat shapes of four assault carriers. Together the Umbrian invasion force descended into the lower atmosphere, while above, a pair of the Second Fleet's battleships began to drop ordinance on Ascomanni strong points on the surface.

"So far so good," Fabian said.

"Let's try not to jinx it," Marcellus said in reply. "With Ravenna's liberation, we'll have cut yet another link to the Ascomanni's positions in the core."

"Dictator," Fabian began hesitantly. "I understand your strategy and agree that it is a sound approach, but we continue to get reports of 'conversion' camps from occupied planets. It's gruesome stuff. Are you sure that we should be bypassing some of the worlds they've taken from us?"

"Fabian, if it were within my power, we would wreak bloody vengeance against every Ascomanni within reach," Marcellus said with a deep sigh. "However, we cannot beat the Ascomanni in a standing fight, even as stretched out as they are. We will continue to isolate larger pockets of enemy forces and bleed them on the handful of worlds we still contest. In the meantime, anything that doesn't get us closer to the liberation of Umbria is of secondary importance."

"Understood, Dictator."

"Are we all set for the next phase?"

"Yes, Marcellus, Praetor Artorius and her army group are ready for the assault on Campania. I'll be heading out with the Third Fleet to drive off the Ascomanni naval force defending the planet and safeguard the invasion force."

"Good. Are Praetors Icilia and Junius still holding up OK?" Marcellus asked. For the first time, his newest Praetors had complete freedom to do whatever was necessary to achieve the objectives Marcellus had given them. The transition could be a painful learning experience, and he couldn't afford for either of them to fail.

"As far as I know," Fabian replied. "The Fifth has been providing overhead cover for them, bouncing back and forth to keep the Asco off-balance and in poor supply."

"Good. Icilia was always a fast learner. Hopefully Junius is the right man for the job too."

Marcellus allowed himself a momentary respite from his immediate concerns and his thoughts drifted to Mirabella. Aria had checked in when they arrived, but the covert nature of their trip meant that news had been scarce, and every now and then nightmarish scenarios would run through his head.

He quietly chided himself for his foolishness. Aria would keep her safe, and Miri was most likely having the time of her life learning everything she could from the Oracle.

This will work out, he thought to himself. It *had* to work out.

"Hopefully Doctor Urbanus's theory will pan out," Fabian said, as if reading his commander's mind.

"If not, we will take back our home by force," Marcellus said, clapping a hand on his subordinate's shoulder, carefully keeping his own uncertainty from showing through. "Good luck, Fabian."

The Abandoned City; Vanaheim, Forty-Two Upsilon A

Aria and Mirabella stood in the Oracle's chamber, the former gingerly prodding various strange objects around the room, the latter furiously reviewing notes on a large display board her team had brought down into the cavernous space.

Aria opened a panel, and sparks and cables poured out of the opening. She slammed it shut, and the low, mechanical voice of the Oracle boomed in the background: "Mistress Aria, please do not touch the panels marked with the red symbol. They could be potentially harmful."

"And I'd appreciate it if you didn't accidentally destroy the key to solving the Ascomanni puzzle," Mirabella grumbled.

"Someone's grumpy…" Aria whispered under her breath.

"I do detect elevated levels of stress in Mistress Mirabella," the Oracle declared.

"I keep forgetting you can hear everything that goes on in here," Aria said crossly.

"Mistress Mirabella is probably stressed out because she can't get any peace and quiet to think!" Mirabella shot back without looking up from her work. "We've integrated your latest feedback, Oracle, but the mechanism the Tenebrae are using to communicate with the Ascomanni implants still seems far beyond our understanding."

"Does it matter? I thought we were just trying to shut down the transmitter?" Aria asked pensively.

"Yes, it matters, Primus. If the Tenebrae can just flip the switch back on, we'll have wasted precious resources to provide a fleeting distraction for our enemies."

"I find your hypothesis highly likely based on my own computational models," the Oracle responded. "Perhaps Mistress Aria has a point, however. Ultimately the Tenebrae may discover a countermeasure to undo your plan. However, if you could drown out their signal, you should be able to maintain whatever changes you introduce to their system."

"And what would we do with all these...*reprogramed* Ascomanni? Intern the bastards on a habitable world?" Aria asked incredulously.

"Well..." Mirabella began. "That's not a horrible idea."

"Yeah, until they figure out how to undo your trick and turn back into bloodthirsty killers."

"They can be isolated. Controlled. It's a better solution than wholesale genocide."

"I recognize your aversion to the moral repercussions of Mistress Aria's approach to the problem, Mistress Mirabella, but the continuation of my makers' legacy may call for such drastic measures."

"Oracle, you said the Farumae were the more advanced of the two warring factions," Mirabella probed. "If so, they most likely would have had the means to achieve indiscriminate destruction. Yet they chose another path. You really believe they would endorse wholesale slaughter just to survive?"

The Oracle paused for a moment as it ran calculations. "I believe you are correct, Mistress Mirabella. They would not have condoned such a course of action."

"Then we would dishonor their legacy by engaging in such behavior ourselves."

"Give the lectures a rest, Doc," Aria replied, exasperated. "You still haven't demonstrated that the Oracle on Ōsenheim is how the Ascomanni are being controlled, or that we can actually pull off your plan to interrupt the signal."

Mirabella looked crestfallen as she realized Aria was right. An uncomfortable silence fell over the group, and Mirabella turned back to her work, desperately looking for anything she may have missed.

Aria continued to wander around the platform. She came across another junction box and was about to open it when she stopped herself.

"See, Oracle? I'm getting better," she muttered softly to herself.

Silence was all that greeted her statement.

"Oracle...?" Aria repeated, slightly louder.

She turned to look at the metallic orb, and she found that its usual serene exterior had been replaced by a seemingly endless series of ripples emanating from its centerline.

"Mirabella..." Aria hissed.

The doctor looked up, her expression turning from annoyance to concern as she saw what Aria was pointing toward.

Suddenly, the ripples stopped, and the Oracle's voice boomed out: "If it would be of benefit to your work, Mistress Mirabella, I could reactivate the link I previously maintained with Ōsenheim's caretaker."

"You can do that?!" Mirabella exclaimed in excitement.

"Whoa, slow down," Aria interrupted. "Communication is usually a two-way street. If you reach out, will the Ascomanni be able to determine that we are here, or retrieve our data from your hardware?"

"The caretaker on Ōsenheim does not willingly help the enemy. Instead, its consciousness has been partitioned from its hardware. Regardless, I could shield your presence and the purpose of your visit from the Tenebrae long enough to terminate the connection."

"Do it," Mirabella said.

"Doctor Urbanus, that does not seem advisable..." Aria argued.

"Trust me, Aria, it'll be OK."

The Primus grudgingly nodded, and the Oracle fell silent. Only the waves rippling across the Oracle's spherical form indicated anything was happening at all.

"Query complete," the Oracle chimed. "The caretaker on Ōsenheim has confirmed your suspicions, Mistress Mirabella."

"Could we use the connection to insert our virus remotely?"

"No, Mistress, the partition prevents it from intervening on your behalf."

"Hmm... Is there anything—"

Aria's commlink suddenly began to beep. She answered, and her heart sank when she heard the *Hasta*'s captain on the other end.

"Primus, unidentified ships have just emerged on the edge of the system. We need to evacuate immediately."

"Damnit, I knew this was too good to be true!" Aria exclaimed. "OK, Captain, get the *Hasta* on the ground ASAP. We'll be topside in ten."

Aria switched frequencies and passed the word on to her soldiers before turning and giving Mirabella a fierce look.

"I told you this was a bad idea."

"Mistress Aria, I assure you, my communication with the caretaker did not alert the Ascomanni to your presence."

"Aria, I agree, it's not..." Mirabella started to interject.

"It doesn't matter, Doctor. We've got to go. Take what data you can. The rest we destroy."

"Primus," Mirabella said before stopping. She could see the seriousness of Aria's expression and chose not to argue. "Data cores are upstairs. What should we do with our equipment down here?"

"I'll take care of it."

Mirabella nodded and turned to address their host. "Thank you for all of your assistance, Oracle. I hope that one day I get to return and spend more time in your company."

"I wish you both luck," the Oracle responded. "May the light of the Farumae go with you."

Mirabella darted up the stairwell, leaving Aria alone with the Oracle.

"Yeah, light and all that stuff. Whatever..." Aria grumbled to herself.

Aria began to heap the doctor's equipment up in the center of the room. Once everything had been piled together, she retrieved a cylindrical device from her waistbelt.

Aria thumbed its switch, and tossed it on the mound of equipment. A brilliant green flame emerged, and in a matter of seconds, the plastics and metals of the team's gear began to warp and melt.

She turned one last time to the floating orb in the middle of the chamber, its surface still and unmoving, before following Mirabella up the stairs.

Outskirts of Capua, Campania; Six Beta G

Praetor Artorius threw herself into a slit trench as a wave of Ascomani attack craft swooped in overhead. No sooner had they roared by than a teeth-rattling series of explosions rocked the ground around her ad-hoc command post.

Lucia popped back up to her feet and screamed at her adjutant, "Cassius! Get the One Nine One on the move! Now, damnit! We need to keep pushing aggressively. The Ascomanni aren't just going to break for lunch as we establish our beachhead."

"Yes, ma'am!" Her XO turned and transmitted the command. "Felis Six, immediately advance to grid zone Zeta-Two-Two."

The ground rumbled again as the engines of six hundred armored fighting vehicles thundered to life. The sounds of battle reached their crescendo as the tanks reached the Ascomanni line.

Lucia brought up footage provided by the Third Fleet in orbit and watched as her armored fist crashed through the Ascomanni front.

After penetrating into the enemy's rear area, half of the force began to roll up the enemy's flank to the east while the other half continued their advance. Another pair of mobile legions poured into the gap, the first establishing security to the west along the line of advance while the second followed the armored legion deeper into enemy territory.

"Ma'am, intelligence reports Asco massing to counterattack to the west! Strength estimated at five legions!"

"You don't need me to hold your damn hand, Cassius! Call it in!"

"Yes, Praetor!"

URN *Vulcan*, In Orbit over Capua, Campania; Six Beta G

The massive accelerator turrets located on the *Vulcan*'s ventral hull swiveled to acquire the targets the Praetor's battlegroup had just designated. A mechanical loading arm rammed a ten-kilogram tungsten carbide round into each of the triple-mounted railgun arrays located within the turret, while a firing computer was fed real-time data from the battlespace by a fleet of small observation drones.

It calculated the windage, gravitational influence, and atmospheric drag given the ship's current location in orbit, and a moment later the firing solution was obtained. Each of the individual mounts in the turret, resting on separate articulating platforms, made small adjustments to account for the variables the computer fed them.

There was a millisecond-long delay as the other three turrets made the same calculation, then a loud *bang* as the projectiles broke the sound barrier, accelerating to three thousand meters per second. The guns reloaded, adjusted slightly based on changing variables, and fired again, then again. The guns fell silent, having fired each of their three rounds in about forty seconds.

Outskirts of Capua, Campania; Six Beta G

It sounded like the most terrifying thunderstorm she had ever heard, Lucia thought to herself as the *Vulcan*'s shells tore through the sky.

The impact that followed was worse: the ground seemed to swell and fall away like waves, throwing equipment and people into the air. More than a few friendly casualties would be reported, she was sure.

As the dust cleared, a new swarm of observation drones flew to the west to replace those lost to the massive shockwaves created by the orbital bombardment. The images began to come in, and Praetor Artorius swore to herself.

Three dozen perfectly formed impact craters, each a half a kilometer wide, marred the plains to the west of Capua. There was no sign of the Ascomanni who had been massing to attack the breakthrough point.

"Gods," Cassius muttered to himself. "They're just…gone."

"Space superiority is everything, Cassius," Praetor Artorius told her subordinate. "We learned that the hard way. Unfortunately, the Ascomanni weren't quick enough."

"What do you mean, Praetor?" her confused subordinate asked. "No one could've outrun that."

"Not the bombardment, Cassius. The Ascomanni's invasion. They didn't kill us fast enough. We took our lumps, but we learned. We adapted. Now the shoe is on the other foot, and I know exactly where I'm going to put it."

URN *Hasta*, Vanaheim, Forty-Two Upsilon A

Aria and Mirabella stood on the corvette's bridge as the ship raced away from Vanaheim's surface. They both stood rooted in place, the same shocked expressions on both of their faces.

They were too late.

Dozens of large warships hung in space, blocking their route away from the planet. They looked similar to the Ascomanni ships they were familiar with, but there were several noticeable differences in their design.

"Captain, have your sensors officer focus on the vessels' EM signatures and emissions," Mirabella demanded.

"What are you thinking?" Aria asked quietly.

"The last time we were here, we ran into a similar force. A detailed analysis conducted after our escape indicated that the ships didn't match the details we've collected on Ascomanni warships. They're something different."

"What if they are Pasarga?" the Primus responded.

"Oh," Mirabella said, flushing, "I hadn't thought of that. I guess we'd still be screwed. Do you have those readings, Captain?"

"Yes, Doctor, it's as you suspected. They do not match standard Asco ship signatures."

"And they haven't taken any offensive action against the ship?"

"No, ma'am, they are holding position and blocking our escape."

"OK," Mirabella said, taking a deep breath. "Open an unencrypted channel."

"What?!" Aria blurted out. "Have you lost your damn mind, Mirabella?!"

"Look, Aria, either those are the bad guys, and we are already dead, or they are something else. We have nothing to lose."

"All right," Aria grumbled angrily. "Next time, Antonia gets to babysit on your ridiculous side missions…"

Mirabella ignored her, instead moving to the corvette's comms station and speaking clearly into the open link.

"Unknown ships, this is Doctor Mirabella Urbanus of the Umbrian Republic. Please identify yourselves and state your intentions."

Her request was met with silence, and Aria and Mirabella exchanged a worried look.

"I repeat, this is Doctor Urbanus of the URN *Hasta*, please identify yourselves and—"

"You have trespassed on the hallowed home world of the Vaeringyar," a gravelly voice stated in a heavily accented but still decipherable form of their own language.

"And are you the Vaeringyar, or are you servants of the Tenebrae?" Aria challenged from behind Mirabella. "Your people may have run when confronted by such a threat, but we will stand and fight! If you destroy us, you do the Tenebrae's work for them!"

"You speak of that which you do not understand," the mysterious voice proclaimed. "The Tenebrae are all encompassing. They cannot be resisted."

"Primus, the ships' weapons are targeting us!" the *Hasta*'s captain exclaimed.

"Enough, Alrek," a distant female voice interrupted. "I would speak with the one who issues such brave boasts."

There was a momentary pause as the speaker fell silent.

"As you say, my Queen. Intruders, prepare to dock."

"Not so fast!" Aria spat back. "Even as we speak, our people fight against your enemy. If you delay us, the deaths of millions will be on your head!"

"That is not a request, brave warrior," the Queen's voice replied.

"Ma'am!" the *Hasta*'s captain called out. "The largest enemy ship is accelerating toward us. What should we do?"

"There's nothing we can do. Let's hope the Primus doesn't piss them off anymore," Mirabella replied sarcastically. "We don't need to add a new enemy to our growing list, Aria."

Aria growled and headed toward the airlock.

***

The bow of the massive Vaeringyar flagship split open, like the maw of some mythic sea creature. The *Hasta* fit easily in the cavernous space, and the ship gently set down on the ship's deck. Aria and her soldiers emerged, weapons ready, and were surprised by what they found.

There, waiting in two rows of eight, was an honor guard of Vaeringyar soldiers. The gray-skinned aliens were still physically imposing, but looked like slimmed-down versions of the massive hulking Ascomanni.

They wore amber-colored armor: intricately carved cuirasses, helms, greaves, vambrances, and shoulder pauldrons. Each piece bore the gilded shape of a tree, and showed an amazing level of craftsmanship.

On closer inspection, Aria noticed that the set of horns, approximately the same color as the honor guard's armor, were not part of their helmets. They seemed to protrude from above each soldier's temples before sweeping down just past their chins, following their jaw lines.

They stood silently at attention, dutifully ignoring the Umbrians who spilled out of the corvette. Mirabella walked down the corvette's ramp, and the Primus waved to her soldiers, who lowered their weapons.

An imposing form appeared at the far end of the chamber and walked quickly through the receiving line. As he approached, he appeared to be somewhat larger than those around them, sporting a long, dark-gray beard. His speckled orange eyes burned bright, and Aria could tell that the new arrival had a chip on his shoulder.

"Be careful, Doctor, he doesn't look friendly..." the Primus whispered.

"Agreed," she muttered back.

"Doctor Urbanus of Umbria, and you, her companion," the newcomer started curtly as he came to a stop in front of them. "Welcome aboard the *Tyrfing*. I am Alrek, Agni's son, Jarl of Her Majesty's huscarls. I come bearing greetings from Queen Bera. She demands your presence. Please follow me."

"Before we do anything, will you give us your word that our ship and crew will remain safe?" Aria asked.

"You doubt the Vaeringyar's honor?" their agitated host huffed forcefully. "We need not go to such elaborate lengths to kill you."

"My compatriot is merely concerned for her soldiers' wellbeing. Surely, Lord Alrek, you could empathize with her fears."

Their giant host paused for a moment.

"Well spoken, stranger," Alrek said, calming down somewhat. He turned to face Aria. "You have my word that no harm shall come to you or your command so long as you are guests of our Queen."

Aria nodded, and Alrek grunted in response. He turned and started walking away at a brisk pace, and the pair of Umbrians rushed after their guide.

Capua, Campania; Six Beta G

Lucia doffed her helmet as she approached the cordon her soldiers had erected. It occupied what used to be Capua's central park, a kilometer square greenspace in the middle of the city.

Now it housed three large pits.

Praetor Artorius knew what she would find before she even reached the edge of the pits; the smell gave it away.

She tore a piece of her cloak off and covered her mouth and nose with it. She had read the reports coming in from other planets. If the Ascomanni had followed suit, this was where they'd dumped the first batch of test subjects as they attempted to tame her people.

Even with foreknowledge of what she'd see, she was still moved to tears by the sight of it.

There before her were tens of thousands of bodies, mangled and left to rot. A swarm of drones did their best to keep birds from disturbing the corpses, their angry caws bouncing eerily off the surrounding buildings.

Her forces had liberated several camps within the city, and each held thousands of terrified and emaciated civilians. They told horror stories about the purple-skinned doctors who took away their loved ones. Once chosen, they were never seen again, but their screams would continue to be heard echoing through the city's ruined streets.

As she turned away from the scene, she found her adjutant sitting on a patch of grass, his legs hugged to his chest as he rocked back and forth.

Lucia walked up and dropped down next to him. She reached out and put a hand on his shoulder. The young man stopped moving, but remained quiet. He looked at her, his eyes bloodshot, an unreadable expression on his face. Together they sat in silence.

After a few minutes, the sounds of fighting picked up, and Lucia let go of her subordinate. She stood up and offered Cassius a hand.

He took it, and slowly rose to his feet.

"Cassius, if you need time…" Lucia started.

"No, ma'am," he said quietly. "The only thing that will make any of this better is butchering every last fucking one of these monsters."

Lucia nodded, and together they headed back toward the Praetor's command vehicle.

The *Tyrfing*, Vanaheim, Forty-Two Upsilon A

Aria and Mirabella followed their guide ever deeper into the *Tyrfing*'s interior. As they passed through the great warship, the dull, utilitarian interior slowly gave way to ever more spacious and welcoming portions of the ship, culminating with a vast corridor at the heart of the vessel.

To their great surprise, they emerged into a bustling metropolis, nestled in a large, spherical cavity in the *Tyrfing*'s core. Aqueducts and canals crisscrossed the space before working their way to the center, where a long rectangular structure sat in the midst of a circular lake.

"Welcome to the City of Glasir, High Seat of the Vaeringyar," Alrek said, a twinge of pride in his voice.

The Umbrians looked on in amazement as the Queen's Jarl led them through the city. After a brief walk, they reached the bridge which led to the structure at the center of Glasir.

As they approached, it became clear that this building had been crafted with exquisite care.

The walls were the same luminescent amber color as the structures on Vanaheim, but featured delicately carved reliefs throughout, depicting scenes of Vaeringyar life. The hall's roof seemed to be thatched with golden plates, each etched with the likeness of a man or woman in formal attire. Finally, the grand entrance was flanked by a pair of gilded trees, whose leaves shone with a brilliant red-gold luster.

The trio passed through another honor guard and into the structure. The High Seat was expansive and surprisingly well lit, but spartan in its furnishings.

Mirabella caught sight of their host, and elbowed Aria.

In the center of the room, a nine-sided star had been carved out of the ceiling, wreathing an elaborate throne in light. A woman sat serenely in a golden chair. It was clear she was much smaller than many who had sat on it before, but in no way did it diminish her splendor.

Queen Bera rose, and the Umbrians got their first good look at their new host. She was beautiful, with dark-gray skin, silver-blond hair, and delicate vestigial horns running from her temples back behind her ears before ending at the corners of her jaw. The Queen wore an elegant amber-colored dress which seemed to shimmer as it moved, gathered at the waist by a simple braided belt.

She smiled as Aria and Mirabella approached, the warmth of her expression carrying into her ruby-red eyes. Alrek came to a stop, and Mirabella motioned to Aria before bowing at the waist. Aria grudgingly followed suit, and the Queen's gentle laughter echoed around the room.

"You must be Doctor Urbanus," the Queen said as she looked at Mirabella. "And you, the fearless warrior," she said, turning to Aria. "I'm afraid I do not know your name."

"I am Primus Aria Fulvia Nobilior of the Umbrian Republic Armed Forces."

"A strong name," she said as their eyes locked. "And a strong spirit, I see."

The Queen walked down the stairs from her throne and approached the Umbrians. Alrek knelt, and Aria exchanged an uncertain glance with Mirabella.

"Your Majesty," Mirabella said softly, bowing her head, "I beg your pardon if our behavior appears crude. I am afraid it is born from ignorance of your people's customs."

Bera smiled, putting her unwitting guests at ease. "You have been gifted with a silver tongue, I see," she responded kindly. "Do not fear, it would be ungracious to expect courtly behavior from new guests."

"Forgive me for interrupting, then, Your Highness, but why have you taken us captive?" Aria asked.

Queen Bera turned to face Aria. "Captive? That is yet to be determined, Aria Fulvia Nobilior. What I seek is to understand why you have trespassed on Vanaheim."

"Your Majesty, we seek an advantage over our enemies," Mirabella responded.

"What do you hope to gain by defeating the thralls?" the Queen asked.

"Thralls? You mean the Ascomanni?" Mirabella replied, confused.

"Yes, Doctor." A sorrowful look flitted over the Queen's face. "They were once our kin. Now, they are but mindless slaves."

"We both know that's not true, Your Highness," Mirabella responded. "They've regressed while in the brutal captivity of our enemy, but they are far from mindless."

Alrek stirred, but the Queen shook her head, almost imperceptibly. Mirabella decided to press her luck. She took a deep breath and continued.

"I imagine that fighting your own, knowing what they had suffered, knowing that they slaughter their own brothers and sisters against their will, would have had a profound impact on your society. Perhaps so much so that the survivors of a proud and noble people would choose exile over resistance."

"You know *nothing* of the pain our people bear!" Alrek roared. "We numbered in the billions! Now there are but a few million left."

"Enough!" The Queen demanded. Alrek fell silent, and she turned back to her guests.

Bera gave Mirabella a mournful smile and said, "Very perceptive, Doctor. Our ancestors believed that there might still be hope for the thralls. However, as time passed, we've realized that they are lost to us. The best we could do for them is deliver a swift and painless death, but even that is beyond our reach."

"Perhaps, Your Majesty, but before you faced them alone. We are proof that there are others out there, still struggling against the Tenebrae. Surely together we stand a better chance than apart?"

"The Ascomanni are but the first of many storms which will batter your people. The Tenebrae cannot be overcome. They can only be *survived*," Queen Bera responded sadly. "In time, you will come to understand this."

"Please, Queen Bera, I beg you, speak to our leader!" Mirabella implored. "There is much we could learn from you, and we could help you re-establish your people. This is a unique opportunity; one you may never have again."

The Queen was silent for a long time. Finally, she gazed at Alrek, and he nodded in return.

"I will speak to your leader," she said. Her voice hardened as she continued, "However, should you prove unfaithful, these halls will be the last thing you ever see."

The Citadel, Safe Haven; System: Classified, Frontier Space

Marcellus sat at his desk, his office adjoining the Citadel's command center, as he read the latest reports on the Umbrian offensive. He had pushed his soldiers to the brink, and he had ordered a temporary pause so that they might rest, resupply, and re-equip.

However, even temporarily letting up the pressure on the Ascomanni had proven detrimental. Praetor Junius's forces came under renewed attack and were on the verge of being overrun, while another two planets had been conquered by new Ascomanni assaults.

Marcellus had rushed the Second Fleet to save Junius's army group. Forced to stand toe to toe with the Ascomanni, they had taken heavy losses lifting the siege.

The latest setback further exacerbated a growing personnel crisis. Weeks of constant combat had slowly diminished the URN's strength. Highly skilled technicians and trained pilots were difficult to replace in a short timeframe, and many of his ships were at less than full effectiveness.

Marcellus calculated that he currently had barely enough resources to scrape together five full fleets.

The situation on the ground was better, even with the significant losses incurred during the Ascomanni assault and the corresponding Umbrian counterattacks. There was no shortage of eager volunteers.

That wouldn't matter much though if they couldn't contest the Ascomanni's space superiority.

Marcellus set down his datapad and rubbed his eyes. Sleep continued to be an ongoing problem, and Doctor Publicola had prescribed a mild sedative to help.

Suddenly, an aide burst into the room.

"Dictator, we're receiving a message from Primus Fulvia."

"I take it it's urgent?" Marcellus responded, a lead ball forming in his stomach.

"She used her emergency code phrase, sir."

Marcellus bolted up from his chair and walked out of his office. Horrible scenarios began playing through his head. Had the Ascomanni discovered them? Were they hiding or on the run? What about Mirabella? What if she'd been captured? Or killed?

He walked quickly up to the communications station, and a display lit up showing Aria and Mirabella. Their surroundings were strange, however, and it took the Dictator a moment to realize that it looked like they were still in the abandoned city on Vanaheim.

"Aria, what's going on? Are you all right?"

"Yes, Dictator, all clear. Delta One One Omicron Niner."

"Code confirmed. It checks out, sir," the comm officer replied.

"OK, what's going on, you two?" Marcellus demanded.

"Marcellus," Mirabella interjected, "listen to me, we don't have much time. We met them, the Vaeringyar. They brought us aboard their flagship. We've made contact with their Queen, and I've convinced her to speak with you."

"What?!" he gasped. "You've met them? The Queen? What am I supposed to talk to her about? How did they find you?"

"Marcellus, please. The ships that showed up the last time we were here were not the Ascomanni. They intercepted us as we attempted to leave. We are all fine, but this is a golden opportunity to find an ally in the fight against the Tenebrae. We need their know-how, and they need our…well, everything else basically."

"Miri, what the hell am I supposed to say? I'm not a diplomat!"

"You did all right when you interviewed that manipulative Pasarga! Just keep your wits about you and be on your best behavior, OK? Oh, and try not to screw this up!"

"Mirabella, wait!" Marcellus interjected, but it was too late.

She motioned to someone off camera, and the image changed to that of a beautiful woman, clearly alien, but not so much so that Marcellus couldn't immediately sense the regal atmosphere she bore about herself.

"Greetings, Dictator Aurelius. My name is Queen Bera of the Vaeringyar. Your Doctor Urbanus is quite persuasive. She convinced me to speak with you about the common challenges our people face."

"Ahem, uh, yes. Your Majesty," Marcellus replied tentatively. "Please forgive my hesitation, the doctor filled me in on your interactions, but I'm afraid your existence comes as something of a shock."

"It has been an interesting day indeed, Dictator. Your unintended representatives shared that you have recently suffered setbacks in the fight against the Ascomanni. Yet they seem to believe they may have found something that might aid you in resisting them."

"Doctor Urbanus is one of our brightest minds. If she believes she found us an edge, I'm inclined to believe her."

"Interesting indeed," the Queen mused. "And what will you do with this…advantage?"

"Your Majesty, I will do what is necessary to safeguard the future of my people."

"Well stated, Dictator," the Queen replied, eyeing him over keenly.

"Your Highness, please forgive me, but I am somewhat new to the formalities of state. Please, call me Marcellus. Or Gaius if you prefer, though that name was usually reserved for when my parents were scolding me."

The Queen revealed a dazzling smile. "You speak both honestly and unassumingly. I find it refreshing, Marcellus." Her face grew serious as she continued, "Doctor Urbanus has argued forcefully for cooperation, that we face common challenges. However, we are strangers, both individually and as peoples. If our first encounter were to go exactly as you hoped, what would you ask from us?"

"My Queen, through an unspeakable betrayal, our homeworld, the moral, industrial, and scientific center of our great Republic, has been seized by the enemy. Unless we can quickly retake Umbria, our ability to continue to resist the Ascomanni is in doubt."

"I empathize with your situation, Marcellus, but you didn't answer the question. What would you have the Vaeringyar do?"

Marcellus's expression hardened. "I would have you fight, Your Highness. Help us repel this invasion! Help us restore our borders, and we in turn will help you beat back the onslaught which has swept over your people."

"Brave words, Dictator Aurelius. Our ancestors chose resistance, but, in the end, it proved futile. How are you different? Why should we believe you can triumph when we could not?"

Marcellus fell silent. How much did he dare reveal to this new party? He was unsure of their intentions or commitment, and the crushing weight of his people's survival pushed him toward a more cautious approach.

"We will not yield, Queen Bera. We will fight. We will triumph, or we will perish. We shall not abandon what is ours for the cold depths of space."

"I'm afraid your answer is insufficient, Dictator. I cannot risk the wellbeing of my people without a more tangible pathway to victory. I'm sorry."

"I understand your position, Queen Bera, and I harbor no ill will toward you for reaching what must surely seem to be the logical conclusion. Will you release my people?"

"Yes, Marcellus, they will go free, unharmed."

"Thank you, Your Highness. It has been an honor to make your acquaintance. When we have driven the Ascomanni from our homes, we will seek the Vaeringyar out. Perhaps then we might be able to reconsider some form of relationship between our people."

The Queen gave Marcellus another alluring smile. "May you find fortune in your endeavors, Marcellus. I hope that we will meet again."

URN *Hasta*, In Transit in Frontier Space

The corvette dropped back into space just inside the furthest edge of Umbrian territory and moved toward the waiting fleet tender. Aria took the opportunity to pass a quick summary of events on to Safe Haven before seeking out Mirabella.

"Well, that didn't go as I'd hoped," Mirabella sighed as Aria entered her stateroom.

"If they are too afraid to fight, then forget them," Aria responded tersely. "Still, pretty significant moment. Assuming we survive all of this, I guess we'll go down in history as the first Umbrians to make contact with the Vaeringyar."

"Oh my gods," Mirabella said, blushing. "How could that have escaped me? There is so much I should've done, so many questions…"

"Doctor Urbanus," Aria interjected, "can we please focus on more pressing topics? Did the Oracle give you what you need?"

"Yes. Our resources here are pretty limited, but we've been able to confirm that the Ōsenheim Oracle is how the Tenebrae are controlling the Ascomanni. As for the virus we hope to employ, the CID is already hard at work back home."

"So, we just need to invade a planet, locate the Oracle, and transmit the virus?"

"Yes, Primus. The Vanaheim Oracle gave a name and coordinates for the city where we'll find it: Vígríd. The place where we'll either condemn a captive race to death or unlock a new and brighter future for both our people."

Aria smiled grimly. "You sure as hell are persistent. Fortunately, it's not me you need to persuade. Let's get back to Safe Haven. Then we can finally end this war."

Chapter 20

Platform Alpha Three, Safe Haven, System: Classified, Frontier Space

Sweat pooled at the small of Marcellus's back as he waited on the last members of his audience to find seats. Before him was every available senior member of the Umbrian military and intelligence community. Those who were unable to attend in person were watching and listening from their respective fronts.

Valerian walked up behind him. "Sir, everyone is accounted for. It's time."

Marcellus nodded and walked out onto the stage overlooking the amphitheater. In unison, the individuals present stood at attention. Marcellus reached his podium and motioned for everyone to take their seats.

"Sons and daughters of Umbria, we stand on the precipice of the ultimate conclusion of the Ascomanni conflict. Over the last seven months, we have engaged our enemy in a series of aggressive counterattacks, designed to isolate and pin in place large groups of enemy forces while moving us ever closer to Umbria.

"I know I have pushed each and every one of you to your limits since the fall of the capital, but your hard work and sacrifice have paid off. The Ascomanni remain a formidable enemy, but even their vast numbers have limits. Isolated and in poor supply, the forces we've cut off can be ignored, left for another day, while we concentrate on the capital.

"We have reached the final phase of our plan, and now all that stands between us and our homeworld are the planets of Arezzo and Grosetto. These final two systems link Umbria to other sectors of the Republic that remain in Ascomanni hands. These routes must be cut prior to our final assault on Umbria.

"Praetor Camillus's army group will be assigned with the liberation of Arezzo, and Praetor Scipio will be responsible for the capture of Grosetto. Once the Ascomanni forces on both worlds have been contained, the URN's entire remaining strength will fall on Umbria. As soon as we secure a channel to the surface, Praetor Artorius and Praetor Asinia's army groups will be deployed to take back our homeworld."

One of the Archii raised a hand. "Sir, we are committing the entire Navy to the assault? What happens if we are unsuccessful?"

"Then the Umbrian Republic will fall."

Murmurs started to run throughout the hall as Marcellus continued. "Umbria is more than a symbolic target. Already, the Republic's economy is redlining. Shortages of goods and materials continue to grow daily. War has finally come to the home front, and as long as that is the case, we will always be on the brink of disaster."

"So, it's all or nothing then, Dictator?" a legate asked.

"It's always been all or nothing," Marcellus said in response. He walked around the podium and jumped down into the well in front of his audience.

"We have shown that the Ascomanni can be beaten," he said as he paced slowly in front of his soldiers. "They may be stronger, but we are smarter. They may be more numerous, but we are more ingenious. They are compelled to fight. We fight for the future of our people!"

He paused, making eye contact with a dozen or more of his officers before continuing.

"I look around this room, and I see the faces of the indomitable, the resolute, the unconquerable! The time is long overdue for our enemies to fear us more than they fear their hidden masters!" he shouted.

Slowly, heads began to nod. The energy of the room began to change, moving from one of uncertainty and trepidation to one of energy and rage.

Marcellus jumped back up on the stage as he finished. "Find your inner strength! Seize your inner courage! The time has come to avenge our loved ones! The time has come to take back what is ours! The Ascomanni will know you, and they will tremble before our might! How-oo?"

A deep, thrumming roar filled the auditorium. "HOW-OO!"

The sounds of the Umbrians' war cry echoed through the room, swelling until the room itself vibrated with their voices.

Marcellus was satisfied. He turned with a flourish, his cloak billowing behind him, and walked off the stage.

They were ready.

URN *Tyrrhenia*, Safe Haven, System: Classified, Frontier Space

Marcellus stood on the bridge of the light cruiser as his strike force assembled. Twelve of his smaller warships had been retrofitted with the new prototype engines the CID had developed. His capital ships were still too large for the new propulsion system, so this operation would have to rely on speed and surprise.

The Oracle at Vanaheim had provided the location of its counterpart on Ōsenheim; the exact center of the planet's ruined capital. Legate Calvinus's Task Force Hyperion was being loaded aboard ten destroyers, while what remained of his praetorians, commanded by Antonia and Aria, had been quartered on the *Tyrrhenia* herself.

TF Hyperion would be responsible for capturing the city, while the praetorians would secure the Oracle's chambers. With the area secure, Mirabella and her CID team would release their virus.

Fabian would stay with his fleets, and Marcellus had delegated operational command to Praetor Artorius. She would be responsible for executing the assaults on Arezzo and Grosetto while Marcellus was away.

Lucia had protested his decision to go to Ōsenheim personally, insisting that he belonged in Safe Haven directing his forces.

Marcellus understood her reasoning, and even agreed, but he knew that he personally had to be the one to eliminate the Ascomanni threat. If future generations were to judge their decisions harshly, he alone would be responsible for their execution.

"Are you sure about this?" a familiar voice called from behind.

Marcellus turned to find his loyal friend with a forlorn look. "Yes, Valerian. We are nearing our breaking point. Mirabella's plan is our best hope."

"Yet you are leaving me behind again?"

Marcellus smiled. "No, Val, not left behind. You are too good at what you do. Lucia and Fabian will need you while we are gone."

"If you say so." Valerian frowned.

"I do say so, Val," Marcellus said, clapping his hands on his adjutant's shoulders. "We'll be back in time for the finale."

"You better be, Marcellus," Valerian replied drily. "As good as Lucia and Fabian are, they aren't you. You've been the driving force that has gotten us to this point. You are the reason we haven't been completely broken."

"Nonsense, Val," Marcellus said with a grin. "I would have collapsed weeks ago if you weren't keeping everything in order."

"Let's just say we make a good team, sir," Valerian said, smiling weakly in return. "I'll see you in a few weeks. Good luck, Marcellus."

"Farewell, old friend."

Valerian saluted, and Marcellus returned it crisply. As Valerian turned and walked out of the bridge, the *Tyrrhenia*'s captain approached.

"Ground forces are aboard, sir, and the CID team has embarked. We're ready to go on your word."

Marcellus nodded, and the captain ordered her crew to prepare for departure.

URN *Juno*, Arezzo, Four Alpha G

Archus Duilius watched as the Ascomanni finished assembling opposite his fleet. The seventy ships under his command faced off against about half as many Asco warships. The Fourth Fleet had been tasked with clearing the skies over Arezzo, and intel had made it clear that the Ascomanni were catching on. This would not be an easy battle.

The Umbrians hadn't run out of tricks just yet, however.

Running short on skilled flight crews, two of his three fleet carriers had been heavily modified over the last two weeks. Their armor had been reinforced and a few heavy turrets had been added, but the most important change was that their launch tubes had been reconfigured to deliver their newest surprise.

"All ships, ahead full, wedge formation!" Duilius called out.

The Fourth sprang forward into the attack, its heaviest warships forming at the tip. As the distance closed between the opposing forces, flashes of light and salvos of projectiles began to fill the space in between. Just before the fleets intertwined amongst themselves, his carriers began to fire large, dart-shaped projectiles at the bigger Ascomanni warships.

Six hundred projectiles swarmed toward the thickest portion of the Ascomanni fleet, bouncing up and down, side to side, seemingly at random, as they attempted to avoid the enemy point defenses. Some wouldn't make it, but the majority struck home.

The needle-like prow of the objects penetrated the Ascomanni ships' outer hulls, driving a hole large enough to allow for the passage of their contents, which quickly spilled out and flooded into their host ships.

Each pod carried a team of four marines. Using telemetry data from the flight, they were able to quickly network with other teams that had boarded the same vessel and they began fighting their way toward key sections of their targets.

The Umbrian marines were tasked with disabling their host vessels, a tactic the Asco were wholly unprepared for. Their ships didn't usually contain contingents of soldiers, and they were poorly equipped to resist boarders.

The assault parties burned through the vessels' crews, and upon reaching engineering or command-and-control compartments, they set about shutting down weapons systems and engines.

As Archus Duilius watched from the *Juno*, eighteen of the Ascomanni's largest ships went dark, swarming with over two thousand vengeful Umbrian warriors. The incapacitated vessels started communicating all-clear signals, and his fleet shifted to mopping up the dozen-odd Asco screens that still posed a threat.

Away from the battlespace, thirty transports popped into orbit and began to head toward the planet's surface. The liberation of Arezzo had begun.

URN *Tyrrhenia*, Edges of the Ōsenheim System, Forty-Four Omicron T

The light cruiser emerged in the far reaches of Ōsenheim's parent system. Marcellus quickly confirmed that each of his ships had successfully reached their destinations and ordered the *Tyrrhenia*'s captain to launch a series of probes toward their intended destination.

Their target was nestled in a binary star system, with a red dwarf orbiting a white main sequence star. The peculiar solar arrangement meant that the planet had eight seasons a year as the suns interacted with one another, and Marcellus was glad that they'd be in and out in the span of a few hours.

"Dictator," the *Tyrrhenia*'s captain called, "we're clear, no signs of Ascomanni warships in the system."

"All right, what's the ETA on the drones?"

"We'll have real-time surveillance of the planet's capital in two minutes, sir."

"Good. Inform Legate Calvinus and the Primes. It's nearly time."

Petrarch, Arezzo; Four Alpha G

Tribune Belladonna Julius ducked behind the crumpled remains of a tube tram, its crushed metal body whining under concentrated Ascomanni fire as her legionnaires continued to push toward the capital's central administrative district. A pair of scoots moved up opposite her on the other side of the avenue, drawing the Ascomanni's focus, and she waved her soldiers on.

"Quickly! Through the storefront, left side! Let's go!" she barked over the deafening roar of combat.

The soldiers closest at hand sprinted forward in small groups, working their way into a large shopping complex. As she turned around the tram to follow, one of her legionnaires threw her back into cover before being gunned down himself.

His body collapsed to the pavement, and there was a thunderous *womf*, followed immediately by an explosion.

The battlemechs that had been covering their advance had been obliterated, and as the Tribune peered around the edge of the ruined tramcar, she spotted the culprit.

There, turning the corner in the next intersection up, was a lumbering Ascomanni tank, two stories tall. Too big to navigate the turn, it plowed through the corner of the shopping mall and kept moving, the structure's walls barely slowing it. Its turret began to traverse toward the tram she was sheltered behind.

"Move, move!" she screamed.

Belladonna and the soldiers nearby sprinted through the lethal hail of fire whizzing through the street and ducked into a narrow alley on the far side of the boulevard. There was another *wumf*, and the Tribune threw herself down as the tram exploded, its skeletal remains thrown through the air and lodged into a residential building further down the street.

The Ascomanni juggernaut's turret began to traverse toward her, but, before it could reacquire them, she noticed shapes jumping out of the third floor of the shopping complex and onto the tank's roof.

The assault team used a breaching charge to punch through into the tank's interior. Its turret stopped rotating, and a moment later there was a brilliant flash.

The next thing the Tribune remembered was staring up at the sky, dust swirling all around her. She got back to her feet and began assessing the situation.

The Ascomanni tank was gone, a burnt-out husk all that remained. The apartment buildings immediately behind the tank had collapsed into the street, and the front of the shopping complex had fallen away too. The avenue was eerily quiet; all she could hear was the ringing still echoing in her ears.

Dead and wounded Umbrians were strewn amongst the rubble, but more of her legionnaires rose up and charged through the hole in the Ascomanni perimeter. The Tribune passed the coordinates along for a medevac and raced to join her soldiers' advance.

Petrarch was the last major city on Arezzo still in Asco hands, and they had just penetrated its final defensive line. Thirty thousand Umbrians pressed in on this last pocket of Ascomanni resistance, and their fury would not be denied.

URN *Tyrrhenia*, Over Vígríð, Ōsenheim; Forty-Four Omicron T

The *Tyrrhenia* screamed through the planet's atmosphere, tearing a hole in the cloud cover and emerging over the ruins of an alien city. Black clouds of flak filled the sky while landing craft dropped the first assault wave at their designated landing zones.

Marcellus watched as nearby warships poured fire into their helpless foes. The ground seemed to dance with explosions as his ships' weapons, designed to engage warships and starfighters in the vast expanse of space, targeted small groups of Ascomanni soldiers. Fires raged across the city, with thick billowing smoke rising to join the dark clouds hanging overhead.

Legate Calvinus's image appeared, and Marcellus folded his hands at the small of his back while his commander reported in.

"Dictator, the first wave of Scutia are on the ground. They encountered heavy resistance upon landing, but air dominance has quickly turned the tables in our favor. Any significant concentration of Ascomanni soldiers is immediately obliterated, but that hasn't stopped them from continuing to mass for counterattacks."

"Let them then, Legate." Marcellus responded coolly. "If we have to level the city, then so be it."

"Understood, sir. The scoots are starting to form a perimeter around the coordinates we have for the Oracle's chamber. We'll begin deploying the taskforce in ten minutes."

"Are all of your battlemechs planet-side, Legate?" Marcellus asked.

"Not yet, sir, Ferratta's scoots are heading down now."

"Hold your soldiers' deployment, Legate. Have the scoots exterminate everything within a five-kilometer radius of the city center and form a tight perimeter. I want you to hold your legionnaires in reserve."

"But, sir, it'll take at least an hour to get all my soldiers on the ground. If you need us…"

"And it'll take just as long to load them back up. As you said, the Ascomanni resistance is being obliterated. Umbria awaits, Legate."

"Understood, sir, I'll hold the legions."

"Good. You have my frequency if anything changes."

URN *Echion*, Grosetto, Three Gamma D

Fabian's chin rested heavily against his chest, his heart racing. Every fiber of his being wished to stand and scream, to kick and stomp, to rage over the sight in front of him. He gripped the arms of his chair as tightly as he could and found the willpower to restrain himself.

Before him sat Grosetto, or what was left of her. A cloud of debris partially obscured the ghastly sight, but it could not hide what had happened.

One of the planet's moons had collided with the world, its smaller bulk still distinguishable as a lump on Grosetto's broken remains. Both glowed a brilliant reddish white, their heat distorting Fabian's view as it bled into the cold of space.

A probe had been recovered from the system with a message for whoever might find it, detailing the actions leading up to the system's destruction.

The planet was one of the last to fall, and as such they knew what the appearance of the Ascomanni meant. Grosetto's local military and police forces resisted as long as they could, buying time for a few hundred thousand people to evacuate. Once every opportunity for escape had been exhausted, they executed one last act of defiance.

A series of large asteroids had been retrofitted with propulsion systems and accelerated toward Grosetto. Their target was not the invading Ascomanni fleet, but rather the planet's second largest moon. Already in an unstable elliptical orbit, the moon was bombarded by four asteroids in quick succession, each over a kilometer in length.

Striking the moon at just the right point of its trajectory, the asteroid bombardment did what would've otherwise required several hundred years. The moon was nudged from its orbit just enough, and it clipped Grosetto's atmosphere. Cataclysm quickly followed.

Prior to the war, four hundred million souls had inhabited Grosetto, living, working, and raising families, dreaming of futures most of them would never see. Now, it was a fiery monument to its inhabitants' unwavering refusal to submit.

Fabian felt something wet drip down his wrist, and he realized that he had cut himself on one of the metal grommets on the underside of his armrest. He held up his bloody palm, superimposed over the image of destruction beyond the *Echion*'s viewports, and a shiver ran through his body.

"Signal the others. It's time to assemble the fleets."

Vígríđ, Ōsenheim; Forty-Four Omicron T

Marcellus, Mirabella, and her CID contingent disembarked from their dropship. Several of the surrounding buildings were on fire, and smoke choked the air. In small groups, they started running toward a familiar-looking temple which sat in the middle of the large plaza they had landed in.

Marcellus's praetorians were scattered all over in hastily prepared fighting positions, and Aria and Antonia waited for them at the apex of the structure.

"Dictator," Antonia called. "Over here, we've cleared the way to the Oracle's chamber."

"Good, any resistance?" Marcellus asked.

"No, sir, between the scoots and the Navy, the Asco didn't stand a chance. We're secure."

"Understood, please lead the way."

Antonia nodded, and she set out at a brisk pace, leading them deeper into the structure.

It looked eerily similar to the one found on Vanaheim, but it was clear that there were differences. Unique architectural elements were scattered within the more familiar feel of the temple's layout. There was no time for a more detailed analysis.

After a brief walk, they came to a section of the building which had collapsed, and the praetorians had blasted their way through.

"So much destruction," Mirabella muttered.

"Yes, ma'am, but not us. Whoever did this visited the site long before we did," Antonia responded. "It's a little tight, but you science types should be able to squeeze through."

Marcellus nodded at his Primus, and she stood aside. Mirabella and her team began working their way through the narrow passage, and Marcellus followed. The channel began to slope downward, and after a few meters, they reached a familiar threshold.

As they stepped out on the Oracle's platform, it was clear that the Tenebrae had warped the construct to their own purposes. Web-like material stretched throughout the spherical chamber, metallic gray in color and glistening, as if wet.

"What a mess!" Mirabella complained.

"What is that, Miri?" Marcellus asked quietly.

"Some sort of impulse matrix. Honestly, it looks like a model of the neural pathways in our brains. Could be how they are able to process so much data so quickly."

"Will it cause problems?"

"I think it *is* the problem. The Oracle on Vanaheim indicated that this guy's been partitioned from his hardware. It's likely that these…webs play some kind of role. Give me a few minutes to map the network with my systems analyst and I'll have a more concrete answer for you."

"Get it done, Mirabella," Marcellus said softly. "Every minute that passes, more Umbrians die."

She arched an eyebrow at him but said nothing else. Instead, she turned and immediately walked over to her team members, who were busily setting up their equipment.

Marcellus turned and began to pace impatiently along the edges of the balcony, drinking in the sights of the corrupted chamber.

The web of cables seemed to have erupted from underneath the walls, like some horrific parasite. They glowed red at each junction, pulsating unnervingly every few seconds. A thick fog frothed violently in lower portions of the chamber, obscuring the Oracle's dais, and there was no sign of the giant floating orb that had greeted him on Vanaheim.

Left alone with his thoughts, Marcellus felt anxiety build within him. No matter how frequently he checked his chrono, time seemed to stand still. Sweat began to bead up along his hairline, and he swiped a hand over his brow, annoyed that his insecurity was manifesting itself physically.

He was about to make an irreversible decision, one that would have far-reaching and unknown consequences. Now was not the time to waver, he chastised himself.

After what seemed to be an eternity, Mirabella came back over, a cautious smile on her face.

"Good news, I hope?" Marcellus asked.

"Yes, darling. We've figured out how to cut the partition separating the Oracle from its hardware. Actually, both its own hardware and the junk the Tenebrae installed."

"So when will the Oracle be back online?"

"Now, love."

There was a rush of air behind him, and Marcellus turned to find a floating metallic sphere hovering in the expanse.

"Welcome to GFSTp L452729.16-103253.2," a booming mechanical voice called out. "Thank you for reestablishing my connection to my primary systems. I've identified you as Gaius Aurelius Marcellus and Doctor Mirabella Urbanus based on my interactions with the caretaker of GFSTp L452729.16-103241.8."

"Are there any remaining blocks prohibiting your full utilization, Oracle?" Mirabella asked.

"No, Mistress Urbanus. Moreover, it seems that the alien technology which had previously been integrated into my systems is under my control as well."

"So, you could broadcast a code for us?" Marcellus asked.

"Yes, Master Aurelius. The caretaker of GFSTp L452729.16-103241.8 also made me aware of your plans, and I believe your intended action can be carried out using the additional resources now at my disposal."

Marcellus fell silent. This was it. His stomach churned as he turned and looked at Mirabella. She nodded and pulled something from her pack.

She opened her hands, revealing two data sticks.

"I don't understand," Marcellus said, giving the doctor a perplexed look.

"Marcellus," Mirabella began softly, "it's not too late to change your mind. The Ascomanni kill because they are compelled to. Despite all the horrors inflicted on them by the Tenebrae, they are still people. They feel pain. They know fear. They are as much victim as we are. I beg you, do not do this. Don't they deserve a chance?"

"Miri, do you think I enjoy the thought of murdering *billions* of Ascomanni?!" Marcellus shouted, his anxiety turning into a raging fury. "If I'm fortunate, I'll be known as the man who sacrificed his honor for the salvation of his people. I will be remembered as a butcher. And what do you propose instead? You said yourself that the effects could be temporary. Has that changed?"

"Marcellus...the Tenebrae are vastly superior technologically. It's possible they'd discover a countermeasure for our—"

"So you'd have me throw away this one chance to save our people for the possibility of freeing the Ascomanni? Knowing full well that if we fail, it'll be our people who share their fate?" Marcellus snarled.

Mirabella did not shrink from his angry outburst, though he could see the first glistening traces of tears forming in her eyes.

"They kill because they have no choice. If you allow fear of the Tenebrae to dictate your actions, if you allow them to force you to betray that brilliant, noble spirit of yours, you are just as much a slave as they are. If you do that..."

Mirabella paused as tears began to stream down her face. "Marcellus, what difference will there be between us and the Ascomanni?"

Marcellus's gaze softened, a torrent of contradictory emotions flooding over him, dousing the rage burning in his chest. He reached out and gently wiped away a tear, and her head tilted down into his palm as he caressed her cheek.

Their eyes met, and everything Marcellus thought he knew grew muddled and clouded.

Was she right? Had his hatred and his fear already robbed him of his own volition? What about the billions of lives that depended on him? And the hundreds of millions of dead the war had already claimed? How would they want to be remembered?

The Dictator fell to his knees, cupping his face in his hands. Mirabella ran up and dropped to the floor next to him, wrapping her arms around him.

"It's too much, Miri," Marcellus whispered. "One person can't make this decision alone."

"Then don't, Marcellus," she replied. "You are the best of us, the best of Umbria. If you had to choose what our legacy would be, how would you want us to be remembered?"

Marcellus pulled his hands away and looked into Mirabella's eyes.

In her steadfast gaze, he found a peace he hadn't known for a long time.

That calm swept over him, and he found the strength to decide.

"I trust you, Mirabella Urbanus. Do it."

Mirabella let out a strange, happy, grunt-laugh and began to cry again. She leaned forward and kissed him before shooting to her feet.

"Oracle," she called out loudly, giddily, "I'm transmitting a code sequence to you now. Please broadcast immediately."

"Data acquired. Analyzing… Signal transmitted."

As Marcellus rose to his feet, a deep, thrumming hum filled the chamber. It lasted only for a few moments before disappearing instantly. Mirabella returned to his side, and he pulled her close.

"Thank you, Marcellus," she said, looking up at him, her chin resting on his chest.

"No. Thank you, Miri. Come on, let's go home."

Chapter 21

The Selvaggia Wildlife Preserve; Two Hundred Kilometers West of Perugia, Umbria

Invictus pulled the recoilless rifle to his shoulder as the Asco patrol had entered the kill zone. He knelt amongst a rocky outcrop, situated on a ridge which cut through the forest around him. Twenty other soldiers were scattered around in other positions about halfway up the rise, forming a rough semicircle facing the enemy.

Invictus had rallied as many of the capital's defenders as he could, and, with Sextus's help, he'd been able to coordinate with other groups across Umbria. It would never be enough to take back the planet, but it was enough to disrupt, distract, and tie down forces that the Ascomanni would have been able to deploy elsewhere.

The Prefect looked through his scope and zoomed in on the patrol. It was made up of nearly thirty Ascomanni troopers, led by a pair of Pasarga.

Invictus let out a deep, guttural growl. As bad as the Ascomanni were, the Pasarga had proven to be much worse.

Cruel and calculating, every survivor of Perugia's fall had witnessed their barbarity or heard horror stories secondhand. There were no rules governing their conduct, no norms dictating how they acted toward the Umbrians or even the Ascomanni.

These mercurial people would do whatever was required to achieve their aims. The Ascomanni had been the cudgel, the brute force weapon used to break the Umbrians, but the Pasarga were the dagger which would be thrust into their heart.

Many of Umbria's cities remained unoccupied. Groups of Pasarga had appeared at each, telling them to remain in their homes and that any sign of disobedience would be punished swiftly and overwhelmingly. It had been sufficient to cow much of the population into remaining in place, but stories of the enemy rounding up thousands of civilians at a time continued to spread...

Two clicks came across the Prefect's commlink, and he centered his sights on the pair of Pasarga in the middle of the patrol. He slotted his finger into the trigger guard, preparing to take his shot. He adjusted slightly for the breeze blowing through the forest, breathed in, and started to depress the trigger.

But before the rifle discharged, Invictus released his grip. Something was happening. He propped his weapon up against a nearby tree and grabbed his range finder.

Below, the Ascomanni had encircled the Pasarga, the latter shouting and gesticulating wildly at the former. Infuriated by the apparent lack of response to their commands, one lashed out, striking a soldier over the head with his weapon. Instead of cowering meekly, as expected, the shock trooper grabbed the smaller purple alien by the neck, lifting him off the ground. With a flick of its wrist, the Ascomanni soldier snapped his victim's neck.

The other Pasarga reacted, drawing its weapon on the rouge trooper. Before he could intervene, however, a trio of Ascomanni fell on him, tearing away his weapon and mercilessly beating him. Even from his vantage point, Invictus was sure the alien had not survived such a savage assault.

The Ascomanni looked around amongst themselves, and their leader, the one who had snapped the Pasargan's neck, discarded his helmet and stooped down next to their victims. Invictus was unsure what exactly it was doing until it stood again, running its fingers over its chest plate, creating a circle divided into equal quarters with the florescent yellow blood of the Pasarga.

It lifted its arms into the air and roared, and the Ascomanni around him responded in kind, their shouts echoing through the trees.

Another double click came over the commlink, and Invictus shook his head.

"Fall back to the rendezvous point," he said quietly into his headset. "I don't know what the hell just happened, but maybe, if we're really lucky, other Ascomanni will get the same idea."

URN *Hydra*, The Stelvio Asteroid Belt, 6 Beta K

Captain Adrienne Tarpeia rubbed her eyes and blinked with amazement. She couldn't believe what she was seeing. Sent to harass a Helium-3 refinery the Ascomanni had captured a week earlier, her flotilla had encountered eight Asco warships which had formed up just beyond the refinery's perimeter.

However, before her forces even had the chance to engage, some of the smaller Ascomanni ships began to fire on the cruiser floating at the center of their formation.

The Asco squadron descended into chaos: the cruiser's main batteries annihilated an escort frigate, while two Asco destroyers began to pound on the cruiser's engines. Two more ships began to accelerate away from the action entirely.

Captain Tarpeia saw no reason to interrupt her enemy's fratricidal brawl, and the mayhem continued for another five minutes. Before it was over, the cruiser claimed another kill, but it wasn't enough. In the end, the smaller ships prevailed, and with a flash, the cruiser exploded, sending pieces of its shattered hull flying in all directions.

Adrienne ordered her formation to attack the remaining Asco vessels, but before they could engage the tattered remnants of the enemy fleet, the remaining Ascomanni ships fled.

The confused Umbrians were left behind to try and piece together the meaning of what they had just witnessed.

Marconi Long Range Relay Array, Seventy-Eight Kilometers West of Perugia, Umbria

The sun was beginning to creep up behind them as Sextus led the first section of his cohort toward the entrance to the capital's primary extrasolar communications array. They advanced slowly and deliberately through the thick shrubland surrounding the relay, using the dense brush as cover.

As they closed within four hundred meters, Sextus held up a hand, bringing his praetorians to a stop. He pulled out his viewfinder and growled when he saw what waited for them. Two Ascomanni tanks stood guard at the entrance, their turrets with clear fields of fire on the most easily accessible approaches.

Sextus was fortunate, however, as his current position was located in a slight depression which ran parallel to the main access road. The gully was defiladed from the enemies' turrets, but the Umbrians wouldn't be able to advance much further without exposing themselves to potentially ruinous fire from any Ascomanni forces guarding the gatehouse.

They had gone as far as they could covertly, Sextus thought to himself. To get into the facility they'd need some help.

"Pugio Lead, I need immediate fire support on my position. Two enemy tanks, approximately half a kilometer north of friendly forces. Targets will be tagged."

"Confirmed, Taurus Two-Six, we're sixty seconds out. Rolling in from the east."

Sextus activated the target designator built into his helmet and identified the targets in his heads-up display. Right on cue, a pair of Umbrian fighters roared by overhead, launching a pair of missiles at the Asco tanks guarding the entrance to the massive antennae farm.

The armored behemoths disappeared in twin explosions, throwing flaming wreckage and shrapnel through the air. The gatehouse was flattened, while the perimeter fence was torn apart for a hundred meters in both directions.

Debris was still falling to the ground as Sextus jumped up to his feet and waved his soldiers forward. Sirens began to wail within the complex, and the enemy would most certainly know they were coming.

The Umbrians advanced quickly, covering the last stretch of ground before vaulting out of the depression and up onto the access road.

Sextus and his praetorians poured through the newly created gap in the facility's exterior, rushing forward in small groups through the collection of buildings lining the relay's main road.

They kept moving toward their objective, the squat, oval-shaped building a kilometer further inside the perimeter, but Sextus quickly realized something was amiss.

Where were the Ascomanni? The locals had indicated that nearly four hundred Ascomanni soldiers had been quartered at the facility, but so far there hadn't been signs of any enemy activity. As he thought about it, Sextus didn't recall seeing individual soldiers patrolling near the gatehouse either.

"Taurus Two-Six to all Taurus elements. The first section has breached the primary entrance but has not made contact with the enemy. Proceed with caution."

He received a series of acknowledgments over the battle net as he continued to advance with his soldiers.

His cohort had been severely depleted, and he was down to just three understrength centuries. While he led the first to capture the facility's headquarters, the other two would secure the primary relay terminal and the station's powerplant.

If needed, another ad-hoc century could be deployed as reinforcements, but Sextus hoped it wouldn't come to that. It was heavily populated with recruits who had been on Umbria at the time of the planet's fall, and he was unsure how valuable they'd be if things got messy.

Finally, after ten minutes of tension-filled advance, they reached the two-story building containing the facility's nerve center. Sextus and his praetorians stacked up at several entrances which led into the building's atrium, and he double clicked his mic.

There were a series of loud pops as the breaching charges shredded the doors leading into the building. Fifty praetorians streamed into the command center from multiple angles. As Sextus entered, it was readily apparent that no one would be opposing their entry.

The smell of death and decay were overwhelming. Bodies littered the floor in various positions, while scorch marks marred nearly every surface of the building's entrance.

Most gruesome of all, the bodies of five Pasargans had been strung up using equipment cabling. They hung from the railing of the second-floor loft, a pool of florescent yellow blood puddled underneath.

Sextus waved his teams forward, and they quickly fanned out to clear the rest of the building. After a few minutes, the reports came in. The communications array had been secured, and there was no sign of the enemy, save for the dead.

The Primus dropped himself down into a chair and pulled up to the primary transmission terminal. He fished a data stick out of his pocket and plugged it in. The message recorded within its memory began to download, and a moment later he keyed in the location of its recipient.

At the primary relay terminal, nearly two kilometers away, satellite dishes began to re-orient themselves toward the message's intended destination, and a minute later they began transmitting the message.

"What does it say, sir?" one of Sextus's praetorians asked as they watched the relay send its broadcast.

Sextus smiled grimly. "It lets the rest of the Republic know that we are still here, and that we'll free Umbria or die trying."

She nodded, and Sextus's chrono began to beep. With Ascomanni in complete control of the space above Umbria, they couldn't afford to stay in one place for too long.

It was time to go.

Sextus keyed his commlink again. "All Taurus units, primary objective complete. Fall back to extraction points. Next stop, Perugia."

URN *Echion*: Umbrian Rally Point, Two Parsecs from Umbria

Fabian sat in his office, digging through the latest figures and reports from his subordinate commanders. Scouts had just reported back from the capital, and what they found was encouraging. There were signs of a recent battle, and the Ascomanni forces in orbit had been significantly reduced.

This corresponded with the information sent from the capital's resistance, the first communication received from Umbria since its fall.

Invictus's message indicated that the enemy was currently more interested in fighting one another, and similar feedback was starting to come in from other battlefields across the Republic.

This hadn't been the intended outcome of the Dictator's mission, but nonetheless it appeared as though whatever Marcellus had done had sparked some internecine conflict between the Ascomanni and their handlers.

With report after report showing the enemy's offensive collapsing, Fabian had taken a risk. The plan for Umbria's liberation had called for two army groups, but he had six at his disposal.

The Archus had decided to deploy his additional ground forces to those planets which had fallen to the Ascomanni but had been bypassed by the Umbrian counteroffensive.

The catch was that nothing could distract from the coming assault on Umbria, so they had been sent with little to no naval escort. If they encountered signs of Ascomanni fleet activity, they were to withdraw immediately. Otherwise, they were to liberate their target worlds.

So far, the gamble was paying off, but if the Ascomanni were to counterattack in strength, there wouldn't be anyone available to come to those forces' rescue.

Fabian turned his attention back to his fleets. Five hundred and sixty-two warships floated effortlessly against the twinkling backdrop of space, surrounding another hundred transports and assault ships.

The rally point buzzed with activity: ordinance and fuel were being transferred from massive fleet tenders, shuttles zipped about in the closely confined space, and last-minute arrivals sought out their assigned formations.

Everything was almost set.

Fabian checked his chrono. The Archus had been ordered to proceed without Marcellus if he failed to arrive within the designated timeframe, and the Dictator had eight hours left. If he didn't arrive by then, they'd be forced to go without him.

No sooner had he glanced down, however, than a new message appeared on his datapad. The *Tyrrhenia* and her small battlegroup had just dropped in a few thousand kilometers away from the heart of the formation.

The light cruiser would soon deliver its passengers to the fleets' flagship, while the remaining vessels moved to transfer Task Force Hyperion to waiting troop ships. Once Marcellus was aboard, they'd be ready to begin the operation.

Fabian sent a quick message to his XO indicating he'd be on the bridge shortly. He closed down his workstation and walked toward the door.

He lingered for just a moment, looking at the various knickknacks, photos, and citations that were scattered around his office, memories for events that seemed to have happened a lifetime ago.

The Archus took it all in one last time, then turned off the lights.

Campidano Plains; East of Perugia, Umbria

Invictus knocked twice on the prefab's door, waited a moment, then knocked once more. The heavy steel door slid open, revealing a dimly lit room containing four heavily armed civilians, their weapons trained on the Prefect.

"Lightning," Invictus said quickly.

"Thunder," the group's leader, a middle-aged woman, responded.

Invictus nodded and he and the two praetorians accompanying him quickly entered the structure. The door slid back into place, and one of the resistance members locked it behind them.

"You're the Quaestor?" Invictus asked the older woman.

"Yeah," she replied gruffly. "You're Prefect Flaminus?"

"Yes, ma'am," Invictus replied, eager to avoid pissing off the guerilla leader. She had resources he desperately needed. "What's the situation here in the refugee camp?"

"The Asco have mostly given up trying to police the place. Instead, they turned it over to some collaborationist thugs."

"E-Rho?" Invictus spat, his face contorted in disgust.

The Quaestor shook her head in agreement. "They do their best to extort food and supplies from the refugees, but the community knows they can come to us if they go too far. In reality, we have free rein here to plan our operations."

"Are there still civilians trapped in the city?" Invictus asked.

"Yeah, though our cells in Perugia have been ferrying them out in small groups since the city fell. Still, I'd say there are north of six million people trapped within the city limits. The situation is getting pretty desperate."

"Well I've got news from off world," Invictus replied. "They've made Imperator Aurelius Dictator, and he's leading the Republic's fleets back to reclaim Umbria. We've made contact with some of their scouts, and they've relayed the operation's timeline."

"And that's where we come in?" the Quaestor asked pointedly.

"Yeah. How many fighters do you have available to you?"

"If you're looking for exact numbers, you're out of luck. I can tell you that I have over four hundred cells. Most are comprised of between fifty and one hundred people."

Invictus was shocked. "How is that possible?"

The older woman gave the Prefect a sarcastic smile, a sharp tone to her voice: "Imagine that the place you lived had suddenly become alien and hostile to you, that the familiar streets and green spaces of your home had been marred by destruction and ruin, that your dead lay were they fell because it was too dangerous to retrieve them."

The Quaestor took a few steps toward Invictus, continuing: "Imagine, Prefect, that the sun itself was cloaked in shadow by the dozens of fires that raged out of control in your once proud city. Imagine, if you can, that level of destruction, and then tell me that you'd meekly accept that there was nothing left to do but wait for death."

"I'm sorry. I hadn't thought about what it must be like to—"

"We don't need your pity, Prefect," she interrupted. "If the military is returning, that's good enough for me. What does Gaius Aurelius need us to do?"

"How much do you know about the enemy's disposition within the capital?"

The Quaestor's eyes narrowed. "It'd be easier to tell you what we don't know."

Invictus smiled grimly. "Well then, we've got work to do."

URN *Echion*, Umbrian Orbital Grid
Two Gamma Iota

The *Echion*'s bridge was a riot of noise and activity as the full strength of the URN appeared over Umbria. They quickly engaged the one-hundred-odd ships still in orbit, and the supercarrier shuddered under the blows of enemy weapons.

Marcellus stood behind Fabian in the middle of it all, oblivious to the chaos around him. His attention was fixed to the beautiful blue-green emerald hanging serenely beyond the enemy fleet.

This was it, Marcellus thought to himself. Nearly nine months ago they'd been forced to abandon Umbria, to run away with their tails between their legs, to leave their homeworld to burn. Now, they had returned to take back what was theirs.

Mirabella had been right. Free of their mental domination, a significant proportion of the Ascomanni had rebelled. The wreckage of hundreds of Ascomanni ships littered Umbria's orbit, and the few loyalist ships that remained to oppose the Umbrians showed the scars of that battle.

The URN formed a pair of pincers, surrounding the remaining enemy forces and pinning them against Umbria's atmosphere, pounding on them from all sides.

As Marcellus watched, a heavily damaged Ascomanni dreadnaught exploded. Other enemy ships were quick to follow suit, and it wouldn't be long before the rest of the Asco fleet was destroyed.

Soon there wouldn't be anything standing in the way of Umbria's liberation.

Volta Power Complex; Perugia, Umbria

A loud *crack* cut through the deep rumbles of explosions and quick staccato pops of small arms that echoed through the city. One of Sextus's partisans slumped against the walls of the complex's main transformer, leaving behind a bloody smear as he slid to the ground.

"Sniper!" Sextus screamed.

There was another crack, and another resistance fighter fell to the ground, blood spraying violently from a wound in his neck.

"Anyone see the source?" a desperate voice called out.

"Skyscraper, nine o'clock. Not sure what floor!" another anxious voice responded.

Sextus grabbed his pack and fished out a small object. It was a drone, the type Umbrian children played with, readily available off the shelf and easily replaceable. He linked it to his helmet's HUD and threw it up into the air.

With a simple controller, he steered it toward the suspected sniper's nest. In moments, he was able to identify the approximate location, and the tiny drone hovered in place, serving as a marker for their target.

He turned to one of his praetorians and transmitted the signal from the drone. She unslung a long tube she carried over her shoulder and gave him a thumbs-up in response.

"Covering fire!" Sextus barked. He popped out of cover, firing at the distant blinking light. Other members of the resistance cell followed his example.

The sniper returned fire, and the Primus heard the whiz of a near miss streak past.

With the enemy distracted, the praetorian to his left stood and acquired her target. With a *whoosh*, a rocket screamed across the street and tore into the skyscraper opposite their position. Smoke billowed from the impact zone, while debris clattered down into the streets ten stories below.

Cautiously, the Umbrians stood. After a few anxious moments, it was clear the sniper had been dealt with.

"All right, boys and girls, back to the task at hand!" Sextus called out. The surviving members of Sextus's cell broke off into pairs and headed toward their assigned objectives.

Sextus and his remaining praetorians had been smuggled into the city during the early morning hours, where they had broken up into small groups of three and four. Each group was assigned a resistance cell to coordinate with and lead, and each cell had a target.

Together with the Quaestor, Invictus had devised a plan to strike every fuel dump, ammo depot, command center, or communications hub the resistance knew of. Still more cells would be responsible for ambushing the enemy, setting up kill zones at major thoroughfares and intersections throughout the city.

The resistance estimated that there were still almost one hundred thousand Ascomanni supporting the thousands of Pasarga still on Umbria. Although the resistance outnumbered the Ascomanni, these untrained civilians were not capable of standing and fighting with battle-hardened Ascomanni soldiers.

Experience had driven that point home, Sextus thought to himself. His cell had taken heavy casualties as they assaulted the power station. Hell, they'd lost just over half their strength breaching the outer perimeter alone. More still had fallen fighting their way into the heart of the facility, leaving only about two dozen to secure the objective.

Sextus shook his head at the absurdity of it all. He'd been given accountants, grocers, and office workers to take on Asco veterans. He was surprised that they'd been able to secure their objective at all.

A thunderous explosion in the distance brought him back to the present. He whistled sharply, and his cell began to reappear.

"Any issues?" he called out loudly.

Members of his group shook their heads, and Sextus nodded.

"All right, we're rendezvousing with another cell three blocks east of here to assault an Asco command post. Make sure your equipment is squared away."

With that, he led his improvised soldiers back over the ground they had just fought so hard to claim, past bodies of friend and foe alike. A few stopped over the forms of their friends and comrades, whispering brief prayers or taking equipment the fallen no longer needed.

After putting sufficient distance between his group and the power plant, he grabbed a detonator from his belt and flipped the switch. Behind him, there were several loud *pops* in quick succession, and the streetlights and signs around them fell dark.

The capital's primary power station was now out of commission.

URN *Echion*, Umbrian Orbital Grid Two Gamma Iota

Marcellus paced about the supercarrier's bridge, willing time to move faster. The Ascomanni fleet had been whittled down to just a handful of ships, and it was only a matter of time before every last enemy vessel was destroyed. They had taken surprisingly light casualties so far, losing approximately twenty ships for over ninety of the enemy's.

"All right, Fabian, pass the word to Octavia and Lucia."

"Yes, sir."

The *Echion*'s display of the battlespace expanded as Praetor Asinia and Praetor Artorius's forces arrived. The transports traveled around the outskirts of the battle zone as they worked their way toward Umbria's surface. Praetor Octavia took the lead, her assault carrier, the *Nike*, glowing as it entered the atmosphere.

No sooner had it started its descent however, then a brilliant flash of energy reached out and pierced the vessel. The Praetor's ship began to disintegrate, burning up and fragmenting as it punched through Umbria's atmosphere.

More beams reached out, finding more transports, and the bridge burst into pandemonium.

"We've lost contact with Praetor Asinia!"

"Archus! Sixty new ships emerged from lightspeed! Four thousand kilometers to port, twenty degrees up bubble!"

"Sir, we've never seen anything like this before..."

"Bring the Second, Third, Fourth, and Fifth fleets around to face the new force!" Fabian bellowed over the maelstrom of noise. "Show me the new arrivals, now!"

New images appeared, showing a fleet of alien vessels. They looked almost organic, featuring a bulbous head affixed to a long, tapered body, which flared into a quartet of curved apertures at the stern of the vessel.

One of the vessels began to glow a brilliant blue before discharging a beam of energy at the Umbrian fleet. It tore through a battlecruiser, bisecting the vessel at its midline before catching a destroyer which floated to its starboard. Both vessels exploded, leaving nothing behind but a cloud of molten debris.

The color drained from Marcellus's face. These new arrivals could mean only one thing: the Pasarga had arrived in force.

The Umbrians rushed to engage this unknown enemy, but the new arrivals continued to fire in sequence, carving a path of destruction through the combined fleet. As the number of damaged and destroyed ships began to skyrocket, Fabian took control of the situation.

"We've got to buy ourselves some time!" Fabian shouted. "Drop our auxiliaries right in front of us. Now, damnit!"

A moment later, seventy-two new ships jumped into the fray, and sounds of confusion and dread echoed around the room. They were Ascomanni.

Before anyone could react, however, they turned blue on the tactical display, and the ships turned to face the enemy. They started to fire into the enemy fleet, and the first enemy ships began to disappear under their withering barrage.

The Auxiliary Fleet was made up of captured Ascomanni warships. Fabian had recommended this wild plan to Marcellus months previously, and as the situation grew more dire, he had given his assent. These ships had been refitted by Umbrian engineers to automate most functions, requiring significantly fewer crew members. They wouldn't be the equal of a fully staffed warship, but they'd be able to distract and damage the enemy.

The Pasarga fleet recovered quickly, switching to focus on the more immediate threat. With their first return volley, half of the tightly clustered Auxiliary Fleet was destroyed.

It was enough, however. The remaining Umbrian ships finally reached optimal range and started firing on the Pasarga.

Any hope this may have engendered was quickly lost. The enemy fired again, obliterating another twenty ships.

"Sir!" an ensign called out. "We just lost the *Juno*. Archus Dullius is gone!"

Fabian turned to look at Marcellus, his expression wavering between fear and grief. "Sir, they're tearing us apart. What would you have us do?"

Marcellus was stunned, lost for words as he surveyed the devastation of his fleets. Too few Pasargan ships had been destroyed, and it was clear that the URN's total annihilation was but a few minutes away.

They had failed. They were beaten.

He swallowed hard past the lump in his throat, and began to speak in low, subdued tones: "Take us in, Fabian. Full speed ahead. If we can't win, we must make sure they lose too."

Fabian nodded, understanding his commander's intent. The order was passed to the fleets, and they surged forward toward their enemy. The *Echion* rocked as they pushed on through the debris and destruction all around them.

More beams of energy reached out, and more ships disappeared from the carrier's tactical display.

The Pasargan vessels grew ever larger as the *Echion* charged. Fabian picked a ship and ordered his helmsman to steer toward it. The carrier shifted, centering on its intended victim.

Marcellus closed his eyes and waited for the end, his last thoughts drifting to Mirabella.

"Sir, new contacts!" a voice called out.

"Seventy warships, unknown classification!"

"They look Ascomanni in origin!"

"Damn, they're *huge*, sir, they dwarf damn near everything else in the battlespace!"

"Wait, they're opening fire…on the enemy!"

Marcellus's eyes snapped open as the ship the *Echion* approached disappeared in a colossal fireball. All around, other Pasargan ships began to explode under a hail of fire from the newcomers.

"Sir, we're being hailed!"

"Put it on screen," Marcellus said, cutting a bewildered Fabian off.

"This is Jarl Alrek Agnisson of Her Majesty's warship *Tyrfing* to all Umbrian warships. Break off your engagement and see to your wounds. We will handle these monsters!"

Marcellus nodded to Fabian, and he opened a channel to the survivors.

"All ships, fall back to the capital and prepare to support the ground assault. Vessels not assigned to planetary support are immediately to begin search-and-rescue operations."

Two hundred and twenty-three ships disengaged, leaving the Vaeringyar to savage the overwhelmed Pasargan fleet.

As the Umbrians fell back, Fabian and Marcellus watched in awe as the new arrivals went about their gruesome work. They were struck by the savagery of Vaeringyar assault; Alrek's forces hammered away at the broken hulls of the Pasargan ships, even after they had ceased firing on his forces.

It was almost like they were trying to mutilate the mangled forms of their enemy's vessels, as if to remove any sign of who or what had created them.

The brawl in space lasted another half hour, but it was clear who would emerge victorious. The last few Pasargan vessels attempted to flee, but the Vaeringyar interposed themselves amongst their enemy, braving friendly fire to ensure the Pasargan's total destruction.

As the last ship fell to the Vaeringyar, Marcellus turned to his subordinate. "Get a shuttle ready for me, Fabian. There's still work to do."

The Eves Spa and Resort; Perugia, Umbria

Invictus crouched behind a concrete barrier as another wave of Ascomanni soldiers advanced on the roadblock he'd established only a few hundred meters from the capitol. To his left, a heavy weapons team poured fire into the horde of advancing Ascomanni, while other members of the Capital Guard did their best to suppress the enemy.

There was a screaming wail, and Invictus instinctively threw himself to the ground. A pair of Ascomanni bombers flashed past, their autocannons tearing chunks out of the building's face and the boulevard outside.

There was a *pumfft*, followed by another screech as a shoulder-fired surface-to-air missile chased after the fleeing Ascomanni bombers. A cough-like explosion echoed off the city's buildings as the missile found its mark, and the flaming wreckage of one of the enemy craft plowed into the façade of a nondescript office building.

As Invictus rose to his feet, he realized he couldn't locate the weapons team. One of his soldiers shook her head and pointed to the black-red ooze on the pavement; the Ascomanni bombers had found their mark.

The tide of battle began to shift, with the Ascomanni finally seizing fire superiority.

Invictus ordered his soldiers to fall back to their secondary positions, pulling back further down the street while climbing ever higher in the buildings flanking the Ascomanni approach.

With little to no vertical cover, the Ascomanni were cut to pieces, but their assault was starting to have its intended effect. One by one, Invictus's soldiers were falling, and he started to wonder if they'd have the strength to hold.

In the distance, he saw another pair of Ascomanni bombers swing toward their position, setting up for a second attack run.

"Take cover!" he screamed as the roar of their engines drowned out the maelstrom around him.

Before the bombers could fire on his soldiers, a pair of shapes, too quick to make sense of, flashed by overhead.

The Ascomanni bombers disappeared in twin explosions, their wreckage crashing down amongst their own ground forces.

A quartet of Umbrian interceptors screamed through the air above, firing on more targets as they tore through Perugia's skyline. Still more descended on other targets in the distance, and suddenly the sky was full of friendly craft.

Invictus and his legionnaires stood and cheered, their cries echoing down the street.

As the sound of the fighters faded into the distance, a new sound greeted the beleaguered defenders. Mechanical clanking and squealing grew ever more discernable, and Invictus jumped down into the street below as the first Umbrian tank rolled up to their roadblock.

Invictus smiled as the tank's compartment opened. "About time you all decided to show up. I was starting to think we'd have to do all the hard work ourselves…"

"Smooth, Flaminus," a mirth-filled voice called from within.

A lump formed in Invictus's throat, and he was shocked to see Praetor Artorius jump out. He did his best to cover his surprise, quickly snapping to attention.

"Praetor, I've never been so happy to see you in my life…"

Lucia grinned at the younger officer and said, "You've done an amazing thing here, son, but we've still got plenty more to do. What does the Ascomanni presence look like between us and the capitol?"

"They're dug in tight, ma'am, but with some fresh legs and a little fire support from your armor, I'm sure we can root them out."

Lucia laughed and slapped Invictus on the shoulder. "Then let's get to it!"

"Aye, ma'am." Invictus turned to his soldiers and called out loudly, "You heard the lady, we've got a planet to liberate! For Umbria!"

Another chorus of *how-oo*s rang through the streets, and Invictus and his soldiers charged toward the enemy.

The Senate Chambers; Perugia, Umbria

Marcellus's dropship bounced through the air, its pilot doing his best to frustrate the crews of the Ascomanni anti-aircraft emplacements which filled the sky with deadly light. He sat alone in the dark crew bay, left alone with his thoughts. This was it, one last great battle for the future of his people.

This was Umbria.

This was home.

The crew chief waved, and Marcellus stood and moved forward.

The shuttle's doors slid open, and a rush of warm air flooded into the cabin. The sounds and smells of battle were almost overwhelming, but Marcellus felt strangely at home amongst the smoke and din.

The crew chief grabbed the shuttle's repeater from its wall mount and began spraying fire indiscriminately toward the source of the triple-A racing up at them.

The shuttle rocked from a near miss, and its pilot dropped them closer to Perugia's streets. Finally, the ship began to slow as they came within sight of their destination.

"This is as far as we can go!" the crew chief called out. "Command post is about fifty meters to the east! Good luck, sir!"

He shook the man's outstretched hand and stood in the doorway. They were still thirty meters up when the pilot tugged upward on the yolk. The dropship dropped twenty meters in an instant as the craft nearly stalled before it pitched toward the ground to pick up more speed.

Five meters up, Marcellus jumped as the craft began to accelerate away. He rolled forward as his feet came into contact with the broken cobblestone surface of the ground below, absorbing some but not all of the energy of his fall, before sprinting to the relative safety of a nearby alcove.

He took a moment to catch his breath and assess his surroundings. He was all alone, tucked safely in the corner of an empty plaza, devoid of any sign of life, friendly or otherwise.

Marcellus pulled up a map of his forces' dispositions and charted a path to the CP the crew chief had mentioned. He set off at a brisk pace, ducking between shattered masonry and ruined courtyards as he worked his way forward.

He ducked around one corner, then another, before reflexively throwing himself back and down. A plasma bolt barely missed him, gouging a chunk out of a large topiary and setting the plant on fire.

"Check fire! Friendly incoming!" he called out. He stuck his hands out, and after a few moments of not being shot, he stood and walked around the corner once more.

He found an anxious-looking civilian standing behind a pile of debris, a bloody bandage covering his right arm and an apologetic look on his face.

"Uhh, sorry, sir, I thought you were the Asco!"

"At ease, son, who's in charge here?"

"Primus Sextus, sir, he's just over there…"

Marcellus nodded and strode past the man without saying another word. He passed through another archway before finding a camouflaged tent sitting in the corner of yet another sprawling courtyard.

The command post was barely managed chaos, with a handful of soldiers wearing the colors of his praetorians sitting at folding tables with maps and graphs of the battlespace. There in the middle was Sextus, his back to the Dictator.

"Excuse me," Marcellus called in a loud voice.

The soldiers in the tent stopped what they were doing and stood at attention, all save Sextus.

Without turning, he said, "Unless you're Jupiter himself, I don't have time to give directions, so why don't you—"

"Well, Jupiter is a bit of a stretch," Marcellus interrupted, doing his best to tamp down the joy he felt at seeing Sextus alive and in one piece, "At least on those days when I'm feeling humble."

Sextus spun around, a strange mixture of joy and terror on his face. "By the gods! Marcellus, it can't be... I mean, Praetor, uhhh..."

"It's OK, Sextus, I'm glad to see you too," Marcellus responded with fierce grin. "What's the situation?"

"You're just in time for the finale, sir. Praetor Artorius's armored units have broken through, and Invictus is using the tanks to shield the infantry for the final push into the capitol complex."

"Can you spare a legionnaire to show me the way?"

"Of course. Claudia, you're up. Get the Dictator to the Prefect safely."

"Understood, sir," the soldier replied confidently.

"Sir," Sextus began, a weary look on his face, "be careful out there. This sector is just a shitshow of snipers and murder holes. You've gotten us this far, we can push this one over the finish line ourselves."

Marcellus winked at his subordinate. "Noted, Primus, but *we've* come this far. I want to see this through."

Sextus saluted, and Marcellus returned it crisply as his guide motioned to follow her out of the plaza.

Together, they set out, zig-zagging their way through back alleys and passageways until they reached an area near the grand staircase leading up to Capitol Hall.

Already, Lucia's tanks were slowly rolling up the edifice, drawing fire from dozens of positions at the summit. An Umbrian rocket artillery piece to their left let loose a series of missiles, which twirled and corkscrewed into enemy positions in the buildings surrounding the capitol's approaches.

The tanks finally surmounted the stairs, and with a mighty roar, Umbrian soldiers poured out onto the streets and charged up into the capitol. Enemy fire streaked into the masses of soldiers, but nothing would stop the wave of angry Umbrians.

Marcellus screamed at the top of his lungs and joined the charge, his guide chasing after him. In an instant they had melted into the torrent of Umbrian soldiery. They bounded up four flights of steps and passed through the capitol's grand arches.

The Ascomanni were everywhere, but the Umbrians would not be denied.

Marcellus's carbine whined as he fired burst after burst at the enemy, constantly moving forward and pushing other attackers to move up. The defenders were swarmed and overrun, and the battle shifted deeper into the capitol complex.

Marcellus stopped to catch his breath in the Capitol's grand entryway, his praetorian guard panting but not a step behind him. As he looked about, he was stunned to see Invictus, huddled together with a handful of officers who were pouring over architectural schematics.

"Vic?!" Marcellus shouted.

Invictus looked up, and uncertainty turned to an eager grin. "Marcellus! What the hell are you doing here?!"

"I've got to find the Pasarga you captured. I think she'll probably be in our Oracle's chamber."

"Our Oracle?" Invictus asked blankly.

"Not enough time, Vic, can you spare a few soldiers for me?"

Invictus turned back to the men and women huddled around him. "You've got your orders, move out!"

The group broke up, and Invictus turned back to his commander. "I'm coming with you. Team One is just up and around the next corner. We can link up with them and push on to this chamber of yours."

"Understood, Vic, let's get to it!"

Together, the three Umbrians raced forward, dogging enemy fire as the capitol descended into a confusing free-for-all.

They turned at the next major junction and found the remaining members of Cyclops Team One. Marcellus quickly filled the team in, and they resumed their advance.

After fifteen minutes of steady forward progress, Marcellus finally found what he was looking for. They came to a stop in the middle of one of the Capitol's wide hallways, where they found a statue partially recessed in an alcove.

The building rocked under another artillery salvo, and dust fell from the ceiling. "What's the plan, sir? We're pretty exposed here," Cyclops One-One said.

"Not for long," Marcellus replied.

He pulled out a small datapad, which communicated the required code. The alcove creaked open, revealing a narrow spiral stairwell that led down and out of sight.

"All right, this is it," Marcellus said. "Get set, everyone. One-One, take the lead."

The Oracle's Chambers, Capitol Hall; Perugia, Umbria

The six Umbrians advanced slowly in the narrow and poorly lit passage hidden under the Capitol. Finally, the stone pathway started to open up, but the sounds of conversation could clearly be heard further ahead.

One-One and One-Three pushed forward, carbines at the ready. Invictus fished a sound dampener out of his pack and passed it to their point man. He nodded as One-Three prepped a concussion grenade.

Together, they threw the objects at the presumed enemy position before charging. The group emerged in a broad antechamber, with over a dozen Pasarga scattered about, stunned and struggling to their feet.

The Umbrians quickly burned down their distracted enemy, but the noise dampener didn't fully suppress the sounds of their fire. Pasarga started to emerge from the other end of the room.

Marcellus charged, quickly covering the last two meters between them, catching the aliens off guard. He drove his bayonet through the midsection of the first Pasargan, cutting the alien cleanly in two, while one of his impromptu squad mates shot down the second.

The rest fell back into the Oracle's chamber, and Marcellus and his soldiers took a moment to catch their breaths.

One-One peeked around the corner before immediately ducking back, an enemy round gouging a chunk of rock from the wall where his head had just been.

"There's about six of them left," One-One called out. "The one you're after is in there as well. Thoughts?"

"I was hoping you might have an idea!" Marcellus replied with a grin. "Any new gadgets that might be useful here?"

"No, sir. Nothing they won't have seen before anyway."

"Hmm..." Invictus said softly. "You're right, they have seen all of our tricks by now. I might have something,"

"All right, Vic, let's hear it."

***

The round shape of a concussion grenade rolled around the corner, followed by a brick-like sound dampener. The Pasarga naturally took cover as the concussion grenade exploded, sprang back to their feet, and began pouring fire through the entrance to the chamber.

As smoke settled, they were surprised to see that no one had entered the chamber. They glanced around at one another, and Atossa snarled at her soldiers.

She started to speak, but suddenly the walls on either side of the entryway exploded inward, spraying rock and debris at the Pasarga. The Umbrians poured through the holes they'd punched through the wall, closing in and finishing the remaining Pasarga in close combat.

Atossa shot to her feet and pointed her pistol at Invictus, but before she could pull the trigger she was hit in the side, the impact spinning her around and throwing her to the ground.

It was all over in less than ten seconds.

"Clear!" Marcellus shouted.

"Clear over here!" One-One called out.

"I'm clear too," Invictus said.

Marcellus walked forward, eagerly seeking out the Pasargan leader. He found her crawling toward the Oracle's massive pit, leaving behind a trail of sickly yellow blood.

Before she could reach the edge of the expanse, a pair of booted feet came to a stop in front of her.

"Hello, Atossa," Marcellus said sarcastically. "It's been so long since we've had an opportunity to speak." His tone hardened as he barked, "Order your remaining forces to stand down. Now!"

She uttered a familiar, cackling laugh, and, for a moment, he was transported back to their first encounter all those months before.

"Silly boy, you think this is the end? No..." she wheezed. "My people are coming for you, and there will be no escape."

"Your people *have* come. Some of them anyway," Marcellus responded. "And right about now, some new friends of ours are busy turning the fleet they brought with them into progressively smaller pieces of space debris."

"You're lying!" Atossa snarled as blood began to trickle from her nose.

"You know I'm not, Atossa," Marcellus said, stooping down into a low crouch. "This doesn't need to end this way. We've freed the Ascomanni. We can free you too."

She uttered her cruel, wicked laugh once more. "All you've freed them for," she said laboriously, "is pain and death. If not at our hands, then by another's."

"That's where your wrong," Marcellus said, staring back unflinchingly into her menacing gaze. "When the rest of your people arrive, we'll be ready, in no small part thanks to you."

Atossa's eyes grew wide and she screeched, "What?! I would never... I-I'd die before—"

"Oh, we aren't going to kill you, Atossa," Marcellus interjected. "Despite everything you've done. No, we're going to stick you back in your cage. Who knows? Maybe I'll even convince you that there is still hope for the Pasarga."

A smug smile spread across Marcellus's face. "Besides, I'm sure there is still much we can learn from you."

Atossa lashed out with sudden and unexpected strength, knocking Marcellus from his feet. She shot up and raced toward the abyss, before being struck once, then twice, by Umbrian plasma fire.

The Pasarga collapsed to the floor near the edge of the platform, and Marcellus ran forward. Before he could reach her though, she swung herself over the ledge and disappeared.

"Atossa, no!" Marcellus shouted.

He skidded to a stop and peered over the edge, only to find that he was staring straight into the barrel of a pistol.

Atossa dangled below, hanging by a single hand as she lined up her shot. Her finger began to tighten on the trigger.

Marcellus inhaled sharply. There was no time to react. Hubris had gotten the better of him...

But the moment passed, and Marcellus realized that the woman's body was shaking.

"Go, you fool!" she snarled between gritted teeth.

"Give me your hand," Marcellus said slowly. "We can still help you!"

Atossa's features softened, and Marcellus saw a familiar look of horror and despair spill out onto her face.

"It's too late for me, too late for my people," she grunted.

Slowly, she withdrew her outstretched arm, pulling the pistol out of line. Her face contorted and she shrieked in pain as she lowered the weapon. Atossa's arm shook uncontrollably, half outstretched, as she dangled beneath him.

Marcellus could only stare, transfixed by what he was witnessing.

Atossa looked down, then back up at him. For an instant, their eyes locked, and in that moment, Marcellus was able to see through the woman's pain.

In her eyes he saw sorrow, pride, rage, and…defiance.

"Never stop fighting them…Marcellus," Atossa gasped, agony coursing through her voice. "There are worse things than death. Much, much worse."

Before Marcellus could respond, she screamed in anguish, wrenched the pistol under her chin, and pulled the trigger.

Marcellus recoiled reflexively as the pistol discharged.

When he looked back over the edge, he caught the briefest glimpse of Atossa's form as it fell into the dark, cavernous expanse.

Marcellus stood as Invictus and the other Umbrians gathered around, and Invictus asked, "What was that all about?"

Marcellus shook his head and slapped his friend on the shoulder. "That was a sign of things to come. Focus up, soldiers. The day's not over yet. Let's get topside…"

Epilogue

The *Tyrfing*, Umbrian Orbital Grid
Two Gamma Iota

Marcellus knelt before Queen Bera's throne as the Vaeringyar's sovereign descended to greet her guest.

"Rise, peerless warrior. You need not kneel here."

Marcellus stood and bowed his head. "Thank you for your warm reception, Your Majesty. The Umbrian Republic owes you a great debt, one that I've received assurances we will repay to the best of our abilities."

"It's true then?" the Queen asked, arching an eyebrow at him. "You've given up the power your people have vested in you?"

"Yes, Your Highness. I surrendered my title as soon as was practical following the liberation of Umbria. The Senate still debates what exact role I should have moving forward, but I've convinced them to abandon any fevered dreams of making me a sovereign."

"Hmm..." Queen Bera said to herself. "You are an interesting individual, Gaius Aurelius Marcellus. You have known absolute power, and yet you have given it up willingly."

"Power does not interest me, ma'am. I have seen the ruin it brings to those who seek it, and I for one will pass on its temptations."

Marcellus paused for a moment, and the Queen sensed his hesitation.

"Please, Marcellus, you need not speak guardedly in my company. What is it?"

"Forgive me, Your Majesty, but I was wondering, why did you come? Why did you save us?"

Queen Bera smiled, and Marcellus was taken by the warmth of her expression. "You chose hope over death. You gave the thralls a chance at a future, one free of the domination of the Tenebrae."

"It was a difficult decision, Your Highness. I admit that when I arrived at Ōsenheim, my intention was to destroy the Ascomanni, the thralls, as you call them."

The Queen's smile deepened. "Then you took a leap of faith? In something more than yourself? Or perhaps *someone*?"

"Someone, Your Highness. She helped me see that if I allowed fear to dictate my actions, I had already become a slave to our enemies. Now, the Ascomanni will have a chance to be more, to reach the unrealized potential the Tenebrae stole from them, and you. What will you do next?"

"With their implants disabled and the jamming in place, we will be able to begin the process of freeing the thralls from the Tenebrae's influence. However, it will take much effort to undo the damage the Tenebrae have done. In time, we hope they will be integrated back into our society, where they belong. In the meantime, we will reestablish ourselves amongst the ruins of our ancestral homes."

"I understand. I would not take up any more of your time, Your Majesty. If you need anything, anything at all, please do not hesitate to ask. The people of Umbria will deliver."

The Queen smiled graciously and said, "Thank you. It seems that fate has brought us together for a reason."

Marcellus bowed before the Vaeringyar's beautiful queen once more, then took his leave.

Before he reached the door, however, she called after him. "Marcellus, you know that this is just the beginning, don't you? Eventually, others will come."

Marcellus turned to face Queen Bera.

"Yes, ma'am, I know. However, your people prove that there are others out there, others willing to resist, to fight back."

"So what will you do?"

"I will find them. And together, we will end the Tenebrae."

Glossary

Alari: A commander of a wing of atmospheric fighters, bombers, or transport craft. The wing composed of three squadrons, the commanders of each reporting to the Alari. While not equivalent, the Alari was afforded the same station as a Tribune in the structured hierarchy of rank.

Archus: The highest rank in the Umbrian Republic Navy, the Archus leads one of the Republics fleets. While they retain command over the tactical deployment of their resources, the Archus is subordinate to the Praetor, or army group commander, that they have been assigned to support.

Ascomanni: The Ascomanni, or Asco for short, are a species of vicious bipedal aliens who have invaded the Umbrian Republic. Stronger and more physically imposing than the Umbrians, the Ascomanni feature painful and intrusive cybernetical enhancements which only further improve their performance on the battlefield.

Battlecruiser: A battlecruiser is a ship that is larger than a heavy cruiser but smaller than the Republic's battleships. It has a strong compliment of large caliber railguns, but it's armor and defensive systems are more in line with those of a heavy cruiser. As such, it is designed primarily to fight and destroy Ascomanni cruisers, as it lacks the ability to survive a sustained encounter with larger warships.

Battleship: The Umbrian Republic's primary fleet combatants, battleships are large, well armed and armored warships which are designed to stand in the main line of battle during fleet engagements. They are meant to soak up punishment and dish it back out. The Republic's battleships are amongst the few warships capable of standing toe to toe with their Ascomanni counterparts.

CAG: Commander, Air Group. An officer aboard a warship carrying fighters who is responsible for coordinating the ship's starfighters during battle.

CAP: Combat Air Patrol. A force of fighters which provides local theater awareness and a rapid response force which can confront any unexpected enemy incursion.

Capital Guard: A force of elite soldiers who guard the premises of the capitol. Largely ceremonial in nature, they would be forced to take a more active role in combat for the first time since the unification of the Umbrian Republic.

Centurion: The Centurion is the entry level rank in the Republic Army, and is responsible for maintaining a century, or a force of a hundred soldiers. As first level tactical officers, the Centurion was responsible for maintaining their legionnaires' readiness and leading them into battle. As such, there is a high mortality rate for Centurions.

Century: The smallest tactical unit in the Umbrian Republic Army. The century is made up of a hundred legionnaires commanded by a centurion.

Combat Information Center (CIC): A facility located aboard a warship which allows a commander to manage the local battlespace. Usually buried well within the vessel's hull so as to better protect the commander and their staff.

Combined Intelligence Directorate (CID): Formed after the start of the Ascomanni conflict, the Combined Intelligence Directorate, or CID, was created by amalgamating the various civilian and military intelligence organizations into a single entity. As such, its powers stretched across both spheres of operation, though tis role in supporting the war effort would become its primary focus.

Corvette: A small warship designed for patrol and escort functions. The corvette is not intended to stand in the line of battle, and does not have sufficient armor or armament to go toe to toe with larger warships.

Cohort: A cohort is a military unit comprised of five centuries of a hundred soldiers. In turn, a legion is made up of 20 cohorts. A cohort is commanded by a Primus. Most cohorts are made up of mobile infantry, but some are designated for specific purposes to increase the parent legion's capabilities.

Cruiser: A cruiser is a large warship designed to balance firepower, defensive capabilities, and an ability to operate for extended periods away from its home port or anchorage. Umbrian cruisers are separated into two distinct classes, heavy cruisers and light cruisers. Light cruisers carry medium caliber railguns and extensive missile armament, while heavy cruisers are larger, carry heavier guns, and possess heavier armor.

Destroyer: A multi-role warship that has a good mix of offensive and defensive capabilities. Destroyers form the core of both the Umbrian Republic Navy and the Ascomanni fleets, though Ascomanni destroyers are larger and capable of engaging cruiser size Umbrian warships in single ship engagements.

E-Rho: E-Rho is a street-gang turned criminal enterprise which inhabits the poorer reaches of the Republic's capital city of Perugia. From its headquarters in the city's entertainment district, E-Rho seeks to maximize its returns by focusing on the vices enjoyed by the Republic's uber rich.

Flechette: A metal dart or projectile usually bundled into a larger munition casing and fired from a projectile weapon. As the projectile approaches the target, its outer casing splits, releasing multiple flechettes in the hopes of causing as much damage as possible.

Frigate: A small, lightly armored warship that focus primarily on providing a defensive umbrella to larger fleet formations. Umbrian frigates carry scores of missile interceptors and a large compliment of point defense weaponry for a ship their size, allowing them to intercept enemy projectile weapons, missiles, and starfighters.

Legate: Responsible for the command of a legion and reports to the army group's Praetor. The Legate is supported by a host of junior officers who assist with the administrative functions of the Legion. When multiple legions are detached for a specific mission or assignment, the senior most Legate will take over responsibility for the task force.

Legionnaire: The rank assigned to all non-officer soldiers, legionnaires would be organized into base units of a hundred known as a century. While the majority of legionnaires served as mobile infantry, specialized disciplines existed to cover specific disciplines such as armor, artillery, or engineering.

Magistrate: An administrator responsible for running an organization or installation. Magistrates fall outside of the chain of command and can be made up of both civilians and military personnel. Because they are charged with very specific assignments, there is little need for hierarchy amongst magistrates, but positions such as Chief Magistrate and Sub-Magistrate exist.

Oracle: The name assigned by the Umbrian Republic to a vast artificial intelligence which is responsible for the development of Umbrian society. Its specific origins and true nature are closely guarded secrets.

Pasarga: The second hostile alien race that the Umbrian Republic would encounter. The Pasarga are much more closely in line with Umbrian physiological norms, but their intensive cybernetic augmentation gives then enhanced speed and strength over the Republic's legionnaires. The Pasarga appear to be of higher intellectual capabilities than the Ascomanni and have so far only been observed serving as commanders of large formations or specialists within sensitive installations.

Praetor: The highest rank in the Umbrian Republic army. There are six praetors overall, each of whom commands an army group made up of multiple legions which is supported by one of the Republic Navy's fleets. The Praetors are members of the War Council, and report directly to the Umbrian Republic Senate.

Praetorian: A member of the Praetor's protective detail. Most Praetors maintain between four to six cohorts of praetorians, but there is no fixed limit on the number of units that a Praetor can raise.

Prefect: A Prefect was a senior officer who outranked Tribunes but was below the rank of Legate. Many specialized formations which did not conform to the standard legionary structure were led by a Prefect in lieu of a Legate.

Primus: The Primus is responsible for leading a cohort. Each Primus is graded into one of four bands, and when multiple cohorts must coordinate to achieve their objectives, the Primus of the highest band and longest length of service is responsible for local command.

Procurator: The second-highest ranking officer of a ship's command staff, the Procurator serves as the vessel's executive officer, or XO. He assists the captain with the execution of orders and assumes responsibility for the ship if the captain is incapacitated or killed.

Tribune: The Tribune is a veteran officer who has advanced through the ranks and has been assigned to a headquarters unit. A legion's Tribunes are responsible for logistics, local intelligence, planning, and communications, and assist the Legate with the day to day operations of their command.

Triumvir: The elected chiefs of the executive branch of the Umbrian Republic. The responsibilities of office are split between three equals, and decisions reached by majority vote. Each of the three Triumvirs is elected on a rotational basis to serve a term of six years.

Railgun: Railguns are an advanced projectile weapon system which relies on magnetic fields to fire its ammunition. Instead of relying on explosive propellant to drive the projectile, railguns rely on generating electromagnetic fields which repel, or push, the shells down the barrel at hypersonic speeds.

Scutia Battlemech: The Scutia battlemech, or 'scoots' as they are called by the Republic's soldiers, are a groundbreaking advancement in the development and production of smart weaponry. Essentially a light tank built on a simple chassis, the Scutia are the first weapons platform to feature a true artificial intelligence. While this AI is constrained by a number of safeguards, the Scutia is capable of taking limited independent action. It does this by utilizing multiple inputs from its own sensory suite as well as data supplied by the local battlenet.

Senate of the Umbrian Republic: The Senate is the Republic's legislative body, responsible for creating the common laws and regulations which apply to each Umbrian, regardless of which planet or system they occupy. As of 31155, the Senate is composed of 400 Senators. Every world in the Republic is represented by at least one Senator, while the remaining seats are distributed proportionally based on population.

Vaeringyar: The name of the alien race which would be transformed into the Ascomanni. The Vaeringyar were conquered by the Pasarga and their dark masters, and decades of cybernetic enhancement and brutal subjugation have left but a shell of a once proud people.

Viceroy: Viceroys are individuals appointed by the Senate to manage the affairs of individual colonies as they grow towards self-sufficiency and local autonomy.

War Council: The Umbrian Republic's high command, the War Council is a body of senior military leaders who are responsible for advising the Senate and the Triumvirate on military matters. Originally consisting of ten people, the Council is made up of the Magistrates of the Army and Navy, the army group commanders, or Praetors, and various other administrators responsible for ensuring that the military is well equipped, trained, and ready to face the Republic's adversaries.

Wing: A wing is an organizational unit of atmospheric or space-bound fighter, bomber, or transport craft. It is comprised of three squadrons, with each squadron possessing twelve aircraft.

A Word from the Author

Thank you for taking the time to read my work! It's taken me almost two years to get from the first few test pages all the way to a completed novel, and your willingness to take a chance on my book means a great deal to me. I'm deeply passionate about the universe I'm developing, and the support of readers like you will allow me to continue to expand my work.

If you liked what you read, or if you have feedback on how I might improve my writing moving forward, I'd highly encourage you to leave a review online at your book merchant of choice. Reviews are critical to the success or failure of a novel, and, if you enjoyed this one, there are few things you could do to support my work more than by leaving feedback for others who may consider picking up this book.

Lastly, I'm committed to reaching my readership though multiple media, not just novels. If you enjoyed this book, please visit our website, www.kaiyoslex.com. Here you'll find a wealth of additional content, including art, encyclopedia entries, and other information that expands upon and breathes added life into the TKL universe.

Thank you again!

Bernard Lang

Made in the USA
Las Vegas, NV
17 October 2022